W9-CMU-416

THE TIGER WARRIOR

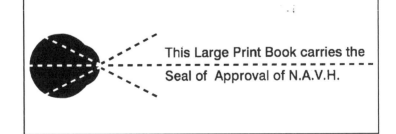

This Large Print Book carries the
Seal of Approval of N.A.V.H.

THE TIGER WARRIOR

DAVID GIBBINS

WHEELER PUBLISHING
A part of Gale, Cengage Learning

GALE
CENGAGE Learning

Detroit • New York • San Francisco • New Haven, Conn • Waterville, Maine • London

LIBRARY OF CONGRESS CATALOGING-IN-PUBLICATION DATA

Gibbins, David J. L.
  The tiger warrior / by David Gibbins. — Large print ed.
    p. cm.
  Originally published: New York : Bantam Books, 2009.
  ISBN-13: 978-1-4104-2226-2 (alk. paper)
  ISBN-10: 1-4104-2226-7 (alk. paper)
  1. Marine archaeologists—Fiction. 2. Archaeological
  expeditions—Fiction. 3. Treasure troves—Fiction. 4. Large type
  books. I. Title.
  PR6107.I225T54 2010
  823'.92—dc22   2009034728

Published in 2010 by arrangement with Bantam Books, a division of Random House, Inc.

3 1969 02000 7919

Printed in the United States of America
1 2 3 4 5 6 7 14 13 12 11 10

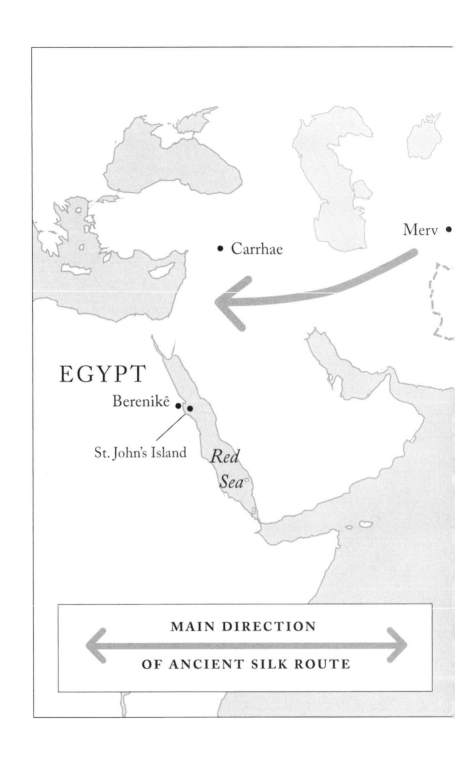

Merv •

• Carrhae

EGYPT

Berenikê •

St. John's Island

Red Sea

MAIN DIRECTION
OF ANCIENT SILK ROUTE

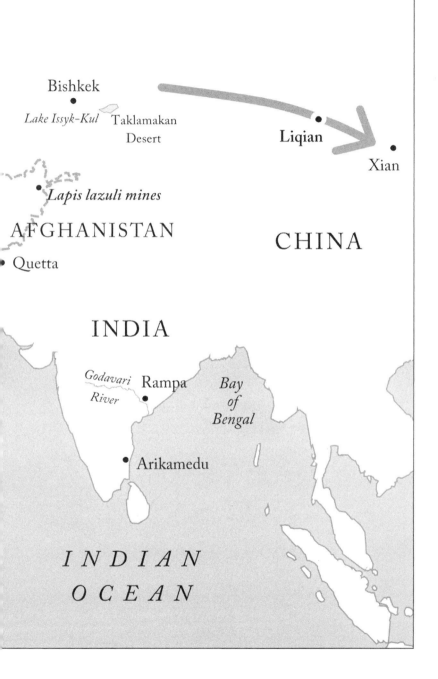

Bishkek

Lake Issyk-Kul Taklamakan
Desert

Liqian

Xian

Lapis lazuli mines

AFGHANISTAN

CHINA

Quetta

INDIA

Godavari Rampa
River

Bay
of
Bengal

Arikamedu

INDIAN

OCEAN

. . . after this, toward the east and with the ocean on the right, sailing offshore past the remaining lands on the left, you come upon the land of the Gangês; in this region is a river, itself called the Gangês, that is the greatest of all the rivers in India, and which rises and falls like the Nile. Close by this river is an island in the ocean, the very farthest part of the inhabited world toward the east, beneath the rising sun itself; it is called Chrysê, the land of gold. Beyond this land, by now at the most northerly point — where the sea ends at some place in the outer limits — there lies a vast inland place called Thina. From there, wool, yarn and silk are transported overland by way of Bactria to Barygaza, and by way of the river Gangês back to Limyrikê. As for this place, Thina, it is not at all easy to get to; for people only rarely come from it, and then only in small numbers. The place lies directly beneath Ursa Minor, and is said to be anchored together, as it were, with parts of the Black Sea and the Caspian Sea, where they turn away . . . What lies beyond this region, because of extreme storms, immense cold and impenetrable terrain, and because of some divine power of the gods, has not been explored . . .

From the *Periplus of the Erythraean Sea*
Egyptian Greek, *c.* First Century AD

In the ninth month the First Emperor was interred at Mount Li. When the emperor first came to the throne he began digging and shaping Mount Li. Later, when he unified the empire, he had over seven hundred thousand men from all over the empire transported to the spot. They dug down to the third layer of underground springs and poured in bronze to make the outer coffin. Replicas of palaces, scenic towers and the hundred officials, as well as rare utensils and wonderful objects, were brought to fill up the tomb. Craftsmen were ordered to set up crossbows and arrows, rigged so they would immediately shoot down anyone attempting to break in. Mercury was used to fashion imitations of the hundred rivers, the Yellow River and the Yangtse, and the seas, constructed in such a way that they seemed to flow. Above were representations of all the heavenly bodies, below, the features of the earth . . . After the interment had been completed, someone pointed out that the artisans and craftsmen who had built the tomb knew what was buried there, and if they should leak word of the treasures, it would be a serious affair. Therefore, after the articles had been placed in the tomb, the inner gate was closed off and the outer gate lowered, so that all the artisans and craftsmen were shut in the tomb and were unable to get out. Trees and bushes were

planted to give the appearance of a mountain . . .

Sima Qian, *Records of the Grand Historian*
Second Century BC

PROLOGUE

Lake Issyk-Kul, central Asia,
autumn 19 BC

The sun hung ominously in the eastern sky, reddened by a swirl of dust from the desert beyond. The man reached the top of the hill, shifted the armor on his shoulders and eased the great sword on his back. Below him lay the boulder-strewn foreshore, and beyond that a great body of water that seemed to stretch off to infinity. He had tasted the water, and it was more fresh than salt, so they had not reached Ocean, and the horizon ahead was not the fiery edge of the world. He strained his eyes to see where the lake narrowed and the towering snowcapped mountains dipped, to the pass that led beyond, under the rising sun. The trader had told him these things, but still he was not sure. Were they already dead? Had they crossed the river Styx? Was this Elysium? For the first time he felt a pang of fear. Do the dead know they have passed beyond?

13

"Licinius!" A voice bellowed up. "Get your arse back down here!"

The man cracked a tired smile, raised his arm then looked down to the others. They were waiting on the far side of the icy torrent he had forded to get here, where the meltwater that filled the lake rushed through the treacherous canyon they had traversed the night before. Earlier that morning the trader had led him to the secret place where the boat was hidden. *The trader.* Licinius could still smell him, smell the fear. He had chained him to a rock behind the hill. It would not be long now. He remembered what the man had said, over and over again, desperately, as they dragged him along. That he knew where to find the greatest treasure in the world. The tomb of an emperor, the greatest the world had ever known, somewhere over the eastern horizon. He would show them the way. They were guaranteed the riches of kings. They would live like emperors, each of them. They would find immortality. *Immortality.*

Licinius had been sceptical. The others had been entranced. It was what they had wanted to hear, the lure that had drawn so many to their deaths along this route. But Licinius was still not sure. He glanced to the horizon again, then looked south. *Had he made the right decision?* He looked back to the lakeshore. On the far side was their camp, rectangular, surrounded by sharpened stakes facing outward. The ground had been hard, baked like rock, and they had been beyond exhaustion the night before, but they had dug a ditch and heaped up the stony soil into a rampart, as they had been trained to do. And they had good reason. They had a terrifying new enemy, one who had first come for them after they had attacked the Sogdians and captured the trader. It was an enemy they had heard but hardly seen, had grappled with in the terrible swirling darkness of the canyon the night before. An enemy who had taxed all their strength and guile as soldiers. *As Roman legionaries.*

They had route-marched for weeks now. Twenty-five miles a day, when the going allowed it. But the nightmare had begun a lifetime ago. Two hundred miles east from the Mediterranean coast to the battlefield at Carrhae. Fourteen hundred miles from there to the Parthian citadel of Margiana, chained and whipped by their captors. Anyone who faltered was beheaded on the spot. It had left only the toughest. And now, thirty-four years later, they had escaped and were on the march again, a thousand miles over desert and mountain, in scorching heat and icy cold, through storms of dust and snow that veiled their past as if it were a shadowland. They had followed the route of Alexander the Great. On the edge of the desolate plain beyond Margiana they had passed the last of his altars, a great plinth that marked the eastern limit of his conquest. They had dug for treasure there, no longer mindful of the wrath of the gods. They had found a few coins, nothing else. Ahead of them had risen a forbidding wall of mountains, and the caravan route. Others from Margiana had escaped this way almost twenty years before, and word had come back, rumors that had spread among the prisoners like wildfire, of great armies beyond the mountains, armies that would pay a king's ransom for mercenaries, for soldiers who had once fought for Rome.

And now there was another reason. Licinius remembered what the trader had told him. *A great tomb, buried under a pyramid of earth, built by seventy thousand slaves. A tomb that he, the trader, could open up for them. The tomb of the greatest emperor the world had ever known, an emperor who would make them forget Alexander. A tomb that contained all the riches of the world, riches that would be theirs for the taking, in a place where they would be treated like gods.*

They had been fifty strong when they had broken out of the citadel, fleeing through the breach they had made in the walls with all the gold they could carry. Half of them had been cut down before they were out of sight of the walls. The caravan route, the route of the traders, had been sinuous, confusing, not one road but many, and more than once they had been tempted up a blind alley, gone higher and higher, through narrower defiles until they came out on snow, places so high an eagle could not fly, where fire burned with a pale flame, where they had gasped for breath, knowing their own mortality, trespassing in the home of the gods. They had come down again, and marched on. They had needed to find a guide. They had needed food — desperate, ravenous with hunger, they had become no better than the wild dogs who circled travelers in these parts, preying on the stragglers and the dying. And fate had cast her dark spell on first one companion, then another. They had been attacked by others like them, marauding bands who preyed on the caravans, but now they were stalked by some darker force that had followed them, hunted them down since they had pushed the trader ahead and told him to find a way out of this place of nightmares.

Licinius saw Fabius begin to make his way up the hill. He watched the others wade out to the boat, carrying the sacks of booty, led by Marcus, the shipbuilder from Aquileia, who would try to keep it afloat. He felt his own bag, the shape in it. He had wrested the bag from the trader when they found him. There had been another bag, identical, and he had given it to Fabius. The trader had pleaded with them not to open the bags, and to keep them separate. They had humored him, needing him. Licinius still did not know what lay inside. He would open it as soon as he had dealt with the trader and found somewhere to sleep that night. The rest of the booty had been taken from the Sogdians. The traders had been leading camels across the plain, heading west, laden down with bags of precious stones, textiles, shimmering cloth they called *serikōn.* The legionaries had killed them, all but one. They killed everyone they came across. It was what they did. Then they had made a pyre of it all, the bodies, the textiles, everything, and gorged themselves. They had been famished, and had gnawed at the bones like dogs. They had found wine, skins of it, and had drunkenly fashioned crude branding irons from the camel bits. They had branded themselves. He could still smell the burning flesh. He looked at his forearm, squeezed it, watched the blood oozing out, coagulating. There would be a good scar, one that would cut through all the other scars, the scars of whipping and beating, the old scars of battle. It hurt like Hades, but he relished the pain. It helped him focus. It was how they had been trained. It was how they had survived thirty-four years enslaved, whipped by day and chained by night, building the walls of the Parthian citadel. Most had died. Those who remained were the toughest. He held his fist in a hard ball and

18

grunted. The mark of the brand was a number seared into their souls. *XV*. Fifteenth Apollinaris. The lost legion. A legion of ghosts. *Their legion.*

It was as if their souls had been locked within them, frozen for the past thirty-four years. Ten thousand had marched from the battlefield at Carrhae. They were only nine now, one fewer than the day before. *"Frater,"* he whispered, remembering Appius. *"Ave atque vale.* Hail and farewell. Until we meet in Elysium." They had spent the night in a fearful place, full of crumbling canyons and dead ends, rent with the moans and howls of the spirits who lurked within. The sky had blackened and crackled with lightning, as if Jupiter himself were slashing at the fabric of the heavens. The wind had shrieked up behind them like a dragon breathing fire through the canyons, licks of poisoned breath seeking them out, reaching into every nook and cranny. They had huddled down under interlocked shields, the *testudo,* the tortoise, as they had been trained to do, under square shields they had made for themselves, while the rain thundered down and the arrows of their enemy slammed in. Appius had gone half-mad, screamed at their enemy to show themselves, to fight like men, and had broken free, and then an arrow had taken him. Licinius had dragged him back under, gurgling, wide-eyed, and held him with an iron grip even after he had passed beyond, shaking and convulsing. Death in battle as it really was, not as Licinius had once sculpted it in stone for his patrons in Rome. He had gone half-mad himself, smearing his body with the blood, and had unhorsed the bowman, bellowing in rage and grief, clamping and twisting the man's throat, tearing his eyes out. They were human, he had screamed, not demons, and if they were human they could be defeated. He had wrenched away the horseman's great dripping sword, its gauntlet in the shape of a tiger, ripped off the scale armor, throwing it over his back, and had taken the severed head in his hand, held by the long plaited hair and knot. But the other legionaries had already gone, taking Appius' body with them, leaving him to struggle behind, and he had slipped and dropped the head in the maw of some mighty waterfall.

Hours later he had come upon them, the dwindling band, with the trader in tow, on the edge of the lake. They had found boulders with mysterious carvings, and they had laid Appius there with his weapon, a broken bronze dagger-axe. They had put coins on his eyes, one coin from the altar of Alexander the Great, the other a strange coin with a square hole they had taken from the Sogdians. They could not risk the smoke from a pyre, but he, Licinius, the former sculptor, had used a chisel he had fashioned to gouge out a few words on a rock beside the body. He had put the sacred number of their legion on the stone, so Charon would know where to take Appius when he came for him, to join all the others who shadowed them, the ghost legion.

Fabius reached him and sat down, looking east. Licinius sat beside him, angling the sword on his back out of the way, the gleaming metal tiger gauntlet above his shoulder. Fabius was from the Alps, tall, with blue eyes and red hair, still visible amid the gray stubble. For a while they said nothing. They were blood brothers, the last of the *contubernium,* the eight who had answered the call to arms when Julius Caesar had marched on Gaul, who had messed and camped and fought together through all the glory days of the legion. Like Appius had been. Licinius glanced at the place where they had laid him, then took something out of a pouch on his belt and passed it to Fabius. It was a small, smooth stone, light in weight, with a hole in the center. Fabius took it, and held it up. "The color of honey," he said. "It has something inside it. A mosquito."

"I took it from Appius' body," Licinius said. "It was an heirloom, passed to him by his mother. It's a strange stone he called burnstone that comes from the shore of the sea to the north of Germania. You remember the patterns on the shields of the Gauls we fought at Alesia, the swirling animals? You can see the same, etched on the stone. Appius' mother was a German, you know. He said this stone was for children. It brought them luck. He hoped one day he might have a child. I promised I would take it if I survived him. Somehow he kept it, all those years in the quarries."

"I hate to think where he hid it," Fabius said. "But knowing Appius, it makes sense. He was always talking out of his arse."

"We will miss him."

"Until Elysium."

Licinius closed his pouch. "It's yours. We are old, but not too old, and maybe one day you will escape from all this and find a woman and have a child. My time for that has passed. I had a child once, a boy whose hair would now be flecked with gray, but for me there will be no more. Hold it, and remember Appius. Remember me, *frater*. Remember all of us, this day."

Fabius said nothing, but held the stone. Licinius looked him over. Macrobius, the leatherworker, had fashioned sandals from camel skin, good, sturdy marching sandals, tied up their bare calves to the knees. With those, they could go anywhere. Apart from that, they looked like barbarians. Fabius wore armor and weapons he had pillaged along the way, a leather jerkin rigid with dried blood, shreds of Parthian chain mail crudely sewn into it. The chain was in the Roman fashion, better able to counter a sword thrust, but Licinius' new shirt of segmented metal squares might stop a few arrows and would help to keep the wind at bay. Fabius had their prized weapon, a short bronze thrusting sword covered with intricate foreign patterns, dragons and tigers and demons. It was like a Roman *gladius,* perfect for close-quarters fighting. The great sweeping sword on Licinius' back was a slashing blade, as sharp as swamp grass, and had decapitated his enemy the night before as if it were a head of cabbage. But sweeping blows left the body exposed, and were not the Roman way. He would get Rufus the metalsmith to cut the sword down to size. But then he remembered. Rufus was gone too. And it scarcely mattered now. He extended his bare arms, and held out his hands. "Look at us. I hardly feel the cold anymore. My skin is like camel leather. And when I kill now, I do it with my bare hands."

"Maybe we are becoming gods."

"The gods are our brothers who have gone before."

When Licinius heard Fabius speak he still heard the voice of a young man, but when he looked he saw a man ravaged by the years, gray-stubbled and hoary, halfway to Elysium already. The day before, blind drunk and freshly branded, they had shorn their hair and beards, preparing for the final battle. They had not expected to survive the canyon, and when they joined the others in Elysium they had wanted to look right. Licinius felt his scalp. It was rough, hard, like every surface of his body, like the freshly sawn marble he had once traced his fingers over in their workshop in Rome. He felt the weals around his wrists, as thick as elephant hide. *Thirty-four years in chains.* They were survivors, but he felt they were living ghosts, men whose souls had departed that day on the scorching battlefield of Carrhae.

"You are remembering? The battle?" Fabius said quietly.

"Always."

The expedition had been ill-fated from the start. Crassus had been their general. Crassus who saw himself as equal to Caesar. Licinius snorted. Crassus the Banker, Crassus who had only wanted gold. They had despised him, loathed him even more than their Parthian enemy. When they crossed the river Euphrates, there had been peals of thunder, crashes of lightning, and a fearful wind, half-mist, half-hurricane. Then the sacred eagle standard of the legion had turned face-about, of its own accord. *Of its own accord.* And yet they had marched on. It was not the defeat that was unbearable, it was defeat without honor. Crassus, too weak to die by his own sword, had to be slain by his tribune. Poor Caius Paccianus, *primus pilus* of the first cohort, whose fate it was to bear the closest likeness to Crassus, had been paraded around by the Parthians in a woman's red robe, trumpeters and lictors on camels ahead of him, the dripping heads of Roman dead suspended from axes all around. The Parthians had filled his throat with molten gold in mockery of Crassus, a man who had thought that pay and promises of gold were the only guarantee of a soldier's loyalty.

But that was not the worst. The worst was to lose the eagle, ripped off its standard and taken away before their eyes. From then on they were ghosts, all of them, the living and the dead.

"Does the trader give us any news of Rome?" Fabius asked quietly. "You're the only one who can speak Greek. I heard Greek sounds when he was pleading with us."

"He's been many times to Barygaza, a place on the Erythraean Sea where traders come from Egypt. That's where the Sogdian caravan was heading, and that's where he learned his Greek." Licinius paused, not sure how Fabius would take it. "There is some news, my friend, about Rome."

"Ah." Fabius leaned forward. "Glorious news, I hope."

"He says the wars are long over. He says there is a new peace." He put his hand on

Fabius' shoulder. "And he says Rome is now ruled by an emperor."

"An emperor?" Fabius looked hard at him, his eyes ablaze. "Julius Caesar. Our true general. He's the only one. It must be him."

Licinius shook his head. "Caesar is long gone. You and I both know that, in our hearts. And if he'd become emperor, he'd have come looking for us. No, it's someone new. Rome has changed."

Fabius looked downcast. "Then I will seek Caesar in Elysium. I will serve no other as emperor. I have seen what emperors do, in Parthia. We are citizen-soldiers."

Licinius held out his hands again, gnarled, scarred, caked in blood and grime, the ends of two fingers missing. "Citizens," he said ruefully. "Thirty-five years ago, maybe. Are these still the hands of a sculptor?"

Fabius leaned over on one elbow. "You remember Quintus Varius, who the Parthians made foreman of the southern sector of the walls? First centurion of the third cohort? He'd been a builder on the Bay of Naples before joining up, knew all about concrete. He persuaded the Parthian vizier that the dust that choked us for all those years was the key ingredient of concrete, like the volcanic dust of Naples. Of course it was nothing of the sort. Varius was executed years ago, some trivial thing, but we put that dust with our mortar ever since. Those walls we spent thirty-four years building won't last another ten. You mark my words. They'll crumble to dust. That's a citizen-soldier for you. Brings all his skills as a civilian to bear."

"And a citizen-soldier can go back to civilian life."

"What are you thinking?"

"The trader said something else."

"Spill it, Licinius."

"He said this emperor has negotiated peace with the Parthians. He said he had seen a new coin, celebrating the peace as a great triumph. He said the eagles have been returned."

Fabius shook his head angrily. "Impossible. He's spinning you tales. He knew who we were, knew about our looted Parthian treasure. Word must have spread about us along the caravan route. He was eager to please, and thought a tall tale of an emperor would satisfy us. Well, he was wrong. We should have butchered him along with the others."

"Then we would never have got here. He guided us through the canyon."

"We would have died fighting. Death with honor."

"If the eagles have been returned, then we can return too, with honor."

Fabius paused. "The eagles would be this emperor's triumph, not ours. We would be an embarrassment." He peered at Licinius. "But I know you too well, brother. You are think-

27

ing of your son."

Licinius said nothing, but squinted at the rising orb above the eastern horizon, casting a shimmering orange sparkle on the surface of the lake. *His son.* A son who would not know him, who had been little more than a babe in arms when he had marched off. A son who would have carried on in his father's trade, as generations had done before. Licinius thought about what Fabius had said. *I have seen what emperors do.* Emperors did not just enslave and terrorize. They also built palaces, temples. There would be work for a sculptor, in this new Rome.

"Don't be deluded," Fabius said. "If what the trader says is true, the world has changed. Rome has forsaken us. We only have ourselves. The band of brothers. Everything else is gone."

"My son might still be alive."

"Your son is probably in Elysium by now. He too may have become a citizen-soldier, fought and died with honor. Think of that."

There was a muffled yell from somewhere beyond the hill. Fabius grabbed his sword handle, but Licinius stayed him. "It's only the trader. He's chained up."

"I thought you'd killed him. That's what you came up here to do."

"I wanted to see that he was telling the truth. That the boat wasn't some kind of wreck."

28

"Tell me again what he said. We need to set off now. Dawn is upon us."

"He said that where the great orb rose, glistening, was Chrysê, the land of gold. To get there, you must first cross the lake, then go over a pass, then traverse the desert, a place worse than anything we have yet endured, that sucks men in and swallows them up forever. You follow the camel caravans east, and you come to a great city called Thina. And there the bravest will find the empire of heaven. All the riches of the world await those who can defeat the demons that had stalked the trader, a treasure awaiting us, his new masters."

The trader had talked too much. He had told them all they needed to hear. He had kept nothing back. That had been his mistake. He had not been used to bargaining with the Fates.

The trader had told Licinius something else, while he was chaining him up. To the south, due south, was another route. Great mountains stood in the way, then the kingdom of Bactria, and beyond that a mighty river, the river Alexander the Great had crossed. And south from there, for untold miles, through jungle and along coast, was a route to a place called Ramaya, where there were Romans. There were untold dangers. *Always beware the tiger,* he had said. But at this place, like Barygaza, the goods of trade

— the riches from Chrysê and Thina, the *serikōn* and the precious jewels, the jade and the cassia and the malabathron — would go in ships across the Erythraean Sea, and from there you could make your way to Rome. *To Rome.*

Licinius grasped Fabius' hand hard, as hard as he could, their special bond since they had arm-wrestled as young recruits. They both relaxed and embraced, before pushing each other roughly away. Old men, playing like boys. He reached for the bag he had taken from the trader, and gestured at the other one on Fabius' belt. "Before we go. We don't have to placate the trader anymore with promises. May as well look at what we stole from him."

Fabius sprang up, pulling on his belt to ease the weight of the chain mail on his hips. "Time for that later." He pointed at the fore-shore, where the others were sitting at the oars gesturing up at them. "The boat's ready."

"The boat to the other side has been waiting for us for a long time, brother."

"I don't mean Charon, you fool. I mean our boat. The boat to freedom. The boat to untold wealth. We're going east, to *Chrysê.*"

"You go on ahead. I have to finish with the trader. His time has come."

"*Ave atque vale, frater.* In this world, or the next."

Licinius stared at Fabius. *He knew.*

30

Fabius bounded down the hill without looking back. Licinius got up and went in the other direction, toward the place where he had left the trader. The sky to the west was darkening again, over the pass they had come up, flickering with lightning, and he felt the first drops of rain. The air was eerily still, just as it had been before the maelstrom the night before. They would be caught in it if they did not set off now. He knew that Fabius would not linger, and the others would follow him. He was their centurion. And Fabius knew they had no time to lose. There would be other boats, hidden like the one they had found, left by other travelers. There was the route around the shore. Their enemy had horses, and could move quickly. Licinius looked at the pass again, and saw the jagged ridges of the gorge silhouetted by distant flashes of lightning. The rain was suddenly pelting down, and he slipped down the slope. The boat was obscured by the hill now, and to the south all he could see was the misty foothills of the mountains. He turned into the hollow. The trader was still there, splayed on the ground, his arms chained above his head around a boulder.

Licinius drew the great sword from under the leather loops on his back, put his hand inside the golden gauntlet and grasped the crossbar. He stared at the image of the tiger, then wiped the blade across his forearm. He found a cleft in the rock and pushed the blade into it, then bent it until it snapped, leaving the gauntlet attached to a jagged point about two feet long. That was more like it. More like a Roman *gladius.* He turned on the trader. The man had thought there was a chance, had led them through the canyon to this place, but now he knew. Licinius knelt down, close enough to smell the man's armpits, his breath, the way animals smelled when they were cornered, trapped. He put the broken edge of the blade below the man's chest. He could see the heart pounding.

Here, there was no right or wrong.

They killed. *That was what they did.*

The man looked up. Licinius remembered his son. It was like looking down at a child, just as helpless. But this was different. The man's breath was short, rasping, his face contorted with terror, his mouth drooling. A foul smell came from below, and Licinius turned his head away, nauseated. He knelt up to put his weight behind the sword, and for the first time saw that the man was different from the other Sogdians, his eyes less slanted, his cheekbones higher, a wisp of a moustache over his lips. His skin was that of a city-dweller, not a desert nomad. Then he remembered what the man had said. He himself had come from this land far to the east, this great inland city. He said he knew the tomb. He said he knew how to get inside. He said he

32

was the caretaker. He'd been babbling, desperate to please.

The man was trying to speak now, looking toward the bag Licinius had taken from him. He spoke in a hoarse whisper, the Greek so heavily accented Licinius could barely understand it, the words scarcely comprehensible.

His grandfather had seen it and grasped it, the greatest star in the heavens.

His grandfather, two hundred years old, had kept the secret.

He, Liu Jian, had taken it, to return it to its rightful place, and they had come after him.

"Now they will come after you."

The man tried to raise his head from the ground. His Greek was suddenly clear, as if he knew the words would be his last. "You have taken the celestial jewel that belongs above the emperor's tomb. It is in two parts. One part is blue, lapis lazuli from the mountains of Bactria, the other green, peridot from the island in the Erythraean Sea. You must take what you have to the lapis lazuli mines, and hide it there. That is the only place where the power of the stone will not be felt. You must never put the two stones together, to make the jewel whole. Only the emperor may have immortality. Those who follow will pursue you, relentlessly. They must never be allowed to have the power."

The man slumped back, lips trembling. Licinius remained still. He suddenly realized.

The treasure the trader had babbled about the day before, the treasure of the emperor's tomb. It was not in that far-off place to the east. *It was here.* He felt the bag at his waist, the shape within. He leapt up, and stumbled to the edge of the hollow, looking out over the lake. He was too late. The others were already far offshore, pulling for their lives. They had seen the coming storm. *Fabius would never know.* Licinius turned back to the trader. He felt hollow, in limbo. Had he forsaken the greatest treasure of all, the lure of immortality, for a hopeless dream of finding his son?

He turned toward the looming darkness. The wind stung his eyes, laden with red dust that seemed to swirl around the lake from the east, whipped into a frenzy by the storm coming up the pass. Then he heard it, above the distant rumble of thunder, at first barely discernible, like a pounding of blood in his ears, then insistent, louder. *A drumbeat.* He remembered the night before. Horses, rearing up, black horses with yellow eyes, the red dust swirling in and out of their nostrils, their life-breath. Horses slick with blood, their own blood, as if they were sweating it. Horses that pulled chariots, crossbowmen barely visible, and in front of them the rider with the skin of the beast draped over his armor, the face framed by savage teeth, only darkness within.

And now they had come again.

Licinius turned back to the trader and drove the blade in hard, crunching through the spine. The man died wide-eyed, the blood from his last heartbeat spurting out of the wound. The body convulsed, the muscles clasping the blade, and Licinius got up and put his foot down to pull it out. He stood there, blade dripping, and peered back through the darkness and the rain. Then he saw it. A silhouette on a ridge, looking toward him. Hooves pawing the ground, skin glowing red, breathing out the dust that glowed with the sun, the snarling head and jagged teeth above, a great sword held high and glistening.

He remembered what the trader had called it.

The tiger warrior.

Licinius turned south.

He began to run.

1

The Red Sea, present-day

"Jack, you're not going to believe what I've found."

The voice came through the intercom from somewhere in the blue void ahead, where a silvery stream of bubbles rose from beyond a rocky ledge to the surface of the sea nearly fifty meters above. Jack Howard took a last look at the coral-encrusted anchor below him, then injected a burst of air into his buoyancy compensator and floated above the thick bed of sea whips bending in the current, like tall grass in the wind. He powered forward with his fins, then spread his arms and legs like a skydiver and dropped over the ledge. The view below was breathtaking. All down the slope he had seen fragments of ancient pottery, Islamic, Nabatean, Egyptian, but this was the mother lode. For years there had been rumors of a ships' graveyard on the windward side of the reef, but it had been just that, hearsay and rumor, until the unusually strong tidal currents in the Red Sea that spring had scoured the plateau and revealed what lay before him. Then there had been the rumor that set Jack's heart racing, the rumor of a Roman shipwreck, perfectly preserved under the sand. Now, as he saw the shapes emerging from the sediment, row upon row of ancient pottery amphoras, their tall handles rising to wide rims, he exhaled hard, dropping faster, and felt the familiar excitement course through him. He silently mouthed the words, as he always did. *Lucky Jack.*

The voice crackled again. "Fifteen years of diving with you, and I thought I'd seen everything. This one really takes the cake."

Jack turned toward the far edge of the plateau. He could see Costas now, hovering motionless in front of a coral head the size of a small truck, the growths rising several meters higher than him. Two more heads rose behind the first, forming a row. Beyond them the water was too deep for coral to flourish, and Jack could see the sandy slope dropping off into an abyss. He flicked on his headlamp and swam toward Costas, coming to a halt a few meters before him and panning his light over the seabed. It was an explosion of color, bright red sponges, sea anemones, profusely growing soft corals, with clown fish darting among the nooks and crevices. An eel drooped out of a hole, mouth lolling, eyeing

Jack, then withdrew again. Jack looked down through a waving bed of sea fans and saw fragments of amphoras, so thickly encrusted as to be almost unrecognizable. He peered again, saw a high arching handle, a distinctive rim. He turned to Costas, his headlamp lighting up his friend's yellow helmet and the streamlined backpack that held his trimix breathing gas.

"Nice find," he said. "I saw sherds like this coming down the slope. Rhodian wine amphoras, second century BC."

"Switch off your headlamp." Costas seemed riveted by something in front of him. "Take another look. And forget about amphoras."

Jack was itching to swim over to the wreck he had seen in the sand. But he lingered in front of the coral head, stared at the dazzle of color and movement. He remembered the words of Professor Dillen, all those years ago at Cambridge. *Archaeology is about detail, but don't let the detail obscure the bigger picture.* Jack had already known it, since he had first gone hunting for artifacts as a boy. It had always been his special gift. To see the bigger picture. And to find things. *Lucky Jack.* He shut his eyes, flicked off his headlamp then opened his eyes again. It was as if he were in a different universe. The profusion of color had been replaced by a monotone blue, shades of dark where there had been vivid purples and reds. It was like looking at an artist's charcoal sketch, all the finish and color stripped away, the eye drawn not to the detail but to the form, to the overall shape. *To the bigger picture.*

And then he saw it.

"Good God."

He blinked hard, and looked again. There was no mistaking it. Not one, but two, sticking out of the sand, curving upward on either side of the coral head, symmetrical, gleaming white from centuries of burial in the sediment. He remembered where they were. The Red Sea. The eastern extremity of Egypt, the edge of the ancient Graeco-Roman world. Beyond here lay fabled lands, lands of terror and allure, of untold treasure and danger, of races of giants and pygmies and great, lumbering beasts, beasts of the hunt and of war that only the bravest could harness, beasts that could make a man a king.

They were tusks.

"I'm waiting, Jack. Explain your way out of this one."

Jack swallowed hard. His heart was pounding with excitement. He spoke quietly, trying to keep his voice under control. "It's an *elephantegos.*"

"A what?"

"An *elephantegos.*"

"Right. An elephant. A statue of an elephant."

"No. An *elephantegos.*"

40

"Okay, Jack. What's the difference?"

"There's an amazing papyrus letter, found in the Egyptian desert," Jack said. "Maurice Hiebermeyer emailed it to me on *Seaquest II* as we were sailing here. I asked him for anything in the papyrus records that might refer to a shipwreck. It's almost as if he had an instinct we'd find something like this."

"Wouldn't be the first time," Costas said. "He's an oddball, but I've got to hand it to him."

Jack's mind was racing. He reached out and touched the tip of the nearest tusk. It was silky-smooth, but powdery, like chalk. "The letter mentions a shipwreck. It's one of very few ancient documents to mention a shipwreck in the Red Sea. Maurice knew we were planning to dive here, on our way up to his excavation at Berenikê."

"I'm listening, Jack."

"It tells how a ship dispatched from the port at Berenikê had sunk. The letter was meant to reach a place called Ptolemais Thêrôn, Ptolemais of the Hunts. That was an outpost somewhere to the south of here on the coast of Eritrea. It was where the Egyptians procured their wild animals. Because of the shipwreck, the men in the outpost hadn't received their grain. The letter assures them that another *elephantegos* was under construction at Berenikê, and would soon be on its way with all the supplies they needed."

41

"Elephantegos," Costas murmured. "You mean . . ."

"Elephant-transporter. Elephant-ship."

"Jack, I'm getting that funny feeling again. The one I always get when I dive with you. It's called disbelief."

"Have you looked beyond? There are two more coral heads. Exactly the same size. Three of them, in a row. Just the number you'd expect. Chained and roped down just as they would have been in a hull."

"You're telling me this thing in front of me is an elephant. A real elephant. Not a statue."

"We know ivory can survive burial underwater, right? We've found tusks and hippo teeth in the Mediterranean. And the coral around here grows pretty fast, quicker than it would take for an elephant skeleton to crumble. There may be no bones left inside there now, but the coral preserves the shape."

"I need a moment, Jack. Remember, I'm just an engineer. I need to stare this thing in the face. This could be the one archaeological discovery that finally does it for me, Jack. I think I might cry."

"You can handle it." Jack floated back and stared at the ghostly apparition that loomed in front of them, one of the most amazing things he had ever seen underwater. He switched on his headlamp again. "Those tusks aren't going to survive long. We need to get them reburied. But before that we need a film team down here, pronto. This is headline stuff."

"Leave it to me, Jack. I've got a channel open to *Seaquest II.*"

Jack glanced at his wrist computer. "Seven minutes left. I want to have a look at those amphoras in the sand. I'll be within visual range."

"I think I've had enough excitement for one dive."

"I'll meet you halfway for the ascent."

"Roger that."

Jack drifted back toward the sandy plateau, letting the current take him. It had picked up slightly during their dive, raising a pall of fine silt that hung a meter or so over the seabed, briefly obscuring the amphoras from view. Ahead of him a school of glassfish hung in the water like a diaphanous veil, parting to reveal a reef shark swimming languidly along the slope. He heard the muffled roar of the Zodiac boat on the surface gunning its outboards, circling to keep position. A banging from the boat marked their five-minute warning. He glanced back at Costas, now some twenty meters away, then dropped down into the suspended sediment. Costas might not be able to see him, but Jack's exhaust bubbles would be clearly visible. He stared ahead, concentrating on his objective, his arms held out in front of him with his hands together, his legs slowly kicking a frog stroke. He was in perfect control of his buoyancy. Suddenly he saw them, a row of four amphoras, intact and leaning in the sand, another row poking up beyond. He exhaled hard, emptying his lungs, knowing his life depended on his equipment delivering that next breath, the edge of danger that made diving his passion. He dropped down, then inhaled just above the seafloor, regaining neutral buoyancy. The amphoras were covered with fine sediment, sparkling with the sunlight that streamed through the water from the surface forty-five meters overhead.

He saw more rows of amphoras, then a scour channel with darkened timbers protruding below. He drew in his breath. "Well I'll be damned."

"Got something?" Costas' voice crackled through.

"Just another ancient wreck."

"Couldn't beat an *elephantegos*," Costas retorted. "My *elephantegos*."

"Just some old pots," Jack said.

"It's never just old pots with you. I've seen you empty the gold inside to get at the pot. Typical archaeologist."

"The pots are where the history lies," Jack said.

"So you keep telling me. Personally, I'll take a sack of doubloons over a pot any day. So what have you got?"

"Wine amphoras, about two centuries later

than the Rhodian ones with the *elephantegos.* These date from the time of Augustus, the first Roman emperor. They come all the way from Italy."

Jack finned toward the row of amphoras. His excitement mounted. "These are outward-bound, no doubt about it. They've still got the mortar seals over the lids, with the stamp of the Italian estates that made them. This is Falernian wine, vintage stuff. Costas, I think we've just hit pay dirt." He looked back. Costas had swum up from the coral head and was hanging in the water at the halfway point, already rising a few meters above the seafloor. "Time to go, Jack. Two minutes to our no-stop limit."

"Roger that." Jack's eyes were darting around, taking in everything possible in the remaining moments before the alarm bell sounded. "Each of these wine amphoras was worth a slave. There are hundreds of them. This was a high-value cargo. A Roman East Indiaman."

"You mean actually going to India?" Costas flicked on his headlamp, bringing out the colors in the seabed around Jack. "Doesn't that mean bullion? Treasure?"

Jack touched one of the amphoras. He felt the thrill that coursed through him every time he touched an artifact that had lain beyond human hands since ancient times. And shipwrecks were the most exciting finds of all.

Not the accumulated garbage of a civilization, castoffs and rubbish, but living organisms, lost in a moment of catastrophe, on the cusp of great adventure. Adventure that always came with risk, and this time the dice had fallen the wrong way. This had been a ship heading out into a perilous monsoon, for a voyage of thousands of miles across the Indian Ocean. Jack knew the draw of the east from his own ancestors who had sailed there in the time of the East India Company. They had called it *The Enterprise of the Indies,* the greatest adventure of all. Untold treasure. Untold danger. And for the ancients, the stakes were even higher. Somewhere out there lay the fiery edge of the world. Yet along its rim, as far as you could go, were to be found riches that would humble even a mighty emperor, and bring him face-to-face with the greatest secrets imaginable, with sacred elixirs, with alchemy, with immortality.

The alarm sounded, a harsh, insistent clanging that seemed to come from everywhere. Jack took a deep breath and rose a few meters above the amphoras, then began to fin toward Costas. They would excavate. So much of archaeology was below the radar of recorded history, about the mundane residue of day-to-day life, but here perhaps they had found something momentous. It was a shipwreck that might have been a turning point in history, that might have determined

46

whether Rome would ever rule beyond the Indian Ocean. He looked at Costas, who was staring down into the pool of color in his headlight, reflecting off the sand. Jack checked his dive computer, then saw Costas still staring, transfixed. He followed his gaze, and looked down again.

Then he saw it. Yellow, glinting. Sand, but not just sand. A fantastic mirage. He blinked hard, then exhaled and sank down again until his knees were resting on the seabed. He could scarcely believe what he was seeing. Then he remembered. A Roman emperor's lament, two thousand years ago. *All our money drained off to the east, for the sake of spice and baubles.*

He looked up at Costas. He looked down again.

The seabed was carpeted with gold.

He picked up a glittering piece, held it close. It was a gold coin, an *aureus,* mint, uncirculated. The head of a young man, strong, confident, a man who believed that Rome could rule the world. The emperor *Augustus.*

"Holy cow," Costas said. "Tell me this is true."

"I think," Jack said, his voice sounding hoarse, "you've got your treasure."

"We need to put this site in lockdown," Costas replied, flicking a switch on the side of his helmet. "All outside radio communication off. We don't want anyone else picking up what we say. There's enough gold here to fund a small jihad."

"Roger that." Jack flipped off his switch. He savored the moment, holding the gold coin, looking at the glittering spectacle in front of him, the rows of amphoras in the background. Costas was right. Jack was an archaeologist, not a treasure hunter, but in truth he had scoured the world for a discovery like this, good, old-fashioned treasure, an emperor's ransom in gold. *And it was Roman.*

He looked up, saw the Zodiac far above, sensed the darker shadow of *Seaquest II* a few hundred meters offshore. He flashed an okay signal to Costas, and jerked his thumb upward. The two men began to ascend, side by side. Jack glanced back at the receding seafloor, the details now lost in the sand, the amphoras indistinguishable from rock and coral. He had dreamed of this for years, of finding a wreck that would take him back to the greatest adventure the ancient world had ever known, a quest for treasures of unimaginable value, treasures that were still beckoning explorers to this day. His whole spirit was suffused with excitement. This had been the dive of his life. They had found the first ever treasure wreck dating from ancient Roman times. He saw Costas looking at him through his face mask, his eyes creased in a smile. He whispered the words again. *Lucky Jack.*

2

Three hours later Jack dipped the nose of the Lynx helicopter and swung it around in a wide arc from the helipad on *Seaquest II,* lingering for a moment to set the navigational computer for the Egyptian coast some thirty-five nautical miles to the northwest. They would fly low, to prevent the nitrogen in their bloodstreams from forming bubbles, risking the bends.

Jack glanced past Costas' helmeted form in the copilot's seat toward *Seaquest II.* On the stern was the word *Truro,* the nearest port of registry to the campus of the International Maritime University in Cornwall, England, and fluttering above it was the IMU flag, a shield with a superimposed anchor derived from Jack's family coat of arms. She was their premier research vessel, custom-built less than two years before to replace the first *Seaquest,* lost in the Black Sea. From a distance she looked like a naval support ship. On the foredeck Jack saw a team in white flash overalls beside the forty-millimeter Breda gun pod, raised from its concealed mount for live-fire practice. Several of the crew were former members of Britain's elite Special Boat Service who Jack had known in the Royal Navy. They were near the coast of Somalia, where the threat of piracy was ever present; in a matter of days they were due off the war-torn island of Sri Lanka. But in all other respects *Seaquest II* was a state-of-the-art research vessel, bristling with the latest diving and excavation technology, with accommodation and lab facilities for a team of thirty. She was the result of decades of accumulated experience when they'd put their heads together and come up with a blueprint for the ideal vessel. Not for the first time Jack silently thanked their benefactor, Efram Jacobovich, a software tycoon and passionate diver, who had seen the potential in Jack's vision and provided the endowment that funded their exploration around the world.

"We're locked on," Jack said into the intercom. "Good to go."

Costas pointed at the horizon. "Engage."

Jack grinned, pushed the cyclic stick forward to dip the nose again, then flipped on the autopilot. As they gathered speed he glanced at the bridge wing and saw Scott Macalister, a former Canadian coast guard captain who was *Seaquest II*'s master. Beside him stood a tall, slender girl, her long dark hair blowing in the breeze, shielding her eyes against the glare and waving at them.

"Rebecca seems to be doing nicely," Costas said.

"For her first expedition, I can't believe how well she fits in," Jack replied. "She's almost running the show. Pretty impressive for a sixteen-year-old."

"It must be in the blood, Jack."

They could see the reef now, the dark blue of the abyss rising through shades of turquoise until the coral heads at the top of the slope were visible, some of them nearly breaking the surface. They passed over the wavering yellow forms of two Aquapod submersibles, just about to dive on the ancient ships' graveyard fifty meters below. Within hours the Aquapods would have completed a full photogrammetric and laser survey of the site, something that would have taken weeks of dives and painstaking hand measurements in Jack's early days. After surfacing from their dive and returning to *Seaquest II* he had gone straight into an intensive video conference with the Egyptian Antiquities Authorities, the Egyptian Navy, and the staff of his friend Maurice Hiebermeyer's Institute of Archaeology in Alexandria. With *Seaquest II* committed months before to a voyage into the Pacific, another IMU vessel would take over the excavation, and an Egyptian navy frigate would be on station for the duration. The

51

excavation would complete a hat trick of ancient wreck investigations by IMU over the past few years: a Bronze Age Minoan shipwreck in the Aegean, St. Paul's shipwreck off Sicily and now this. Jack fervently hoped he would be back in time to work on the site himself, but for now he was thrilled to have set the wheels in motion. He relaxed back in his seat, breathing out the excess nitrogen in his bloodstream and feeling his body recoup its strength after the dive. He was exhausted, but elated. He was itching to reach their destination, to discover what Hiebermeyer had been badgering him to see for months now in his excavation in the Egyptian desert.

"Check out that island." Costas gestured at a barren, rugged outcrop in the sea below them, about two kilometers across and rising to a peak several hundred meters high, the rock scorched white and seemingly devoid of vegetation. It looked like a place of extremes, unable to support life.

"That's Zabargad, known as St. John's Island," Jack said. "The ancient Greeks called it Topazios, the Island of Topaz."

"I can see rock tailings, old mine workings, around the edge of the mountain," Costas said.

"It was the only ancient source of peridot, the translucent green gem also called olivine," Jack said. "The island's a minerologist's dream, an upthrusting of the earth's crust.

The Chinese revered peridot because it's like jade, a sacred stone. They thought it had healing qualities. The best gems were the treasures of emperors."

"Was it mined by convicts?" Costas asked.

"You've got it. The mother of all penal colonies," Jack said. "To most of the prisoners here, this was the end of the earth."

Costas took a deep breath. "It reminds me of Alcatraz."

"A longer swim here than San Francisco Bay, and a few more sharks."

"Did anyone ever escape?"

"Before I try to answer that, look at this." Jack reached into his front pocket and took out a small envelope. He passed it to Costas, who tipped out the object inside onto his palm. It was the gold coin Jack had picked up on the seabed, glistening and perfect, as if it had come straight from the mint.

"Jack . . ."

"I borrowed it. A sample. I had to have something to show Maurice. Ever since we were schoolboys he's been telling me that nothing equals the treasure from Egyptian tombs."

"Dr. Jack Howard, the world's premier maritime archaeologist, loots his own site. What will the Egyptian authorities say when I tell them?"

"The authorities? You mean Herr Professor Dr. Maurice Hiebermeyer, the greatest living

Egyptologist? He'll probably give me a pity-ing look and show me a jewel-encrusted mummy."

"I thought you guys only liked bits of broken pot." Costas grinned, and held the coin up carefully between two fingers. "Okay, so why show me this now?"

"The portrait on the obverse is Augustus, the first Roman emperor. Now check out the reverse."

Costas turned the coin over. Jack saw a shield in the middle, a standard on either side. The standard on the right was topped by an orb, signifying Rome's domination over the world. The one on the left had an *aquila,* the sacred eagle that legionaries would fight to the death to protect. They were the *signa militaria,* the Roman legionary standards. Jack pointed to the inscription in the middle. "Right. Now read out the words."

Costas squinted. *"Signis Receptis."*

"That means 'Standards returned.' This coin was one of Augustus' prized issues, about 19 BC, only a few years after he became emperor. Augustus was consolidating the empire, following decades of civil war. His son Tiberius had just concluded a peace treaty with the Parthians, who ruled the area of Iran and Iraq. They agreed to return the standards that had been taken from defeated Roman legions years before. Augustus treated the return as a personal triumph, and had them paraded through Rome. It was a huge propaganda score for him, though too late to help the men who had fought under those standards and been unlucky enough not to die on the battlefield."

"What does this have to do with convicts?"

"Backtrack to 53 BC. Rome is still a republic, ruled by the triumvirate of Julius Caesar, Pompey and Crassus. Already things are falling apart, with personal rivalries and ambitions that would lead to civil war. Military prestige is what matters. Pompey has his, having cleared the sea of pirates. Julius Caesar is getting his, campaigning in Gaul. Crassus is the odd one out. He decides to seek glory in the east, and to hunt for gold. The difference was Pompey and Caesar were both seasoned generals. Crassus was a banker."

"I think I can guess what happened."

"The Battle of Carrhae, near modern Harran in southern Turkey. One of the worst defeats ever suffered by a Roman army. Crassus was a useless general, but his legions fought for Rome, and for their own honor. They fought hard, but were overwhelmed by the Parthian cavalry. At least twenty thousand were slaughtered, and the wounded were all executed. Crassus was killed, but a Roman soldier was dressed up as him and forced to drink molten gold."

"Fitting end for a banker."

"At least ten thousand Roman soldiers were

captured. Those who weren't executed were sent to the Parthian citadel of Merv, and probably used as slave labor building the city walls. That's the connection. Mines, quarries, slave labor. The lot of prisoners of war in antiquity. Merv wasn't cut off by sea like St. John's Island, but was marooned in the desert wastes of what's now Turkmenistan. At that time hardly anyone knew what lay beyond the lands conquered by Alexander the Great in the fourth century BC, beyond the Indus and Afghanistan." Jack flipped open the computer screen between the two seats, and clicked the mouse until an image came up. It showed a scorched landscape of ruins and dusty tracks surrounded by a vast, decayed rampart, flattened in places to a rounded hillock. "That's what's left of Merv," he said. "Those are the walls of ancient Margiana, the name of the city at the time of the Parthians."

"They look like earthworks, not masonry."

"They were made of mud-brick, over and over again, a new wall built on top of the eroded remains of the previous one. But at some point there may have been a failed experiment with mortar. We found a recently exposed section where one of the walls had collapsed, and it was filled with a whitish powdery substance. Almost like concrete that hadn't set properly."

"When were you there?"

"The Transoxiana Conference in April," Jack said. "The Oxus was the ancient name for the great river that runs near here, from Afghanistan toward the Aral Sea. The ancient Greeks and Romans saw it as the limit of their world. The conference focused on contacts between the west and Central Asia."

"You mean the Silk Road?"

"The time when Chinese and central Asian traders were first appearing in places like Merv, soon after Alexander the Great swept through there."

Costas peered at the picture. "Hang on. Who's that? I recognize that person."

"Just there for scale."

"Jack! That's Katya!"

"She chaired my session of the conference. It's right up her street. She's been studying ancient inscriptions along the Silk Road. She invited me. We weren't doing any diving in April, so I could hardly say no."

"Jack. Well, well. You've been seeing Katya again. That's what this is all about, isn't it? Jack Howard, underwater archaeologist, flying off to a heap of dust in the middle of a desert. Turkmenistan, is it? That's about as far away from a shipwreck as you could find."

"Just keeping up with old colleagues." Jack grinned, and closed the screen.

Costas grunted. "Anyway. These Romans. Prisoners of war. I asked whether any of them ever escaped."

"From St. John's Island, I doubt it. From Merv is another matter. Hardly any of Crassus' legionaries could have survived to the time Augustus repatriated the standards, more than thirty years after the battle. But there were rumors in Rome for several generations after."

"What kind of rumors?"

"The kind you hear about but can never source. Rumors about a band of escaped prisoners, legionaries who had been captured at Carrhae. Prisoners who didn't go west, back to a world that had forsaken them, but instead went east."

"You believe this?"

"If they'd survived all those years of toil in the Parthian citadel, they'd have been the toughest. And they were Roman legionaries. They knew how to route-march."

"Let's see. Heading east. That's Afghanistan, central Asia?"

Jack paused. "Some of the rumors come from much farther east. From the ancient annals of the Chinese emperors. But it'll have to wait. We're almost there." Jack pointed ahead to a great tongue of land that jutted out into the Red Sea. "That's Ras Banas. It's shaped like an elephant's head. I thought you'd like that."

"How could I forget?" Costas murmured. "My *elephantegos.* Never in a million years did I think I'd find ancient elephants underwater."

"Dive with me, and anything's possible."

"Only if I provide the technology."

"Touché."

Jack lowered the collective and the helicopter began to descend. "I can see the excavation now. I can even see Maurice. Those shorts of his are like a signal flag. I'm going to put us down on a rocky patch just in from the shore to avoid making a dust storm. Hold fast."

The scene that confronted them as they stepped out of the helicopter was one of desolation, enormous expanses of sunbaked ground with nothing but the sea glinting behind. Despite Jack's best efforts they had raised a whirlwind of sand as they landed, and the view now was refracted through a film of red dust as if the air itself were glowing hot. Inland to the west Jack could just see the line of low mountains that marked the edge of the coastal desert, on the route to the Nile; to the east, the rugged peninsula of Ras Banas curved out into the sea. Tucked in at the head of the bay a few hundred meters away were the ramshackle huts of the Egyptian customs outpost, and beyond that lay a shallow lagoon about a kilometer across enclosed by a thin sandy spit on the seaward side. It seemed a place on the edge of human existence.

Costas stood beside Jack, wearing a straw hat and garish wraparound sunglasses, wiping the dust and sweat from his face. He pointed into the haze. "Here he comes." A portly figure trundled out of the dust down the small hill beside them, his hand already outstretched. He was shorter than Jack, a little taller than Costas, but whereas Costas had the barrel chest and brawn of his Greek island ancestry, Hiebermeyer had never managed to shake off the impression that his entire being revolved around sausage and sauerkraut. It was an illusion, Jack knew, for a man who was continuously on the move and had the energy of a small army.

"He's still flying at half-mast, I see," Costas muttered to Jack.

"Don't say anything. Remember, I gave him those shorts. They're a hallowed part of our archaeological heritage. One day they'll be in the Smithsonian." He glanced at Costas' own baggy shorts and luridly colored shirt. "Anyway, you can hardly talk, Hawaii-Five-Oh."

"Just getting ready," Costas said. "For where we're going in the Pacific. You remember? Holiday time. Thought I may as well kit up now."

"Yes. About that." Jack cleared his throat just as Hiebermeyer came up and shook hands warmly with him, and then with Costas. "Come on," he said, continuing down the hill without actually stopping.

"So much for small talk," Costas said, swigging at a water bottle.

"He's been wanting to show me this place for months," Jack said, slinging his faded old khaki bag over his shoulder and following. "I can't wait."

"Okay, okay." Costas tossed the bottle back into the helicopter and followed Jack down the hill, catching up with them about fifty meters from the water's edge. Hiebermeyer took off his little round glasses and wiped them, and then opened his arms expansively. "Welcome to ancient Berenikê. The holiday resort at the end of the universe." He pointed back up the slope. "Up there's the Temple of Serapis, down here's the main east-west road, the *decumanus.* The town was founded by Ptolemy II, son of Alexander the Great's general, who ruled Egypt in the third century BC and named the place Berenikê after his mother. Flourished mainly under the Roman emperor Augustus, declined after that."

"So where's the amphitheater?" Costas looked around. "I don't see anything at all."

"Look down."

Costas kicked at the ground. "Okay. A few potsherds."

"Now come over here." They followed Hiebermeyer a few meters farther toward the shore. He had led them to the edge of an excavated area the size of a large swimming pool. It was as if the skin had been peeled off the ground. They saw rough rubble walls of coral and sandstone, forming small rooms and alleyways. It was the foundations of an ancient town, not an immaculately laid out Roman town like Pompeii or Herculaneum but a place without any architectural pretension, where walls and rooms had clearly been added organically as they were needed. Hiebermeyer leapt down with surprising agility onto a duckboard that lay across the trench. He bounded over to the far side and pulled a large tarpaulin away, then gave a triumphant flourish. "There you go, Jack. I thought you'd like that."

It was a row of Roman amphoras, just like the ones they had seen on the wreck that morning, only these were worn and many had broken rims. "All reused, as you can see," Hiebermeyer said. "My guess is these went all the way to India filled with wine, then were brought back here empty and reused as water containers. Water's a precious commodity here. The nearest spring's on the edge of the mountains, miles away. We don't even have electricity. We use solar panels to run our computers. And we have to bring our food in, just as they did in ancient times from the Nile Valley. It really makes you empathize with the past."

"It sounds like a lunar colony," Costas murmured.

Hiebermeyer replaced the tarpaulin and pulled up another one beside it, revealing a pile of dark stones about the size of soccer balls. "Ballast," he said. "It's basalt, volcanic, foreign to this area."

"Ballast," Costas repeated. "Why?"

"An outward-bound ship, filled with gold and wine, is going to sail along fine. A ship returning with peppercorns is going to bob around like a cork. You needed ballast. This stone's been sourced to southern India."

"Maurice!" Jack exclaimed, patting him on the back. "We'll make a nautical archaeologist of you yet."

"India," Costas said. "Someone's going to have to fill me in."

Jack turned to him. "For millennia, the ancient Egyptians received goods from beyond the Red Sea, but always via middlemen. Then, after Alexander conquered Egypt and the first Greek merchants appeared along this coast, someone told the Egyptians and the Greeks how to sail across the Indian Ocean using the monsoon. They sailed out from Egypt with the northeasterly monsoon, came back with the southwesterly, achieving one round voyage a year. It was dangerous and terrifying, but the winds were as predictable as the seasons. It opened up an amazing era of maritime discovery. The first Greek sea merchants hit India soon after Berenikê was established. After the Romans took over

Egypt in 31 BC, everything revved up. Under Augustus as many as three hundred ships left from here annually. It was big investment, big risk stuff, just like the European East Indies trade fifteen hundred years later. Gold, silver, wine went out; gems, spices, pepper came back."

"And not just that," Hiebermeyer said, leaping out of the trench and wiping the sweat from his forehead. "Now for what I really wanted you to see. Follow me up the hill." A scorching gust of wind blew up, stinging their eyes. Costas crouched back against it, then trudged up behind the other two men.

"We've been talking about the Battle of Carrhae, Crassus' lost legions," Jack said.

"I'm always ready to hear about a Roman defeat," Hiebermeyer replied, grinning at Jack.

"Come on. The Romans didn't rule Egypt that badly. If it wasn't for them, you wouldn't be here, sunning yourself beside the Red Sea. This is basically a Roman site."

"I'd rather be in the Valley of the Kings," Hiebermeyer sniffed.

"Talking to Costas about Carrhae set me thinking about another Roman defeat," Jack said. "One never forgotten by the emperors. The lost legions of Varus, destroyed in AD 9 in the Teutoberg Forest."

Hiebermeyer stopped in his tracks. "That was my first real taste of archaeology as a boy, hunting for the site of the battle. My family owned a lodge nearby, outside Osnabruck in Lower Saxony."

Jack shaded his eyes and looked at Costas. "The Romans were pushing into Germany. It was the glory days of Augustus. The possibilities seemed limitless. Then it all went horribly wrong. Varus was inexperienced, like Crassus, and took three legions into unknown territory. They were ambushed by the Germans and annihilated, twenty thousand men at least."

"What's your point?" Hiebermeyer said, walking slowly again up the hill.

"The decline of Berenikê, after Augustus. It's bizarre, at the height of the empire when the Roman economy was booming. It's as if the British government had suddenly pulled out of any interest in the East India Company in the late eighteenth century, when the biggest fortunes were being made."

"The defeat stopped the Romans in their tracks," Hiebermeyer said. "The Rhine became the frontier. Augustus nearly went insane over those lost legions." Jack nodded. "I wonder if Augustus had second thoughts. He looked east, to Arabia, to India, the lands beyond this place, where everything was ripe for conquest. He looked, and he said no. The empire was big enough. They couldn't afford another defeat. And the risk out here, the cost of failure, was huge."

"And not just military," Costas said.

"Go on."

"Massive fortunes were involved, right? Shiploads of gold and silver. That means only the wealthiest investors, including the emperor himself. What are the chances of shipwreck on a voyage out here, one in three, one in four? Let's say it happens, and the emperor loses big-time. His own cash. A high-risk investment gone wrong, and then those legions wiped out. It's all too much. He pulls the plug on India."

Jack stopped. "That's a hell of an idea."

"I'll sell you it for a cold beer," Costas said, wiping his forehead.

"Find me a wreck out here full of mint issues of Imperial gold, and I might believe you," Hiebermeyer said, trudging determinedly up the slope ahead of them. Costas looked questioningly at Jack, who grinned and followed Hiebermeyer.

"Speaking of shipwrecks, thanks for the hint, Maurice," Jack said loudly, catching up.

"Huh?"

"That translation you emailed me. From the Coptos archive. The ancient shipwreck. The *elephantegos*."

"Ah. Yes."

"We found one."

"Ah. Good."

"We found an *elephantegos*."

"Ah. Yes. Good." Hiebermeyer stopped,

clearly deep in some other train of thought, nodded sagely, then carried on walking. After a few moments he stopped again, dead in his tracks, and peered at Jack, his mouth open in astonishment. Jack caught Costas' eye, and the two of them continued up the slope. Hiebermeyer followed them to the edge of another large excavation trench, where he was suddenly preoccupied by the busy scene in front of them. He gesticulated at a group of students and Egyptian workers under a tarpaulin in one corner. A dark-featured Egyptian woman quickly came over and climbed out of the trench in front of them, her hair tied back under a bush hat. She spoke quietly to Hiebermeyer in German. He nodded and turned to Jack. "You remember Aysha? She dug with me in the mummy necropolis in the Fayum. She's in charge there now, but I got her down here as soon as we started finding what you're about to see."

"Congratulations on your doctorate." Jack shook hands warmly with her.

"And on your assistant directorship of the Institute in Alexandria," Costas said.

"Someone had to look after Maurice," she said.

Jack smiled to himself. Two years ago Aysha had been Hiebermeyer's top graduate student, a naturally gifted excavator who had more patience than Maurice did for the minutiae of a dig, able to spend hours dissecting a shred of mummy wrapping where Maurice would have quickly become flustered. She was never subservient to him, always quietly in control. She was his perfect foil, and he was never pompous with her. Jack looked at them together for a moment, and then banished the thought. It was impossible. Maurice would never allow the distraction.

"You must miss New York City," Costas said. "I get back whenever I can."

"When I finished at Columbia, I kept the apartment," Aysha said. "When this dig's over for the season, I'm back in NYC for a sabbatical. The apartment's where we arranged with Rebecca's guardians for her to meet up with Jack for the first time. They stayed there together in the spring."

"Thanks again for that, Aysha," Jack said, smiling at her. "You know she's with us on *Seaquest II*?"

"Of course. She emailed me this morning. A running commentary on your friend's appalling jokes."

"When you're back in Queens, say hello to my barber, Antonio," Costas said wistfully. "Corner of Fourteenth and Twenty-second. For ten years he cut my hair. While I was at school. Five bucks a go. Gave me my first shave. Taught me everything I know."

"Of course, Costas," Aysha said, rolling her eyes. "Next time I make a hair appointment."

"No appointment needed. You just show up."

Jack laughed. Hiebermeyer stamped his foot impatiently, and Jack saw his expression. "Okay, Maurice, what have you got?" Hiebermeyer nodded at Aysha, who ushered them to the edge of the trench. "It's a Roman villa," she said. "Or I should say, what counts as a villa in this place. The owners used the best available materials and put some expense into it. The walls are made of blocks of fossil coral, the main building material here, but they're veneered with slabs of gypsum that must have been hauled by camel caravan from the Nile. The little columns are Egyptian gray granite, quarried in the mountains to the west of here. The really fascinating thing is that he's got a polished wooden floor, completely at odds with Roman tradition. The wood's teak, from southern India. It's reused ship's timbers."

"And I see some modern conveniences," Jack said, pointing over to the corner where the workers were excavating.

"It's a water cistern, dug into the rock, lined with impervious concrete. Alongside it there's an economy version of a Roman bath. He's built himself a frigidarium, lined with pottery tubes for insulation and an ingenious system for keeping the room damp."

"He must have spent a lot of time in there," Costas grumbled, wiping the sweat off his face. "I don't know how anyone could stand this heat."

"They didn't, for half the year," Aysha replied. "This place was pretty well abandoned for months on end, between ships leaving from here to catch the northeast monsoon and then arriving back with the southwest. I think this guy was a traveling merchant, on the move a lot. I think this was just his pad when he was in town. And I think he probably had another place, in India."

"In India!" Costas exclaimed.

"Aysha, show them, will you?" Hiebermeyer said, clearly relishing the moment.

Aysha nodded, and led them under a tarpaulin shelter beside the trench. On a trestle table were trays full of finds, mainly fragments of pottery. "Some of this is Indian, Tamil style," she said, passing Jack a sherd in a polythene bag. "That one has a Tamil graffito on it, possibly the word Ramaya. It could be the name of the merchant himself, but I think it's the name for the Roman community in south India, the name the local people there gave it."

"You think this guy was Indian?" Costas said.

"Or his wife," Aysha said. "Take a look at this." She pointed to a chunk of sandstone about thirty centimeters across, highly eroded but with a carving on the front. It showed a woman, with pronounced hips and breasts, in a swirling motion as if she were dancing, between pillars with spiral fluting surmounted by a decorative architrave. "When she was found, my British assistant called her the Venus of Berenikê," Aysha said. "Typical western perspective. For my money, she's Indian. The swirl, the decoration, are clearly south Indian. I think she's not a classical goddess at all, but a *yaksi,* an Indian female spirit. You might expect to find this in a cave temple in Tamil Nadu, the farthest point we know Roman merchants visited along the coast of India, on the Bay of Bengal."

"And look at this." Hiebermeyer pointed at an airtight box with a thermostat alongside. "That's silk."

"Silk?" Costas said. "You mean from China?"

"We think so," Aysha said excitedly. "We think this shows that silk wasn't just coming overland via Persia to the Roman Empire. It was also arriving by sea, from the ports of India. It shows that traders were leaving the Silk Route somewhere in central Asia, and going south through Afghanistan and down the Indus and the Ganges to reach the ports where they met up with merchants like this one. And yes, Costas, it brings China one step closer to the Roman world."

"Maybe that's where all the gold was going," Costas said. "Not to buy pepper, but silk."

"Another nice idea," Jack murmured.

"Find a shipwreck of that trade, and that would be a cargo worth excavating," Hiebermeyer said. "Even I concede that. An ancient East Indiaman."

"I think we might be just one step ahead of you there, old boy," Costas replied, kicking at a rock, glancing at Jack. But Hiebermeyer bounded away to the other side of the excavation, where he lifted up an aluminium case and carried it carefully back toward them, the sweat now pouring off him.

Costas picked up the rock, and Jack watched him. It was a gemstone, uncut, deep blue with speckles of gold. "Check this out."

Aysha looked over, then gasped. "It's lapis lazuli! Maurice, look! Costas has found a piece of lapis lazuli!"

Hiebermeyer put down the case and took the stone from Costas, raising his glasses and peering at it, turning it over and wiping it. "My God," he muttered. "It's the highest grade. From Afghanistan. That's another piece of the jigsaw puzzle. They also traded for this. Lapis lazuli was worth a fortune too."

"Months of painstaking excavation and you would never have found it," Costas said, looking at Hiebermeyer deadpan.

Hiebermeyer's eyes narrowed. "Where, might I ask, did you pick this up?"

Costas pointed down, grinning. "You just have to know where to look."

Hiebermeyer snorted, then carefully placed the stone on a finds tray. "Something of Jack's knack has clearly rubbed off on you. And now for the real treasure."

"There's more?" Jack said.

Hiebermeyer tapped the case. "I've been waiting for *Seaquest II* to arrive. We need full lab facilities, infrared viewers, multispectral imagery. We need a place to look at this properly, not out here, in this oven," he said, wiping his face. "We're finished here for the season. It's become too hot. My Egyptian foreman will close up the site. Aysha and I have already said our good-byes to the team, and we're ready and packed."

"You mean you want to go right now?" Jack said.

"You've got spare cabins, haven't you?"

"Of course. I'll radio the captain. You can join us for a cruise on the Indian Ocean."

Costas peered skeptically at Hiebermeyer. "How are your sea legs? We might hit the monsoon."

"My sea legs are fine." Hiebermeyer looked pointedly at Jack. "It's his I'm worried about."

"That hasn't happened for years," Jack said defensively. "Not since we were kids, Maurice. And that was a sailing dinghy. One that you built. Very badly."

Aysha looked wide-eyed at Jack, the hint of a smile on her lips. "I am hearing this right? The famous Jack Howard gets seasick?"

"He calls it the Nelson touch," Costas said. "Lord Nelson, England's greatest admiral. Sick as a dog every time he put out to sea."

"I do not get seasick," Jack said. "I just empathize with my heroes."

"Well, that's good," Hiebermeyer said. "Because with what I've got here in this case, you won't be having much time to stare at the horizon. Are you really taking us to Arikamedu?"

"Where?" Costas peered at Jack suspiciously. "You've got that look."

Jack cleared his throat. "Where the Romans who sailed from here landed in southeast India. It's an amazing site. Roman pottery in India. The Archaeological Survey of India are planning a new excavation. I'm official advisor for their underwater unit, and I promised to look in when *Seaquest II* was next in the Indian Ocean. Maurice and Aysha have never been there, and it seems crazy not to give them the chance if they're going to be aboard with us anyway. I've already called our contact at Arikamedu and prepped him. He can't wait to see us."

"I thought we were going to test my new submersible off Hawaii," Costas grumbled. "And find a beach. And prop up a nice little palm-fronded bar."

"Just a small diversion first," Jack said.

Costas stared at him. "Yeah. Right. A diversion."

74

Jack looked at the carving of the dancing female spirit, then at the sherd with the Tamil graffito. *Ramaya.* He put it back down carefully on the table, and glanced up at the others. "Well, if you're ready, I think we're good to go. The sooner we do, the sooner we find out what it is you've got in that case."

Hiebermeyer picked up the case. Jack and Costas each shouldered a rucksack lying ready by the tent, and Aysha took a briefcase and a smaller bag. They waved back at the group in the trench and began to walk down the slope toward the helicopter. Hiebermeyer seemed lost in thought again, but suddenly stopped, put the case down and peered at Jack. "I just remembered. Talking about the dinghy reminded me. And then going to southern India. You've got family history out there, haven't you? Your great-great grandfather, wasn't it, the soldier? Something he found in the jungle, back in the nineteenth century. You used to go on about it when we were at school. How you'd love to get out there. As I recall it was somewhere in Tamil Nadu, the Eastern Ghats. If you're at Arikamedu, you won't be that far off."

Jack stared intently at Hiebermeyer. "I've always wanted to see if I could find out more. You're right. I'm passionate about it. This is too good an opportunity to miss. It'd be a small diversion, a day or two. I think I can set it up with the Survey of India. And there's a connection with the Romans, I'm sure of it. I've got a gut instinct."

"Uh-oh," Costas said, stopping beside them. "Not just a diversion. A gut instinct. That's serious."

Jack grinned, then dumped the rucksack and reached into his own bag and extracted a small brown envelope. He took Hiebermeyer's hand, held it palm-up and gently tipped out the gold coin. Aysha gasped, and Hiebermeyer held the coin up, the sun glinting dazzlingly off the image of the emperor. "I guessed you'd found something like this, Jack. You were leaving a trail of hints. I do know you pretty well." He held up the coin again. "It's fantastic," he murmured. "The crumbled walls, these scraps of ancient Berenikê, they tell a human story, but this place was really about what passed through it, incredible riches, the wealth of an empire. To understand what actually went on here, you have to hold this. To hold treasure. That's what fueled this place, treasure on an unimaginable scale."

"And the sea trapped one load in its net," Costas said.

"There are more of these coins?" Hiebermeyer said.

"Thousands of them," Jack said. "All mint issues. All Imperial gold."

"It's the mother lode," Costas said.

Hiebermeyer relaxed his shoulders, gave a

broad smile and put his other hand on Jack's shoulder. "Congratulations, Jack. You remember what I used to call you, when we were boys? Lucky Jack." He handed back the coin, picked up the case again then took Costas by the arm, steering him down the dusty slope toward the helicopter. "Now, tell me about these elephants."

"You're not going to believe it."

"Try me."

3

Three days later Jack stood outside on the flying bridge of *Seaquest II*, leaning on the railing and looking out toward the eastern horizon. The sun had risen in a clear sky for the first time since they had left the Red Sea, and Jack enjoyed the warm radiance as it reflected off the water. It had been three days not entirely to his liking. The monsoon had hit them as soon as they rounded Arabia, and they had sailed directly across the open ocean toward the southern tip of India. The only saving grace was the twenty-knot speed with the wind behind them. Jack could barely comprehend how ancient Greek and Egyptian sailors had done it, bucketing and wallowing in the swell, hundreds of miles from land with only the direction of the monsoon for navigation. It would have been a tremendous feat of courage, and sailing out of sight of land would have been their worst nightmare. Especially if they had been seasick. Jack swallowed hard, and tried to forget the last seventy-eight hours. The worst had not happened, but it had been close. He felt dog-tired, but also like the survivor of a near-fatal illness with a new lease on life. And it had also been exhilarating, the hours he had spent rooted to this spot, lashed by wind and spray, his eyes roving continuously, searching for the line of the horizon, in the tumult of the swell and flickering blackness that had seemed without end.

The captain's face popped out of the bridge door, and a hand holding a steaming mug. "We're entering the Palk Strait now. We've got a local pilot coming to navigate us through and I'm putting the ship on alert. The Sri Lankan navy's fighting a gun battle with Tamil Tiger boats just off the northern tip, and we'll be within range."

"Okay. Thanks." Jack took the mug gratefully and turned back to the sea. He watched the launch carrying the pilot come alongside, skillfully matching their speed while the pilot was hooked into a chair and winched on board. He could see land now on both sides, the southern tip of India and the northwestern coast of Sri Lanka. The narrows ahead were another obstacle facing ancient sailors, treacherous shallows and reefs that only local craft could ply. But once through, the sailors were near the end of their voyage, at the place where they met traders coming from the east, from Chrysê, the semi-mythical land of gold, from the farthest places known to westerners. Jack looked at his watch. Maurice had promised that this would be the morning to reveal his find before they reached the Roman site of Arikamedu. Maurice and Aysha had been holed up continuously in the ship's lab belowdecks, piecing together whatever it was that Maurice had brought on board from his excavation in Egypt. Jack was itching to join them. He would go down and see for himself once he had finished his coffee. Especially now that belowdecks was a realistic proposition, not the lurching nightmare of the last three days.

A hand touched his arm, and he turned to Rebecca. She was dressed in jeans and an IMU T-shirt. "Feeling better?" she said. Jack nodded, smiling. Her accent was American, and her voice was developing the depth that Jack had found attractive in her mother. Rebecca was black-haired, as Elizabeth had been, but had Jack's blue eyes. There was a sadness in them, a sadness that would always be there, and Jack's heart went out to a child who had experienced the loss of her mother, and had grown up apart from her real parents. Jack had only known he was a father since the appalling circumstances of Elizabeth's disappearance and death in Naples less than a year before. Elizabeth had left him sixteen years earlier when she had succumbed to family pressure to return to Naples, and

Jack realized she could only have known she was pregnant once she had been sucked back into the dark underworld from which she never found an escape. She had not wanted to risk bringing up her daughter in that world and had sent her to New York. Rebecca had grown up strong and confident under the guardianship of her mother's friends, and when Elizabeth had explained to her the reasons why, the dark backdrop of her life in Naples, she had understood as only a child could, absorbed in the excitements of her own life. But the death of her mother had been devastating, and after Jack had first met Rebecca in New York, his friends at IMU had become a second family to her. Jack had gone with her to Naples for the commemoration held by her mother's colleagues from the archaeological superintendency on the slopes of Mount Vesuvius, overlooking the Roman site that had been Elizabeth's lifelong work, and the modern city whose dark tentacles had taken her life. Jack knew they were still there, those who had used her, worn her down, even among her own family, but there was to be no retribution; that cycle had been the poison that killed her. His choice, the one Elizabeth would have craved, was to walk away and take their daughter with him, to create a new and exciting world for Rebecca that would help her package the past in a place where it would never threaten to take hold of her. Jack would never know whether Elizabeth had intended to tell him about their daughter, but he could not afford to dwell on it. His responsibility now was Rebecca's happiness. He put his hand on hers. "I feel fine," he said. "I just needed some off-time."

"For three days? You? Dad." She had only just begun calling him that. "It's me, remember? You don't need to play the hero."

Jack gestured at what she was holding. "What's the book?"

"A guy called Cosmas Indicopleustes. That means Cosmas, sailor of the Indian Ocean. He was an Egyptian monk who came here in the sixth century AD. I was doing background reading, like you asked. Being your research assistant. I found this in your library."

"What does he say about Sri Lanka?"

She opened the book and read:

"The island being, as it is, in a central position, is much frequented by ships from all parts of India and from Persia and Ethiopia, and it likewise sends many of its own. And from the remotest countries, I mean Tzinitza, it receives silks, aloes, cloves and other products, and these again are passed on to marts on this side. And the island receives imports from all these marts which we have mentioned and passes them on to the remoter ports, while at the same time, exporting its produce in both directions. And farther away is the clove country, then Tzinitza, which produces the silk. Beyond this there is no other country, for the Ocean surrounds it to the east."

She closed the book. "Okay. Tzinitza is China, the clove country is Indonesia. What he's saying is that Sri Lanka was a kind of clearinghouse, midway between two worlds. Captain Macalister suggested I look at the Admiralty chart. I saw how treacherous this strait is, a deathtrap for big ships. So what Cosmas was saying was, ships from Egypt came here, off-loaded their stuff onto local craft, then waited. The local craft took it over the shallows to the other side, loaded it on big ships coming from the Bay of Bengal, Indonesia, even China. And the same thing happened in reverse. You can really picture it out here, those big fat-hulled Roman ships where we are now, and over there on the other side Chinese junks, with all kinds of canoes and catamarans in between. Pretty cool, huh?"

"Pretty cool," Jack replied, grinning. "Cosmas was writing five hundred years after what the Romans we're talking about at Berenikê, but basically it's the same scenario, until the Arab conquest of the Middle East and north Africa shut down the sea routes to India. Cosmas provides the most detailed account we have of the ancient trade that went on here. Good work, research assistant."

"Think outside the box. That's what Uncle Costas tells me."

"Uncle Costas?" Jack said.

"Hiemy says I'm a lot like you. I don't know whether that's praise or not."

"Who?"

"Hiemy. You know, your old buddy. Herr Professor Dr. Hiebermeyer. That's what Aysha calls him, Hiemy."

"Of course," Jack said. "Hiemy."

"Aysha's in love with him, you know."

"Hang on a second. One thing at a time."

"Just getting you up to speed. You've spent the last three days with your head in the clouds."

Jack laughed. "Well, I've been waiting. Hiemy's been holed up like Caractacus Potts working on Chitty Chitty Bang Bang. He's been like that ever since we were at school. Every time he calls me up with a new discovery, insists that I come and see it, I agree to go, and then he realizes he needs more time to make absolutely sure. So before going I usually wait until he's come to see me personally three times. Then I know. It's a fine art."

"I'm sworn to secrecy. I could tell you what it is, but I can't. That was his condition for allowing me to help them in the lab."

"That's part of the game too." He looked into her eyes, thought for a moment, then spoke carefully. "I've been thinking about

84

your mother a lot over the past days. You know when I saw her last year I hadn't been in contact with her since before you were born and when I did see her, it was for only a few moments in the archaeological site at Herculaneum. But I've got a perfect memory of her from when we were together all those years ago, like a favorite old film that will never change. You're in that film now too. It's as if we're a family together. I can see a lot of her in you."

"When she told me about you the last time I saw her, she said the same about you," Rebecca said. "She was planning to contact you after my sixteenth birthday, you know. She said she always meant to, once I was old enough to look after myself. My birthday was a month after she disappeared." Rebecca looked at Jack with unfathomable eyes, and then draped her arms around him and rested her head on his shoulders. Jack held her tight, and smiled. "Maybe she was right," he said. "Maybe there is a bit of me in you."

"Not the seasick bit, I hope."

"I do not get seasick."

"Yeah, right." She leaned back into the bridge and yelled, "Dr. Jack Howard, famous underwater archaeologist and commando extraordinaire, gets seasick."

"Time you were back in school," Jack grumbled.

"Hah. We're on the high seas. I've been

reading about that too. Out here, no laws apply."

A hand clamped her shoulder, and Scott Macalister stepped out from behind her, smiling at Jack. "Young lady, only one law applies, and that is the law of the captain. Anyone signed on under the age of eighteen is my personal responsibility." He placed an old brass sextant into her hands. "Navigation class at 1600 hours." At that moment a white streak appeared a few hundred meters off the starboard bow. "Tracer rounds," he said. "Everyone inside, now." He ushered them into the bridge and shut the door, pulling down a steel plate over the window. He took out his binoculars and peered through the bulletproof glass of the front screen. "That was a spent round from the gun battle a couple of miles away, but better safe than sorry."

"Ben's been teaching me to shoot with a twenty-two," Rebecca said.

"I don't think you're going to be taking on the Tamil Tigers with a twenty-two," Macalister murmured, eyes still fixed to his binoculars.

"I hope you were wearing ear protection," Jack said.

"I can look after myself." She turned around and walked toward the rear hatch that led down to the accommodation decks.

"Maybe she does have a bit of me in her,"

Jack muttered, looking apologetically at Macalister. "Teenagers."

"Come on, Dad," Rebecca called. "They're ready for you in the lab. That's what I came up to tell you. I helped Aysha with the final pieces. You're going to love this. It's my present to you for rescuing me from school."

Jack felt a surge of excitement, and turned to Macalister. "Okay, Scott. Let me know when we clear the strait, will you? And I want the Zodiac prepared. Our meeting with the Archaeological Survey of India people at Arikamedu is at 0900 hours tomorrow, and I don't want the schedule to slip."

"Will do, Jack." Macalister jerked his head toward the hatchway. "You'd better follow the boss."

The main laboratory on *Seaquest II* was the size of a school classroom, set below the accommodation block and above the engine room. The wet cleaning and conservation of finds was carried out in a room behind, with a cluster of desalination tanks for timbers and other artifacts too delicate to be taken out of water. Jack thought of the complex like a field hospital for the stabilization of finds that would then be transferred for long-term treatment to the IMU museum at Carthage in the Mediterranean or the IMU campus in England. The lab was a dry facility for the cleaning of finds such as pottery that could safely be removed from water for short periods. Farther forward were rooms for analytical work, including multispectral imagery, thin-section petrology and mass spectrometry. The complex was designed to allow basic questions to be answered during an excavation when time might be pressing.

Jack followed Rebecca inside. Four long tables had been drawn together to form one surface, their legs locked into runnels on the floor. Above them a cluster of fixed tungsten lights bathed the tables in a warm glow. Aysha and Hiebermeyer were hunched together over a camera stand. Aysha was nudging something into place on the black baseboard under the camera, and Hiebermeyer was poised over the viewfinder, holding the remote shutter control. They looked as if they were performing a strange embrace. Rebecca glanced at Jack, pointing at them as if to rest her case. They both waited silently while Hiebermeyer clicked the shutter, and then Aysha slid the object back onto the table. Hiebermeyer turned toward them. "Jack!" In the tungsten light his face seemed to have a feverish glow, and his eyes were red-rimmed. "Sorry to keep you in the dark for so long. I just wanted to be absolutely sure."

Rebecca went around to the far side of the table and sat on a stool, surrounded by the books and notepads she had accumulated over the past few days. Costas had also been summoned and came through the door behind Jack, and they moved to the table. On the surface were hundreds of fragments of pottery, some of them tiny, only a centimeter or two across, others the size of small saucers.

"We playing jigsaw?" Costas said.

Jack's pulse began to race. *"Ostraka!"* He leaned over the table. Aysha ushered Costas to a stool. "It's the Greek word for potsherd," she said. "But archaeologists use it for sherds with inscriptions on them, where the pottery was used as a writing surface. In the ancient world, papyrus was a fairly valuable commodity, used only for top copies. If you wanted a writing surface for day-to-day use, for jotting notes, writing letters, composing rough drafts, you just found the nearest old amphora and smashed it up."

Jack circled the table, staring at the sherds, his mind racing. "They're Roman amphora fragments, Italian, first century BC or first century AD. It's the same type as the wine amphora we saw at Berenikê. And the writing's Greek, as you'd expect in Egypt at that time. Greek was the lingua franca ever since Alexander conquered Egypt. The writing all looks as if it's in the same hand. I'm assuming you found all of these sherds in the merchant's house you were excavating?"

Hiebermeyer's face gleamed. "It's an astonishing find. I still can't believe it." He paused, looking Jack steadily in the eye. "You ready for this? Okay. What you're looking at is the only known ancient text of the *Periplus Maris Erythraei*. The only one actually to date from the Roman period when it was first written."

Jack gasped. *The* Periplus of the Erythraean Sea. *The greatest travel book to survive from antiquity.* It was exactly what you might find at Berenikê, in an outpost on the edge of the empire. Not a great work of literature, not a lost history or a volume of poetry, but a travel guide, an itinerary for sea captains and merchants. He cleared his throat. "Copy, or draft?" he said.

"Draft."

Jack exhaled forcefully. *Draft.* This was even more extraordinary. A draft could mean emendations, material deleted from the polished version. All the rough notes that get edited out. Precious words and phrases. He peered at Hiebermeyer. "I hardly dare ask. Have you seen anything new?"

Hiebermeyer was bursting with excitement. "I saw it within days of starting the excavation at Berenikê. You remember when I tried to speak to you in Istanbul? Little did I know then how many more sherds we'd find, and how long it would take. This has been an exercise in patience. I couldn't have done it without Aysha." He turned and looked at Aysha, who nodded. He reached over and clicked a control panel. The plasma screen on the wall beside the table showed a CGI of the sherds in 3-D, jumbled together. "This is how they looked in the excavation. We call it the archive room, but really it was more like a study. After drafting each sentence on a large amphora sherd, we believe the author transferred it to papyrus and then tossed the sherds in a corner. Some sherds survived almost intact, others broke into pieces. I realized we were going to have to record all the spatial relationships in situ if we were going to stand any hope of piecing it all back together. That's been Aysha's job. She's been wonderful."

"Somebody had better fill me in," Costas said.

"*Maris Erythraea,* the Erythraean Sea, translates as Red Sea," Aysha said. "Which to the ancients meant all the seas east of Egypt — the Red Sea, the Indian Ocean, what lay beyond. *Periplus* means to sail around, and was the term for a nautical guide, an itinerary."

"The nautical guide of the Erythraean Sea," Costas murmured.

"It's truly one of the most amazing documents to survive from antiquity," Jack said. "The *Periplus* wasn't written by an aristocrat, by a Claudius or a Pliny the Elder, but by a working man with his feet on the ground. Yet it tells of a journey far greater than any fantasy of Odysseus or Aeneas, a true-life account of exploration and trade to the nether regions of the ancient world. The whole text seemed hard to believe until archaeologists began to find Greek and Roman remains where we are now, in southern India."

"So the guy who lived in the villa, the merchant, was the author?" Costas said.

"I'm absolutely convinced of it." Hiebermeyer clicked the console again, revealing an aerial shot of the excavated house in Berenikê they had visited three days before, looking down over the ancient port and the Red Sea. "We know from a Roman coin embedded in the foundations that the archive room was built soon after 10 BC, and the whole house was abandoned about AD 20. Because these sherds hadn't been swept out of the room, we're guessing that the text dates from just before the abandonment, about the early years of the reign of the emperor Tiberius."

"You mean when the trade was beginning to decline?" Costas said. "What we were saying in Egypt a few days ago, about the emperor plugging up the bullion flow?"

"Correct. But I don't think that was why the house was abandoned. Everything points to this man being old, retired. Aysha?"

She looked up. "Luckily, we've got a lot of scholarship to go on. Before this find, the earliest surviving text of the *Periplus* was a medieval copy dating from the tenth century AD, and it's been studied in translation since the nineteenth century. What we've found confirms what many scholars have thought, but adds a fascinating new dimension. First of all, it's clear from the vocabulary, the analogies, that he was Egyptian Greek. Second, there's no doubt that he himself had sailed the routes described in the *Periplus,* as far down Africa as Zanzibar, then around Arabia to northwest India, and using the monsoon route to southern India. He's done it enough times to know a lot about navigation, but it's clear that he's a merchant, not a sea captain. He's mainly interested in naming the ports, telling how to get to them, and listing the goods to be traded there. In southern India it's predominantly bullion, meaning gold and silver Roman coins that were exchanged for pepper and a fantastic range of other spices and exotica, some of it transshipped from far distant places."

"Any idea of his specialization?" Costas asked.

"You remember the piece of silk we showed you at the excavation? We think that was it. He would have had contacts with the very farthest reaches of the trade, with traders who had come west through the Strait of Malacca from the South China Sea, and down through Bactria, modern Afghanistan, from central Asia. From the Silk Road."

"I think I've got you," Costas said. "The book was a retirement project. He finished it, he croaked and the house went on the market, but there were no buyers."

"Eloquently put, as always." Hiebermeyer pushed his little round glasses up his nose. "Unusually for an Erythraean Sea merchant, he didn't retire to Alexandria or Rome, but seems to have stayed in the Egyptian port that had probably been his base all his working life. Perhaps he was given some sort of administrative role, maybe as *duovir,* prefect of the town, to supervise it during the off-season when it was largely deserted. But few wealthy men able to afford a villa actually wanted to live in Berenikê, and his house was impractical, especially with the high-value trade winding down."

"Maybe he didn't die there." Rebecca looked at Aysha, who nodded encouragingly. "Aysha thinks he had a wife, and she was Indian. One sherd had a female Indian name, Amrita. She showed me pictures of some of the stuff they found, other sherds with Tamil graffiti, fragments of Indian textile, pottery from southern India. Maybe the *Periplus* was his last say as a trader, and after finishing it he took his family and left on a final voyage to the east, never to return."

Costas rubbed his chin. "Nice thinking. Maybe after all that time trading in India, he went native."

Jack was absorbed in a cluster of small potsherds placed close together, clearly the remains of two large sherds which had been smashed. "Look at this," he exclaimed. "Amazing. I can read the words *Ptolemais Thêrôn,* Ptolemy of the Hunts. That's the elephant port on the Red Sea, Costas. And over here, Rebecca, on this other sherd, I can see *Taprobanê.* That's what Sri Lanka was called, five hundred years before Cosmas Indicopleustes sailed here." He straightened up and looked at Hiebermeyer. "Well? This is all fantastic. But I know you too well. What did you really want me to see?"

"Spill it, Hiemy," Costas said.

Hiebermeyer's eyes bored into Costas. He turned to Jack. "We've got a little under a third of the *Periplus* here, about a thousand words. It's very similar to the tenth century copy, with only minor differences in wording and grammar. With one exception."

"Go on," Jack said.

Hiebermeyer pointed at a large sherd beside Rebecca, and they all crowded around. The sherd was about the size of a dinner plate, and was covered with fifteen lines of fine writing, the ink barely discernible in places against the whitish surface patina on the pottery. The text had been written within the sherd, and was not broken off at the edges. "It's an intact section, like a paragraph," Hiebermeyer said. "It's where he describes sailing beyond the Arabian Gulf and looks toward India, just before reaching the port of

Barygaza at the mouth of the Indus."

"You mean the section where he puts on his archaeologist hat," Jack murmured.

Hiebermeyer nodded. "Generally he only digressed where it was of practical value, for example showing where a certain local tribe was to be avoided, or describing an inland region to give an idea of where the trade goods came from. There are two fascinating exceptions, both concerning Alexander the Great. In one place he describes how Alexander penetrated as far as the Ganges but not to the south of India. He says how in the market in Barygaza, near the mouth of the Indus, you can find coins, old drachmas, engraved with inscriptions of rulers who came after Alexander."

"Apollodotus and Menander, the first Seleucid kings," Jack said.

Hiebermeyer nodded. "Western traders going to India would have been well-versed in the story of Alexander, and doubtless there were locals who saw a quick buck in passing off Seleucid coins as relics. Alexander lived in the fourth century BC, three hundred years before the *Periplus* was written, but the story was still so big that people coming out here might have felt the dust of conquest had barely settled. Our merchant knew all about sharp dealing and was warning his readers that the relics were bogus. He wasn't the kind of man who was duped by these stories. That makes me think we should take his second reference seriously, what you see on this sherd."

"I've spotted the word *Alexandros*," Costas said, peering down at the sherd. "My ancient Greek's a little rusty."

"Here's the translation." Hiebermeyer picked up a piece of paper covered with his indecipherable handwriting. *"Immediately following Barakē is the gulf of Barygaza and the shore of the land of Ariakē, the beginning of the kingdom of Manbanos and of all India. The inland part, which borders Skythia, is called Abēria; the coastal part is Syrastrēnē. The region is very fecund, producing grain, rice, sesame oil, ghee, cotton, and the Indian cloths made from it, those of ordinary quality. There are numerous herds of cattle, and the men are very large and have dark skin. To this day there are still preserved around this area traces of Alexander's expedition: archaic altars, the foundations of encampments and huge wells."*

Jack nodded. "Archaic altars. That sounds like the familiar text."

"But not the next sentence." Hiebermeyer paused, and pushed up his glasses. *"And from Margiana, the citadel of Parthia to the north of here, the Roman legionaries captured at Carrhae escaped east, taking the Parthian treasure with them toward Chrysê, the land of gold."*

Jack reeled as if he had been physically

97

struck. "That's incredible," he said, almost whispering. "That's not in the *Periplus*."

"Isn't that what you were telling me about in the helicopter, Jack?" Costas said. "Crassus, his lost legions?"

"Hearsay and rumor," Jack murmured. "Until now." He took a deep breath, and looked at Rebecca. "After the Roman defeat at Carrhae in 53 BC, the Parthians took thousands of legionaries prisoner, possibly as many as ten thousand. Their fate fascinated the Romans for generations. The poet Horace wrote of it in one of his odes, wondering if Roman veterans had taken native wives and fought as mercenaries for a foreign ruler. Then Augustus' son Tiberius negotiated peace with the Parthians and the captured legionary standards were returned, a great triumph for Augustus that closed the chapter on the defeat."

"Jack showed you the coin from our shipwreck, didn't he, Rebecca?" Costas said. "That celebrates the return of the eagles, the sacred legionary standards."

Jack nodded, his mind racing. "The only other hint from Roman sources is in the *Natural History* of Pliny the Elder, who says the captured legionaries were taken to Margiana, the Parthian capital in present-day Turkmenistan."

"That's what gives the *Periplus* plausibility," Hiebermeyer said. "And look at the Alexander reference. He only tells us what he can verify. Alexander is known to have set up altars during his conquest. They could have been where Alexander took his army across the Turkmenistan desert toward central Asia."

"Of course," Jack replied. "Alexander went past Margiana, modern Merv. And if prisoners were escaping east from Merv, they could have passed these altars on the way east toward central Asia. It all fits."

"Why would the author later delete this reference?" Costas asked.

"It must have been something he felt was true, but could never substantiate," Aysha said. "Ancient coins you can hold, altars you can see, but stories are just that. We imagine he was told the story by a trader, perhaps a Bactrian or Sogdian middleman who brought him silk. But perhaps that trader had broken off contact, had disappeared without a trace as so often happened on the Silk Route. Perhaps as an old man the author may even have doubted his memory. The story of treasure on the Silk Route may have sounded like an adventurer's fable. There was enough doubt in the end for him to strike a line through that sentence on the sherd and ditch it into the refuse pile. It was an anecdote best passed on by word of mouth, that might one day reach the ear of an encyclopedist like Pliny the Elder, and find its way into a cornucopia of fact and hearsay like the *Natural*

History."

"And perhaps it did, but only in small part — Pliny refers to the prisoners in Merv, but nothing about the escape east," Jack said.

"But you talked to me in the helicopter about this, Jack," Costas said. "About how Roman legionaries might have got to China. The evidence in the Chinese annals."

"It's been on my mind for several months now, since I saw Katya."

"At the Transoxiana Conference?" Hiebermeyer asked.

"Katya's his new girlfriend," Rebecca said matter-of-factly to Aysha. "Well, not new, exactly. He met her when he was searching for Atlantis in the Black Sea, but after that she needed some off-time. Then Dad kind of saw someone else for a while, but she was traumatized after another guy she was seeing got spread-eagled. Or something like that. Anyway, she needed some off-time as well."

Costas coughed, and Jack stared hard at the ground, trying to keep a straight face. He cleared his throat. "As I was saying" — he shot Rebecca a look — "the Chinese connection. In the 1950s an Oxford scholar published a radical theory that Roman mercenaries were used by the Huns of Mongolia in a Chinese border war during the Han period, the Chinese dynasty at the time of the *Periplus.* The evidence was a reference to a formation that sounded like the Roman

testudo, the tortoise, where shields are interlocked above. The battle was in 36 BC. Then
a study of the Han annals suggested that Roman prisoners from the battle had been
settled in a town in Gansu on the final stretch
of the Silk Road toward Xian. Someone
noticed that the population of the village
today contains a proportion of fair-featured
people, and so began the legend of the Roman legionaries in China."

"What's the archaeological evidence?" Costas asked.

"There's nothing definite," Jack replied.
"But you wouldn't expect to find much. A
band of Roman soldiers after decades of
imprisonment would have little with them
that was recognizably Roman. Escaped soldiers could have made themselves legionary
sandals for marching, and possibly rectangular wooden shields, the basis for the *testudo*
theory. But otherwise they would have scav-
enged what they could on the way, weapons,
armor, clothing, anything from Parthian and
Bactrian to Sogdian and Han Chinese. But
one thing they could have done was leave
inscriptions on stone. That's what got Katya
interested. It's right up her street. The
Romans loved making inscriptions, mile-
stones, grave markers, stamps of authority in
newly conquered territory. And that's where
archaeology comes into play. A few years ago
a Latin inscription was found in a cave

101

complex in southern Uzbekistan, three hundred kilometers to the east of Merv near the border with Afghanistan." Jack flipped through a notebook he pulled from his pocket, then opened a page with a sketch on it. "Katya drew it for me." He showed them the letters:

LIC

AP.LG

"Fascinating," Hiebermeyer murmured. "The first line's a personal name, probably Licinius. And the second line's Apollinaris Legio, isn't it? That's the legion dedicated to Apollo. That was the Fifteenth legion, wasn't it, raised by Augustus?"

Jack nodded. "Pretty good for an Egyptologist. I remember your boyhood passion was the Roman army in Germany. But this wasn't Augustus as emperor. He raised the legion in his earlier guise as Octavian, adoptive successor of Julius Caesar. The Fifteenth Apollinaris that he raised dates from 41 BC, soon after Caesar's assassination. That's twelve years *after* the Battle of Carrhae. Over the next three centuries it spent a lot of its time in the eastern frontiers of the empire fighting the Parthians. One theory has the inscription carved by a legionary captured by the Parthians and used as a border guard, on the far eastern edge of the Parthian Empire."

"But?" Costas said.

"I've never bought the idea of prisoners of war being used as border guards, let alone one of them making an inscription. Katya and I brainstormed it one day walking the walls of Merv, and came up with another hypothesis. This line from the *Periplus* gives it just that little bit more weight."

"Spill it, Jack."

"At the time of Crassus, most legions were raised for specific campaigns and usually disbanded after six years. We know very few of these legions by number or name, and the same numbers might be used repeatedly. Plutarch and Dio Cassius, the main sources for Carrhae, don't tell us the names of the legions involved. But already a few legions were gaining legendary status, the legions that had served under Julius Caesar in Gaul and Britain in the years before Carrhae. Several of those legions survived to become the most famous of the Imperial army, cherished by Augustus because of their association with Caesar. The Seventh Claudia, the Eighth Augusta, the Tenth Gemina."

"You're suggesting the Fifteenth was one of these?"

"The Fifteenth was founded in 41 BC, right? That's only a couple of years after Caesar was assassinated. The young Octavian was trying to consolidate his strength, and anything that harked back to his illustrious father was seized upon. The historians tell us that a thousand of the cavalry at Carrhae were veterans of Caesar's campaigns. Why not one of the legions too? Our theory is that the Fifteenth Apollinaris wasn't *founded* in 41 BC, it was *re*founded. We're suggesting that Octavian deliberately reconstituted one of Caesar's revered legions, one that had been shamefully lost by the incompetence of Crassus. It would have been a massive show of confidence and of reverence for past glory, exactly the kind of thing Octavian would have done."

"Not so glorious for the surviving legionaries, chained up in Merv," Costas said. "It would have written them off."

"It was too late for them anyway," Hiebermeyer said. "Even if people knew the defeat was caused by the incompetence of Crassus, the survivors still couldn't hold their heads high. They would already have been marching with the dead, looking forward only to finding death with honor so they could join their brothers-in-arms in Elysium."

"But you're suggesting that some escaped prisoner was not above inscribing the name of his legion in a cave on the trek east," Costas said.

"For the survivors, the name of the legion would still have been their binding force, even with the sacred eagle standard gone."

"So they were still loyal to Rome."

"They had fought for themselves, for their comrades, as soldiers always have done. They were proud of being citizen-soldiers, of having civilian professions. They were proud to fight for a commander if they respected him, if he was one among them, *primus inter pares.* They fought for Caesar. They fought for their families. Whether they would have fought for Rome as an empire is another matter."

"And the legion?" Costas asked.

"The legion was sacred," Hiebermeyer replied. "That was where loyalties lay. And within it, the cohort, the century, the *contubernium,* the squad of ten or twelve men who even called each other brother, *frater.*"

"So losing the eagle was bad, big-time," Rebecca cut in.

"The worst. A battle they could lose, Crassus they couldn't care less about. But losing the eagle? A legion that lost its eagle would have been a legion of the dead, never able to show themselves in Rome again. Even to their families."

"Do you think they fragged him, Crassus?" Costas said.

"Crassus signed his own death warrant as soon as he committed them to battle. They probably would have called it assisted suicide."

"These men, if they really did survive and escape, must have been the toughest of the tough," Aysha said.

"There are always a few," Jack said. "Those who escape execution, who survive the beatings and the torture, who have the mental strength to endure. And some of the legionaries with Crassus were men who had been recruited five years before and fought with Caesar in Gaul. They may have been citizen-soldiers, but they were among the most ruthless killers the world has ever known. Men who killed with the spear, the sword, with their bare hands."

"And with the legion a hollow memory, there are no checks, no controls," Costas said.

Jack nodded. "Some of these guys in the late republic saw much more action than the professional legionaries of the empire, and the idea of their civilian lives, their jobs, became a kind of myth. But if you spend your life killing, who knows where the boundaries are? When the time comes, if it ever does, how do you know when to stop being a soldier, and become a citizen again?"

"An age-old problem," Hiebermeyer murmured.

"If they did escape, word would have passed on the Silk Route," Jack said. "That was bandit country, but even there the Romans' reputation would have preceded them. You would not have wanted to encounter these guys."

"What about the Silk Route?" Costas asked. "Are there any more inscriptions?"

106

"Katya's spent the last couple of seasons roaming the mountains and passes of central Asia, searching. A lot of it's still unexplored territory."

"And still bandit country," Hiebermeyer said.

"I seem to remember Katya knows how to use a Kalashnikov," Costas murmured.

Jack opened his notebook again. "A few months ago she hit pay dirt at a place called Cholpon-Ata, on the western shore of Lake Issyk-Kul in Kyrgyzstan. That's hundreds of miles east along the northern Silk Route from the place with the Fifteenth Legion inscription, on the edge of the Tien Shan Mountains and the pass that leads down to the Taklamakan Desert and China. For years now archaeologists have known about this place, a desolate boulder-strewn landscape where there are hundreds, probably thousands of petroglyphs, shallow-cut rock carvings of ibexes, other animals, hunters. Most were carved by Scythian nomads. But it would also have been a staging post along the Silk Route for traders who had survived the trek from the west, and before embarking on boats toward China."

"How big is the lake?" Rebecca asked.

"It's the second biggest mountain lake in the world after Lake Titicaca. There are many stories of sunken settlements, of treasure. There's a lot to be found. The Soviets used the lake as a submarine and torpedo testing site."

"Can we go?" Rebecca said. "I want to meet Katya."

Jack smiled. "It's on the cards. Last year, Katya stumbled across a boulder there that might have an inscription on it. The boulder was almost entirely buried, and the permit for an excavation had only just come through at the time of the conference. She's out there now."

"Not alone, I hope," Aysha said.

"She has Kyrgyz collaboration," Jack said. "That means one guy and a creaky old tractor, as far as I can tell."

"You've spoken to her recently?" Costas eyed Jack.

"This morning."

Costas grunted. "So we might be able to join some dots."

"There's another thing. A really fascinating idea."

"Fire away."

"Well, the dots might not just lead east. They might also throw a curveball south."

"Map, Jack," Costas said.

Aysha reached over and unrolled a map of the world on the chart table. Jack traced out the features as he talked. "The Silk Route goes west–east, from Merv in Parthia to Xian in China, through the mountains of central Asia. Lake Issyk-Kul lies at the northeastern end of that massif with only one major pass to go before you get to China. But you can also leave the route along the way and break off south. If you do that from Lake Issyk-Kul, you've got a huge mass of mountains to get through, really forbidding places, through eastern Afghanistan, but then you break into northern Pakistan and the jungles of India. From there, if you're a traveler from the west in the first century BC, the Roman world is within reach again."

Costas' eyes narrowed. "Are you suggesting that escaped Roman prisoners may have gone that way?"

Jack paused. "One of Katya's colleagues, a man named Hai Chen, is an independent scholar based in Xian who's made a lifelong study of the Roman connection. He encouraged Katya to explore Kyrgyzstan, the petroglyphs at Issyk-Kul. He believes passionately in the story of Crassus' lost legionaries, but with a twist. He's originally a linguist, an expert on analyzing foundation stories and mythology among peoples with a strong oral tradition. As a young man he spent several years in Chitral, a kind of Shangri-la in northeastern Pakistan, the first place you'd come to after breaking through the mountains from the north."

"The people who believe they're descended from Alexander the Great," Hiebermeyer murmured.

"The mythologies of the region — Vedic, Hindu, Buddhist — are full of stories of travelers from afar, princes, pilgrims, holy men dispensing wisdom. Sometimes they're on a quest, or princes on a transformative journey, like Buddha himself. Imagine the *Canterbury Tales, Sir Gawain and the Green Knight,* Hercules' Labors, Moses in the desert. Sometimes the arrival fulfills a local prophecy, and the traveler becomes king."

"Didn't Fa-hsien come through the mountains?" Hiebermeyer asked.

Jack nodded, and glanced at Costas. "A Chinese Buddhist monk who came to India in the early fifth century AD in search of the holy texts of his religion. His *Records of the Buddhistic Kingdoms* is one of the great early travel books. He came to Gandhara, the ancient Buddhist state of northern India. But Katya's colleague Hai Chen wasn't on the trail of a Buddhist monk. He'd heard of someone else. The traveler he recorded from the oral stories was a *yavana,* meaning westerner. And this *yavana* was no monk but a warrior, one who ruled with a golden hand. He came to Chitral for a short time, and then left. Farther south Hai Chen heard another legend of a god-king called *Haljit Singh,* Tiger Hand. He too left, and went south."

"Where are we leading with this?" Costas said.

"If you're our Roman, once you get through

110

the mountains of Afghanistan, past Chitral, the way's open to the west. You have two options. You can travel down the valley of the Indus southwest to the head of the Indian Ocean, to the port of Barygaza, near modern Karachi in Pakistan. From there you can sail to Arabia, then the Red Sea toward home. But there was another option. If you want to make contact with fellow *yavanas,* with other Romans in India, the better route was to go southeast, down the valley of the Ganges to the Bay of Bengal. You'd end up passing extensive tracts of jungle in eastern India. Look at the travels of the monk Fa-hsien. He took that route, and sailed south all the way to Sri Lanka. Then look at the *Periplus.* It describes the same route, just looking in the opposite direction. Listen to this." Jack picked up the modern edition of the *Periplus* on the table, and flicked through it until he came to the page he was looking for. *"After this, toward the east and with the ocean on the right, sailing offshore past the remaining lands on the left, you come upon the land of the Ganges; in this region is a river, itself called the Ganges, that is the greatest of all the rivers in India, and which rises and falls like the Nile."* Jack gestured toward the porthole, where the shore was just visible. "Remember, the author of the *Periplus* was recalling being here off southern India, looking north. It was probably as far as he ever came. But he knows men who've come

111

down from there, maybe Indian middlemen from Gandhara, maybe even traders who have come all the way down from central Asia — Bactrians, Sogdians, even western Han Chinese."

"The kind of trader who would have told our *yavana,* our escaped Roman, which way to go," Aysha said.

"But probably not lived long enough to guide him there," Jack said. "All a Roman legionary needed was a pair of stout marching sandals and a clear view of the sun and stars. With that, he was set. A guide would never have kept up with him."

"It's all about the monsoon, isn't it?" Costas said.

"What do you mean?"

"Well, why a legionary looking for fellow Romans might not go to this place at the mouth of the Indus, Barygaza," he said, pointing at the map. "It's a lot closer to Egypt. But ships can sail there from the Red Sea pretty well year round, hugging the coast, sometimes taking a direct open-sea route during the monsoon season. There was no need for a permanent western presence at Barygaza, to maintain the port during the off-season. The native traders could do that. But the south of India was a different story. I take it the Egyptian shippers only got there and back during the monsoon season, taking the open-sea route across the Indian Ocean?"

112

Jack nodded. "The coastal route down western India was too treacherous. The author of the *Periplus* makes that pretty clear. It was like the Skeleton Coast of west Africa, beset with reefs and infested with pirates."

"So for half the year Arikamedu and the other south Indian ports are empty of business. But it's crucial that they operate during the sailing season. You need people there during the off-season, your own people, people you trust. That's my point. If you're going to search for fellow Romans in India, you go south, not west. That's what our traveler would have been told. And that's what this is all leading to, isn't it? We're talking about a grizzled old legionary who wants to make contact. Maybe he's too ashamed to go home, but something drives him to try, some hope, a dream."

"Maybe he had a family, all those years ago in Rome before he marched off to war," Aysha said. "They were citizen-soldiers. They had a life before joining up."

"We can only speculate," Jack said. "Maybe he had a dream, cherished over all those years of captivity. Going to Barygaza might have put him on a ship to Egypt, yet with little foreknowledge of what to expect, committing him to discovering a truth he may never have wanted. But going to the south of India, to Arikamedu, would have put him directly in contact with other Romans. They would have

113

told him of the civil wars, of the new order, the sweeping away of all that had been before, the passing of the Rome he had known. Maybe he would have had some hint of this from traders they'd encountered on the Silk Route, but he needed to know for certain. Maybe he knew all along that a return voyage could never be more than a fantasy, laden with disappointment and grief. But he still had to make contact, a yearning that could only be satisfied by talking to those who had come from the world he had left."

Hiebermeyer peered at Jack. "It sounds as if Katya's colleague might have been following this trail. Did he go farther south?"

Jack pursed his lips. "He was planning an expedition to the tribal peoples of eastern India. Katya said he'd had a revelation about some character in Hindu mythology, a Roman connection. He seemed to know exactly where he was going, but he was secretive about it, didn't want her to get involved. Katya thinks it was here, just in from the Godavari River Delta." Jack pointed to a spot north of Arikamedu, in from the east coast of India. "He was going to reveal everything to Katya when he got back. He was due at the Transoxiana Conference, but never made it. That was almost four months ago."

"Is any of his research published?" Hiebermeyer asked.

"No. He was always secretive. Katya said

he always seemed to regret anything he revealed. He was suspicious of everyone around him. And it wasn't just a scholar with unorthodox ideas battling against the academic establishment. She said it was as if he had some great secret. He thought he was being followed. He always seemed to be putting people off the scent. Katya said he'd been like that as long as she could remember."

"So how can we trust what he told Katya?" Hiebermeyer asked.

"Because he's her uncle," Jack replied.

"Her uncle!" Costas exclaimed. "Good God. This gets more mysterious by the minute. Uncles tell their nieces things, don't they? And they're both archaeologists, linguists. He must have let her in on a bit more of the secret. Didn't she say *anything* to you?"

"She said he was like one of the Silk Route explorers of a hundred years ago, searching for an elusive treasure he could never seem to find."

"What treasure, Jack?"

Jack paused. "You're right. Katya knew more than she was letting on, but I wasn't going to press her. One thing did happen, though. In the hotel at the conference she showed me her uncle's work on Chitral. It was his doctoral thesis, one of the few times he wrote anything down. She hadn't read the section before about the legend of the god-

115

king called *Haljit Singh,* Tiger Hand. When she read that, she visibly paled. I told her about an artifact I had and where it came from, and she nearly fainted. After that she said nothing. End of topic. But she was more troubled than usual. I think there are dark forces at play. Someone who wants her uncle stopped. And that was when she began to get seriously worried about his whereabouts."

"So is that really why we're going to the jungle, Jack? To find Katya's uncle? To find what he was after? The elusive treasure?"

Jack stared at the map for a moment, then looked out of the lab at the open door of his day cabin. "There's more to it than that. A lot more." He glanced at the clock. "We're due at Arikamedu early tomorrow morning. Before that, there's something I want you all to see. A little treasure trove of my own."

4

The great bronze doors of the chamber swung shut, and the heat and smell of the desert were instantly gone. The man inside pressed the remote control, and a thin shaft of light lit up the long black slab of the table and the high recesses of the ceiling above. Then it was gone, and darkness enveloped him, a darkness so complete it seemed to suppress his very being, to make him at one with the elemental force around him. He was sitting cross-legged on the cool marble floor, his palms turned upward in the lotus position, the silk of his robe sliding against his skin when he reached down to the control pad. For years he had played, created, in front of a screen, always yearning to be within, and now he was here, controlling a world of imagery and sensation that seemed one step from the celestial existence that would soon be his.

He had already set the sequence in motion. It would prepare him for what was ahead, cleanse him, focus him, as it had done count-less times before when he had come to this place. From somewhere in the darkness came a trickling sound, then the noise of a small waterfall, just enough to conceal the sound of his own breathing, to remove all sense of himself. He felt the strength course through him, *shuide,* the power of water. He closed his eyes, and sensed them all, *wu de,* the five powers, earth, wood, metal, fire, water, each one overcoming the last, just as the dynasty of Qin had overcome the reviled Zhou, the power of water extinguishing the power of fire. And with the power of water had come darkness, a time of inchoate forms, of endless winter, of death, a sweeping away of all that had been. And into this emptiness had come *Shihuangdi,* the First Emperor, the Celestial One, who had remade the universe in his own image, a universe where his will was felt in every corner of existence, a will that none could escape. And now the Brotherhood, in the sixty-sixth generation since the tomb had been closed, prepared for the moment when the celestial universe of *Shihuangdi* would fold out into reality, when his earthly war-riors would ride once again. But before then they had one final task. That was why he had summoned the others here today.

The man opened his eyes. A cool alpine breeze had come upon him, bringing with it the sweet fragrance of mountain flowers. The

118

darkness was gone, replaced by a thin, crepuscular light, and he had the sensation of being raised high into the sky, of levitating. The image of a mountainous landscape appeared, projected as if wrapping around him, gnarled turrets of rock jutting out of a sea of cloud below, serried peaks visible in the distance, olive-green and pastel-brown, surmounted by leafy groves of emerald-green, coursed through with a fantastic architecture of villas and courtyards and pagodas, structures that blended in as if they were natural protrusions of the rock. This was what the First Emperor had seen. *Shihuangdi,* who went to the highest peaks in his realm, who claimed this space between heaven and earth as his own, who inscribed the rock with the record of his accomplishments, who proclaimed his power over earth and cosmos. The image receded into the background, and an inscription took its place, lines of white Chinese symbols against a dark background. The man began to whisper the words, sacred expressions of power:

Great is the virtue of our emperor
Who pacifies all corners of the earth,
Who punishes traitors, roots out evil men
And, with profitable measures brings prosperity.
Tasks are done at the proper season,
All things flourish and grow;

119

The common people know peace
And have laid aside weapons and armor;
Kinsmen care for each other,
There are no robbers or thieves;
Men delight in his rule
All understanding the law and discipline.
The universe entire
Is our emperor's realm . . .

He repeated the final phrase. *The universe entire is our emperor's realm.* His clipped accent and precise vowels sounded in keeping with the message, everything ordered, in its place, in control. He inhaled slowly, then relaxed completely. He hardly needed to breathe. He felt the blood drain from his heart. The power was within him, the power of *shuide.* He seemed to levitate again, far above the clouds and peaks, to the very edge of space itself, to the liminal zone between heaven and earth. Above him was darkness, suddenly suffused with a million brilliant stars, the constellations revolving in slow motion. Below him the earth was reduced to a featureless sphere. But then as he watched the surface began to sparkle, and was suddenly coursing with rivers, streams of quicksilver. *The hundred rivers, the Yellow River and the Yangtse, and the seas surrounding them.* The sparkle came from a thousand palaces and temples, from a million precious treasures. He seemed to swoop down, and to float above a misty stream, among geese and swans, cranes and herons, with tinkling music in the background. Then the scene disappeared, and the warriors were there, all around him, extending off in ranks as far as he could see, waiting. Some held spears, some wore armor. Generals stood in front of foot soldiers, cavalrymen held horses at bay. The protectors of the universe. The army of the Qin. They who would rise again, who would march forth when heaven and earth came together, when the power of water was replaced by the power of light. *The power that he himself would wield.*

The man tensed in anticipation. There was a blinding flash of green, then blue, as if the sun had been caught in a giant revolving prism in the darkness above. Then the two colors seemed to commingle and become a dazzling white. The rivers of quicksilver flowed again, sparkling and shimmering. Reeds shot up beside them, vivid green, trembling with life. Birds arched their necks upward, drawing in the light. And all around him the warrior army seemed to stir, the gray monotone becoming pastel, colors more defined with every second — flesh glowing, robes of vivid blue, armor shimmering silver, banners of red emblazoned with the roaring golden tiger that furled and rustled like the river reeds. He could feel the warmth. He reached out, exultant.

Then it was gone. He was sitting in a dark chamber again, alone in front of a low table like a raised tomb. He let his hands drop onto the surface. It was cold, hard, real. Everything before had been a phantasm. A phantasm he had created. But it was a premonition of what was to come. *The celestial jewel would shine once again.*

He looked at the low table, its polished surface gleaming. He could see the Chinese characters carved in front of each place, six on one side, six on the other. *Xu, Tan, Ju, Zhongli, Yunyan, Tuqiu, Jiangliang, Huang, Jiang, Xiuyu, Baiming, Feilian.* He reached out and traced his fingers in the lines, faultlessly cut by laser into the marble. They were the twelve, the Brotherhood, the trusted guardians of *Shihuangdi,* the First Emperor, those who awaited the return. One place would be empty. He clenched his fists until the knuckles were white. *The one who had strayed.* The one who had been tempted to search for the jewel himself, who had succumbed to his own greed, had taken his eyes off the true path. They had hunted him down, as they had hunted down all who had failed to follow the path of *Shihuangdi.*

He relaxed his hands and closed his eyes, suffused by the power of the Qin, the all-encompassing. Soon the empty place at the table would be filled again. They had found another whose ancestry traced back through the clan, to those who had ridden, armored, weapon-girt, over the steppeland from their homeland to Xian, at the side of he who would become *Shihuangdi,* First Emperor. The initiate had been taught the skills of *zhishau,* the swordsmanship of the Qin, how to strike mortal fear into the heart of all enemies of *Shihuangdi,* how to vanquish them. He would complete the murderous task that would assure him his place at the table. *The place of the tiger warrior.*

The man touched the control pad, and the thin shaft of light spread outward to reveal a crossed pair of swords lying in front of him, their blades shimmering as if they were speckled with a thousand jewels. He put his hands into the gleaming gauntlets, curling his fingers around the crossbars, feeling the power of the blades as they extended out from the snarling tigers that adorned each fist. He tensed, and he was suddenly there, among the heavenly steeds, thundering over the steppe, foam-flecked, cutting through the mist of red that streamed off their necks, the glistening sweat of blood. He felt the exaltation of the warrior, of knowing that all would be swept before him. He felt himself cry out, and all he saw was crimson, all he heard was panting, rearing, stamping.

Then the image was gone. He sat back, letting the swords down. Soon there would be a sixth power. *The power of light.* Just as water had conquered fire, so light would conquer darkness, the light of the celestial jewel, the light of his own soul, the reborn emperor. The man breathed in deeply, and pulled off the swords. Ahead of him a crack of light appeared in the doorway, and shadowy forms began to file in, silently assuming their places at the table. The Brotherhood was reunited. The jewel would be found. *The tiger warrior would ride again.*

Jack sat in his day cabin below the bridge deck of *Seaquest II,* his hands behind his head as he contemplated the old wooden traveling chest against the bulkhead in front of him. He had removed the wooden frame that had been used to batten down the chest during the monsoon, and had opened the third drawer down so he could see the contents. It was one of his most prized possessions, an officer's traveling chest of the eighteenth century, made of camphor wood that still exuded a faint smell of the Orient. For generations his ancestors had taken the chest to sea with them, from the merchant adventurers who had built the Howard family fortune in the early years of the East India Company to his own grandfather, who had carried it with him through the Second World

War and last brought it ashore more than forty years ago. No Howard had ever suffered shipwreck before the loss of the first *Seaquest* in the Black Sea two years before, and Jack had made the decision to install the chest when the new vessel was under construction. But the chest meant more than just good luck. It contained the clues to a quest that Jack had yearned to follow since he was a boy, when his grandfather had first shown him the contents of that drawer.

Jack felt a surge of excitement as he looked at the chest. Hanging on the wall behind it was an old East India Company musket, and below that was the sweeping steel blade of a *tulwar,* an Indian sword with a distinctive circular pommel and handguard. Both had been the possessions of the first Howard to live in India, the colonel of a regiment of the Bengal army at the time of the Napoleonic Wars. Below the sword were two Victorian photographs, one showing a woman and a child, the other a well-dressed young man with dark features and full lips, and a twinkle in his eye. The features came from the man's Portuguese-Jewish grandmother, the wife of the Bengal army colonel. Below the picture in elegant handwriting were the words *Royal Military Academy 1875, Lieutenant John Howard, Royal Engineers.* It was the graduation picture of a young man brimming with Victorian confidence, about to set out on the greatest adventure of his life. Yet a mere four years later something would happen that would transform those eyes, and give them the unfathomable look that Jack sometimes saw in his own daughter. Finding out what happened to his great-great-grandfather had been a personal quest of Jack's for as long as he could remember.

He glanced at the open drawer. On one side was a small stack of leather-bound books and a notebook, with the same handwriting on the spines. On the other side were two box files containing a mass of papers, letters, manuscripts, some of it material Jack had barely begun to delve into. And between were the artifacts he had just been unwrapping. He took out a small red box containing a brass pocket telescope, the ivory surround of the cylinder shrunk with age. For the thousandth time since he had been a boy he extended the telescope to its full length, only a few inches, and peered through it. And just as he always did, he tried to imagine what John Howard had seen through it on that fateful day in the jungle. Jack shut his eyes, closing his mind off from the present, then opened them again, but the view remained the same. Yet he knew he was on the cusp of it now, only a helicopter trip away from the place where the history that he had spent years trying so hard to imagine might finally come to life.

"Cool telescope." Rebecca had come quietly into the room and was standing beside Jack. He passed it to her, and she peered through it. "That was your great-great-great-grandfather's," he said. "He brought it back from India, where he used it in a war in the jungle not far from the Roman site we're visiting tomorrow morning."

Rebecca looked at the pictures. "That's him, isn't it, and his family? I can see you in him. I can really feel his presence, holding this. Whenever we do school trips to museums, I always want to touch things. I got into a lot of trouble at the Metropolitan Museum once. They don't have to be great works of art, just little things. They seem to take me back into the past."

Jack smiled at her. "Look around this room. There are artifacts from almost every expedition I've been on. Most of them are little things, just as you say, shards of pottery, worn old coins. But they're what makes it real for me. When I sit here and write, I always have something in my hands."

"Uncle Costas says you're a magpie. He says you're really a treasure hunter." She passed back the telescope and traced her finger over the coat of arms carved into the front of the chest, an anchor over a shield with the Latin words *Depressus Extollor* carved underneath.

Jack laughed. "Uncle Costas had better

watch what he says."

"Uncle Costas says that without him, you'd be going nowhere in a rowboat."

"And without me, Uncle Costas would be sailing a desk to nowhere in some technology park in California."

"No, he says without you, he'd be on holiday in Hawaii."

"Ever since we planned the Pacific trip, he's had Hawaii on the brain. Everything else on the way, Egypt, India, is just a distraction, and he's tolerating it only because I'm his dive buddy and I save his life occasionally."

"We've already talked about it. He says he's giving you two days, and then he's going to ask to be dropped at the nearest international airport. He needs a week before we arrive to get everything set up for the submersible testing."

"He means he needs a week to test the lounge chairs at Waikiki. He's just a beach bum."

At that moment Costas bounded in, wearing a garish flowery shirt over baggy shorts, with wraparound sunglasses pushed up his forehead. "Aloha!"

"Aloha!" Rebecca replied, grinning mischievously at Jack.

"Thought I may as well get ready," Costas said. "We may not have time to change."

"I hear you," Jack said.

Costas spied the object Jack had just finished unwrapping. "An elephant! I was getting withdrawal symptoms."

Jack passed it over, and Costas held it up carefully to the light. "It's made of lapis lazuli," Jack said. "The same stone as that fragment you found at Berenikê. It's the highest grade too, from the mines in Afghanistan. You can see the sparkle of pyrites in the layers of blue. It's been handled a lot, played with. It was among my great-great-grandfather's possessions, given to him when he was a child. He had wanted to give it to his own son, his firstborn, on his second birthday. But that never happened."

"It's beautiful," Rebecca said reverently, taking it from Costas and stroking the trunk. "Can I have it? I mean, can I borrow it and keep it in my cabin? It's kind of a shame to have it stuffed away in that old chest."

Costas wagged a finger at Rebecca. "Careful what you say about that chest. It follows him everywhere. It makes him feel like an old sea dog. Whenever he's got some downtime, he comes and sits with it."

Hiebermeyer and Aysha came in, and they all sat down on the chairs Jack had arranged in an arc around the chest. Costas peered in the open drawer and gestured at another object inside, an old revolver. "The Wild West?"

Jack gave a wry smile. "Right period, wrong continent. The period we're talking about, the 1870s, saw major international confrontations — the Franco-Prussian War which nearly destroyed Europe, the Afghan War which brought Britain head-to-head with Russia. But it was also a flashpoint for colonial conflict. Within a few years you've got Custer's Last Stand in America, the Zulu War in South Africa, and jungle rebellion in India. And in each case it's unclear which side got off best."

"Your ancestor John Howard," Aysha said, as Costas carefully lifted the revolver out of the drawer to inspect it more closely. "He was a British army officer?"

Jack nodded. "Now that we're all here, I want to tell you about him. In 1879 he was a lieutenant in the Royal Engineers, recently posted out to India as a subaltern in the Queen's Own Madras Sappers and Miners. That was one of the premier regiments in the Indian army, based in Bangalore in south India but used on expeditions all around India and the frontiers. They were surveyors and builders, but they also trained as infantry, so were about the most useful troops around. Each of the ten companies had two British officers and several British NCOs, but the sappers were all Madrasis, including the native officers — the jemadars and subadars — and the native NCOs, the havildars and naiks. The Madrasis were proud men, a warrior caste. For a young British officer, service with a regiment like the Madras Sappers was about the best experience of soldiering you could have. Lieutenants commanded companies and the senior subalterns had the responsibilities a major would have today. All of the Royal Engineers officers had gone through the equivalent of a graduate degree program in engineering before coming out to India."

"India must have been a shock to the system coming from cold and drizzly England," Costas said.

Jack shook his head. "Not for Howard. He'd been schooled in England, but he was born in India in 1855 just before the Indian Mutiny, in the final years of the East India Company before the British crown took over. His father had been an indigo planter in Bihar, on the border with the Himalayas and Tibet, and his grandfather had been a colonel in the East India Company army. So India was in his blood. That helps to explain how he survived the jungle conditions of his first active deployment."

"This place we're going to," Costas said.

"After more than two decades of peace following the mutiny, India was heating up," Jack said. "There was war again in Afghanistan, for the first time in forty years. Most of the Madras Sapper officers were deployed there, but not Howard. The reason was another conflict, a tribal uprising that flared up in 1879 in the jungle of the northern

Madras presidency, in the foothills of the Eastern Ghats Mountains along the Goda-vari River." Jack pointed at the map above his desk. "Ever since the mutiny, the Indian government had put down any hint of internal uprising with an iron fist. A brigade-sized expedition was dispatched to the jungle, including two companies of sappers. But these revolts were regarded as civil disturbances, so there was little military glory and no medals for officers despite the hard campaigning involved. And this revolt, called the Rampa Rebellion after the local district, dragged on for almost two years, longer than the entire Afghan campaign. Howard was there almost from beginning to end."

"It must have been pestilential, during the monsoon," Hiebermeyer said.

Jack nodded. "Rampa had all the extremes of jungle warfare, in common with the jungle campaigns of the following century, in Burma, Malaysia, Vietnam. Malaria was a huge problem. A few years later, the surgeon-major of the Madras Sappers was Ronald Ross, later Sir Ronald Ross, the man who confirmed the link between mosquitoes and malaria. But at the time of the rebellion there was limited understanding of it and the men dropped like flies. And that's where Howard's Indian background comes into play. He had some resistance to the fever, and that must have been a factor in his continued deploy-

ment. He was the only officer fit enough to do the job."

Costas pulled back the hammer and rotated the cylinder on the old revolver, a long, elegant piece which had turned a plum color where the blueing on the metal had come away. "Eighteen fifty-one Colt Navy, London make," he said. "I used to shoot one of these with an uncle of mine in Vermont who was a black powder enthusiast." He turned the pistol over and traced his fingers over the letters and numbers stamped into the wooden grips. "Army markings?"

"That's UC, Upper Canada, the letter A for the Frontenac Troop, number fifty," Jack explained. "This was one of a batch of revolvers bought from Colt's London factory to arm cavalrymen of the Canadian militia, based in Kingston on Lake Ontario. The surgeon of the Madras Sappers, Dr. Walker, had grown up in Kingston, served in the militia himself and acquired this pistol as surplus in the 1870s when the militia converted to cartridge revolvers. Walker took it to India and gave it to Howard to complement an identical Colt revolver he'd inherited from his father, who used it during the Indian Mutiny. Always best to have a pair of cap-and-ball revolvers, as they took so long to reload."

"Where's the other one?"

"Howard took it with him when he disappeared."

"Disappeared?"

"One day years later in northern India he packed his bag and left, never to return. No one knows for certain where he went or what happened to him. I've been obsessed with it ever since I heard the story as a boy. I used to read Kipling, and accounts of explorers on the Silk Road, and imagine him on some great final adventure. He's always been there in my mind when I've gone off on quests of my own. Now that we're so close to the jungle, to actually being on his trail, I'd love to get to the bottom of it. But more about that later. Let's not jump the gun."

"I've found something on the rebellion," Rebecca said, holding up a notebook with Victorian marblized covers and faded ink handwriting on a label. *The Rampa Expedi-*

tion 1879, by John Howard, Lieutenant, R.E."

"That's his diary," Jack said. "It's the only personal account to survive from the rebellion. Almost everything else I've reconstructed from records in the India Office collections in the British Library, from the military and judicial proceedings of the Madras government which oversaw the jungle tracts. The rebellion was overshadowed by the Afghan War, and pretty well lost to history."

Rebecca carefully opened a page, then began to read. *"The difficulties of surveying really begin when the mapping is being pushed forward into an unknown country, especially if the surveyors are hampered with having to keep with troops, and their vision frequently obstructed by bad weather."*

Jack nodded. "Survey was his specialty. He'd just come out of the School of Military Engineering at Chatham, two years of intensive training. There's a lot of youthful enthusiasm in the first pages of the diary. But that soon changes."

Rebecca read another section toward the end of the book. *"The causes of that outbreak have been fully described; the administration was slack; our officers turned a deaf ear to the complaints of an oppressed people, and the ancient spirit which appealed to the sword at length asserted itself, amongst a brave and hearty race of mountaineers. Once that spirit is roused, and we are forced into a campaign in a wild, difficult and malarious tract — no man can say how long the petty warfare will last, or what slumbering elements of disorder will be stirred up against us. All that can be predicted is that the enemy will seldom be seen, that fever will fill the regimental hospitals, and that when peace comes at last, it will be the peace of desolation. All that these hill clans require of us is that we shall protect them in the tranquil enjoyment of the few contracted and simple objects of personal liberty and comfort which constitute the main sources of their happiness."*

"Love the language," Costas murmured.

"That pretty well sums it up," Jack said. "Years later the Indian nationalist movement tried to make out that the rebellion was part of a general uprising against the British, but that's revisionist history at its worst. These were jungle people who basically wanted to be left alone. Most of them had never even seen a European face before. Their main contact with the outside world had been with lowland people, with corrupt Indian police constables and with traders who extorted them. There was little economic gain for the British in the jungle and they put less competent officials in charge, a lower grade of district officer who rarely bothered to inspect the tracts themselves. Then the Indian Forestry Act interfered with their traditional slash-and-burn agriculture. But the spark was some petty official in Calcutta failing to exempt the hill peoples from the *abkari* tax on alcohol. The jungle people lived for their toddy, the palm liquor which sustained them through the monsoon months when there was nothing else to do."

"I see what you mean," Costas murmured. "Not exactly a glorious war. A long way from the geopolitics of Afghanistan."

"But war was still war," Jack said. "Take away grand strategic purpose, and you question far more. And these officers were a long way from the closed-mind, stiff-upper-lip caricature. The Royal Engineers attracted men of high intellect and curiosity. Today they'd be scientists, civil engineers, explorers. Much of what we know about the anthropology and natural history of India comes from what these men did in their spare time. And much of their work was not spent soldiering, but in surveying and mapping, and building roads, bridges, dams, aqueducts and irrigation systems, railways, public monuments, the infrastructure of the nation today. You had to speak the language to operate effectively in India, and many of these officers were gifted linguists, empathetic with their soldiers and the people around them. You can see that in the diary. The tone may seem a little lofty to us today, but guys like Howard saw human beings in their gun sights, not primitive tribals. They were tough soldiers, unswervingly loyal to the British crown, and would kill without hesitation, but they knew they were not always on the moral high ground."

"There's a reference to a book here, on the final page of the diary with writing on it," Rebecca said. "It's all smudged black." She lifted the book and sniffed it, pulling a face. "It stinks like rotten eggs."

"Black powder residue," Jack said. "He must have had it on his hands when he wrote that. He'd have just been shooting. Look at the date. Twentieth August 1879."

"I can barely read it, but the note says, *Campbell, Wild Tribes of Khondistan, page 177.* Then it says, *Lord help me.*"

Jack took one of the two leather-bound volumes from the drawer and opened it to a marked page. "This is the actual book. He had it with him when he wrote that final diary entry. In the margin of the book he's written, *Captain Frye, an admirable officer, an oriental scholar of the highest rank, who occupied himself most zealously in the acquisition of the Khond language.* He clearly wrote that some time earlier, perhaps when he'd first read the book before going into the jungle. But the passage of text beside the note is circled in the same ink as that last diary entry, slightly smudged. He must have read it again that day in the jungle. Listen to this:

"A curious circumstance occurred to this excellent officer when in the hills. He was informed one day of a sacrifice on the very eve of consummation; the victim was a young and handsome girl, fifteen or sixteen years old. Without a moment's hesitation, he hastened with a small body of armed men to the spot indicated, and on arrival found the Khonds already assembled with their sacrificing priest, and the intended victim prepared for the first act of the tragedy. He at once demanded her surrender; the Khonds, half-mad with excitement, hesitated for a moment, but observing his little party preparing for action, they yielded the girl. Seeing the wild and irritated state of the Khonds, Captain Frye very prudently judged that this was no fitting occasion to argue with them, so with his prize he retraced his steps to his old encampment."

"Human sacrifice?" Costas exclaimed, looking horrified. "India? In 1879?"

"That book was published in 1864, fifteen years before the Rampa Rebellion. The full title is *A Personal Narrative of Thirteen Years Service Amongst the Wild Tribes of Khondistan for the Suppression of Human Sacrifice.* The author, John Campbell, was an army officer charged with the task, and Frye was his assistant."

"But they failed."

Jack pursed his lips. "They succeeded. That was the public face of it, anyway. The British didn't interfere much with ritual in India, but they drew the line at human sacrifice and female infanticide. What they did was drive both practices underground. Who knew what went on in the depths of the jungle, miles from prying eyes. Even today the sacrificial ritual survives among the tribal peoples, though they use chickens instead of humans. Or so we're told."

"And in 1879?"

"The rebel leader, Chendrayya, openly executed several native policemen he'd taken captive, giving the executions the semblance of sacrifice in defiance of the British. On one occasion he used a sword, probably a *tulwar* like the one on the wall over there." Jack opened the book to an engraving in the frontispiece. It showed a semi-naked woman tied to a pole with a priest in front and a crowd pressing around her, brandishing knives. "But there are hints that actual human sacrifice was also carried out. These involved a *meriah,* a man, or woman, even a child, who was bought into slavery by the sacrificing tribe, well-fed and well-treated for months in advance, then intoxicated with palm toddy and lashed to a stake."

"How did they do it?" Rebecca asked quietly.

"It's pretty unpleasant. They ripped the victim apart with their bare hands and knives. Each man took a strip of flesh home to bury in his own soil before nightfall that day as a kind of fertility offering."

Rebecca looked pale. Costas took the book. "Why did they do it? Who was the god?"

"I'm coming to that."

"And that date? Twentieth August 1879?"

"That's the lynchpin date of the rebellion, and also somehow of Howard's life. Something happened that day, something I've been trying to fathom out ever since I first saw the diary as a kid." Jack picked up the diary. "Here's what I know. On that day, a party of thirty sappers were led into an ambush by four hundred rebels, armed with bows and poison arrows and matchlock muskets, as well as some old company muskets they'd stolen from the police. The sappers fought their way back through the jungle to the river. It was one of the biggest fights of the rebellion, with dozens killed and wounded. One British official died, a civil service man responsible for this area who'd accompanied the troops. That day was big enough to hit the news, and was even reported in the London *Times* and *The New York Times,* with the name of the officer commanding the sapper party, Lieutenant Hamilton. His account of the fight was printed in the *Madras Military Proceedings.* Otherwise there are no eyewitness records of that day. But I'm certain something else happened."

"Executions?" Costas murmured. "Sacrifice?"

Jack looked at the book. "Hamilton's foray took place from a river steamer, *Shamrock,* which had been on its way upriver to a place where the sappers were going to hack a road into the jungle. Lieutenant Howard, my great-great-grandfather, was in overall charge, as the senior subaltern present. As well as Lieutenants Howard and Hamilton, there was another sapper officer, Robert Wauchope, recently returned from Afghanistan, an Irish-American who was a close friend of Howard's. We've already encountered Dr. Walker, the Canadian. He probably had his hands full with cases of jungle fever. I've pinpointed where Hamilton's party came out of the jungle on the riverbank, where the *Shamrock* must have been. It was the site of a native village. The rebels congregated there and put on a show for them. A pretty spectacular one. Howard was on the steamer. He saw something, or did something, that profoundly affected the rest of his life."

"What do you mean?"

Jack paused. "He'd been at the top of his class at the Royal Military Academy, one of the officers flagged for great things, perhaps a future army commander like Lord Kitchener, another Royal Engineer. But after the jungle, it was as if he did everything he could to avoid active service again. He'd been detailed to join the Khyber Field Force in Afghanistan, but instead was deployed in Rampa until the end. Then he left the Madras Sappers for secondment to the Indian Public Works Department, and after that went back to England to spend ten years teaching survey and editing the journal of the School of Military Engineering. These were respectable career moves for a Royal Engineers officer, but not for the ambitious soldier he had once been. Even after he returned to India as a garrison engineer in the 1890s he passed up on chances of campaigning. It was only at the end of his career that he was poised for active service again, on the Afghan frontier, twenty-five years after the Rampa Rebellion."

"What about devotion to his family?" Rebecca said. "Couldn't that have influenced him?"

Jack looked across at the faded photograph above the chest, showing a woman in a black dress holding a baby, her faced turned down to the child, indiscernible. He turned to Rebecca, nodding slowly. "Howard married young, straight out of the academy. They had a baby boy they adored. They lived in the military cantonment at Bangalore, headquarters of the Madras Sappers. The boy died while Howard was in the jungle several months after that day in August, struck down with convulsions one morning and buried that evening. It was weeks before Howard even knew. His wife never got over it, though they had three more children. Howard was utterly devoted to them, and told his children that he took up his job at the School of Military Engineering in England to get them away from the diseases that had killed their brother, and to be with them when they were at school."

"He put family before career," Aysha said. "Nothing wrong with that."

Jack pursed his lips. "But there was more to it than that. Even after they'd grown up and he'd returned to India, he passed up chances. I'm convinced something happened on that day, 20 August 1879."

"Sounds like something traumatized him,"

Costas said.

"There's one other thing." Jack leaned over and opened the lower drawer of the chest. "You remember I mentioned an artifact I'd spoken about to Katya, when she and I saw her uncle's reference to the *Haljit Singh,* the Tiger Hand? The one that nearly made her faint? This was it." He took out a gleaming brass object almost the length of his forearm, and placed it carefully on the table between them. It was semi-cylindrical, and one end had been formed into the shape of a head, with protruding ears and a wide, leering mouth. "Howard brought this back from Rampa. This, the revolver, the little telescope and a few primitive arms captured from the rebels are just about the only artifacts that can be pinned to the campaign. Any guesses what this is?" Jack asked.

Hiebermeyer pushed up his glasses and leaned over, lifting it up gingerly to look underneath. "Well, it's clearly a piece of armor, for the lower forearm and hand," he asserted. "In the hollow under the head there's a crossbar, and the mouth has a hole in it the size of a blade. My opinion is that this was once a gauntlet with an attached dagger or sword blade."

"Full marks," Jack said. "Not a thrusting blade, but a long, flexible blade, for sweeping cuts. It would have been awkward in unskilled hands, but with the gauntlet and the crossbar,

145

rather than a conventional sword handle, the blade would have become like an extension of the arm. The swordsman could deliver a massive sweeping blow, easily enough to slice bodies in half with a razor-sharp blade. They were fearsome weapons, designed to be used from horseback."

Rebecca touched the nose. "Those eyes look Chinese."

"It's called a *pata,* a gauntlet sword," Jack said. "This one's unique, and only a few other brass ones are known. Steel *patas* were used by the Marathas, the warrior-princes the British fought in southern and central India in the eighteenth century. But the British scholar who first studied *patas* thought they originated much earlier, among the Tatar ancestors of the Mongols in northern China. They could have come into India with the Mongol invaders, with Timur the Great in the fourteenth century, or Genghis Khan. Or one might have come much earlier by way of the Silk Route and then been copied. Most of the Indian *patas* of the seventeenth or eighteenth century are made of steel, and don't have this decoration, the hammered-out head. My instinct is that this one is older, much older, possibly even of ancient date."

"So what's the connection?" Costas said.

"You asked about the god, the sacrificial god in the jungle," Jack replied. "There were several, one of them a kind of earth goddess, another a god of war. But there's only one shrine we know of, and that's to Rama, the god who gave his name to the district. The legend of Prince Rama is wrapped up in Hindu mythology, but the version of Rama worshipped in the jungle was distinctive, possibly of very early origin. The shrine is mentioned in the records of the Rampa Rebellion because the rebel leader Chendrayya sacrificed two police constables there. It lies directly inland from the point where the *Shamrock* picked up Lieutenant Hamilton and his sappers after their foray in the jungle. And I believe it was where my ancestor found this *pata.* It was the only permanent structure in the jungle other than the huts of the villagers, and exactly where you'd expect such an unusual object to be stored, even venerated."

"And you want to go and check it out," Costas said.

"I need to see what he saw. To see if there's anything still left."

"Rama," Hiebermeyer murmured, tapping his fingers on the table. *"Rama."*

"What is it?" Costas said.

"Just thinking aloud."

Costas picked up the *pata* and stared at the face. "What is it? A god?"

Jack looked across. "It's a tiger."

"A tiger god?" Costas asked.

Jack slipped the *pata* over his hand, holding

the crossbar. "Not tiger god," he said, turning it slowly on his arm. "It's what we always called it when I was growing up, what my grandfather told us to call it. He must have learned it from his grandfather, from John Howard. It's what made Katya nearly faint when I described it to her. *Tiger warrior.*"

Early the next morning they stood on the bridge wing gazing out over the bow of the ship. *Seaquest II* had passed through the Palk Strait between India and Sri Lanka, navigating the treacherous channel at only a couple of knots speed. They had just watched the pilot disembark and power off in his speedboat. The northern tip of Sri Lanka was now receding off the starboard stern quarter, and the captain had reduced the alert level as they entered Indian territorial waters. The Breda gun turret had been lowered out of sight below the foredeck and the security team was stowing the two general purpose machine guns, which had been mounted on either side of the bridge. Ahead of them lay the Bay of Bengal, a shimmering expanse of water seemingly stretching out to infinity. The sea was dead calm, and it was as if they were motionless, mired in a haze of sea and sky with no visible horizon.

Jack sensed the whiff of excitement that had first drawn western explorers — his own ancestors — into these waters. The eastern sky seemed full of allure, and with the risks that made the draw that much more beguiling. Jack had been thinking about the Romans again. Here, two thousand years ago, they would have been on the cusp of the unknown, the place where the author of the *Periplus* had drawn the line between what he himself had seen, and the world beyond. Ahead lay places half-imagined, which the author knew only from the goods that were brought to him — silk, lapis lazuli, exotic spices and medicaments, carried by traders across great mountains and deserts to the sea. The traders he met would have told him little, and what they did tell might have been deliberately misleading, designed to put him off searching for the sources himself. Yet their tales would have needed little exaggeration. The dangers were all too real, even today. Jack remembered the final lines of the *Periplus. What lies beyond this region, because of extreme storms, immense cold and impenetrable terrain, and because of some divine power of the gods, has not been explored.*

Costas came up beside him, and turned to speak. "Rebecca wants to come with us, Jack. She has three weeks' more holiday from school."

"She can come to the Roman site at Arikamedu, but not to the jungle. It's bandit country out there. The place is a haven for Maoist terrorists. It's heated up since the

Indian government allowed foreign mining speculators into the jungle, and the Maoists have stirred up the tribal people."

"Okay, you tell her."

"She seems to listen to you, Uncle Costas."

"She knows already." Aysha was standing on the other side of Jack. "I told her."

"Oh, thanks, Aysha." Jack's eye was suddenly caught by a spectacular image. The eastern shoreline of India had been visible a few miles off the port bow, but was now lit up by the morning sun as it rose above the haze to the east. It was an extraordinary sight, a thin line of beach and fringing palms glowing orange, as if a channel of fire were ripping up the shore toward the northern horizon. Jack thought of India in 1879, the year of the jungle rebellion. It was an India of Mughal opulence and colonial civility, yet there was another India, a darker place of desperation and cruelty, of starvation, of disease that took half the children and would kill a person within a day. Two decades before the Rampa Rebellion, India had been torn apart by the mutiny of the Indian troops of the East India Company's Bengal Army, an orgy of barbarism and bloodshed. Three years before the rebellion, in 1876, a dreadful famine had settled in the south and killed millions. India seemed a place of temptation, yet a place where fickle mortality sharpened the senses, focused experience on the present. Jack remembered those last words in the diary of John Howard, written somewhere out here in the jungle beyond the line of coast that burned across the horizon. *Lord help me.* What had he seen?

A warm breeze wafted over them as *Seaquest II* picked up speed. Jack turned and went down the stairs to his cabin, leaving the door open. A few minutes later Rebecca came in flopping down on his foldout bed. "I've been reading a story you put by my bed, Rudyard Kipling's *The Man Who Would Be King.* It was published in 1888, and the book's signed John Howard, Captain, R. E."

"Go on," Jack said.

"It's about two British adventurers, former soldiers, who go north to Afghanistan in search of a fabled lost kingdom. They find it, and one of them becomes king, ruling like a god. But he accidentally cuts himself and the people see his blood and realize he's mortal, and he comes to a sticky end. I also found James Hilton's *Lost Horizon,* published in 1933. That's about Shangri-la, somewhere in the mountains to the northeast of India, the fabled place where people were nearly immortal."

"These are both modern legends," Hiebermeyer said, walking into the cabin with Aysha, both carrying steaming mugs of coffee. Costas followed behind.

Rebecca shook her head determinedly, and

pointed at a book on the desk. The cover showed an image of an exploding volcano at sea, superimposed on an underwater photograph of a rock-cut stairway leading to a dark entranceway surrounded by mysterious symbols. Across it was the single word *Atlantis.* "My mother sent a copy of that to me even before I knew you. That first chapter on the ancient Greek philosopher Plato. Atlantis is also a modern legend, but there was a kernel of truth in it."

"So you think we're looking for a lost kingdom, for Shangri-la?" Hiebermeyer said dubiously.

Rebecca shook her head and pointed at a small pottery statue of a Chinese warrior used as a paperweight on Jack's desk. "I've been thinking about that warrior."

"Uh-oh," Costas murmured. "I think we're in for a bit of Howard lateral thinking."

"You remember, Dad? You took me to the terracotta warriors exhibit at the British Museum in London the day after we flew in from New York." She turned to Aysha, suddenly breathless with excitement. "It's amazing. This guy, the First Emperor, had himself buried with everything, and I mean everything, under a mound the size of an Egyptian pyramid. They haven't even excavated it yet, can you believe it? There's only some ancient Chinese account of what it's like. There's a complete model of the world with mercury rivers, and even the heavens. The stars were jewels. And around the mound is what they've actually dug up, those warriors, all life-sized, thousands of them. It's the coolest thing you've ever seen."

Hiebermeyer began tapping his fingers. "What's your point, Rebecca?"

"I think it's all about immortality."

"That's what tombs are usually about," Hiebermeyer said, still tapping. "Equipping people for the afterlife."

"I don't mean the afterlife, I mean immortality," she said impatiently. "With the First Emperor, it was a complete obsession. You remember, Dad? In the exhibit it said he sent out a huge expedition in search of some fabled islands in the Pacific, the Isles of the Immortals. I asked whether you'd ever hunted for them."

Costas had a faraway look in his eyes, and began humming the Hawaii-Five-Oh tune. "I think I know where they are."

Rebecca's face crumpled with frustration. "You're not taking me seriously."

Jack looked at the statue. "The Chinese concept of the afterlife was close to the notion of immortality. You didn't go to heaven as we might understand it. Instead you remained in a kind of parallel universe, shadowing the real world. For the First Emperor of China, *Shihuangdi,* in the third century BC, the idea of heaven couldn't offer him more than he already had on earth. That's what the terracotta army was about, a copy of what he had at his command during his mortal life."

Rebecca was silent, looking down and fiddling with her fingers. Aysha leaned forward and looked at her. "I know what you're driving at. It's the allure of the east, isn't it? Do you think that's what Howard was after, when he disappeared? For some, it was remote fantasy valleys, Shangri-la, lost kingdoms, heaven on earth, places where you could live forever in earthly paradise. For others, it was where you might find the secret of immortality. Always it was the allure of eternal life, the greatest of treasures."

"But what about our Roman legionaries?" Costas said. "Is this what they were after too? I thought all they wanted was glorious death, to join their brothers-in-arms in Elysium."

"Out there, on the Silk Route heading east, they may have thought they were in that shadowland already, marching alongside their dead companions," Jack said. "But they were still alive, and we should never underestimate human desire. For those among them who still hankered after it, immortality might have seemed their only hope of ever making it back to Rome."

"How could they have known what lay ahead?" Aysha murmured. "What might have drawn them on?"

154

"I was getting to that," Rebecca said. "The First Emperor's tomb was at the end of the Silk Route, right? Full of treasure, just as it is today. If traders coming down from the Silk Route could tell the author of the *Periplus* about legionaries escaping from Parthia and heading east, then traders could also have told the legionaries about the fabled tomb of the First Emperor. Maybe a trader told them the story in the hope they'd spare his life."

"Maybe we're being too mystical about this," Costas said, rubbing his stubble.

"What do you mean?" Rebecca said.

"Maybe you have the right idea, but it wasn't some mystical allure. Just good old-fashioned treasure."

"Dad says you're wrong about him, he's an archaeologist, not a treasure hunter."

"When I see an elephant, I call it an elephant." Costas stood up. "We need to get to the Zodiac. And I wasn't being flippant. Hawaii is paradise. The west shore of Kaua'i, you know? There's a beautiful beach with some shady palms just beyond Hanalei, and the perfect little bar."

"Dad says you're a beach bum," Rebecca said.

"Now you know why I have to go."

Jack turned to Rebecca. "Keep on reading John Howard's diary. There might be more in it I've missed. And pretty good thinking, by the way. We might just sign you up. All you have to do now is learn to dive."

"It's a done deal, Jack," Costas said. "I'm taking her out from Kaua'i next week."

"She might not want to, of course," Jack said. "She might want to learn to fly helicopters instead."

"Oh, I'll do anything for Uncle Costas," Rebecca said, waving a diving textbook at them as she followed Hiebermeyer and Aysha out of the door.

Jack turned to Costas, his expression serious. "I'm dog-tired, but I'm looking forward to this." He jerked his head toward the pile of khaki clothes and jungle boots beside his bed. A shoulder strap and holster lay on top, the butt of his Beretta 92 automatic poking out. "It's been a while since I've worn that."

"Too long, Jack. We don't want to lose the edge."

Jack was suddenly exhilarated. It had been an extraordinary twenty-four hours since he had first seen the shards with the text of the *Periplus,* and he was still reeling. They had begun to fathom out a story from the past, a lattice of possibilities and connections. Already he had begun to see images, the first few pictures in his mind that told him his instincts were right. Gnarled, weatherbeaten faces — Roman faces — the sheen of sunlight off a blood-soaked blade, swirling snow, then something else, the image of a warrior, something he could not shake from his mind.

He turned and looked at the pictures above the sea chest, the faded images of the British officer, of his wife and child. Jack felt as if he were about to walk into that image and join his ancestor on his foray into the darkness, to a place Jack had yearned to know all his adult life. He took a deep breath, picked up the holster and looked at Costas. "Good to go?"

"Good to go."

5

Godavari River, India, 20 August 1879
Lieutenant John Howard, Royal Engineers, took off his pith helmet and wiped his brow. The sun was bearing down directly on the deck of the steamer now, and it was deuced hot. The brass helmet plate of the Queen's Own Madras Sappers and Miners gleamed up at him, lovingly polished by his batman that morning. But it presented an excellent mark for a sharpshooter, and he rubbed his grimy palm into it, and then replaced the helmet on his head. He reached out to touch the metal casing of the paddlewheel, the last spot of shade along the side of the vessel, but the metal was like a furnace. A lump of coal rolled out from under an oilskin in front of him and he kicked it despondently. At least they had managed to get that dry. He had seen speckles of iron pyrites in the coal, and had remembered an alarming demonstration of spontaneous combustion in damp coal at the School of Military Engineering. It would

have been a less than glorious end to his first field command, immolated on a sandbar in a godforsaken river gorge in the jungle of eastern India, without ever having fired a shot. He was beginning to realize that war was like that.

He watched a crocodile swim languidly by, seemingly oblivious to the drama unfolding at the river bend, then shifted to face the fore-deck of the vessel, pulling his Sam Browne belt around so his holster was out of the way, and keeping his head below the iron plating they had erected as bullet-proofing in the river port at Rajahmundry. He glanced at the nameplate, *Shamrock,* then at his men. Kneeling behind the plating were a dozen Madrasi sappers, their cartridge pouches open and their Snider-Enfield rifles at the ready. Beyond them was the seven-pounder gun, with canisters of grapeshot and a sponging rod laid alongside. Colonel Rammell had urgently requested mountain pack guns for the mules but instead they had been sent two muzzle-loading field pieces with fixed carriages, useless in the jungle. At the last minute the sappers had installed one on the river steamer, and had devised a block and tackle to keep the recoil under control. Beyond the gun the lascar boatmen were still engaged in a futile effort to kedge the vessel off the sandbar which had held them fast for almost two days now. During the night another boat had come upriver, delivering a replacement officer and taking away some of the sappers broken by jungle fever, but every effort of the crewmen had failed to dislodge the steamer. That was another reason to pray for the return of the monsoon. With the river in full spate, they would float off and be able to continue their voyage upriver to Wuddagudem, where they were supposed to be hacking a road out of the jungle. Their mules were still standing patiently in the lee of the deckhouse, with racks of picks and axes stacked beside them. One of the lascars was there too, lying unconscious on a stretcher. His moans and cries had made the previous night intolerable. The afternoon before, the boatmen had taken the anchor out in the little boat and dropped it a hundred feet away, and the unfortunate lascar had been at the capstan when the hawser had broken and snapped back, mangling his legs. Surgeon Walker had dosed him with brandy and laudanum but there was nothing more he could do. The lascar had been their only casualty of the expedition so far, and Howard was too tired for another night like that. He fervently hoped the man would not last the day.

There was a lazy whine overhead, followed by a dull thump and a puff of smoke from the opposite shore. A copiously moustached figure walked into view from behind the deckhouse and planted himself firmly behind the line of riflemen, his hands behind his back and his heavy Adams revolver drawn. He turned toward Howard, and a bloodshot eye bore down on him from under the peak of his pith helmet.

"Shall we give them a volley, sir? Put the wind up them. Fucking savages."

"Sergeant O'Connell. Might I remind you we are desired by government to open negotiations to induce the rebels to free the native constables they have taken captive."

"Poppycock, sir, if I may say so."

"You may. Meanwhile, hold your fire."

The moustache twitched. "Very good, sir."

Howard took out a brass and ivory pocket telescope from a pouch on his belt, raised his head slightly over the plating and peered through the telescope at the far bank. There were dozens of them now, streaming down from the village, lean, dark men clad in loincloths, some carrying bows and arrows and others long matchlock smoothbores. He could see that some were more extravagantly made up, their long hair combed and braided forward and embellished with red cloth and feathers. Some of them carried skin drums and brass trumpets. Along the foreshore clusters of men were digging pits in the sand and erecting three bamboo poles in a line against the edge of the jungle. They had lit large bonfires, and the swirling black smoke drifted over the river, obscuring the scene

161

from the steamer. It was unsettling to view, flashes of activity revealed and then obscured in the smoke, impossible to discern the intent. At any moment they might pull out their canoes and mass for attack. Howard turned to the sergeant. "Their last fusillade was up in the air. There's something odd going on over there. They're right on the edge of the riverbank, as if they want us to see them, taunting us. If they start aiming at us, you can let fly. On my command. You understand?"

"Sir." The sun-scorched face stared resolutely forward.

Howard looked out at the scene again. A week ago, washed by the rain, this had been a place of shimmering beauty, the great gorge of the Godavari snaking its way through hills of sparkling green, rising on either side five hundred feet or more, with the ridges and peaks of the Eastern Ghats beyond. But now, it was as if a heavy miasma had risen up from the river and choked the valleys in veils of mist. The river was a lifeline, the only place where the sun burned through, and everywhere else was cloaked, sinister. He could sense the fear and superstition of the spirit world, the hundred gods and demons these people believed lurked in the jungle. His first patrol ashore had deeply unnerved him, and it was not just the rebels waiting in ambush. There was something else there, something that had kept these dark places remote and impervious from the march of progress across the continent. He could understand why their native bearers from the coastal lowlands feared and despised this place, and refused to come with them beyond Rajahmundry. He took a deep breath and raised his eyeglass again toward the reed-roofed village that spread along the opposite riverbank, and the increasing throng of natives who swirled and danced around the fires on the sandy fore-shore. He turned to the Indian officer beside him, a ferocious-looking Madrasi in a turban, with piercing dark eyes. He spoke to him in Hindi. "Jemadar, pass the word for Mr. Wauchope, would you?"

"Sahib."

A few moments later a tall figure ambled out from the deckhouse, carrying a small open book in one hand. He wore dust-colored khaki, the new fad among officers fresh from the northwest frontier, and his puttees were bound with strips of colorful Afghan cloth. He was bareheaded and tanned, with a thick crop of black hair and a full beard. Howard had spoken to him briefly when he had arrived during the night with the reinforcements, hearing the latest news from Afghanistan, but Wauchope had promptly gone to sleep in what counted as the officers' quarters under a mosquito net beside the deckhouse. Howard was looking forward to having another officer on deck, one who was famously unruffled, just what was needed to keep them all from becoming unhinged by the darkness and sorcery of this place.

Wauchope peered at the tumult on the opposite shore, pursed his lips, then nodded at Howard. He had sharp eyes, intense like the jemadar's, but with humor in them. "I was looking for the saloon," he said, with a pronounced drawl. "I have come to realize that this is not exactly a Mississippi River steamer."

"I never understood why you left America, Robert."

"My family is Irish, remember." Wauchope slouched down beside the railing, and fished out a pipe. "Not poor Irish, but landowning Irish of English origin. My father moved us to America because he felt powerless during the famine, and could not bear to return afterward. We have a long tradition of soldiering. For me, it was either West Point or the Royal Military Academy. After having lived through the American Civil War as a boy, I never wanted the possibility of facing my brother on the field of battle." He tapped his pipe. "I was inclined to seek my glory abroad."

"I was here in India during the mutiny, you know," Howard said. "A babe in arms. I don't remember it and my mother never told me what I saw, but I used to have bad dreams. Not anymore." He paused, then he gestured at the book. "What are you reading?"

Wauchope deftly struck a match with his other hand and lit his pipe, sucking on it as he flicked the match overboard. He raised the spine of the book toward Howard. "Arrian. The life of Alexander the Great. We found some ancient ruins up beyond the Indus, and I'm sure they're Greek altars."

"The frontier's got you hooked, Robert."

"I've put in for the Survey of India, you know. They've got a vacancy on the Boundary Commission. I was heading back from the Afghan campaign to tie up my affairs with the regiment in Bangalore when I was diverted here as a replacement."

"We've been dropping like ninepins. Every officer who steps into the jungle is prostrate within a week. It's the worst fever I've ever seen."

"You seem to have survived it."

"I was born here, remember? Any child who survives the Bengal summer is set for life."

"Surgeon-Major Ross in Bangalore thinks it's the mosquitoes."

"Of course it is." Howard swatted his neck, and peered up at the sky. Beyond the hills a black swathe of cloud had appeared, forked by distant lightning. "And we're not safe from mosquitoes anymore on the river. The monsoon's pushing them out over us like a pestilential blanket."

"Pity." Wauchope drew on his pipe, closing his book. "If you only allowed yourself to be struck down by the fever, you'd be invalided from here and then sent to Afghanistan. That's where careers are being made. There'll be no medals out of this place."

"I'm detailed for the Khyber Field Force. They say the war there isn't over yet. But I've wanted to be near Edward and Helen in Bangalore. Colonel Prendergast has been most understanding."

"Ah." Wauchope put his hand on Howard's arm. "How is your little boy?"

Howard's face fell. "He's not good, Robert. He's been sickly all year. You know what that can mean for an infant out here."

Howard's voice hoarsened. "I cherish him dearly. Poor Helen is beside herself." He turned away, blinking hard, then knelt up again and peered over the plating. He passed his telescope to the other man. "See what you make of that."

Wauchope glanced at Howard with concern, then peered through the glass at the foreshore. "Good Lord. There must be five hundred of them, maybe more."

The scene had changed from a few moments earlier. There were now crowds of men milling around the bonfires, and there were gourds, the palm liquor flowing freely. The men with braided hair wielded swirling batons, now weaving them into spirals, now figures of eight and back again. Drums were being beaten, discordant, out of unison, then together in a monotonous beat. Suddenly an extraordinary apparition materialized out of the smoke. A dozen men appeared with extravagant headgear of bison horns, great curved horns that perched precariously on their heads. They wore tiger skins, and their faces were red with kumkum powder. As they came forward the air was rent with shrieking, so loud it set Howard's teeth on edge. The men advanced in a line toward the riverbank, retreated, then advanced again, kneeling down and pawing the earth in imitation of fighting bulls.

"I believe they are invoking the bloodred god of battle, Manecksoroo," Howard murmured. "Asking to turn battle axes into swords, bows and arrows into gunpowder and bullets."

"They have real bulls too," Wauchope said, passing the telescope over. Howard peered through, and grunted. "So that's it." He snapped shut the glass, then turned and leaned back against the railing. "Bull sacrifice. That's what those pits are for. They mix the blood with grain and throw it into the forest clearings, to induce fertility of the soil. This could go on for hours, until they are stupefied with the toddy."

"I thought sacrifice had been suppressed,"

Wauchope said.

"Human sacrifice, yes, decades ago, but not animal sacrifice, though it's discouraged." Howard slumped, suddenly overwhelmed with lassitude. "This is what those idiots at the Board of Revenue don't understand. I've brought Campbell's book on the suppression of human sacrifice with me. You can read it yourself. He says we can't use morality to persuade a people to give up their age-old customs. Our morality means nothing to them. You have to show them that their life will be improved as a consequence. If you then take away their greatest pleasures, they will return to their old ways. We broke the cycle by showing them their land could be fertile without needing sacrifice. Now a stroke of the pen in Calcutta and it is all undone. It was all lurking just below the surface, just inside the jungle, but now they want us to see it. You can hardly blame them."

"Tell me about these people."

"They're Kóya," Howard said. "Descendants of the ancient Dravidian inhabitants of India, here at the time of Alexander the Great. But you couldn't get a greater contrast to the civilization of the Mughals or the Sikhs. These people are more akin to your Red Indians. They hunt in the jungle and burn small clearings for crops. Hardly any of them have a notion of the world outside."

"Maybe no bad thing," Wauchope murmured, drawing on his pipe. "Do we have their language?"

"I possess a slight colloquial knowledge of the vocabulary. But we have our interpreter, who tells me about their customs." Howard jerked his head toward a small, wiry man of indeterminate age sitting cross-legged on the foredeck, his skin deeply tanned and wearing only a white loincloth. His hair was dark brown, almost auburn, curly like his straggle of beard, and his face was wizened. In one hand he was holding a bow and arrows, and in the other a tubular section of bamboo about a foot long. His only embellishment was a gold chain hanging from the top of one ear to the lobe, with a small pendant dangling below. He was smoking a cheroot, and his eyes seemed dazed.

"He's half-cut on palm wine," Howard said. "It can't be helped. It's their lifeline during the monsoon. That's what this rebellion is all about. How much did Colonel Rammell tell you?"

Wauchope shook his head. "I only had time to report my arrival at the field force headquarters in Dowlaishweram. The boat with the sapper reinforcements was already waiting to take me upriver. And Rammell and his adjutant were both prostrate with fever. Like almost all the other officers."

Howard exhaled forcibly. "Well here's the nub of it. If some imbecile on the Board of Revenue hadn't decided to impose a tax on palm toddy, then we wouldn't be here. That, and the native policemen. For months at a time the only outside presence among these people has been the constables, lowlanders the hill people despise. The British superintendent of police and the agency commissioner hardly ever come up here because of the jungle fever. The constables are free to intimidate and exploit the hill people as lowlanders always have done. And now that we need them, they're worse than useless. Hardly a man of them can be got to smell gunpowder. The rebels' first act was to capture half a dozen of them. It's good riddance as far as I'm concerned."

A ragged volley erupted from the riverbank, but no sound of bullets overhead. "Matchlocks again, Sergeant. Hold your fire."

Wauchope peered over the metal plate at the smoke. "Where do they get their powder?"

"When I took my first party into the jungle last week, I searched a village and seized their guns, all matchlocks," Howard replied. "The women were making saltpeter by urinating into bags of manure suspended over pans, and then letting the liquid that seeped out crystallize. Ingenious, really. They're always burning jungle to open up new patches for cultivation so they have plenty of charcoal, and sulphur they get from traders. The powder's pretty poor, but it's good enough for small game. Some of them also get powder and ball from the lowland moneylenders who enslave them in debt. But I fear they now have a new source of weapons."

A bullet smacked against the smokestack of the steamer, causing an almighty clang, followed by a sharper crack from the shore. "Speak of the devil." Howard peered through his glass again. "An old East India Company percussion musket, native police issue. Some of the constables have supplied the rebels with arms and ammunition in return for their own safety. The police really are perfectly use-

171

less. They can be trusted to do nothing, they are disobedient and insubordinate. But Government wishes us to employ them. That's what happens when a war is run by clerks in Calcutta. And there's another problem. In the infantry regiments deployed in the field force, there are sepoy officers who still can't use maps properly, even the rudimentary ones we've made of this place. Without a map and bearings you're lost in the jungle. But all of our sappers are excellent map readers. So here we are, the Queen's Own Sappers and Miners, employed as infantry and police. It really is a most lamentable state of affairs."

"What's the quality of the official maps?"

Howard snorted. "That's the final rub. We've had to make them up as we go along. When Lieutenant George Everest came here in 1809 with the Great Trigonometric Survey, they hadn't even set up their trig posts on the hills before they were all struck down by fever. Half of them perished, and Everest never came back. This place is a great black hole smack in the middle of India. It may as well be Baluchistan, or the depths of central Asia." He glanced at the foredeck, and saw O'Connell glaring at him, his lower lip quivering. "Very well, Sergeant, bring your men to the ready. Another ball in our direction and you can open fire. First volley above their heads. Wait for my command."

"Sir." O'Connell instantly barked an order in Hindi and the line of rifles came up to the horizontal along the deck railing, followed by the clicks of hammers being pulled back to full-cock. O'Connell was positively chomping at the bit, breathing like a bull ready to charge.

"I had a look at your native fellow when I came on board." Wauchope pointed his pipe at the man. "The pendant in his ear's a Roman coin, you know. Do you remember when we were cadets, I took you to the coin room in the British Museum? It's very worn, but I think it's from the time of the Roman Republic, possibly Julius Caesar."

"You come across them around Bangalore, and farther south," Howard said. "Edward's ayah has one, a gold coin. I'm told the Romans traded them for pepper."

"Who is he, anyway, our Kóya friend?" Wauchope angled his pipe again.

"He's a *muttadar,* a local headman from Rampa, the village that gives its name to the district. He holds some kind of grudge against Chendrayya, the leader of the revolt. The *muttadar* acts from motives of self-interest. Once satisfied on that point, his time and labor have been most zealously and indefatigably given, when he's been sober enough." Howard lowered his voice. "He's also a *vezzugada,* a sorcerer. The Kóya know nothing of the Hindu religion. They worship

173

deities of their own, ancient Dravidian gods, animistic gods and goddesses. Tigers, hyenas, buffalo. Sometimes the deities possess people, who are known then as the *konda devata*. Sacrifices are made to a dread deity called Ramaya. That hollow bamboo he's holding supposedly contains some kind of idol, the supreme *vélpu*. He calls it the Lakkála Rámu, and it's rumored to be ornamented with eyes of olivine and lapis lazuli. He won't show it to anyone. It's supposed to be kept in a sacred cave, a shrine near Rampa village, to placate the deity. The *muttadar* took it from the shrine when he fled Chendrayya and came to us. But now the deity needs it back, and is apparently becoming agitated. Our side of the bargain is to help the *muttadar* replace it."

"Will you keep your promise?"

"Of course. We need to instill fear among the rebels, and confidence among those who are well-disposed toward us."

"Quite so."

There was a sudden commotion and a curse, and a hatch into the hold opened behind them. An indescribable smell wafted out, followed by a burly man stripped to the waist except for a luridly stained apron. He was only a few years older than the two subalterns, the same age as Sergeant O'Connell, and like O'Connell sported the long sideburns fashionable among a previous generation.

"Surgeon Walker," Howard said, looking at the man with concern. "How goes it in the black hole?"

"Most of the men have had repeated malarious attacks, and are in a very debilitated state." Walker spoke with the hard consonants of his birthplace, Kingston in Upper Canada, and six years at the Queen's University in Belfast. "There are serious after consequences — enlarged spleen, anemia, partial paralysis, extreme emaciation, disorders of the stomach and bowels, and other complaints of a grave nature. Many of the men are passing through the hot stage of a febrile paroxysm, and their sufferings and distress are painful to witness."

"That vile odor?"

"Indeed. A singular putrid efflorescence." Walker wiped something unpleasant off his hand onto his apron. "I'm here for a breath of fresh air. Is Lieutenant Hamilton back yet?"

Howard shook his head and pulled out his fob watch. "He's been gone a full twenty-four hours now. He doesn't have provisions for any longer." He turned to Wauchope. "One of the *muttadar's* men informed us that Chendrayya had been seen in Rampa village about five miles north of here. I sent Hamilton out with what remains of G Company, only 22 men. It was a risk, but we've rarely encountered the rebels in gangs of more than

10 or 20. Until now, that is."

"Let's hope Hamilton doesn't walk into that lot," Wauchope murmured, jerking his head toward the riverbank.

Howard grunted. "I just wish he hadn't taken the infernal Bebbie with him."

"Who?"

"Assistant commissioner for the Central Provinces." Howard paused, trying to control his temper. "Because government in its wisdom decided that this is a police action, all of our forays into the tribal agency are supposed to be led by a civil officer. Some are decent fellows, fine shots. Mr. Bebbie is decidedly not one of those. He gave us a lecture before we set out. How climate will always prevent this being the seat of prosperous industry or great commercial enterprise. How the Kóya are a degenerate race, sunk in the depths of ignorance and superstition. How it is his duty to teach them the value of a moral obligation, and our duty not to upbraid them with the past but to inaugurate them with a better future. His lecture was a magnificent display of language united to a grievous perversion of the facts. It failed to conceal the truth that he's never bothered to come up here into his jurisdiction before and is permanently prostrate with fever. A more worthless specimen and perfectly useless leader of men I have not seen."

"I'm sure Hamilton will keep him in his

place," Wauchope murmured with a smile, slouching back against the side of the boat and lighting his pipe again.

"Our *muttadar* is convinced that one of those men over there on the riverbank is Chendrayya, the rebel leader," Howard said. "If so, Hamilton has been led into a vipers' pit by Bebbie. I told Bebbie not to trust their guide, but Bebbie will not listen to God Almighty, let alone to a mere sapper subaltern." Howard closed his eyes. Another musket ball smacked into the funnel. He opened his eyes, nodded at Sergeant O'Connell, and raised his left arm. Then, sensing a commotion on the river, he quickly peered through his glass again. "Hold your fire!" he shouted. "I think I see Hamilton." They all followed his gaze. Half an hour earlier he had ordered the steamer's boat out into the river ready to pick up the returning party, and now they could see the boat coming around a sandy bluff at the river bend, concealed from the village. The four lascar seamen were pulling like fury against the current. In the middle was a throng of Madrasi sappers with their bayonets fixed, and the pith helmet of a British officer was visible at the stern. Behind them on the sandy bluff, loinclothed men with long matchlocks began to materialize out of the jungle and they heard cries and a ragged crackle of musketry. White smoke rose where the rebels had been

firing and joined the river mist, briefly concealing both the boat and the rebels. When
the smoke cleared the rebels had gone from
the bluff, and Howard caught a glimpse of
the last of them running along the sandbank
toward the throng below the village, brandishing their matchlocks and whooping and hol-
lering. A few moments later the boat had
pulled around to the protected lee side of the
steamer. There was a clatter as the men
disembarked and came on deck, immediately
slumping down below the railing. They
reeked of sweat and sulphur, and looked
exhausted. Hamilton, the last on board, made
his way over to where Howard and the others
were standing. He took out his Adams revolver and swung out the cylinder, dropping
the empty cartridge cases. His hands were
shaking, and his face was streaked with the
greasy residue of gunpowder. He looked
drawn, but exuberant. He was the youngest
subaltern on the Madras establishment, and
this was his first taste of the sharp end of
soldiering.

"We were camped for the night, deep in the
jungle," he panted, squatting down as he
reloaded the revolver. His voice was hoarse,
and he took a few deep breaths to control it.
"We were told by our guide that a gang of a
hundred rebels was at a nearby village. We
marched at three a.m. to surprise them at
dawn. Our guide brought us out into a small

178

clearing in front of the village, where we were spotted. He disappeared and we never saw him again. A shot was fired at us, followed by five or six in quick succession. I got the men into skirmishing order and opened fire on the rebels; they quickly retreated into the jungle. Once there, the rebels, knowing their way about, had a decided advantage on us. If only they'd stand and fight in the open, we could put down this rebellion in a week."

"This happens every time we try to engage them," Howard murmured to Wauchope. "Go on."

"We were getting short on ammunition. They were trying to draw us deeper into the jungle. I decided to retreat, and after a lull they followed, keeping up a hot fire on us all the way. Sometimes they were visible as they flitted from tree to tree, and we were able to pick a few off. Twice I halted the sappers and confronted the attackers with heavy fire, but they always took refuge behind trees. Altogether we expended over a thousand rounds, but we accounted for only ten of the enemy for certain. Frequently the rebels have been encountered in this way, and got off with small losses in killed and wounded. I think, if our men had used buckshot cartridges, the effect would have been greater."

Howard nodded. "Very well. Put it in your report."

"What's the butcher's bill?" Walker asked.

179

"Their matchlocks don't have much power beyond about fifty yards. One of the sappers has a ball embedded in his skull."

"Let's be having him then." Walker gave a ghoulish grin and rolled open a pouch of forceps and pliers from his belt, taking out the largest and wiping it on his apron. "A real wound after that stinking mess below."

Hamilton pointed to one of the sappers with a bloody bandage around his head and Walker got up. Hamilton then turned back to Howard and Wauchope, his eyes gleaming feverishly. "We did score one small victory though." He nodded at the sapper standing behind him, who dropped a burlap bag containing something heavy at Howard's feet. "Tamman Dora. We shot him in the village yesterday. One of the sappers is a Ghurka and has a *kukri* knife. Here's the proof."

"Good God, man." Wauchope recoiled, holding his nose. "It stinks like rotten meat. Get rid of it."

Hamilton kicked the bag aside, then squatted down, looking at them intently. "Apparently he was one of the rebel leaders. This could be just what we need. Show that lot we mean business." He jerked his head toward the riverbank.

"Who told you he was a rebel leader?" Howard said quietly. "Your guide?"

"He was convinced of it. And the man put up a hell of a fight. I emptied my revolver into him and he still kept coming."

"You mean the guide who led you into an ambush? Couldn't he just have been using you to settle some old score?"

Hamilton glanced at the bag and then back at Howard, flustered. "Someone else can confirm the identification. Your *muttadar.*"

"You'll be lucky if there's anything identifiable in that bag now," Wauchope said.

"I maintain that we have killed a rebel leader," Hamilton insisted, urgently now.

"Very well," Howard said, pursing his lips. "You must write an account to go in my report to Colonel Rammell, when we finally get off this wretched sandbank." He paused, looking at the sappers, then looked back at the empty boat. "I've just realized. Someone's missing. Where's Bebbie?"

"I was coming to that. Struck down by cholera."

"Alive?"

"Just. You know how quickly it can take a man. He was prostrate by the time we reached a place to hold out near Rampa village. Then the most curious thing happened. He picked up a Kóya arrow and managed to cut himself. We thought he'd be done for. But the arrow had some kind of paste on it, not the usual poison. Apparently they prick themselves with it. Within half an hour he was on his feet again. We've all noticed that the natives seem immune to the worst depredations of the fever. But by late evening the effect wore off, and he became delirious. When we marched on the rebels he insisted on staying at Rampa. He wanted to parley with the village headmen. I left four sappers with him and a promise to return. It was all I could do."

"Confound the man," Howard muttered angrily. "If only he'd parleyed with these people six months ago, none of this would have happened." He looked at Hamilton. "You'll have to go back. I won't leave any of our sappers out there. Have your havildar break out another ammunition box and get your men some water."

"Done." Hamilton nodded to his havildar, who had understood and immediately marched off.

"Now's the time to go, if you have to," Wauchope said languidly, angling his pipe toward the riverbank. "I don't think any of that lot will notice you leaving. The palm wine is flowing freely."

"One of us will accompany you," Howard said.

Hamilton turned to Howard. "I'd like both you and Robert to come. It would be a chance for Robert to go up-country and get a taste of it. And there's something else I want you to see. Robert, you have a bent for things ancient, don't you? And, Howard, you're always going on about old languages?"

Wauchope perked up and knocked out his pipe. "You've found some antiquity?"

"In the shrine. I just stumbled into the entrance for a moment, but you'll have to see."

There was a crackling sound from the fore-shore, like gunfire but different. Howard took out his eyeglass and peered intently. The Kóya were dancing around the fire, tossing in lengths of bamboo. The bamboo was bursting with a bang as the air between the knots expanded. It was a fireworks display, the flaming splinters spraying the air like sparks. Howard caught Sergeant O'Connell's eye and shook his head vehemently. Then the air was rent by a succession of shrieks. He looked again. The dancing was suddenly frantic, joined by drum beating and the blowing of buffalo horns. A naked man appeared, his body daubed profusely with black and white spots, leading a buffalo calf toward the pit by the shore. The animal was bellowing and pawing the ground. Behind them the dancers parted and another man appeared, wearing only baggy dark pantaloons but carrying something gleaming in his right hand.

"Chendrayya," Howard muttered. "Just as the *muttadar* described him."

"He's got a *tulwar*," Wauchope murmured.

The man in the pantaloons raised his right hand, revealing the curved sword feared above all others by British soldiers in India,

183

able to cut a man in two in a single stroke. In a flash the sword came down one way and then the other behind the buffalo, cleaving the air. For a split second there was silence, and then a terrible bellow as the calf fell backward off its legs, leaving the feet stuck grotesquely in the sand. Blood spurted from the severed limbs into the pit. The dancers leapt on the calf like a pack of frenzied hyenas, tearing the flesh off with knives and their bare hands. Blood spurted and flowed into the pit, the animal's heart still pulsing even as it was torn from beneath the rib cage. Then the drumbeat began again, slow, insistent. The dancers drew back from the carnage, their heads and arms drenched in blood, and carrying their dripping trophies, slowly circling around. The *muttadar* on the foredeck began babbling incomprehensibly, then said the same words over and over again in the Kóya language, all the time drooling and beating his head, averting his eyes from the scene on the foreshore.

"What on earth is he on about?" Wauchope said.

"Meriah." Howard spoke in little more than a whisper.

"Meriah? You mean human sacrifice? Good God."

Three men were thrust forward to the edge of the pit. They were darker-skinned, wearing the tattered remains of lowland pantaloons,

184

their hands tied behind their backs. They seemed stupefied, unable to stand upright, and were kicked to their knees by the man in body paint. Howard watched in horrified fascination. *The captured police constables.* There was nothing he could do.

"Sir!" O'Connell bellowed.

Howard suddenly saw something else. "Wait!" he shouted. "There are women and children there! Hold your fire!"

In an instant the *tulwar* flashed again. Two heads flew off, and blood gushed into the pit. The third constable fell forward, shrieking. The painted man pounced on him and pulled him into the pit, holding the struggling form down in the bloody mire until it was still. For a moment there was silence. Then the man stood up, his back to them, facing Chendrayya, and raised his arms outward, blood and mucus falling from his arms in a diaphanous sheen of red.

"That was for our benefit," Howard murmured to Wauchope. "For it to be a true *meriah* sacrifice, the victim has to be ritually prepared. Those constables were executed. What they did to the buffalo was sacrifice."

"You mean they do that to humans too?" Wauchope said, aghast, his composure gone.

"They supposedly tear their victims to pieces with knives, leaving the head suspended from a pole. No European has ever seen it."

185

The drumbeat began again. The painted man in the pit pulled a heavy dripping garment over his shoulders. Howard could see it was a tiger skin, sodden with blood. The first drops of rain were spattering against the deck of the steamer, and steam from the fires mingled with an efflorescence that seemed to rise from the mangled carcass of the bull and the bloody pit beside it. Chendrayya looked across at the steamer, seeming to stare directly at Howard, then turned and made his way up the sandbar to the place where the three poles had been erected earlier. The frenzied dancers in front of him parted, revealing a group of white-clad women around one of the poles. Howard squinted against the mist that swirled over the river. The women were flourishing boughs, and the pole had the effigy of a bird suspended from it, a cock. Howard swallowed hard. With a sickening feeling, he realised there was more to come. Three victims, one to each pole, west, middle, east — sunset, noon, sunrise.

"This will not be quick," he murmured to Wauchope.

A man was led out in front of the women, his hair shorn, garlanded with flowers, wearing a clean white garment. His neck was held between a cleft bamboo and he already seemed half-dead, whether from slow strangulation or toddy was impossible to tell. Eager hands reached out to catch the saliva that was drooling from his mouth, smearing it into the red turmeric on their own faces. He was dragged toward the far pole, out of sight in the crowd. The incessant slow drumbeat suddenly rose in a frenzied crescendo, and the group of women around the central pole parted. Howard looked, and nearly retched.

It was a child.

A boy, not much older than his own son, was tied to the pole. His head was lolling like the man's, but his body shuddered, still alive. Four of the women held out his little arms and legs. The man in the tiger skin approached, and picked up a pole, like the handle of an axe. He tapped the boy on the head with it, and then tapped each of the boy's limbs. Only they were not taps. Howard had been seeing everything in slow motion, and as his mind replayed it he saw the little limbs each crack and flop away, broken like boughs of dry wood. The women let go, and the small body flopped like a rag doll from the chain that held his neck. A rope tied to the top of the pole was pulled, and the cock began to whirl around and around, followed by the women who circled it. Among the swirling robes there were flashes of blades held in readiness, glinting. The boy raised his head, and Howard was sure he heard crying, the helpless crying of a child, that seemed to reach out to him, that seemed to come from a child of his own.

It was unbearable. Howard reached over and took the Snider-Enfield rifle from one of Hamilton's sappers crouching next to him. It had a repair behind the receiver, a darker piece of wood, but it was sound. He pulled the hammer to half-cock, flipped open the breechblock with a sharp turn of his right hand, pulled back the ejector and tipped out the spent cartridge case. He spat on his finger, pushed it into the chamber and wiped out the fouling, then smeared the stinking black residue on the railing. He reached over to the leather case on the sapper's belt and took out the last remaining cartridge. He was acting without thought now, his whole being focused on the mechanical acts of the drill. He dropped the cartridge into the breech and pushed it home, then snapped shut the block. He brought the rifle to his shoulder, pointing the muzzle a few inches below his target. With his right thumb he pulled back the hammer to full-cock, and he hooked his forefinger around the trigger. He closed his left eye, and raised the muzzle steadily until the foresight was in line with the notch of the backsight. Slowly, almost imperceptibly, he pressed the trigger, without the least motion elsewhere, his eye on the object in his sights.

It was a target, nothing more.

The rifle kicked against his shoulder, but he seemed to hear no sound, as if his senses had frozen the moment before, sealing the image on his retina like a photographic negative. All he felt was a dizzying speed, as if he himself were hurtling at twelve hundred feet per second toward his target. He blinked, and the image was gone. His ears were ringing, and all he could see was a cloud of smoke from the muzzle, and then a swirling maelstrom on the foreshore. He let the rifle fall on its butt and lurched heavily forward on one knee, desperately trying to stop retching. He heard a bellow from Sergeant O'Connell and then the immense crack of a volley from the line of riflemen beside him. He turned and saw O'Connell's face bearing down on him, flushed, eyes red-rimmed, the very image of Fury unleashed. He saw the lips move, then heard the voice. "That should do it for you, sir. Fucking cannibals." Howard looked around and saw Wauchope staring at him, and he breathed hard. *He must stay in control.* He straightened up and looked at O'Connell. "There will be hell to pay if we cause a massacre, Sergeant. The civil authorities will send us out of here in chains. We can only shoot if we're fired on. I'm trusting you to exercise restraint."

"You put that boy out of his misery, sir," O'Connell said. "That took uncommon courage, sir. God bless you."

Howard felt faint, and turned quickly back to the rail, holding it tight. Wauchope took out his revolver, spinning the cylinder to check that the chambers were loaded. He shoved it back in his holster and put his hand on Howard's shoulder. "Now's the time to go and find our sappers and Bebbie," he said quietly. "O'Connell's volley dropped the devils who had been tormenting that little boy, but the rebel leader and the rest had already moved to the other two victims. I fear the sacrifice has taken place. But the rebels are too far gone with toddy to see us go. They're perfectly besotted."

Walker came up from where he had been operating on the wounded sapper, wiping his hands on his apron. "Those who aren't dead drunk will be going home with their pound of flesh," he said. "They have to bury their offering in their own plot of land before nightfall, to ensure the efficacy of the sacrifice. They will be dispersing far and wide to their villages."

Hamilton looked at Howard. "Well?" Howard fingered his own holster, and looked again across the river. His mouth felt dry, and his heart was fluttering. He was not sure what he had just done, or if it was a horrible dream. He took a deep breath and nodded. "Very well. The jemadar and Sergeant O'Connell can look after things here." He glanced up the deck to the *muttadar,* who was cowering beside the seven-pounder gun, clutching his bamboo tube. "And the *mutta-*

dar can come with us. He can bring his precious cargo. Even if Bebbie's beyond our help, at least we can uphold our end of the bargain." He looked up at the wall of black cloud that was now towering over them, and felt the drops of rain on his face. "It's time we got his sacred idol back where it belongs. And got our sappers the hell out of there."

6

Lieutenant John Howard hitched up his sword and eased himself back against the burnt stump of a tamarind tree, then drained the last of his water bottle. He had watched the dozen Madrasi sappers take up position around the edge of the jungle clearing, and now he could relax for a moment. He swatted at a mosquito that had bitten through the thin cotton of his uniform, which was soaked with sweat and clinging to him like a second skin. The smear of blood on his leg could have come from the mosquito or from the myriad small cuts where the jungle grass had slashed his face and arms as if with knives. He was grateful to Surgeon Walker for insisting that he bind his calves and ankles with puttees of coarse cloth. Even so he knew that any open wound out here could be bad news, and he hoped they were back on board the river steamer under Walker's watchful eye before any virulence set in. He pulled out his fob watch. Four hours to sundown. Another hour and they would turn back. He knew with utter conviction that they could not survive the night out here.

He put away the watch. His right hand was still shaking, the hand that had pulled the trigger less than an hour before, and he clenched it into a fist, willing it to stop. With his other hand he unfastened his holster flap and extracted his Colt revolver, checking the cylinder to see that the percussion caps were still firmly lodged on each chamber.

"You ought to get yourself a cartridge revolver, you know." The officer squatting alongside had been eyeing him with concern, and Howard realized that Wauchope must have seen his shaking hand.

"My father used this to defend us during the mutiny. It worked then. Call it superstition."

"If it wasn't for the noise giving us away, I'd be sorely tempted to use mine on those dogs," Wauchope said. "In Afghanistan I saw a pack of wild hounds rip a wounded man to pieces in seconds."

Howard holstered the revolver, then looked around the clearing. They were in a patch of tangled thorn and scrub that had once been a native Kóya clearing, abandoned after the soil had become exhausted and now reverting to jungle. At intervals half a dozen dogs sat silently watching them, long, lean beasts like the dogs the regiment kept for *shirkar,* for hunting fowl and small game in the hills around the cantonment at Bangalore. These were hunting dogs too, and had paced silently alongside them as they made their way up from the riverbank along the jungle path, through dense groves of tamarind eighty, even ninety feet high, festooned with huge creepers and vines dripping with condensation. It had been eerily quiet all the way, as if the beasts and birds of the jungle were in limbo, uncertain whether the monsoon was about to break over them, whether to cower down or to burst out in their usual deafening cacophony. Or perhaps they were fearful of another presence, the evil spirits the *muttadar* said lurked in the jungle after a sacrifice, waiting while the natives returned to their villages with their bloody strips of flesh — spirits that would only be sated when the offerings were buried.

Howard felt he was in the grip of an overactive imagination, tipped into some kind of unreason he could scarcely control, and he closed his eyes. It was the first glimmerings of fever, perhaps, an unfamiliar state for him. He looked at the dogs again, and felt his bile rise. Hunting dogs, but gorged on carrion of the most bestial kind, their maws still glistening red and dripping. The shrieking mob had left them the bones and gristle by the riverbank, and the dogs had remained behind, lapping at the bloody mire in the pit. For a dreadful moment Howard felt as if the dogs were here for him, as if his act in pulling the trigger had not dispelled the awful ritual but made him part of it, as if he had become a sacrificial priest who might provide another ghastly feast before the day was done.

"It's hopeless," Wauchope said. "I fancied I saw a heliograph flash a moment ago, but it must have been a trick of the eye, a brief ray of sunlight on wet vegetation. There's no chance now." He began folding away the instrument in front of him, a wooden tripod with a small mirror on top and a lever for tilting it to flash Morse code. Howard snapped back to reality, and opened his compass. He took a bearing, then shook his head. The champagne quality of the jungle air recorded by Lieutenant Everest sixty years before only came after the deluge, and that had yet to happen. When they had halted in the clearing ten minutes earlier, an attempt at heliograph signaling had seemed possible, with the jungle-shrouded hilltops still visible through the mist in the valleys. But now a heavy fog had descended and the damp penetrated everywhere, even condensing in the bores of the sappers' rifles. He glanced at Wauchope. "Were it not for the prodigious vegetation the *Shamrock* should still be within our line of sight," he said. "But according to Hamilton, from now on we drop down into the jungle beside a stream until we reach the village. You may as well stash the heliograph here. It's no use to us now."

Another figure in khaki and a pith helmet came up through the tangled vegetation, then stooped over at the edge of the clearing to pick up something from the ground. His eyes were ringed with exhaustion, and Howard wondered if he had been right to let Hamilton lead them back to this place so soon after his arduous escape from the rebels. Once again he let his anger with Assistant Commissioner Bebbie course through him, the sustaining emotion that seemed to keep him level. If it had only been Beddie who had needed saving, they would have left him to the tigers and hyenas, but the fact that he had four sappers guarding him made it imperative that they do all they could to mount a rescue.

Hamilton slumped beside them and tossed out a handful of spent Snider cartridges. "This is the place all right. This is where we stopped and gave them a volley," he panted, his voice dry and hoarse. "We dropped three, maybe four, but they took their fallen and bolted into the jungle." He looked intently at Howard, his eyes strange, burning, the beginnings of fever. "We use rifles and bayonets the length of halberds, deploying infantry tactics designed for the field of Waterloo. We need smoothbore carbines, buckshot, revolvers, knives. We need to follow them into the jungle, track them down, kill them as a beast kills its prey. We need to play their game but get better at it, let animal instinct take over from decency. We need to become savages."

Howard looked at him. "Most of all, we need to find the wretched Bebbie and get out of here. You say you can't choose between the trails ahead?"

"We were being pressed back. Only now do I realize there are three trails up the valley out of this clearing. We'll have to trust the *muttadar.*" He jerked his head toward the semi-naked figure squatting by himself on the edge of the clearing, his head swathed in the maroon turban Bebbie had given him as a sign of government authority, his hands clutching his precious length of bamboo. Howard took a deep breath, and looked hard at Hamilton. Perhaps they were all becoming unhinged. Perhaps it was the fever. He saw the yellow eyeballs, the blanched cheeks. He remembered Surgeon Walker's words. *A low fever of the malignant, lingering type.* He felt a sudden chill, and a shiver ran through him. His hand was still shaking. He hoped to God it was just his nerves. He looked at Wauchope. "All right. Tell the havildar to keep the men five paces apart. Rifles at half-cock. And remember, these people can track us like tigers."

Half an hour later they squatted down beside

a trickling stream deep in the jungle. Since leaving the clearing they had descended into a dark tunnel of foliage, all sense of the sky blotted out by the thick canopy. It was a pestilential place, infested with clouds of mosquitoes that seemed to rise from every stagnant pool, bird-sized spiders that leapt into the men's hair every time a helmet was removed, and leeches that lurked in every damp spot and attached themselves without the slightest provocation. Now it was as if they had come up for air, the sky visible above them in patches of dark cloud lit up with distant flashes of sheet lightning. Howard wiped his dripping face and pushed his water bottle into a brackish pool in the stream. Suddenly a shot rang out. Howard dropped the flask and unholstered his revolver, jerking upright. Hamilton was standing a few yards ahead with his own revolver leveled at the ground. A giant cobra had slid across the path, and Hamilton had foolishly shot it. Howard cursed him under his breath for the noise. And it was only wounded. The cobra leapt up, bouncing and writhing around like a demented dancer, and attached itself to the leg of one of the sappers. The man shrieked and fell insensible to the ground. Hamilton unsheathed his sword and decapitated the snake. The *muttadar* gestured wildly, then vanished into the jungle and quickly reappeared chewing a ball of green matter, which he forced into the sapper's mouth. Within seconds the sapper opened his eyes, sat bolt upright and began hyperventilating, his breathing calming down as he was held by two other soldiers.

Howard looked in some astonishment at the scene, reassured himself that the sapper truly was recovering, then reholstered his revolver and began filling up his bottle again. The *muttadar* watched him do it and then bounded up and pushed his hand away, and pointed at the *khukri* knife in the belt of one of the sappers. Howard looked at him quizzically, then nodded at the havildar, who leveled his big percussion pistol at the *muttadar* and gestured for him to go ahead. The *muttadar* took the *khukri* and went over to a grove of thick-stemmed bamboo growing on the stream bank. He tapped the nearest one just above a knot with the back side of the *khukri,* and they heard a dull sloshing sound. He stood back and swung the *khukri* at the bamboo, slashing it sideways to avoid creating splinters. A cupful of clear sparkling water gushed out onto the ground. The sappers quickly came up behind him, holding out their empty canteens as he went from trunk to trunk, expertly slashing with the razor-sharp blade.

"Give the water first to Sapper Narrainsamy," Howard said in Hindi. "We need him to be able to walk."

He watched the sapper who was leaning against a tamarind root, being passed a water flask by the havildar. Now Howard looked around apprehensively. The sound of the gunshot and the shriek had ignited the jungle, and the few cautious chatters and peeps had become an explosive cacophony of screeches and yelps and howls. Somewhere in the background came the throaty rumble of a tiger, rising to a mighty roar that shook the ground. The dogs that had been with them all along suddenly bolted, yipping frantically and disappearing into the jungle. The sappers all dropped their canteens and grasped their weapons. The *muttadar* fell to the ground in a ball, shaking and moaning and chanting a mantra to himself, words that Howard had heard him say before.

"He says it's a *konda devata,* a possessed female in the shape of a tiger," Howard murmured to Wauchope. "She'll devour anyone staying in the forest at the time of a sacrifice. It's she who should lick the blood of the sacrificial victims, not the dogs."

"A real tiger is enough for me," Wauchope muttered, revolver in hand.

"Sorcery and superstition," Howard said in Hindi, nodding sternly at the havildar and speaking a few words of reassurance to the sappers who had taken fright. He remembered his own nervous imagination in the jungle clearing, but he steeled himself to dispel it. They were all depending on him. He looked at the streambed, and then at Hamilton. "Do you recognize this?"

Hamilton nodded. "We left Bebbie and the sappers about half a mile upstream from here. The stream was nearly dry when we came down, but it's a narrow defile and will become a torrent with the rain. The jungle on either side is impenetrable. You can see the sky through the canopy. It's nearly black. We need to move."

Howard led them forward. At first the gradient was tolerably level, and the stream-bed was firm sand and stones. Here and there outcrops of deep red sandstone broke through the bank on either side, and giant moss- and fern-covered boulders forced them to struggle up the bank and back down again to the streambed. As the gradient increased the streambed narrowed into a small ravine, the eroded sandstone banks on either side rising twenty feet or more above their heads. They could now see evidence of the previous monsoon, where the river had threshed over the rock in a raging torrent, leaving uprooted trees and rolling rocks down the bed. The banks were too high to climb now, and Howard knew they stood no chance if the monsoon broke. Already there were flashes of forked lightning and distant peals of thunder. The wild beasts seemed to be howling in concert with the elements, sometimes jarringly discordant, sometimes to the same beat, like a devilish orchestra tuning up, a preamble to the unleashing of the heavens that would surely come.

Howard tried to ignore his fear and struggled on, a few yards ahead of the others. As he rounded a boulder, something rolled down the muddy bank just in front of him. It was a red gourd the size of a human head, and he kicked it forward unthinkingly. As he did so he saw a marking. He sloshed ahead, turned it over then quickly stamped his foot into it before the sappers could see. It had been a crude representation of a man hanging on a gallows. The *muttadar* had told him about these. They were more than just a warning. They were beacons to the *konda devata,* meant to attract the evil spirit like the smell of dead meat to a hyena. Howard's heart was pounding, and he looked up at the impenetrable wall of the jungle above the riverbank, blinking away the drops of rain. He could see nothing. But it was not only a tiger that was stalking them. They were close to the village, and there were others in the jungle, flitting forms. He looked ahead along the boulders to where the streambed rose into a tumbling rapids, and he fancied he saw a child, a form in a shawl with arms outstretched, beckoning him. He caught his breath. *He must be hallucinating.* He remembered the riverside scene, what he had done, and the image was gone. He struggled forward until he reached the base of the rapids. The stream was already rising against them, a red-brown torrent where it cut through the sandstone. Two freshly felled trees on either side were exuding dark-red sap that stained the banks. It was as if he were walking into a gush of blood. He wondered if he was being drawn into a world of sorcery and horror that he had made his own when he pulled that trigger. He half-fell forward, then suddenly sank up to his waist. He was caught just in time by Wauchope and Hamilton, who had come up behind him.

"I should have remarked on it," Hamilton gasped breathlessly. "The waterfall had liquefied the streambed and it's like quicksand. We had the devil's own time getting down here. Under those choked-up leaves and ash it's a death trap."

"How close are we now?" Howard said, struggling to keep collected.

"Just over the waterfall. There's a bridge, and then we're on the trail from the village to the shrine. We left Bebbie and the sappers in a clearing just in front of it."

"We're being followed," Howard said.

"That gourd? I saw you look at it," Wauchope said.

"Why don't they kill us?" Hamilton said. "They could shoot us like pigs in a slaughterhouse."

Howard looked at the *muttadar,* who had been scampering over the boulders with natural agility and had materialized silently beside them, his precious bamboo container held tight. "I think it's the *muttadar.* He's a sorcerer and even though the rebels know he's betrayed them, perhaps there's some kind of spell that prevents them from harming him."

"His idol?" Wauchope said.

Howard nodded. "That's the only reason he's here with us, and has led us this far. He's as terrified as all these people are of the jungle demons, the *konda devata,* but I believe he knows he will be allowed safe passage back to the shrine to replace what he had taken. And because we've dared to go into the jungle among the spirits that haunt it after the festival, they might think we have some kind of supernatural power ourselves."

"They are utterly irreclaimable savages," Hamilton muttered, his face now flushed with the fever. "The only supernatural power they'll get out of me is a volley of lead from our Sniders."

"Hold this." Wauchope handed Howard the end of a rope he had taken from the haversack of one of the sappers, and leapt up onto the boulder at the base of the waterfall. He held his sword out of the way and climbed nimbly from rock to rock, paying out the rope. He stopped at the top, some thirty feet above them, just visible in the mist, and gestured with his free arm for them to follow. Over the next ten minutes they all clambered up after him one by one, the sappers with their rifles slung over their backs and going barefoot. At the top was a small bamboo bridge over the shingly steambed, and they trooped across it into a clearing surrounded by patches of feathering reed. About fifty yards ahead the jungle began again, rising high over another rocky hillock. The havildar suddenly gesticulated and one of the sappers ran forward, toward a small cluster of fellow sappers with bayonets fixed, visible below a boulder on the far side of the clearing. There was a sudden scream of warning in Hindi from one of them, but it was too late. The sapper had disappeared without a sound. The others cautiously went forward, Hamilton and Howard in the lead, and they peered down.

"Good God, no," Hamilton whispered. "I knew this was here. I should have warned them. I am not in my right mind."

A horrible gurgling sound came from below, then stopped. Howard leaned over, feeling nauseous. *A tiger trap.* The hole was deep, at least ten feet, and stakes of fire-hardened bamboo rose out of the ground. The sapper had fallen in a seated position, and a stake had caught him in the nape of his neck and driven right through his skull, a bloody spike that thrust a foot or more above his turban. The force of the impact had nearly decapitated him, and his neck was stretched out grotesquely, the rest of his body skewered on the bed of spikes in front. Howard swallowed hard, then stood back to let the other sappers see. He took the havildar aside and had a quiet word with him in Hindi before turning to Wauchope and Hamilton.

"I asked him to recover the rifle and ammunition," he said. "They'll want to take him out and bury him."

"That will be an odious task," Wauchope murmured.

"They will not leave him here like this," Howard said. He turned and walked toward the other side of the clearing, his anger rising. Bebbie now had even more to account for. But he saw that they were too late. The four sappers of the detachment, those Hamilton had left to guard Bebbie, were kneeling, with bayonets pointing outward, around a crude bamboo palanquin. On it was a sweat-drenched, half-covered body very far from being alive. Howard knew how cruelly the cholera could ravage a person's appearance, but this was ghoulish in the extreme. The face was gray and the mouth was lolling, full of congealed blood. He came closer. It was not quite right. Bebbie's eyes had clearly come out, only to be pushed crudely back in. As Howard approached, holding his nose against the smell of feces, he saw the explanation. A large hole perforated the middle of Bebbie's forehead.

The havildar followed and spoke rapidly to the four sappers, passing them his water bottle, then let them speak in turn. Howard listened, then turned to Hamilton and Wauchope, his anger still palpable despite the grim finality of the scene. He jerked his thumb at the corpse. "That fool ordered the sappers into Rampa village to parley with the rebels. Their native guide had told him the rebel leader Chendrayya was there. One of the sappers went through the jungle to the edge of the village for a reconnaissance. He saw at least four hundred rebels massed, maybe more. I believe they were the party we saw join the throng by the river. The sapper returned and reported to Bebbie. The sappers had seen what the rebels had done to the captured police constables. The ones we saw executed by the river are not the only victims. Two more were murdered here in full view of the sappers last night, just outside the shrine. But Bebbie still ordered the sappers to go back to the village."

"He must have been delirious," Wauchope said.

"You didn't know this man," Howard said, gritting his teeth. "But before they could go, they were attacked. Shots were exchanged. Bebbie was hit and killed."

Wauchope knelt close to the corpse, and

peered at the gaping blue hole in the forehead. He lifted up the head, raising a swarm of black flies from the sticky mess below. The back of the head was blown off, and fragments of skull were stuck to the ground. He looked up at the other two officers. "That's no musket ball," he said quietly. "That's a Snider bullet. I've seen what our rifles do in Afghanistan."

Howard looked down at the wound, and swallowed hard. He looked at his right hand. It was still shaking. He thought for a moment and then turned to address the havildar in Hindi. "An unfortunate business. He would not have lasted with the cholera anyway. Have them bury him on the spot. And reassure our sappers that they will not be required to parley with the enemy."

"Sahib." The havildar addressed the four men, who nodded at Howard and reached for the collapsible shovels on their haversacks. Howard looked back at the body with contempt. "If he'd done his job this rebellion would never have happened."

"Word will get out that he was shot," Hamilton murmured.

"A musket ball. It is as the sappers describe. They were attacked. That goes in the report," Howard said determinedly.

"If you ever get a chance to make one," Wauchope said. "What do we do now?"

Howard suddenly felt tired, deathly tired,

and he took off his helmet and rubbed his stubble. He put it on again, and peered at the lowering sky. "We leave in twenty minutes. The sappers have that much time to finish up here. Hamilton, be so good as to egg them on. Robert, you and I are going to visit that shrine. You said you might have seen shapes in there, Hamilton? Carvings, inscriptions? At the moment all I want to do is get that wretched *vélpu* in there and be out of here. I don't think the *muttadar* is going to let us leave unless we keep our side of the bargain."

The two men left Hamilton and the sappers behind in the mist, and approached the north side of the clearing where the stream curved around below another waterfall. Through the sheen of spray they could make out three huge boulders, one of which formed a kind of roof over the other two, with a vertical slab of rock blocking the space in between. The *muttadar* had been following them, but as the shrine came into view he pulled off his turban and squatted on the ground, muttering and chanting to himself in the Kóya language, his eyes wide with terror. Howard turned and knelt beside him, trying to coax out some sense. "He has the most intense horror of this place. Nothing will induce him to go any farther."

"I thought this was his temple," Wauchope said.

"He knows he must return the idol, but he dreads the wrath of the *konda devata,* the tiger spirit. He says we must take the idol inside for him."

"But without it, he's defenseless. Surely the rebels will kill him."

"He evidently fears the spirits more than he fears death."

Howard spoke urgently to the *muttadar,* gesturing back in the direction of the sappers, but the man remained immobile, staring ahead as if in a trance. He suddenly reached down with trembling hands and brought a gourd he had been carrying to his mouth, gulping down palm liquor as if it were water. Howard reached over and grasped the bamboo tube from the man's other hand, pulling it until he released it. The container was sealed at both ends with a hard resinous material over a wooden plug. He stood and carried it toward Wauchope, who looked at it with curiosity. "Shall we open it up?" Wauchope said. "He'll soon be too besotted to care."

Howard looked toward the shrine. He thought he could see the shape of a tiger's face in the boulders, the eyes and ears formed by undulations in the rock. He shook his head. "Let's be done with it. I made him a promise. I will not treat these people like savages."

They started forward. A rocky alcove to the

left of the shrine entrance came into view. Two thick bamboo trunks formed a kind of verandah, holding up a roof of poles and palm leaves. In front was a line of posts capped with bleached skulls, some of them of prodigious size — elephants, tigers, wild boar. Behind them were two taller poles, festooned with bedraggled feathers. Hanging halfway down the poles were two blackened masses, dripping and suppurating. Howard had noticed a smell, but thought it was Bebbie. Now he realized it was the sickly-sweet stench of older putrefaction, and he remembered what the sappers had said. *The two other police constables.* He forced himself to look. Knives were suspended from cords beneath the corpses, slowly spinning around. The heads were smashed and scalped, the eyes gouged out. There was movement on the ground. He spied a gorged rat scurrying away, dragging an indescribable lump from below one of the poles. He turned quickly away, swallowing hard to avoid retching, and joined Wauchope at the vertical slab between the boulders. "We need to get away from this place," he said hoarsely, holding himself against the wet rock, his head throbbing.

"We need to finish here first," Wauchope murmured. He was running his finger down the crack on one side of the slab. "It's cut stone. Incredible workmanship. Who made this?"

"Try pushing it," Howard said. Wauchope put his hands on the slab, and it immediately pivoted inward. Inside was a passage large enough for them to stoop through side-by-side, but beyond was pitch blackness. The two men cautiously entered. Howard took out a brass container from his belt pouch and extracted a flint and steel, sparking a length of paraffin-soaked cord and using it to light a small candle. He lifted it up, and was immediately confronted by a crude etching of a lingam, a phallus. He raised the candle higher. All around them were other emblems, crude carvings, stick figures like the one he had seen on the gourd in the ravine. They edged forward. Ahead they could hear the rushing sound of the waterfall through the rocks. Wauchope suddenly tripped and Howard reached out to catch him, dropping the bamboo container with a clatter as he did so. Once Wauchope was upright he picked up the bamboo. One side had splintered, and he could feel something like paper inside. Crouching down, he saw what Wauchope had tripped over, a shallow stone basin full of liquid, still and dark, with a faint metallic tang. He raised the candle over it, and saw his face reflected, as if it were glowing with a deep red aura. Then he remembered what the *muttadar* had told him. *The priest augurs the future in a bowl of blood.* He looked again, but saw only the yellow flicker of the candle.

212

He shifted slightly, then he saw something, gasped, dropped the cylinder again and let his right hand fall heavily into the liquid. It was thick, congealing, warm. He pulled his hand out and shook it hard, splattering gobs of red over the walls of the tunnel, then wiped it on his uniform. "I just saw the most ghastly apparitions," he said hoarsely. "Tigers, devils, scorpions."

"They're on the ceiling above you," Wauchope said.

Howard raised the candle and looked up. *Of course.* There were more etchings on the rock. He had seen reflections. He took a deep breath, and peered ahead. "That must be it. The shrine itself. There seems to be some kind of altar in the center." He picked up the bamboo tube again, and stepped carefully over the basin. Through the flickering candlelight he saw figures that were more rounded, sculptures in relief, front-facing masks and dancing limbs. "I recognize these," he murmured. "My ayah used to take me to cave temples like this when I was a child in Bihar. That's Parvati, wife of Shiva. And Vishnu, striding across the wall, vanquishing a demon." He moved forward into the main chamber, where the walls were barely discernible in the candlelight. "But these ones are different. They look like warriors. I need to inspect them more closely."

"Pass me the candle, would you?" Wauchope had crouched down beside the altar-like structure in the middle, a raised rectilinear shape that had clearly been sculpted out of the living rock. Howard carefully handed over the stub of candle. Wauchope held it close to one side of the stone.

"Good God."

"What is it?"

"It's an inscription. I can read it."

"What language?"

Wauchope did not reply. Howard watched the yellow orb of light move quickly along the side of the rock, and then back again. He could just make out shapes, carved lettering. Halfway along the fourth row the candle sputtered and went out. They were in near darkness, the only light a dull gray coming through the passage from the entrance. "Quick," Wauchope said excitedly. "Strike a light. I think I can read one of the lines." Howard put down the bamboo tube by the altar and hurriedly took out his flint and steel, striking over and over again in the damp air until a spark lit the cord. He cupped his hand over it until there was a flame, and passed it carefully over. Wauchope dangled the flame close to the rock and moved it along. The flame reached his fingers and he dropped it, gasping in pain. There was a hiss as the cord hit the wet floor and they were in near darkness again.

"That's it," Howard said. "Well?"

Wauchope was silent. Howard saw the silhouette of his form, nursing his hand, stock-still and staring blindly at the stone. Then Wauchope swiveled toward him, and Howard could just make out his bearded face in the pale illumination from the entranceway.

"It's Latin. *Sacra iulium sacularia.* Guardian of the celestial jewel. There's more, but that's all I could make out."

"I've heard that before," Howard whispered. "Some memory from my childhood, from my ayah. The celestial jewel. The jewel of immortality."

There was an immense rumble outside, then a clap of thunder. Lightning lit up the interior of the shrine like a flash of gunpowder, revealing for an instant a surging mass of forms that seemed to be crowding in on them, gods and goddesses and demons and glowering tigers, faces contorted in agony and fear, terrifying riders looming above them like the horsemen of the apocalypse. Howard thought he saw Romans. *Roman legionaries.* He felt as he had in the jungle when the noise of the beasts erupted. He put a hand to his forehead. It was burning, and his hand was shaking. He crouched beside Wauchope and they made their way back toward the entrance. The pounding of the waterfall behind the boulders had increased, and they could see the rain lashing down now, giant droplets

215

that spattered into the passageway. Howard realized he was hearing something else, the insistent sound of drumbeats, coming from all sides, sometimes discordant but then steady and rhythmic, just as he had heard that morning from the riverbank. Fear rose in him. He peered into the downpour, searching for the *muttadar*, and then saw a crumpled form, a forest of arrows sticking out of it and a dark stain seeping over the mud. The rain was pulverizing his body, and it seemed to be disappearing before their very eyes. The two men crawled back into the main chamber. Howard pulled out his revolver, and Wauchope did the same. They knelt up in the confined space and shook hands.

"God be with you," Howard said.

"If we ever make it out of here, this place is our secret," Wauchope replied. "I saw something more in that inscription."

"If we rush toward the boulder where we left the sappers, we could make it."

They turned back toward the entrance. Howard reached into the darkness on top of the altar slab and lifted something he had seen earlier, a brass gauntlet with a fist in the shape of a tiger's head, a rusted blade protruding from the tiger's mouth. He felt his own sword pommel, then thought better of it and slipped his right hand into the gauntlet, curling his fingers round the crossbar inside. The head of the tiger looked like the image he had seen on the boulders of the shrine, with a grimacing mouth and slanted eyes. "Tigers seem to be the one thing they're afraid of," he said. "If it's in the shrine, this thing must be some kind of sacred object. Might put the fear of God into them."

"I've got an even better idea." Wauchope picked up the bamboo tube and held it in front of him. "You kept your side of the bargain. You brought the *muttadar's* precious idol back to the shrine. But I think now that he's past caring, we can borrow it for a little longer. If they see that we still have it, the rebels might hold off as they did before."

Through the pounding rain and drumbeats they heard the sharp crack of Snider rounds, then screams. Howard took a deep breath. At least the rebels would not be able to use their matchlocks in the rain. An immense crash suddenly shook them, not thunder this time but the reverberations of an earthquake. They braced themselves. Somewhere behind them was the sound of falling rock, and the boulder above them seemed to shift. Howard remembered the roar of the tiger, and wondered whether it was out there, waiting. He remembered his son. *He remembered what he had done.* He cocked his revolver and held the sword at the ready. For a split second he felt detached from his own body, as if he were standing back and watching the two of them go forward, disappearing through the veil of rain into history. He took a deep breath, and glanced at Wauchope. "Let's do it."

7

Bay of Bengal, India, present-day
Jack reached out with his left hand and pulled the tiller of the outboard engine toward him, bringing the Zodiac broadside-on to the shore and powering down the throttle. Ahead of them, somewhere behind the shoreline, lay the Roman site of Arikamedu. *Romans, in southern India.* It seemed virtually inconceivable, in a setting so completely at odds with all the preconceptions of classical history. Jack snapped back to reality. The wave they had been riding caught up with them in a burst of foam and wake, and the boat pitched sideways in the swell coming from the Bay of Bengal. Costas was sitting on the pontoon opposite him and Hiebermeyer and Aysha clung to either side farther forward. Rebecca was crouched in the bow holding the painter line, her dark hair streaming in the wind. They were all wearing orange IMU survival suits and life jackets. Jack peered at the palm-fringed beach, now only a few hundred yards

distant, and saw where the swell rose over the shallows. He gunned the throttle and the sixty horsepower Mariner engine lifted them along the crest of a wave, pushing them back over deeper water as they headed south parallel to the coast and left the gray form of *Seaquest II* farther behind.

"That must be it, over there," Costas shouted above the noise. He gestured toward shore with his GPS unit while holding on to the fixed rope around the pontoon with his other hand. "It looks like the river entrance."

Jack nodded and powered down again, turning the bow toward land and maneuvering between two lines of breakers that marked the outer reef about two hundred yards offshore. The sea went calm, and he throttled back to idle. "We should be okay if we keep to the channel between the buoys, but keep a sharp eye out from the bow in any case." Rebecca turned and made the okay sign at him. For the first time since leaving *Seaquest II,* Jack allowed himself to relax and look around. They had passed the harbor of Pondicherry and the ruins of the old East India Company fort some twenty minutes before, and were now off the dense green fringe that continued some two hundred miles farther to the southern tip of India, to the edge of the Palk Strait they had sailed through in *Seaquest II* earlier that morning. Jack increased the throttle slightly. They passed a lateen-rigged *nava,* a naked boy in the stern hanging on the arm of the rudder oar. A fisherman's dark eyes followed Jack's as they passed, yet he continued to throw out and draw in his net. Rebecca put her arm out to starboard and Jack pushed the tiller to port, seeing where the water became shallow. Their destination was barely distinguishable from the rest of the shoreline, a backwater that formed a placid channel into the sea, yet it led to one of the most extraordinary archaeological sites in India. Jack had dreamed of coming here since childhood, and to the place in the jungle he planned to visit later. He was tingling with excitement. He glanced back at the *nava,* now framed by the expanse of the Bay of Bengal. The sun gave the water a steely hue, and it seemed sluggish, heavy like mercury, the reflection of the *nava* wavering in slow motion with the residue of the sea-swell.

Jack passed Costas the tiller, then swiveled around and faced the sun in the east, raising his head toward it and narrowing his eyes. That was the other extraordinary image from this place. Somewhere out there lay *Chrysê,* the land of gold. Jack remembered the *Periplus,* words written two thousand years ago by a man who had been at this very spot, who had turned to the east as Jack had done, pondering what lay beyond. Jack squinted again at the *nava.* What had he seen, that

Egyptian Greek who came here so long ago? Had he himself seen the *kolandiophônta* he wrote about in the *Periplus,* great ships that came down from the Ganges? Had he seen other ships that came across the ocean from *Chrysê,* ships with towering braided sails and dragons in their bows, ships carrying bales of silk and untold finery, emissaries of a warrior empire as great as Rome itself?

"I'm cutting the engine," Costas said. "I don't trust these shallows." The clear water of the ocean had given way to a muddy brown as they entered the river outflow. Jack nodded, glancing at the laminated chart clipped on a board in front of them showing the location of the archaeological site. "It's only a couple of hundred meters along the river, on the south side of the channel." Costas raised and locked the engine on the transom, and then picked up a canoe paddle from his side of the boat. Jack took the other one, dipping the blade into the murky water, feeling its warmth. The only sound now was the distant roar of the breakers and the rustle of wind between the palms. They passed a sand spit that marked the river entrance, and entered a channel less than fifty meters wide. The riverbank was a patchwork of red and green, bursts of bougainvillea and the odd mangrove and lemon tree appearing between the coconut palms. It was suddenly hot, an intense, dry heat, and they both shipped their paddles and copied Hiebermeyer and the two girls, stripping down their survival suits to the waist. They drifted past a line of *navas* with drying fish strung from the rigging like lights, and then a group of bathing women and water buffaloes, seemingly oblivious to the fiddler crabs and mudskippers that crawled among them. It was a languid, timeless scene, yet one that was also fragile and ephemeral, in a place swept by cyclones and tsunamis, where the lasting achievements of civilization could only be established inland, beyond the danger zone. Jack thought again of the *Periplus,* and put himself in the mind of the author two thousand years before. It was not only the view to the east that was so beguiling. The view inland, beyond the fringe of palms, also held temptation, and fear. The first Greeks and Romans here were like the earliest European explorers, on the edge of the unknown, thousands of miles of jungle and mountain and desert. All they knew was that somewhere to the north were the lands that had been touched by Alexander the Great. But they had come here not to colonize or conquer but to trade — just as the Portuguese and French and British were to do fifteen hundred years later — with civilizations as old and sophisticated as anything in Egypt and the Mediterranean.

Jack gently paddled the Zodiac over to the opposite bank of the river, and they bumped into a small wooden jetty. A wiry, neatly at-tired man stood watching them, wearing sandals, shorts and an open-necked khaki shirt with the flashes of the Survey of India on his shoulders. Two other men came up and took the painter that Rebecca held out to them, and they helped her, Aysha and Hie-bermeyer off the boat. They removed their survival suits, and without a word Hieberm-eyer bounded off toward the edge of an excavation trench, hitching up his outsized shorts. Rebecca looked back at Jack, who waved her on, and she and Aysha hurried off to catch up. Jack smiled at the man as he and Costas climbed out onto the dock. "You must excuse my colleague. He gets tunnel vision when he sees a new excavation."

The man clicked his heels and held out his hand. "Commander Howard. It is an honor to be making your acquaintance, sir."

"Call me Jack. And I'm only a reservist." He shook hands. "You're Captain Pradesh Ramaya?"

"Indian Army Engineers, seconded to the Survey of India. I'm in charge of the under-water excavation."

"Thanks for emailing the chart," Jack said, stripping off the rest of his survival suit, revealing his khaki trousers. He picked up his old bag from the box in the bow of the boat and slung it over his shoulder, keeping the holster discreetly out of sight. He gestured beside him. "Costas Kazantzakis. Another old navy hand. Engineering too."

"Aha!" Pradesh said, his eyes gleaming, shaking hands. "Which branch?"

"Submarine robotics," Costas said. "Just a couple of years between grad school and meeting up with this character. And you can forget the old navy stuff. I hardly ever had to wear a uniform."

Jack gave him a wry look. "Except when you took a gunboat up the Shatt al Arab during the first Gulf War."

"They put me on an aircraft carrier. Complete waste of my skills. I was just killing time."

"And winning a Navy Cross."

"You can talk. Some reservist. Special Boat Service? Let me think. Those bits of ribbon on your uniform. South Atlantic, Persian Gulf, Adriatic . . ."

"The bits of ribbon the moths haven't eaten, you mean. All ancient history."

"It is a pleasure to meet two such distinguished warriors," Pradesh said, grinning.

"Archaeologists," Jack replied with a smile.

"Him, not me," Costas retorted. "No way. I'm just his stooge. Along for the ride. For the treasure at the end." He finished stripping off his suit, revealing the lurid Hawaiian shirt. Pradesh stared hard, and coughed. Costas looked at Jack defiantly, then at Pradesh. "You from these parts?"

"I'm from the Godavari River region, about two hundred miles north from here. Where we're going after this."

"When I called from Egypt to set up this visit, I had no idea there was any connection," Jack said to Costas. "But when Pradesh emailed back and told me he was from the Madras Engineering Group of the Indian army based in Bangalore, I mentioned my great-great-grandfather."

"The portrait of Colonel Howard holds an honored place in the regimental mess," Pradesh said.

"Colonel?" Costas said. "I thought he was a lieutenant."

"Later," Jack said. "I'll get to that."

"And Colonel Wauchope is one of our most revered heroes," Pradesh said. "His work with the Survey of India in the 1880s and 1890s helped to establish the frontier with Afghanistan. It is an honor to help you. The officers' mess still toasts them on the anniversary of their disappearance."

"They *both* disappeared?" Costas exclaimed to Jack. "You mentioned that Howard disappeared, but *both* of them?"

"Later." Jack put a hand on Pradesh's shoulder and pointed to a cache of diving equipment under an awning a few meters down the shoreline. "I'm itching to see what you've been doing here. We've only got an hour and a half before the helicopter arrives."

226

■ ■ ■ ■

Forty-five minutes later Jack stood up from the worktable under the awning and put down his pencil. He and Costas had been taken on a quick tour of the land excavation, passing a trench where Hiebermeyer and the two girls were kneeling on the baked mud and troweling away along with a group of Indian archaeology students. They had returned to the tent with the diving equipment, and Jack had been making notes on the site plan. He turned to Pradesh. "The Roman material is eroding out into the riverbed. Where Hiebermeyer was troweling just now looks like the edge of a large mud-brick warehouse, but my guess is at least half of it is gone. You've got two or three meters' water depth, and below that many meters of buried sediment. It'll be filled with artifacts, but none of it stratified. With the equipment you've got, you're going to have a big problem excavating it. That's where we can help."

"We've tried using a dredge pump, but the hole fills up immediately and the divers can't see a thing."

"Costas?" Jack said.

Costas snapped shut his radio receiver outside the tent. He came in, raising his sunglasses and wiping the sweat off his brow. "We're good to go. We can use *Seaquest II*'s big pontoon boat to bring the gear in over the shallows."

Jack leaned over the plan, and tapped his pencil at various points. "We suggest you establish a floating caisson, a cofferdam, to enclose an area of riverbed abutting the land site," he said. "You discharge sieved sediment outside the caisson, meaning the water inside remains clear. We have a piece of a kit designed by Costas that we first used in the Black Sea, like a gigantic cookie cutter you place on the area of sediment to be excavated, five meters square. It has an integral dredge pump and can be built up as you excavate deeper, with the pipe outlet on shore where the sediment can be sieved for small finds and organic material. I'll have a couple of our technical people stay here with your team as advisors."

"Because Jack and I are going to Hawaii," Costas murmured.

Pradesh coughed, glancing at the shirt. "So I see. Holiday?"

"Work," Jack said.

Pradesh looked out at the river. "I'm extremely grateful," he said. "Even the smallest find at this site is worth its weight in gold. And the riverbed could be our treasure trove. Now, please excuse me for a few minutes while I let my people know." He hurried off to a group of divers organizing equipment on the jetty, and Jack turned toward the main excavated area of the site. What had the author of the *Periplus* seen when he had disembarked here at this spot, two thousand years ago? It was a jungle clearing on a riverbank, an area smaller than a soccer pitch. In his mind's eye Jack saw mud-brick walls, narrow alleys, flat-roofed warehouses; a line of Roman amphoras along the wharfside, crates of red-glazed pottery from Italy. Arikamedu was like Berenikê on the Red Sea, functional to the point of impoverishment, with no temples, no mosaics — a bartertown on the edge of the unknown, yet a place that belied the enormous value of the goods that passed through it; every scrap of pottery preserved unique evidence for one of the ancient world's most extraordinary endeavors.

"Jack!" Hiebermeyer came bounding up, followed by Aysha and Rebecca. He was pouring sweat. "You remember at Ostia, the port of Rome? The Square of the Merchants, with all the little offices? That's what we've got here, this warehouse building. It's like a stable, with each stall being for one merchant, one firm. And you won't believe whose office we've just found. Aysha spotted it."

An Indian student came up with a finds tray. Aysha carefully took a plastic bag from it and extracted a worn pot sherd. "It's local, south Indian manufacture of the late first century BC."

"There's graffiti on it," Jack said.

Aysha nodded. "It's Tamil. I couldn't believe it when I saw it." Her voice was tight with excitement. "It's the same name as a Tamil graffito we found on the sherd in the merchant's house at Berenikê. The name of a woman, Amrita."

"And now look at the other sherds," Hiebermeyer said, picking one out and showing it to Jack. "The pottery's central Italian, from a wine amphora. Recognize the writing?"

"Numbers," Jack murmured. "They're ledgers, accounts. What you'd expect." He saw some words in Greek. He suddenly gasped. "I recognize the style. Look, the way the letters are sloped. It could be the same hand as the sherds you found at Berenikê with the *Periplus* text!"

Hiebermeyer nodded enthusiastically, then pointed at the excavation. "Here's what I see. We don't know his name, but let's call him Priscus. He's sitting over there in his office with his wife, Amrita. They're a husband and wife team. She's local, perfect for business contacts over here, and her family keeps an eye on their office when they're back in Egypt. You remember we suspected our man was a silk merchant, maybe with a sideline in gems? Well, look at these Greek words. That's *serikōn,* silk. The numbers must be grades, quantities, prices. And look at this one. *Sappheiros.* That's a Greek word for lapis lazuli.

230

It's the word the author of the *Periplus* uses. In antiquity, that can only mean the lapis mined in the mountains of Badakhshan, in Afghanistan."

"You mean this stuff," Costas said, pulling out a piece of shimmering blue stone from his shorts pocket, holding it in front of them.

Hiebermeyer gasped. "That's the piece you found at Berenikê! We can't take you anywhere! What is it with divers?"

"Well, Jack does it sometimes," Costas said, his expression deadpan. "I just borrowed it. For good luck, until we get to Hawaii. Then you can take it back."

Jack suppressed a smile. "Anything else, Maurice?"

Hiebermeyer snorted at Costas, then turned to Rebecca. "Well, your daughter has just won her archaeological credentials," he said. "It was during those few minutes we spent troweling with the students. She has finder's luck."

"That sounds familiar," Jack said. Rebecca opened her hand and showed him a perfect olive-green gem, uncut but brilliantly reflective in the midday sun.

"Peridot," Jack exclaimed, taking the gem from her and holding it up. "From St. John's Island, near Berenikê. Costas and I flew over it on the Red Sea just a few days ago. So you think our man was exporting this from Egypt?"

"And trading it for silk," Aysha said. "Looking at this gem, you can see why peridot might have fascinated the Chinese. It's like refined jade."

"The warrior empire," Jack murmured, holding the piece up to the sun, looking at the green light cast on his other hand.

"What do you mean?" Costas said.

"Just an image I had," Jack explained. "An image of Chinese ships, of warriors coming from the east. But this makes it real."

"And it closes the loop," Hiebermeyer said. "Rome, Egypt, India, lapis lazuli from the mines of Afghanistan, the Silk Route, the fabled city of Xian. Five thousand miles of contact, linking the two greatest empires the world has ever known."

Costas took the gemstone from Jack. He held it toward the sun, with the piece of lapis lazuli in his other hand. The light flashed through them and they seemed to glow together, as if they were enveloped in the same ball of incandescence. He held them closer together, and then flinched, moving them apart. "Hot," he said.

"Probably a focusing effect, like a magnifying glass, concentrating the light," Pradesh said, rejoining the group. "There have always been stories of gemstones doing this, a plausible result of refraction. One of my professors at Roorkee University specialized in it. But I've never heard of peridot and lapis lazuli interacting like this before, especially uncut stones. An interesting research project."

"You're welcome at the IMU engineering lab anytime," Costas said enthusiastically, handing the peridot back to Rebecca and pocketing the lapis lazuli. "But you'd soon get bored with gemstones. There's some incredible underwater robotic stuff I've just been working on. A lot of military applications, right up your street I'd imagine."

"Really?" Pradesh said. "Tell me more."

"Plenty of time for that later," Jack said, shielding his eyes and spying the Lynx helicopter coming in low over the shoreline from *Seaquest II.* He felt the excitement well up inside him. "Are we ready?"

Pradesh nodded, and pointed at two men in jeans and T-shirts with rucksacks and G3 automatic rifles. "A couple of my sappers," he said. "I don't want to aggravate the tribals by showing up in the jungle with soldiers, but there's a very real threat from Maoist insurgents. I don't want to be responsible for the disappearance of the world's most famous underwater archaeologist."

"And his sidekick," Costas added.

Rebecca looked dolefully at Jack, holding up the peridot. "If I've earned my credentials like Hiemy says, does that mean I can come along now too?"

"Not this time." Jack eyed Hiebermeyer. "But Hiemy might let you drive the Zodiac back. Slowly."

"Oh, cool." She put the stone back in the finds tray and clapped her hands.

Jack grinned, and made a whirling motion with his fingers to Costas. "Good to go?"

"Good to go."

8

Three hours after leaving the Roman site at Arikamedu, Jack sat beside Costas and Pradesh on the foredeck of a pontoon boat as it chugged west up the broad expanse of the Godavari River, its bow wave cresting against the current. Jack was riding his own personal wave of excitement. This was his chance to fulfill a dream, to tread the same path as his ancestor, to discover what Lieutenant John Howard had seen in the jungle that day in 1879. Jack grasped the rail and looked out, preparing himself. They had flown by helicopter north from Arikamedu along the coast of India to the port of Cocanada, and then veered inland up the delta of the river. They had swept low over a million acres of paddy and sugar cane, flying through billowing clouds of sweet ferment where the sugar was being processed into jaggery. At Dowlaiswaram, some thirty miles from the coast, they had landed on the great dam that was responsible for the fertility of the delta, and

Pradesh had shown them where the Madras Sappers had been based while they built the dam in the 1860s. The figures were still reeling through Jack's mind as they transferred to the Godavari Steam Navigation Company pontoon boat above the dam for the trip into the jungle. Two thousand miles of irrigation channels, a five times increase in the acreage under cultivation. It had been one of the enduring achievements of British rule in India, yet as they went upstream, evidence of human mastery over nature diminished, and they saw only adaptation, acceptance, just as they had seen on the coast at Arikamedu. Like all great rivers that swelled with floodwaters, like the Nile or the Mississippi, all attempts to harness the water of the Godavari presented only an illusion of success, ephemeral bastions against an overwhelming force that could sweep away the grandest human achievements in a mere instant.

"The Godavari is the second holiest river in India, after the Ganges," Pradesh said, as he steered the boat into the central channel. "I wanted you to experience the final fifteen miles of our trip by river so you could empathize with those soldiers in 1879, going up into the unknown on their paddle steamer, with no idea of what lay ahead."

"Except mosquitoes," Costas said, slapping his leg.

Pradesh nodded. "By the end of the Rampa

campaign, four-fifths of the troops had been laid low by malaria, and many had died. The Kóya people of the jungle have some degree of immunity. They believed the fever was the vengeance of their most dreaded demon, their *konda devata,* the tiger spirit."

Costas peered dubiously into the haze ahead, at the shapes of low-lying hills just discernible to the east. "Is the source of the river up there?"

Pradesh shook his head. "Much farther west. Some say it pours from the mouth of a holy idol near Bombay. Some even say it's joined by a subterranean channel to the Ganges, linking the great waterways of India together."

"Sounds like wishful thinking," Jack said.

"The engineer in me agrees, but it's still an attractive concept. In India, everything from the north seems to flow down, to trickle to the south. Invaders like the Mongols, religions like Buddhism. But hardly any of it permeated the hill tracts, the jungle. Rampa district, where we're going, wasn't even surveyed until 1928. At the time of the 1879 rebellion, it was a big blank on the map. Even now there are hundreds of square miles which have only ever been visited by Kóya and other tribal hunters. Even the missionaries won't go there."

For almost half an hour they carried on upstream without talking, watching the muddy banks as the river gradually constricted from over a mile in width to only a few hundred yards. They glimpsed oxen plowing paddies between lines of coconut palms. They passed women in wet saris bathing in the river, and others thrashing the rocks with washing, risking being swept away in the current. Men in loincloths hung low in the water against the gunwales of their boats, cooling off. Everywhere they saw signs of decay or repair, it was hard to tell which. Jack realized that the tranquility of the scene belied the violence of the coming monsoon season, when the floodwaters would sweep away everything on the riverbanks before them.

They passed a line of wooden posts in midstream, with the tattered remains of fishing nets bowed out in the current between them. To Jack it was as if the nets were there to catch history, fragments of the past dislodged from the jungle ahead. Since leaving Arikamedu, he had been trying to attune himself to the archaeology of rivers, places which could hold treasures, like the fleeces used to catch gold in mountain streams, but at other times were void, swept clear of anything tangible. It was a different kind of archaeology here, more elusive, with none of the certainties of a shipwreck.

Like the coast at Arikamedu the human imprint on the riverbank seemed ephemeral, constantly reforming. The only permanent structure they saw was a beautiful white temple on a rocky island in the river, its roof a swirl of sculpted snakes above painted tiers of gold. Pradesh slowed the boat down, reached into a bowl and tossed a handful of flower petals into the water. "That's Vishnu, asleep under the coiled snake Sesha, the five-headed one," he said. "The deep blue, the blue of lapis lazuli, the color of Vishnu, is the color of eternity, of immortality."

"Are the jungle people Hindu?" Costas asked.

Pradesh shook his head and opened up the throttle again, raising his voice above the noise. "Up ahead there's a hill called Shiva, on the edge of the jungle. Naming it Shiva is a bit like putting a Christian cross on an old Roman temple, only here there was no attempt at proselytizing, no attempt to suppress the old beliefs. Hinduism's like an archaeological site. Strip away the upper layers, and the old gods, the old religions, are all still there. Only where we're going, there's nothing to strip away. That temple's the last bastion of the lowland people against the looming jungle ahead, a place where even their gods fear to go."

After that they saw fewer people along the shore, and then none. The open paddies gave way to scrub and then jungle, a dense green foliage that reached down the slopes and enveloped the shoreline, fringing the river with palmyra and coconut palms that hung over silvery stretches of beach. Mist rose off the trees and tumbled down the riverbanks, leaving a narrow passage in the center of the river where their vision was clear. Soon the jungle-shrouded hills rose three hundred meters or more on either side of the river, the upper reaches barely visible in foggy blue-green silhouette.

A long, flat boat came into view around a bend, drifting with the current, its engine thudding in idle. It was laden with piles of coconuts and lengths of tree trunk, tamarind and mahogany. A policeman in a shabby khaki uniform lounged in the stern, holding an old Lee-Enfield rifle and eyeing them suspiciously as the boat slid past. Pradesh waved at him cheerfully. "The police have always been an issue up here," he said. "The hill people see them as protectors of the low-landers who are given forestry concessions, people who come and cut down their precious hardwoods. And you can hardly imagine that chap standing up to Maoist terrorists, can you? But that opens up a whole other problem. If you militarize the police, you antagonize the hill people more, and if you send in the army to confront the Maoists, you risk a return to the situation in 1879. Sappers are the best option, because the hill people can see them doing useful things, building roads, clinics, schoolhouses. Sappers are soldiers too, but they are a different breed of men."

"So I can see," Jack said, smiling.

Pradesh throttled back and steered the boat out of the main current and into the eddy-waters along the left bank, where the gentle puttering of the motor was drowned out by the screeches and chattering of a band of white-faced langur monkeys who leered at them from the treetops. The boat rounded a bend, and they saw paths leading up from a beach to low-set houses in a jungle clearing, the palm-frond roofs overshadowed by mango and gnarled tamarind trees. For the first time they saw the Kóya, dark, finely muscled men wearing only loincloths, standing under the fronds watching them. One of them sported a leopard skin with a peacock feather pendant hanging from his neck.

"That's the village of Puliramanaguden," Pradesh said quietly. "It means 'Place of the Tiger God.' "

"Tigers," Costas murmured. "Any elephants?"

"Rarely, but plenty of *gaur,* the local bison. The Kóya call this stretch of jungle Pappikondalu, the Bison Hills. The bison are about the size of small elephants. I've heard them at night, thundering together through the jungle, roaring and panting like creatures from mythology. All you can see is the whites

241

of their eyes. Even the tigers steer clear of them."

Costas grunted. "Another choice IMU holiday destination."

They went on farther, still enveloped by the mist along the bank, and reached another bend, the flow of the central channel now visible in the water ahead. Pradesh kept in the lee of the shore until they were only a few yards from the point of the bend, holding the boat almost at a standstill as he waited for the current to pull them out into mid-stream. Jack saw a woman sitting on the tangled roots of a banyan tree. She was very old, and blind. Her eyes were like those of an ancient statue, the paint gone and only the white remaining, yet Jack felt that she was staring directly at him, holding him fast. She seemed like a pietà, a mother anguished, mourning a lost child. Jack remembered the Victorian photo of the mother and child above the old chest in his cabin, his great-great grandmother and her baby. He looked up at the forest canopy above the woman, and through a break in the mist he saw the hills dark against the sky. He felt an intense sense of familiarity, and then it was gone. From around the point a water buffalo lurched into view, lunging on a halter tied to a stake, a sudden, violent movement that set Jack's pulse racing. The current caught the boat and Pradesh gunned the engine, bringing them out into the central channel, away from the woman and around the point, until she was lost in the haze. The river widened and the mist lifted, and Jack knew they were there. The place exactly matched the description in his great-great-grandfather's diary. Pradesh steered the boat back into the still water beside the left bank, and nudged the prow into the beach until it stuck fast. Jack gazed at the opposite shore, a sandbar extending several hundred meters along another bend in the river where sediment had been pushed by the current. The sandbar was cut by a dry streambed he could just make out coming through the jungle. "Over there," Pradesh said, pointing. "That's where it happened."

"I know," Jack replied quietly. "It's just as I imagined it."

"Don't expect to find anything from 1879 on the riverbank," Pradesh said. "That sandbar's swept away every year by the monsoon floodwater, and then reformed anew. We need to go to the riverside village you can just make out higher up, on the fringe of the jungle."

"We're in your hands," Jack said.

Pradesh looked at his watch. "The helicopter's due in an hour. It'll fly us deeper into the jungle. My two sappers will be on board. I didn't want to excite any hostility by having them with us on the river, but I don't want to go into the jungle without them, meaning no disrespect to your nine-millimeter Beretta, Jack."

"You spotted it," Jack said.

"Just keep it out of sight. It's a tinderbox up here. If any of the hill people who don't know me suspect we're government officials, then the game's over. They'll clam up completely. We'll stop here for a break before going over to the village. It may seem odd in this heat, but I'm thirsty for tea."

Pradesh busied himself with the battered old kettle and Primus stove from the boat's store box, and Costas disappeared discreetly ashore. Jack sat alone, looking around. They had left the mist in the narrows behind them and entered an oasis of light, as if the air had been cleansed. The beach opposite swept around in the shape of a sword, the sand a dazzling gold. Behind it rose shimmering tree trunks and great boulders of sandstone that had been scoured clean by the floods. Above that was the jungle canopy, myriad shades of green climbing the steep sides of the cliffs as they converged upstream in the great gorge of the Godavari.

"Ahead of us, where the gorge narrows, the river's only two hundred meters wide," Pradesh said, handing him a glass of tea. "The hills on either side rise to over eight hundred meters, and the river's very deep, almost a hundred meters."

Jack looked at the jungle-clad walls of the

gorge. It was enticing, yet forbidding, like a high mountain pass that promised a lush valley beyond, but threatened grave peril in the crossing. To the few lowlanders who ventured here the promise was the Abode of the Immortals, the Heavenly City. To the first Europeans it was the fabled kingdom of Golconda, the Mountain of Light, where the Koh-i-noor diamond had been mined, somewhere beyond the gorge ahead. Yet before the arrival of steamboats this was the end of the river journey, and most who came here turned back, powerless to resist the current as it tumbled through the gorge, pushing their boats back and letting the river return them downstream to civilization. Jack peered into the water. It was murky, not with mud but with some other darkness, and the sunlight seemed to vanish into it. The canyon walls should have been reflected in the water, but instead he saw nothing. It was disconcerting, as if the river were a black hole that swallowed up reality, leaving him wondering whether the mist-shrouded shoreline was some kind of phantasm, almost too close to his boyhood image of this place to be real. He snapped out of his reverie as Costas came crashing back through the undergrowth and leapt onto the bow of the boat, a picture of dishevelment with his shorts barely on.

"Something threaten your manhood?" Jack said.

"Spiders," Costas panted, sitting back, checking his legs anxiously. "Giant hairy spiders the size of saucers."

"The spiders are harmless, unless you provoke them," Pradesh said, handing him a tea glass. "Just keep an eye out for the cobras. The Kóya use a root as an anti-venom, but I've never been able to find it."

"There's always Jack's Beretta," Costas said.

"Bad karma to shoot snakes," Pradesh replied, wagging his finger. "Anyway, don't worry. We're not going trekking through the jungle. Jack wanted to retrace his ancestor's footsteps, but I convinced him that we should go by helicopter. Jack agreed. He was concerned for your safety."

"My safety? Jack? Yeah, right, that would be a first," Costas grumbled, wiping the sweat off his face and swatting a mosquito. "At least we've all taken our anti-malarials."

"That's another thing," Pradesh said hastily. "They don't always work out here. But I know someone who can give us a little booster in the village."

Jack looked again at the scene, imagining it one hundred and thirty years before. "So what do you know about August the twentieth 1879?"

Pradesh eyed him keenly. "Well, you were right about what happened."

"Human sacrifice?"

Pradesh looked at the riverbank. "I told you I was brought up near the Godavari River, in Dowlaiswaram. Well, my grandfather was actually a Kóya, from this place. The story of that day in 1879 became a kind of legend, kept secret, even from the anthropologists who occasionally came up here asking questions. As far as I know, what I'm about to tell you has never been told to any other outsiders."

"Go on," Jack said.

"The rebels put on a spectacular show. They executed their police captives on that beach, in full view of the sappers on the river steamer trapped on the sandbank. But they also stirred the rest of the Kóya into a frenzy, feeding them alcohol and god knows what else. The tribals carried out three sacrifices that day, the full *meriah.* A man, a woman and a child."

"A child too?" Jack murmured.

"Later, the authorities in the lowlands refused to believe it was a sacrifice, and thought the rebels had given their executions the guise of *meriah* to make them seem more terrifying, as if they were reviving a dread practice the British thought they'd stamped out years before. But the authorities were wrong. That scene on the riverbank was the real thing. Even today, sacrifices are still performed using langur monkeys and chickens, but the *meriah* ritual is still here, lurking just under the surface, and it would take little provocation, the re-lighting of that tinderbox, for it to be revived."

"But what happened?" Jack persisted. "What made my great-great-grandfather end his diary that day?"

Pradesh pursed his lips. "I don't know. Something traumatized him. It would have been a dreadful sight, the child especially, the flesh ripped from them while they were still alive. Maybe he felt impotent, unable to help. You say he was the father of a young child himself? You told me he was in India as a boy during the mutiny, when there were terrible scenes of slaughter. Maybe some latent memory of that horror resurfaced as he watched the sacrifice. By all accounts he was an excellent officer, a tough soldier, so whatever he saw or did, it must have been pretty bad."

"So where do we go from here?" Jack asked quietly.

Pradesh paused. "I know where he and Lieutenant Wauchope went that day."

"Go on."

Pradesh reached into the front of his shirt and took out a pendant hanging on an old leather necklace. "It's a tiger's claw," he said. "The tiger was killed by my grandfather, who was a *muttadar.* That's a village chief, but also a kind of priest. The tiger was attacking a boy playing by the river, and my grandfather shot it with an old East India Company musket the Kóya had stolen years before from the native police. But the tiger is sacred here, and by killing it my grandfather became an outcast, forced to leave the jungle. He met my grandmother, a lowlander, and they lived in Dowlaishweram. But their son, my father, became the district forest officer, and he used to bring me up here. I was adopted by the villagers of Rampa and learned to speak the Kóya dialect. The tribal people revered my father because the officials posted up here are usually lowlanders, and traditionally the lowlanders were seen as corrupt moneylenders who treated the hill people with contempt. My father actually went to Delhi to fight their case for forest rights. He was a great man."

"He must be proud of you."

Pradesh looked downcast. "He might have been. I'll never know. Ever since the time of the British Raj, the cause of the forest people has been hijacked by others. A hundred years ago it was the Indian nationalist movement, who claimed that the tribal uprisings were somehow part of an independence struggle against the British. And now it's the Maoists, the so-called People's War Group. The tribals are angry again because the government has been selling mining concessions, and the PWG have taken the tribals' side. In reality the PWG couldn't care less. It was just a way to get the tribals to leave them alone in their jungle bases where they plan terrorist attacks around India. My father confronted them and was murdered for it."

"I'm sorry," Jack said.

"It's why I've never been posted up here," Pradesh replied ruefully. "My colonel knows my family history. I was too close."

"You don't look the vengeance type," Costas murmured.

"Try me," Pradesh said quietly.

Costas pointed at the claw hanging from Pradesh's neck. "Isn't that going to get us into trouble with any Kóya we come across? I mean, if the tiger's sacred?"

Pradesh shook his head. "Once a tiger's dead and the spirit has left, the skin and claws have great value. The skin is worn by a *muttadar* for dancing and ceremonies, and the claws are distributed among the young men of the village. They're good-luck charms, to ward off the angry spirits when the men are hunting deep in the jungle."

Costas downed his tea in one gulp. "I think I'd opt for an assault rifle."

Pradesh grinned. "That would help too."

"Let's have your story," Jack said. "What the Kóya remember about that day."

Pradesh paused. "It was told to me by my grandfather when I was a boy. For the hill people here it has become part of their lore, shrouded in legend like the foundation myths of the gods. But it concerns your great-great-grandfather."

"Go on."

"The most sacred objects of the Kóya were *vélpus,* a word meaning idols or gods," Pradesh said. "Each family had one, each clan. They were usually small objects that would seem commonplace to us but were exotic to the Kóya, like a piece of wrought iron. Each *vélpu* was kept inside a length of hollow bamboo about a foot long. They were guarded with great secrecy, only brought out on rare occasions to be worshipped. The greatest of them all, the supreme *vélpu,* was called the Lakka Ramu. It was kept in a cave shrine deep in the jungle, and was never opened. It was said that the god inside was too dazzling, and would blind anyone who gazed on it. Perhaps it was glass, maybe a gemstone, something exotic that had reached the Kóya from the outside world countless generations ago. The supreme *vélpu* held the soul of the Kóya people. Without it, they would be living in a shadowland, at the whim of the malign spirits who haunted the jungle, especially the dreaded *konda devata,* the spirit of the tiger. And they have been in that shadowland since 1879."

"What happened?" Costas asked.

Pradesh glanced around and lowered his voice. "My grandfather, the village chief, was a hereditary *muttadar.* By ancient tradition the chiefs of Rampa village had been guard-

251

ians of the jungle shrine where the sacred Lakka Ramu was hidden. My grandfather's grandfather was the *muttadar* in 1879, but he didn't survive the rebellion. I know what happened to him from the rebels who watched the events of that day unfold from the jungle, men of my own clan who slunk back to their villages after the revolt was over and passed the story down to their children. You showed me Howard's diary, Jack, the final entry. On that day the *muttadar* was surrounded by the rebels and shot full of arrows. They knew what he'd done."

"Which was?" Costas said.

"The *muttadar* feared that Chendrayya, the rebel leader, would come to the shrine and take the Lakka Ramu, and use it to control all the hill people for his own purposes. Chendrayya came from another clan, one that had been locked in a feud for generations with the *muttadar's* clan, an ancient dispute over which family should control the shrine. The British officers knew all about tribal feuds from their experiences on the northwest frontier of India, and they used it to their advantage."

"The *muttadar* came over to the British," Jack murmured.

"He took the *vélpu* from the shrine for safekeeping, then he took a huge chance and volunteered himself as a guide and interpreter," Pradesh said. "His condition was that

252

the British officers allow him to return the *vélpu* to the shrine when it was all over. He was on the river steamer with the sappers on that final day in Howard's diary, 20 August 1879. It's in the pages you emailed me, Jack. It fits with what I knew exactly. There was a big firefight that day with the rebels in the jungle, dozens killed and wounded. Then Howard and the others on the steamer must have witnessed that sacrificial scene by the river. The *muttadar* saw it too, and got jittery, went to pieces. It would have seemed as if all the malign spirits of the jungle were converging on him, taunting him for taking the *vélpu*. There's no record in Howard's diary of what happened next, and nothing more in the regimental records at Bangalore. Most of the officers who returned from Rampa just wanted to forget about it. But there's a story told to me by my grandfather. A British official with the sappers, a man called Bebbie, had been taken ill, and was still in the jungle. Howard and Wauchope set off with a rescue party. Bebbie was laid up near the shrine, already dead. The *muttadar* had volunteered to lead them to the spot, providing he could take the idol with him. The British officers probably felt they had no choice. Even with their superior weapons it would have been suicidal to venture into the jungle, a small force of a dozen against hundreds of rebels. They gambled that the presence of the idol

253

would keep the rebels from attacking them. The *muttadar* backed off from the shrine at the last minute, terrified that the god would wreak vengeance on him, and then he was murdered. Howard himself took the idol into the cave."

"And afterward Chendrayya stole it?" Jack said.

Pradesh shook his head. "No. Howard kept his word to the *muttadar.* But then he and Wauchope must have realized that their only chance of escape was to take the idol back with them, to use it as a safeguard just as the *muttadar* had done on the way in. There was a firefight as they emerged from the cave, but when the rebels saw they still had the bamboo *vélpu* they backed off. The two officers retreated through the jungle to the river, with the sappers. And they took something else out of the shrine, another sacred relic. It was a broken sword, attached to a golden gauntlet in the shape of a tiger's head. The Kóya believed it had been worn by the great god Rama himself."

"Well I'll be damned," Jack murmured.

"You know this?"

"Something I haven't shown you yet. A family heirloom."

"You have it?" Pradesh gasped.

"It's brass, not gold, but it must be the same," Jack replied excitedly. "Howard gave it to his daughter, my great-grandmother, and

254

I've inherited it." Jack sat back, exalted. He had known the gauntlet had come from the jungle, but nothing more. This was extraordinary. Then he remembered Katya, her reaction when he had told her about it. And he remembered Katya's uncle, Hai Chen, the anthropologist who had disappeared in the jungle over four months ago. That was the other reason Jack was here. He stared out into the jungle canopy. Maybe Hai Chen had simply walked away. Maybe there had been an accident. Solitary anthropologists had disappeared in jungles before. Then Jack thought of the Maoists, the dangers that lurked out here. He pursed his lips. *Something more was going on.* The pointers were there, but it still didn't add up. He turned back to Pradesh, who said something under his breath, not in English or Hindi but in another language, a soft clicking sound. He looked at Jack, his eyes alight. "The recovery of this object would mean everything to the Kóya," Pradesh murmured. "I hardly dare ask. Do you have the *vélpu* too?"

Jack shook his head. "I'd never heard of that before now."

Pradesh closed his eyes for a moment, and exhaled hard. "What we know is this. The Rampa Rebellion continued for months more, but that day was a turning point. Never again was there a rebel force of that size, and afterward Chendrayya was only able to muster loyal bands of a few dozen, the hard core, many of them already outcasts and criminals. Most of the rebels in the early months had been honest forest men, Kóya and Reddis. Once they saw the murder of the *muttadar* and saw how much Chendrayya coveted their sacred *vélpu,* they lost their ardor for the rebellion. And knowing that the British had the idol — and realised its power over them — would have weakened their resolve still further. They knew they would only ever get it back when the rebellion was finished."

"But you're saying they never did get it back," Costas commented.

"That shrine," Jack said. "It's near a Rampa village?"

Pradesh nodded. "About eight miles northeast of here, through dense jungle. It's named after the god Rama."

"Rama," Jack repeated softly, his mind racing.

"Wasn't Rama a Hindu god?" Costas said.

Pradesh nodded again. "The image of the perfect man, raised to godhead, the seventh incarnation of Vishnu. But it's as I said before — he's an upstart here. The beliefs of the Kóya have virtually nothing else in common with Hindu religion. The legend of Prince Rama, his wanderings and his search for spiritual redemption, is found all over southern India. The Kóya believe this was where he ended up, finding his rightful kingdom in the heart of the jungle."

"Heart of darkness, more like," Costas said, looking at the dense green slopes on the opposite shore, swatting at a cloud of mosquitoes that had enveloped him.

"Is that where you're taking us?" Jack said. "To the shrine?"

Pradesh took a deep breath and nodded, fingering the tiger pendant. "I went there when I was a boy. It was forbidden, but as a lowlander by upbringing I didn't believe in the superstition. No Kóya had visited it since that day in 1879. My grandfather said there was a terrible storm that night, thunder and lightning. An earthquake sealed up the entrance after the two officers had left. To the Kóya that was an absolute sign that the worst horror would befall them if they went anywhere near the place. And now there's another reason for staying away. The shrine's next to a stream in a jungle clearing, and it's been used by the Maoist guerrillas as a base. They caught me once and let me into their camp, and they played with me. That was before they murdered my father. I've been wanting to go back ever since."

"It sounds as if both you and Jack are on a mission," Costas said.

"Your ancestor the *muttadar* also wanted to get to the shrine when he stood beside Lieutenant Howard on the river steamer at this spot all those years ago," Jack added.

"I'd never try to put myself in the mind of a Kóya holy man. He may have been my ancestor, but that's one place I definitely don't want to go." Pradesh looked at Jack, his expression steely. "And my mission's not about ancient gods and spirits and idols. It's about the present day. It's about the duty of a son to the memory of a murdered father."

Jack nodded, then swung his legs out over the bow of the boat, ready to push off. Pradesh sat down and turned on the ignition. "We've got about five hours of daylight left. The chopper should be here in forty-five minutes. That gives us time to visit the village on the opposite shore. There's something I want you to see."

"Let's move," Jack said. "From what you say, we don't want to be out here after dark."

Costas slapped a mosquito on his neck, leaving a bloody smudge. "Roger that."

9

Jack knelt in the bow of the pontoon boat, holding the painter line in readiness as Pradesh swung the tiller and nosed the boat out of the river current into a backwater by the shore. At the last moment he gunned the engine and rammed the keel up onto the sandy beach that fronted the jungle. Jack leapt out with the line, ran a few paces across the hot packed sand and tied it to the stump of a tamarind tree. Pradesh killed the engine and tilted it, then he and Costas jumped out on either side and pulled the boat up as far as they could. Jack tightened the line and looked around. The sand was pristine, as white as he had seen anywhere. He had half-hoped to find something straightaway, some evidence of that fateful day in 1879, but he also half-feared it, as if he were apprehensive of awakening some atavistic trauma inherited from his ancestor. But the sand was spotless, and there was no ancient stain of sacrifice. He saw where the monsoon flood had swept around the curve of the river, churning up the sand and re-creating the beach every year. He looked up to where the gorge narrowed, and remembered the words of a Victorian engineer who had seen the Godavari in full spate: *It foams past its obstructions with a velocity and turbulence which no craft that ever floated could stem.* They had only come a few hundred meters from the opposite shore, but it was as if they had crossed some kind of sacred boundary into another world. Even the air smelled different — tangier, organic — and the light above the fringe of the jungle had a peculiar aura, as if the air itself were stained green and blue at the interface between the canopy and the sky.

"Come on." Pradesh walked across the sand to an opening in the jungle between two trees, a well-worn path up the slope that led to the reed and bamboo houses they had spied from the opposite shore, built above the level of the flood. "This is one of the trackways traced by the sappers in the wake of the 1879 rebellion, but it was neglected after they left. They weren't given the resources to put anything permanent into the jungle, and things haven't changed much since." Costas trudged behind him, and Jack brought up the rear. Costas took out a can of insect repellant from his bag and liberally sprayed his exposed parts, passing it to Jack. "One small step for mankind since 1879,"

Costas muttered, slapping a blood-filled mosquito that had bitten through his shirt. Pradesh turned around and watched. "It's about the only thing that has changed," he said. "Prepare to walk back in time." A huge spider scurried over the rocky path between them, and Jack froze, catching his breath. Pradesh saw him. "Normal animal reaction," he said. "It's the first thing we were taught in jungle warfare training school. You step under the canopy, you instantly lose the veneer of civilization, you become an animal again, feral. You use it to your advantage, the heightened awareness. But it also reawakens primal fear, the survival instinct. Spiders can do it, and snakes."

"And tigers," Costas muttered. "I think I need a drink."

"That's another way of dealing with this place, unfortunately a little too tempting for the Kóya people." Pradesh turned and led them up the path, across gigantic roots of tamarind and teak that had twisted over each other, enveloping the clearance made in 1879. There was a rustling overhead like wind in the leaves, and a troop of monkeys screeched. They reached a level patch and walked past several houses, each a modest affair of bamboo uprights with a roof of overlapping palmyra leaves, surrounded by a narrow verandah fronted by a trellis of bamboo and palmyra leaf stalks interwoven with sprouting bean shoots. Costas pointed at a fresh red mark on the wall. "That symbol looks strangely out of place."

"A hammer and sickle," Jack murmured.

Pradesh glanced back, his lip curled in disgust. "The Maoist guerrillas. They see the Kóya as their allies, but you don't curry favor by desecrating the buildings of your friends. When they're sober the Kóya are pretty contemptuous of them, but the hill tribes have been driven into a corner and are desperate for some backing against the mining companies. The ideology of the Maoists means nothing to them, though, and this will be daubed over soon enough."

Jack and Costas followed him toward the end of the level ground where the jungle closed around the village and began to climb in tangled profusion up the slope. There were signs of life all around, wisps of smoke from fires, half-stacked wood, carved wooden toys, but they could see no one. "Where are the people?" Costas murmured.

"Watching us," Pradesh said. "For them, being invisible is second nature. It's something else you learn in the jungle, how to meld in. They know who I am, but they've had other outsiders here recently, mining prospectors, and they've got reason to be suspicious." He led them into a small clearing beyond the village, hemmed in by soaring trunks of rosewood, satinwood, palm, teak.

He squatted by the base of a hoary old tamarind and pointed to a slab of ochre-red sandstone about half a meter across that had become embedded in the trunk, rising up as the tree grew. Costas knelt beside him. "One of those sacred stones you were talking about?"

Pradesh shook his head. "Look closely. This is what I wanted to show you."

"Okay. I see it's got an inscription on it."

Jack squatted down on the other side of the tree, where the light was better. He touched the stone, feeling the roughness, the condensation. There were several lines in English, crudely carved. He read out the words:

WILLIAM CHARLES BEBBIE
ASSISTANT COMMISSIONER,
CENTRAL PROVINCES
SHOT BY THE REBELS, 20 AUGUST 1879
AGED 41

"That's your guy, isn't it, Jack?" Costas said. "The one who led the sappers into the jungle, the official responsible for this area who'd hardly ever been up here before?"

"That's him all right," Jack murmured, placing the palm of his hand on the stone.

"Pretty basic inscription. I mean, no sacred memories, rest in peace, all that."

"He was lucky to get an inscription at all.

This must have been done by the sappers when they got back from their foray in the jungle. They'd probably buried him there at the shrine, on the spot where he died. I don't think much love was lost."

"Quick burial. Get rid of the evidence."

"What do you mean?"

"Well, if he was fragged. I mean, if those sappers took him out. Who would ever know? They're being shot at from all sides. They were holed up and desperate, and he may have been lording it over them. It sounds as if he was probably putting their lives at risk. An officer like Howard might have understood if he found out, turned a blind eye. He'd have been more loyal to his sappers than to some blundering civil official."

"Possibly," Jack murmured. "And a quick burial wouldn't have excited any interest. People were buried in India the day they died. Howard's little boy Edward was buried in Bangalore only a few hours after he was taken ill, months before Howard even got to the graveside."

Costas yelped, and sprang backward. Jack stared with horrified fascination at what had appeared a few inches from his face. It was a huge snake, a cobra, yellow-brown with dark bands, rising ramrod straight from a hole in the roots in front of Bebbie's tombstone. It flattened its neck and stared at Costas, its tongue flickering in and out, hissing and swaying.

"Okay," Jack murmured through clenched teeth, not moving a muscle. "What do we do now?"

"Keep absolutely still," Pradesh said.

Costas began swaying slightly.

"That means all of us," Pradesh whispered. "It doesn't matter how far away you are. You should see how far these things strike."

"Just getting into the spirit of things," Costas murmured.

"That's something you definitely don't want to do," Pradesh said quietly, his eyes glued to the cobra. It opened its mouth wide, fangs extended and dripping with poison.

Costas stopped swaying. "Got you."

Pradesh reached down slowly, to a gourd wedged between the roots, and scooped up a handful of what was inside. He raised his arm above the snake, and dribbled vermillion powder over it. The snake began to lower, coiling down, somehow soothed, and then it leapt sideways, straightening like a spear and flying several times its body length into the matted foliage on the edge of the clearing. There was a rustle, and it was gone. Jack and Costas remained stock-still, in stunned silence. Pradesh turned to them and grinned. "A little trick I learned as a boy. When I stayed up here with my father. I used to keep one of those as a pet."

"A pet," Costas said weakly.

"It's a portent," Pradesh said. "The rising of the snake signals the beginning of the festival of *Thota Panduga.* That's what's about to happen here." He gestured at the tamped earth of the clearing. "This is where they dance. It's a sacred spot, and not because of Bebbie. Back in 1858, the hill chiefs were hanged here by the British for carrying out human sacrifice. The Kóya don't forget these things. They still sacrifice fowl here, under the toddy-yielding trees. They'll have prepared food last night and left it among the roots, to feast on today."

Jack relaxed slightly, rocking back on his haunches, and looked around. Geckos flickered across the rocks, and ran up a dark brown termite mound in front of the jungle. Insects were everywhere, not just mosquitoes but dragonflies and butterflies, alighting on the flowers that clustered in the sunlight around the edge of the clearing. The jungle seemed to erupt in noise. In the dripping canopy above, Jack saw hanging fruit bats, their wings furling and unfurling. He noticed that the troop of langur monkeys they had heard on the rocky path up from the beach had followed them here, and were sitting on tree roots around the clearing, suddenly chattering and screeching. Beyond them Jack realized he was looking at human faces, men, women and children, several dozen at least, silently watching.

"We've got a friend," Costas said, gesturing.

A man had silently materialized on the edge of the clearing. Pradesh said something in Kóya, and touched the man's hands in greeting. The man was lithe, wiry, with taut muscles, his skin dark brown. He was wearing only a white loincloth, tied by a cord of twisted creepers, and a loose turban, and he was barefoot. He had wide cheekbones and a broader nose than the lowlanders they had seen along the river, and his eyes looked jet-black. He was carrying a bow and a handful of arrows, and he had a curved, viciously pointed dagger in his belt. Pradesh turned and gestured for Jack and Costas to come forward. "This is Murla Rajareddy," he said. "He's a toddy-tapper." Pradesh pointed at an old car tire and a coil of rope against a palm tree, evidently a sling used for climbing up into the canopy. "He uses the knife to cut open the bases of the palm leaves, and then collects the sap in gourds. Now's the best time of year for it. That's what the festival's really all about." Jack saw that the man's torso was scarred with gouges and furrows, some old and healed, some fresh, lines of parallel weals that glistened red beneath some kind of medicinal paste. Pradesh spoke to the man, who replied softly, pointing at his scars. Pradesh turned back to Jack and Costas. "He's also the village tiger hunter, the only one allowed to kill them. He says a tiger came through about ten days ago, and he had a narrow escape. It had taken and eaten a child from another village. He thinks the arrival of the tiger was an omen of what was to come next, the arrival of other outsiders who've been through here recently. I'll ask him about that. It's why they're so suspicious of us. They thought we might be the same."

Jack and Costas shook hands in turn with the man, who bowed his head slightly but kept his eyes on them. He reeked of alcohol. He was surrounded by a cloud of mosquitoes, but he seemed oblivious to them.

"How do they deal with the malaria?" Costas asked.

"They make pills for the fever. It's a paste made from the bark of *Alstonia scholaris,* the root bark of *Ophioxylon scrobiculatum* and the root, stem and leaves of *Andrographis paniculata.*"

"You believe in it?" Costas asked.

"It's worked for me. Sir Ronald Ross established the role of mosquitoes in malaria after treating Rampa veterans, but there was more to learn. Even today, doctors from the lowlands think jungle remedies are the work of witch doctors. The irony is, it's their own superstitions about the Kóya that prevent them from learning from these people."

The toddy-tapper reached down and picked up a gourd from behind the tree. Fat black rats scurried into the darkness of the jungle behind, then turned around, eyeing the men ravenously. Costas looked at them, and gave Jack a baleful look. The man ignored Jack, and handed the gourd to Costas.

"It seems that you're the chosen one," Pradesh said.

"Chosen for what?"

"It's called tiger food." He grinned. "Those who eat it gain magical powers, allowing them to charm the tiger and bind him to them. When the festival's over, you'll be stripped naked and sent into the jungle to find the tiger, a kind of meet and greet."

"Right. So when exactly is that chopper arriving?"

Pradesh checked his watch. "Twenty-five minutes."

"I think I might just go and wait on the beach."

"When you enter into a native ritual, you should never back off. Very bad form, you know. Any anthropologist will tell you that."

"Anthropology, archaeology, it's all the same to me," Costas grumbled. "I'm an engineer. An engineer who's supposed to be on holiday." He peered into the gourd. "Anyway, what is it, exactly?"

"It's fruit from the tamarind tree, the tamar-i-hind. They're like velvety green broad beans, and you suck the pulp of the seeds. They mix it with palm pith and mango kernels. As a special treat for the festival, they've already cracked the seeds in their mouths, and spat out the pulp. The saliva makes it congeal into a paste. Really rather good."

"I didn't hear you say that." Costas looked pale.

"It's their greatest delicacy."

"Do I have to?"

"Count yourself lucky. He might have been fingering you for sacrifice."

"They still do that?"

"You never can be too sure. Old habits die hard. And they've been provoked recently, just as they were in 1879. I suggest you accept his gift."

Costas peered into the gourd, smiled appreciatively at the man then dipped a finger. Taking it out, he licked it, then smiled, nodding enthusiastically. He glanced at Jack, then at Pradesh. He swallowed hard, and for a split second looked like a child about to throw up. "Tell him it was excellent. Got anything to wash it down?" he said hoarsely, still smiling.

"Coming your way."

The man picked up another gourd, and held it out to Costas. Pradesh stopped the man's hand, and sniffed it. "It's *kallu,* palm toddy, fermented in the sun. Sometimes they add poppy leaves to it, sometimes marijuana. But not today. It has to be pure, for the festival." He let the man pass it on. Costas took a cautious sip and then a mouthful, swilling it around and then swallowing it. He exhaled and looked appreciatively at the gourd. "Not bad. A little like cider."

"I was checking it wasn't arrack," Pradesh said. "That's what you get when you distill this stuff. A lethal mix of methyl and amyl alcohols. That's another way the lowlanders exploit these people. There are arrack stills in every village now. Palm toddy kept them floating along, but arrack destroys them." Costas made as if to hand the gourd back, but the toddy-tapper pushed it away, insistent. The man then took Pradesh by the hand and led him to a group of Kóya who had edged into the clearing and were sitting in the shade of a spreading tamarind tree. Pradesh glanced back. "I'll question them about the Maoists," he said. "I need to find out where they're operating." He squatted down beside the group, and Jack and Costas watched intently. At first his questions were met with silence, and then the toddy-tapper became animated, talking hurriedly, putting his fingers by his eyes, pulling them, making a face, then jabbering again, gesticulating at his wrists, his forearms, as if he were drawing on them. He took something out of a little bag on his loincloth and passed it to Pradesh. The other Kóya slunk back into the edge of the jungle, looking fearful, squatting on their haunches with their bows and spears. Pradesh asked several more questions, then put his hand on the man's shoulder and stood up, turning back to Jack and Costas with a look of concern on his face. "I have to go with him somewhere private. He won't talk here. You go to the beach. I'll meet you there."

Fifteen minutes later Jack and Costas were back beside the boat, sitting in the shade of the pontoon. The sun had been burning fiercely, but was now low in the western sky over the river gorge. They had about three hours of daylight left. Jack was tapping his fingers on the side of the pontoon, but then stopped himself. For once someone else was in control, and Jack was unaccustomed to it. But Pradesh seemed to have everything reined tight, and he knew better than Jack how long it would take to get to the jungle shrine and back out again. Jack relaxed slightly, and slid down the side of the pontoon, his elbows on the sand. He watched Costas in amused silence. Costas was sitting on the sand with his knees slightly bent, and the legs of his shorts flapping open. In the distance a river crab had spied a cozy nook, and was hurtling sideways toward him. At the last moment Costas arched upward and the crab shot under him and past the boat, disappearing off down the beach behind them at prodigious speed. Costas saw Jack watching him, and waved the gourd with an innocent look on his face. "What?"

"I think you might have had enough of that."

"I've only had two slurps. Anyway, I'm on holiday. On the beach. At last." He took another slurp and wiped his mouth, gasping. "Okay. Enough to take the edge off the disappointment, no more." He turned the gourd upside down on the sand, then took a long drink from his water bottle. "While we wait, Jack, fill me in. This guy Bebbie. What was he doing here? What was the rebellion all about?"

Jack leaned back and put his arms behind his head. He looked at the palms fringing the beach, and watched another toddy-tapper shimmy expertly down a trunk. He reached over and tapped the upturned gourd. "A tax on toddy. Totally unnecessary, hardly a significant revenue stream, but a massive source of contention for the tribal people. That's how so many colonial conflicts began. A simmering resentment, and then a small administrative blunder that takes catastrophic center stage. And in 1879, with war again in Afghanistan, an internal rebellion was the last thing the government wanted. The reaction was typical. Years of indifference and neglect of the jungle people were followed by heavy-handedness and inefficiency in putting down the rebellion. From the outset the British were hampered by poor knowledge of the people and the jungle conditions. That's where Bebbie comes in. There were many remarkable British officials in the Indian Civil Service, of high intellect and moral rectitude. Bebbie was a lower tier official, assigned to a backwater. For the tribals, there were some outsiders they worshipped, like their memory of the fabled prince Rama himself. Bebbie was assuredly not one of those."

A noise made them turn toward the jungle. It was a new sound, like chimes or distant gongs. It was hard to tell if it was the breeze through the trees, or real. Then it began in earnest, a drumbeat from the direction of the village, three deep beats, a silence, three more beats, intensifying as more drums joined in. Then they saw them, men in loincloths carrying long, double-ended drums, coming out of the jungle on either side of the path, then stepping back, then coming out again with each set of beats. Women appeared between them, wearing bells in their ears, shaking their heads vigorously. They stamped the earth in unison, gathering force with the drumbeat, swelling in numbers, going in and out in line between the drummers. Voices began rising and falling in a plaintive chant. Then the line parted and a man appeared wearing a bison skull on his head, wrapped around with a red sari and mounted with peacock feathers, the horns arching high and dripping red. More men with horns followed, forming a circle on the sand, stamping in and out in unison and chanting.

"Horns of the gaur," Jack murmured. "The other dreaded beast of the jungle. Looks like they've bloodied them already."

"Just with chickens, I hope," Costas said. "But it's still pretty damn terrifying. Add human sacrifice, and put yourself in the mind of a British soldier watching this from that river steamer in 1879. This would have looked like the vision of hell that all those Victorian pastors would have drummed into them as kids. These were heathen savages, and those horned men are a vision of the devil himself."

Pradesh came down the path through the line of drummers and strode toward them. The toddy-tapper had been with him, but stayed behind at the edge of the jungle. Pradesh glanced at his watch, then peered up at the sky, scanning the eastern horizon. "The bison dance," he said. "The first act of the festival. The toddy's flowing freely now. It's a good time for us to leave."

"Before they strip me and send me on a little hike in the jungle, you mean," Costas said.

"Any luck?" Jack asked.

"You saw what the toddy-tapper did with his hands, in the jungle clearing? He pulled the skin of his face to make his eyes slant. He said a man came here before the monsoon broke, about four months ago. He had eyes

275

like that."

"Katya's uncle?" Costas said.

"Could be," Jack murmured. "Hai Chen was Mongolian Chinese. Anything else?"

"The man told the Kóya he was a friend of Christoph von Fürer-Haimendorf. He was an anthropologist who came here with his wife in the 1930s, during the final years of British rule. They stayed in the jungle for several months, and championed the tribals' cause. Christoph befriended my father as a boy, and was always spoken of by the Kóya with great reverence."

"The tribals remember a visitor from almost eighty years ago?" Costas asked.

"Absolutely," Pradesh replied. "And they remember Lieutenant Howard, Jack's great-great-grandfather. In the months after the rebels had been defeated and the main Rampa Field Force had been withdrawn, Howard and his sappers remained behind to clean up and begin road building. Apparently, Howard went out of his way to help the villagers, improving water supply and sanitation, showing them tricks of construction. He was unlike the missionaries who occasionally came up the river. He told them the only gods they should worship were their own. They remembered that. He became ill with exhaustion, and they looked after him here, in this village. He was especially solicitous of the children, and made them toys while he was convalescing. And they remember the day the steamer came to take him away, the day he was told that his own son had died. He was inconsolable, and came out to this riverbank by himself, to the place where the rebels had cajoled the Kóya into carrying out the sacrificial ceremony that day in 1879. It was where they sacrificed the child. Perhaps the sight of that had most affected Howard.

Jack swallowed hard. "That sounds like him," he murmured. "He was devoted to his own children, the ones he had in the following years."

"But he never returned the sacred *vélpu* or the tiger gauntlet," Costas said.

"For some reason he and Wauchope decided to keep them," Jack replied. "Howard may have intended to go back to the jungle shrine and try to find a way back in, but after he was struck down by illness he never returned to the jungle."

Pradesh turned to Costas. "You asked about how the Kóya remember. Because they have no timeline, visitors of a hundred or a thousand years ago are described in the same terms, as 'in the time of their forefathers.' Eventually, those most distant take on the mantle of mythology, and some of them become gods."

"By claiming friendship with von Fürer-Haimendorf, Hai Chen was deploying the oldest technique in the anthropologists' book," Jack murmured. "Gain your subjects' confidence by claiming friendship with a revered visitor from the past. Hai Chen would have known that."

"Apparently, he spoke to them in the Khond language of the northern jungle, well enough for them to understand," Pradesh said. "The Kóya language is a dialect of Khond."

"That clinches it," Jack exclaimed. "Katya said her uncle was an accomplished linguist, and had made a study of the tribal languages when he first began exploring the jungle peoples of India. What else can they tell us?"

"He was interested in their mythology, in ancient traditions, their artifacts. The toddy-tapper told him about the *vélpus,* and the man pressed him to see one. Eventually the toddy-tapper produced his family *vélpu,* already removed from its bamboo container. Ever since the most sacred *vélpu,* the Lakkála Rámu, disappeared in 1879, the *vélpus* have lost a lot of their power, and the family *vélpu* is the least powerful. Even so, the other villagers disapproved, and that's why you saw them backing off in the jungle clearing just now when he produced this." Pradesh held up the object the toddy-tapper had given him, a coin. They peered at it, and Costas whistled. "I've seen those before. Our shipwreck in the Red Sea. It's Roman."

"An early Imperial denarius," Jack said, tak-

278

ing the coin and looking at it closely. "Not gold like the wreck coins, but silver. It's very worn, but the portrait's early Augustus, no doubt about it. Amazing."

"They're found all across southern India," Pradesh said. "We have a numismatist at Arikamedu who's making an exhaustive study of them. She knew about John Howard, as his boyhood collection of Roman coins from India was bequeathed to the Survey of India by his daughter. The coins are usually mint, uncirculated. They were exported by the Romans as bullion. This one was worn because it must have been handled for generations by the Kóya, probably as an ornament, before it gained sacred status and was hidden away as a *vélpu.* The toddy-tapper said that portrait was an image of Rama. He's watching us with eagle eyes over there. I've got to return it before we go."

"Rama," Jack mused. "Anything else?"

Pradesh squatted down. "There is something else. And it's disturbing." He paused. "The man, Hai Chen, arrived here just before the monsoon broke, and wanted to cover as much ground as he could before the jungle became impassable. They sent him with a guide to Rampa village, and from there he went on alone to see the shrine. None of the Kóya would go there with him."

"The cave you were talking about?" Costas said.

Pradesh nodded. "And then a few days later, others came, also like this." Pradesh drew his eyes back with his fingers.

"More Chinese," Jack said.

Pradesh nodded. "But they were different. There were seven of them, and they came by helicopter. They said they were mining prospectors. They were aggressive. The villagers were very apprehensive. They'd had prospectors out here before from the mining companies, and the Kóya hate them. The hills around here are rich in bauxite and the whole area is under threat. But there was something that especially terrified them. The men had tattoos on their forearms, all identical — it was an image of a tiger."

"A tiger," Jack repeated.

"The toddy-tapper was petrified. He thought the *konda devata* had come to punish him for revealing his *vélpu* to Hai Chen. He still thinks they're lurking in the jungle around the village, waiting for the moment to strike. And he has good reason to be apprehensive."

Jack felt suddenly uneasy. "Go on."

"These prospectors' approach to information gathering was slightly different. They grabbed one of the children, a little girl, and held a gun to her head. They wanted to know where the other Chinese man had gone. The anthropologist."

"And the toddy-tapper told them."

Pradesh nodded. "That was over three months ago. The Maoists came here and told them not to go near the shrine. They're used to the Maoists telling them to stay away from their camps, and the shrine's pretty well taboo for the Kóya anyway. But this time it was different. After the disappearance of the Chinese anthropologist, the toddy-tapper knew something else had gone on. Evil spirits had been awakened."

"What's the problem with sending in police troops?" Costas said. "Sounds like enough justification now."

Pradesh shook his head. "Nobody in government's going to buy this story. There's still an ingrained contempt for the tribals among the lowlanders who make up most of the regional government and judiciary, and if any word leaked out that they'd been harassing prospectors solely on the basis of a story from the Kóya there'd be hell to pay. There are powerful elements in government who would happily see the tribals dispossessed and these hills turned into a gigantic strip mine. The financial stakes are huge. Military intervention could only come on the back of Maoist violence in the jungle, and the Maoists are usually careful to avoid that. The jungle is their safe house. My father was murdered by the Maoists in Dowlaiswaram, not up here. If the Maoists shoot at troops it becomes a federal matter, and the next thing you know there would be helicopter gunships hosing down the jungle. Turning this place into a version of the Vietnam War will not help the tribal peoples. You have to tread very carefully. Officially, I'm here on holiday and the two chaps from our assault company who will be with us in the chopper are private bodyguards, employed by you."

"And what you really want to do is kill the Maoists yourself, in your own time," Costas said quietly. "For your father."

Jack glanced at Pradesh, who looked at the ground, saying nothing.

"And what about the anthropologist, Hai Chen?" Costas said.

Pradesh shook his head. "Not a sign of him since then."

The thudding of a helicopter filled the air, drowning out the drumbeat from the edge of the jungle. Pradesh took out his radio receiver and spoke rapidly in Hindi. The helicopter reared up over the river and backed off, dropping down on the opposite sandbank. Pradesh waved at the toddy-tapper, who was gesticulating at the helicopter. "I told them to land on the other side of the river. The Kóya deserve some leeway after the last time one of these landed here. And we don't want them losing control and rushing us."

Jack peered at the dancers. "They look a little too far gone to notice." He stood up and walked back across the sand to where he had tied the painter line. Costas marched off, gourd in hand, to where the toddy-tapper was standing. "I'm just going to say good-bye to my new friend."

"Don't let him whisk you off into the jungle," Jack said. "If you've got that tiger magic in you, we may need it too."

Costas shook hands with the man, pointing at the gourd approvingly. Jack followed, holding the line to the boat, and Pradesh joined them, handing the toddy-tapper the Roman coin. The man packaged it carefully in his little leather pouch, and tied it to his loincloth. "He doesn't seem to be fazed by the chopper," Costas said.

"Some of them are used to it. The Chinese aren't the first prospecting team to come up here. There have been others, multinationals. Sometimes the Kóya are contracted to work as guides. The prospectors pay them in bricks of hashish — it's the mining companies' way of giving something back, showing they really care."

Jack turned toward the toddy-tapper, thought for a moment then took off the Nikon binoculars he had slung around his neck. He had seen several of the Kóya eyeing them with curiosity earlier on. They would be of little use on the trip into the confines of the jungle. He passed them over. The man took them, handling them with care, looked closely at the lenses and the mechanism, then handed them back. He bowed his head to Jack, and spoke a few words to Pradesh.

"He said, if you have no need of them, then neither does he. He said he can see as far as he needs to."

Jack looked hard at the man, and slowly nodded. "Fair enough."

"Anthropology 101, Jack," Costas murmured.

Jack raised his eyebrows. "Yes?"

"Don't mess with the natives."

"Thanks, engineer."

Pradesh pointed at the helicopter. They hurried back down to the boat. He and Costas stood on either side, and Jack threw the painter line over the bow.

"Okay," Pradesh said. "Good to go?"

Costas stared at him, then at Jack. "You said it."

Jack slung his old khaki bag over his shoulder, reaching in to feel the Beretta in its holster. Something was going on, something bigger than he had imagined. He thought of Katya, and suddenly needed to talk to her. He glanced at his watch. Only four hours before the Lynx was due to pick them up from Rajahmundry and take them back to *Seaquest II.*

Costas glanced into the darkness of the jungle, then pointed at the pendant around Pradesh's neck. "I was wondering," he said. "Got any more of those tiger claws?"

Pradesh glanced at him, and began heaving at the boat. "You don't need one, remember? You've eaten tiger food. But don't worry. I won't walk you into a firefight. If there's any sign of trouble, my two sappers will shoot to kill."

"Sounds like a plan," Costas said. "Jack?"

"Let's do it."

10

"Look below us now. Quick, before they vanish. In the jungle."

Jack peered out of the open side door of the helicopter, feeling the downdraft of the rotor against his helmet. Costas did the same on the other side. At first they saw nothing but the lushness of the jungle, draped over the rugged contours of the hills like a thick pile carpet. Then Jack realized there was movement in the gloom below the canopy, a ripple like a spreading shadow, as if the Godavari River behind them had burst its banks and was tumbling through the ravines and gullies of the jungle. He saw individual black shapes in the lead, pounding through the jungle clearings. He heard nothing except the helicopter, but he sensed a rumble like thunder, the sound of a herd of bison as they rolled through the jungle toward some unknown destination.

"They're gaur," Pradesh said through the intercom from the co-pilot's seat. "The Kóya fear them almost as much as the tigers. With a herd this size around, that's another reason for avoiding the jungle path and taking the helicopter."

Jack leaned back inside. He and Costas were strapped into the door seats facing aft, and Jack held on to the mounting where the door gun would once have been. The helicopter was an old Huey, ex–Indian army but now used as a workhorse for supplying remote villages in the jungles of the Eastern Ghats. It had been out of the question for Pradesh to request a helicopter from his own unit, with markings that would have alarmed the Kóya and the Maoist terrorists, and the IMU Lynx looked too much like one of the machines that brought in the mining prospectors. But Jack felt they were adequately protected for the mission at hand, a quick foray that Pradesh hoped would take them less than two hours, so they could be out before sunset. On the fold-down seats opposite were two of Pradesh's sappers, cheerful men from the Madras Engineering Group Assault Company. Each had a weapons case strapped down on the floor in front of them. Jack looked at their faces, at the moustaches and fierce eyes, and wondered if they too had ancestors who had been up here before, men who might have been with his own great-great-grandfather on the jungle path below them on that fateful day in 1879.

"We're only ten minutes away now," Pradesh said. "The clearing with the shrine is ahead of us, and the village of Rampa is about a kilometer to the east, where you can see the smoke rising above the jungle." The two sappers quickly opened their weapon cases, taking out AK-74 assault rifles and pushing in the banana-shaped magazines. They cocked the rifles and held them on their knees, muzzles facing outward. One of them motioned for Jack and Costas to slide their seats along the floor runnels toward the center of the cabin, away from the open doors. Pradesh leaned around, checking that they had moved. "Just in case we encounter any incoming rounds," he said. "According to the Kóya we just spoke to, the clearing hasn't been used as a regular camp by the Maoists for some time now, but the Kóya have been too fearful to go there themselves. They said the Rampa villagers heard a lot of shooting on the day the Chinese mining prospectors went there. There's no telling what we'll find."

"So what's with Rampa village, the name?" Costas said.

"It's derived from Rama, the prince who became a focus for Hindu worship," Pradesh replied. "According to the *Ramayana,* the ancient Sanskrit epic, Prince Rama traveled south from Oudh and spent ten years in exile in the jungle. The place we're going to, the shrine, has always been known as the temple

288

of Rama."

Jack pressed the intercom on his helmet. "I've been thinking about that since we saw that Roman coin from the *vélpu.* When the Romans were at Arikamedu, the most common local name for them was *yavanas,* westerners. But the name *raumanas* also crops up in Brahmin literature. It may just be coincidence."

"Come on, Jack," Costas said. "When have you ever believed in coincidences?"

"It's a fascinating possibility," Pradesh said. "As a Hindu, I took the *Ramayana* at face value. That seemed to account for it. But I know from my Kóya ancestry that a shrine to Rama is completely at odds with jungle beliefs. They have no shrines to their gods, no holy sanctums, not even sacred colors. Their gods are all around them, pure immanence. As Hindus we accept stories of interlopers, as our religion is all-encompassing. But for the animist beliefs of the Kóya, it's a different story. If it wasn't Prince Rama himself, it must have been an equally powerful presence who came here and left a mark."

"Maybe another interloper," Costas said.

"Okay. Here we are now." The helicopter slowed down, angled slightly to port and began to fly a wide circle around a misty patch in the jungle. Jack could see where they had flown up over a ravine, the rugged jungle flank rising up on either side over patches of dull red where the mud must have slipped during the monsoon. Through the dense foliage he could make out the flow of the stream that had carved the ravine, among jumbled masses of boulders exposed in the bed. It was the only obvious route up from the river fifteen kilometers to the south-west, and it must have been where Howard and Wauchope came with their sappers in 1879. They would have been completely exposed to fire from above, and it was hard to see how they were not cut down by the rebels. But Jack remembered Pradesh's story of the bamboo *vélpu,* Howard's promise to the *muttadar.* It was the only explanation for how they could have got through unscathed.

The downdraft from the rotor cleared a swathe through the air, and Jack could see where the stream skirted the east side of the clearing after disgorging from another tumble of boulders that had rolled down from the jungle flank beyond. He could see the trickling waterfall where the boulders extended out into the clearing. In front were three slabs of enormous size, one of them resting on the other two like a gigantic prehistoric lintel.

"That's the shrine," Pradesh said, pointing. "The entrance is under the lintel at the front, but it was sealed off by the earthquake after the two British officers came here, the day the most sacred *vélpu* disappeared forever.

My grandfather said the earthquake was retribution from the *konda devata,* the tiger spirit. The Kóya were already terrified of this place — tigers come here to drink from the stream at night. After the earthquake, hardly any Kóya ever came here again, even into the clearing."

"So how do we get inside?" Costas said.

"My grandfather said there was another entrance through the waterfall at the back. But you have to be very small, lithe. He said he had once done it as a boy, and seen terrifying demons inside. The Kóya elders in Rampa village told the same story to their children. We sneaked up here at night, but the story of demons kept us all from trying to get inside."

"Waterfall archaeology," Costas said. "That's a new one on me."

Pradesh dangled a cord behind his seat. "There is another way."

Costas twisted around to look, his eyes suddenly gleaming. "Detonator cord! Now that's my kind of archaeology."

The pilot came over the center of the clearing, pointing the nose of the helicopter toward the boulders some fifty meters away. He leveled out and began to descend. The rotor had cleared away the mist below them but now kicked up a swirl of dust and leaves. Jack leaned toward the doorway to peer out. Suddenly there was a massive clang and the helicopter lurched sideways, the edge of the door nearly hitting Jack's face. There were more clangs and the crack of gunfire, a jolting noise even through the headphones. The air was split by a series of violent snaps as bullets whizzed through the open doors of the helicopter, missing them by inches. Jack instinctively put his left arm out to keep Costas down. The pilot pulled up on the collective and the helicopter lurched up and away. Jack glimpsed figures below, three of them, in combat fatigues and red bandanas. The pilot leveled out again and the two sappers knelt beside the open door and shouldered their rifles. They opened fire on full automatic, pouring rounds down on their assailants. They stopped, looked out for a second, then fired three rounds each, aiming carefully this time. They snapped off their magazines and quickly reloaded. Jack saw the three figures lying sprawled in the dust, surrounded by dark red stains expanding into a puddle on the clearing floor.

"Maoists," Pradesh exclaimed. "My guess is, not a reception party for us though. There's no way they could have known we were coming. This was an advance party for a larger group, probably a few hours away in the jungle. They usually do their recce in threes. They panicked when they saw we were about to land."

"What do we do now?" Jack said, his heart

still pounding with the adrenaline.

"We stick to the plan. You've seen what my two chaps can do. Chances are the rest of the Maoists are far enough away not to have heard the gunfire. Noise is quickly absorbed in the jungle. The pilot will drop us and then disappear south, so as not to arouse suspicion. The Maoists will be used to seeing this old bird flying to and from the villages with supplies."

Pradesh nodded at the pilot, who made a quick descent this time, bouncing the skids on the hard surface of the clearing. The two sappers were out before the helicopter had settled, kicking the three bodies and checking the perimeter. Jack and Costas unbuckled themselves and stepped out, ducking and running from the whirling rotor. Pradesh followed them, carrying his bag, then the engine revved up to a whine and the Huey rose in a cloud of dust, tilting forward as soon as it cleared tree height and heading off to the south. A few moments later the noise was gone. Jack stood up, shouldering his khaki bag and checking Costas. They took off their helmets and piled them together. The dust was settling on the three dead bodies a few meters away, sopping up the blood. Jack was still coursing with adrenaline. He could see that Pradesh was wired up too, his Magnum revolver held out in front of him, tense and poised like a hunting animal. The whole action had taken only a few seconds, but was replaying in Jack's mind in slow motion. It had happened to him before, when he had been inches from death. He glanced at Costas, who was walking toward a rock outcrop on the jungle fringe, about thirty meters from the entrance to the boulder shrine. The outcrop had evidently been used as a shelter, and the Maoists' rucksacks were there. Costas squatted down, peering at the bags, then at the ground.

"Watch for snakes," Pradesh called out. Costas held up a long, decaying skin, shed from a cobra. "Got you." He let it drop, swatted a mosquito and then picked something else up. "Check this out. Those Maoists had Kalashnikovs, and there are plenty of casings around. In fact, too many for what we've just had. It looks like they've used this place as a shooting gallery before, fairly recently to judge from the state of the brass. And look at this. It's a much older casing. Looks like it was from an elephant gun. Big-game hunters, maybe. There are quite a few of these casings lying around too, but trampled into the ground. Must have been a long time ago."

Jack joined him. "Well I'll be damned," he said. "That's a .577, Snider-Enfield. The rifles the Madras Sappers had in 1879."

"You're kidding." Costas picked up another, looked closely at the rim, then grunted. "Battlefield archaeology. They did it with

294

cartridges from Custer's Last Stand at the Little Bighorn. You can reconstruct fields of fire, the flow of the battle." Costas got up, looking around. "Maybe this rock was where Bebbie met his end. Maybe this was where Howard and Wauchope found him. With the rock behind, it would have been the best shelter around, a defensive position against the rebels while Bebbie and the sappers waited for rescue."

"I think I know what those three terrorists were doing when we surprised them," Pradesh called out. "It wasn't just a recce. They were cleaning up." He had advanced around the back of the rock, his revolver at the ready. Costas and Jack cautiously followed. The jungle smell became stronger, mustier, different from the rusty smell of fresh blood around the bodies in the clearing. Jack knew what it was even before he rounded the corner. A mass of bones and ragged clothes had been pushed into a crevice in the rock. Some were bleached white, but there was still hair to be seen and the limbs were still articulated, with sinews between the joints. Pradesh peered closer, holding his nose, then stepped back, gasping for breath. "Well, that solves one mystery. These are our Chinese, the ones the Kóya saw arriving three months ago. Look, you can see the word *IN-TACON* on their shirts. That's the mining company. They must have been ambushed by the Maoists. That explains all the Kalashnikov cartridges." He picked up a stick, and used it to lift a flap of clothing. "And look at this. Exactly as the Kóya described." It was a section of skin still intact on the arm of one of the skeletons. They could see the remains of a tattoo, probably what had preserved the skin. Jack felt a wave of apprehension. So far it had all been talk, speculation. This was real. The image staring out at them was smudged, half rotted away, but there was no doubt about it. *A tiger tattoo.*

Pradesh waved to the two sappers and pointed so they could see where the bodies were, and then put up six fingers and drew his hand across his throat. He got up, and Jack and Costas followed him back out into the clearing past the three fresh bodies. Suddenly there was an earsplitting crack. Flecks of blood flew off Costas' shoulder, and Jack just had time to see one of the bodies with a pistol raised before Pradesh aimed and fired. The first round took off the top of the man's head, sending brain and bone spattering behind. The man's legs drummed against the ground, but he was already dead. Pradesh fired round after round, slowly and methodically, letting the big revolver return from the recoil and aiming carefully, reducing the man's head to a bloody pulp. Jack reached out and held Pradesh's arm in an iron grip, pulling it away. He fired once more, the last

296

chamber, the bullet ricocheting off the rock behind. "Enough," Jack said. Pradesh turned and stared at him, wide-eyed, enraged. Jack could smell the fresh sweat, the adrenaline. He eased his grip and stared Pradesh straight in the eyes. "You got him," Jack said quietly. "For your father." Jack quickly turned to check Costas, who was dabbing blood from a graze on his shoulder. He looked as imperturbable as ever. "You okay?"

Costas nodded, then turned to Pradesh. "Yeah. And thanks."

Pradesh took a deep breath, nodded then went over and kicked the other two bodies, reloading his revolver as he did so. The two sappers kept their rifles trained on the bodies until he signaled them, and then they returned to the edge of the clearing where they had taken up position before, concealed beside the path entrance. Pradesh snapped his fingers, pointed two fingers at his eyes, tapped his watch and waved toward the jungle. One of the sappers held his rifle at the ready and disappeared down the path. "He's doing a recce," Pradesh said. "If those three Maoists were an advance party, the main group will be following them. They only ever use the existing paths. They're not jungle people at all. The path comes from Chodavaram, past another of the Maoist hangouts. They move between places, a few nights here, a few there. They think they're like Bollywood heroes, like Robin Hood. But they're cowards and murderers and their ideology stinks. I loathe them."

"So we see." Costas grunted, fishing out a bandage shell dressing from Jack's bag and plastering it on his wound.

Jack put his hand on Pradesh's shoulder. "You okay?"

"Couldn't be better."

"You just killed a man."

"That wasn't a man. And it wasn't the first time. I've been in Kashmir. I shot a Pakistani army engineer who was trying to blow up a mountain bridge we'd just built. They shot at us, we shot at them. I did it for my men. I could have chosen to miss him, but I didn't. That time, I threw up. Not this time."

Jack nodded. He had made the same rationalizations himself, and he knew what Pradesh was doing. His ears were ringing, from the adrenaline and the gunfire. They needed to focus on their objective, to keep tight. He gestured toward the boulders where the water was cascading down into the stream. Pradesh took a deep breath, glanced at the corpses, then handed Jack his revolver. He opened his bag and took out a small slab of C-4 explosive wrapped in plastic, and the coil of detonator cord he had shown them in the helicopter. "The obstruction's one small boulder, lodged in the entrance passage," he said. "If I can split it, we may be able to get in." He led them over the clearing to the entrance. The tumble of boulders extended at least fifteen meters out from the face of the waterfall. It looked like an ancient megalithic tomb, yet it was completely natural, the result of a massive landslide far back in history that had eroded away and left the tumble of rock exposed. It was taller and wider than it had seemed from the helicopter, at least twice Jack's height at the entrance. The two massive upright boulders and the lintel formed a passage beneath, blocked up with the boulder Pradesh had described. Rock fragments were strewn on the ground in front. Pradesh knelt down and picked one up. "This is fresh," he said. "Someone's had a go at that boulder with a pick, pretty recently."

Costas knelt down beside him. "The Maoists?"

Pradesh shook his head. "More likely the prospectors. The Maoists may have caught them in the act and gunned them down, or maybe the prospectors gave up here and tried to find another way in."

"Or it could have been Katya's uncle," Jack murmured.

"Whoever it was, it makes the job easier for us." Pradesh crawled in a few meters to the wedged boulder, and packed the explosive in a space underneath. He pressed in the detonator cord, then wound off the spool and backed out of the entrance, carrying on across the clearing about ten meters to another large rock protruding from the jungle fringe. Jack and Costas followed him, and squatted behind the rock. Pradesh clipped on a small electronic detonator, then raised his arm in warning to the sapper who had been glancing at him from his position on the far side of the clearing. Pradesh looked at Jack and Costas, patting his ear with one hand. "Fire in the hole."

They crouched close together behind the rock with their hands over their ears. Pradesh clicked the detonator and a second later there was a crack and a thud. They looked up, and saw a cloud of dust at the passage entrance. Pradesh leapt forward to inspect his work, waiting outside a few moments for the dust to settle before cautiously crawling in. "All I needed was enough explosive to crack the boulder," he said, his voice muffled. "It's perfect."

"Nice job," Costas said, peering in behind. "There's a hole about a meter square. It's wide enough even for you."

"What's that supposed to mean?" Costas grumbled.

"It means you're invited in." Jack took his halogen diving flashlight from his bag, and knelt under the lintel. Pradesh was about six inches shorter than Jack, lithely built, and the hole was a little less generous than he had

300

described. Jack eased himself over the jagged surfaces where the rock had cracked with the explosive, and pulled himself through the hole. The rock wall he felt beyond was smooth, and he knew he was inside the passageway. He heard curses and grumbles as Costas followed, and then a ripping sound. "My shirt. My special Hawaiian shirt."

"I'll buy you another. When we get there." Jack held out his hand, and Costas grasped it, heaving himself through. Jack stumbled forward in the gloom behind Pradesh, seeing only a flickering pool of light in the darkness ahead. Jack lingered for a moment, glancing back through the hole into the jungle clearing. The setting sun flashed off the wet palm leaves on the far side, as if the jungle were suddenly ignited in flame. Jack could still see the sapper squatting against the rock halfway down the clearing, cradling his rifle, staring intently in his direction. He saw the bodies in the dust, and thought of Rebecca. Thank God he hadn't allowed her to come along. He had almost said yes. He glanced at his watch. They had an hour, no more. He turned back and looked into the darkness of the passageway. He felt the rush of excitement he always felt at the threshold of the unknown. He put a hand on Costas' shoulder. He remembered Katya, his promise to find out what had happened to her uncle. She would be waiting. They needed to get cracking.

11

Lake Issyk-Kul, Kyrgyzstan

Katya Svetlanova leaned back against the boulder, shifted slightly to find a more comfortable position and stretched out her legs on the hard baked ground. She put down her digital SLR camera and tightened her long dark hair in the band behind her neck. She looked at the boulder beside her. Swirling forms had been carved into the rock — snow leopards, leaping ibex, a mysterious solar symbol. The carvings had once been painted in primal colors, in blood and ochre, but were now barely discernible, eroded by the wind and scorched by the sun. They had been carved more than two thousand years ago by the Scythian hunters who had roamed these steppelands, who had sat where she was and gazed out over the lake and the mountains. They were ancestors of the Kyrgyz who still lived up here, her own mother's ancestors, nomads who knew the power of the shaman. It was a sacred place, a burial ground, where she could still sense the nomad smells of horses and mutton and sweat, yet it was also a place where others had passed through, extraordinary people — adventurers, traders, warriors, people from immeasurably far to the east and the west. Somewhere there must be an imprint of their passing. She had been photographing the carvings, taking advantage of the long shadows of the late afternoon. It had been a hard day, as every day was out here. Each new boulder offered the promise of an extraordinary discovery, yet the one she craved the most was still eluding her.

She swayed slightly, and the carvings came in and out of view, like a hologram. She was dead tired. It had been five relentless weeks, and now there were only a few days left. She remembered how long the great explorers of the Silk Route had spent searching for lost treasures — decades, a lifetime. Most never found what they had been seeking — fabled lost kingdoms, Alexander's treasure, the Seventh Preciosity, treasures forever just beyond their grasp. Maybe the shamans were right, and this place truly was a heavenly domain, its greatest revelations only attainable to those who took one step farther into the afterlife. Maybe archaeology was really like this, and her time with Jack Howard and IMU hunting for Atlantis had been a magical whirlwind, seducing her into thinking that there was more to life than a career in the

Institute of Palaeography in Moscow, studying other people's discoveries. Jack had warned her, but she needed to find out for herself. She needed to find out whether she had finder's luck.

She took a deep swig from her water bottle, then looked down to where the remarkable blue water of Issyk-Kul lapped the rocky shoreline only a stone's throw away. It was like an inland sea, stretching off to the Tien Shan Mountains to the south, their snow-capped peaks forming a breathtaking backdrop.

Somewhere beyond lay Afghanistan, the forbidding mass of the Hindu Kush Mountains, the passes that led down to India — the Khyber Pass to the east, the Bolan to the west. But the Tien Shan Mountains girt the lake like the battlements of some impregnable castle, and it seemed inconceivable that anyone should have passed through them. Always the eye was drawn east and west, along the Silk Road — the greatest trade route the world had ever known. To the east, the mountains dipped toward the Taklamakan Desert and the heartland of China, toward the fabled city of Xian. To the west, the route led through Kyrgyzstan to Uzbekistan and Persia, and then to the shores of the Mediterranean. As the setting sun cast a rosy tint across the lake, coloring it in streaks of red, Katya shifted around to look at the edge of the canyon that led up from the west to the lake. She always felt uneasy coming up that road, as she knew ancient travelers would have. It was a place her Kyrgyz grandmother had warned her about, haunted by demon-warriors on dark steeds who lurked in every ravine, ready to devour any traveler who strayed into their domain. Katya knew these nomad myths for what they were, folk memories of conquest and horror, of the Huns, the Mongols, human hurricanes that swept through from the east. They were her ancestors too, not of her mother but of her father. She had thought of him lately, the modern-day warlord, of seeing his violent death in the Black Sea two years before, with Jack at her side. She had tried to remember her father before temptation had caught him up and swept him away, like the tides of greed and war that had once coursed through these mountain passes. It was in her blood too, but she could not forgive him, and she knew the weight of this place lay in her search for redemption, in her yearning to find strength in her Kyrgyz ancestry, to hear the words of the shaman in these rock carvings.

"Katya!" A rangy figure appeared above the boulders a hundred yards away. "We're ready." She sprang to her feet, waved and picked up her camera. She loved seeing Altamaty, his bounding enthusiasm. She had not yet told him what she was really after up here.

She was still wary of goalposts, uncertain what failure could do to her. But she suddenly felt revitalized. Standing up, she could see the enormity of their task, a sea of boulders stretching for kilometers along the shore of the lake, and extending for hundreds of meters up the mountain slope where they had been dislodged and brought down over the centuries by flood and earthquake. She and Altamaty had documented almost three hundred carvings already, yet there were dozens of square kilometers still to explore, each boulder to be painstakingly examined, half of them requiring excavation from the rock-hard earth. Maybe she had bitten off more than she could chew. She remembered Jack again, his offer of a research position at IMU. She would have complete freedom, unlimited resources and could continue to be based out here. But she was the only one in the Institute in Moscow who could stand up for her colleagues against the bureaucracy and corruption. She was her father's daughter — her father of the old days, the professor and art historian who had founded the Institute. In truth her feelings had been too raw, and she had found it impossible to accept anything from Jack. Her father had become everything she stood against, a scion of the antiquities black market, a warlord who had taken on the trappings of his ancestors. He had become her enemy, and Jack had destroyed him. But she still had a fire within her, the fierce loyalty of a daughter, the tribal bonding of a warrior clan. Seeing Jack at the Transoxiana conference three months before had brought it all back. She needed to find her own peace before she took any outstretched hand.

She slung her camera, and began scrambling over the boulders. She remembered something else Jack had told her. *You need luck, but you also need to take risks, to be willing to put everything behind a gut instinct.* For Jack that meant committing research ships, his team, Costas, all the paraphernalia of underwater exploration. She looked at the boulders extending in every direction like a giants' cemetery, and at her little tent by the lake. Out here she needed a small army of fieldworkers, and a camp like a military forward operating base. She stopped and took a deep breath. Maybe the time had come to accept that offer. She had not let herself down. She and Altamaty had done all they humanly could. She needed to contact Jack anyway, to find out if he had made any progress in locating her uncle in the jungle. She had been nagged by anxiety for weeks now, and she needed to know. And she wanted to hear his voice. She would set up the satellite phone that evening.

An engine coughed to life and settled into the chugging rumble of a diesel four-cylinder.

Katya crested a rise and saw Altamaty ahead, his *cholpak* felt hat bobbing above the boulders. He was sitting astride their sole piece of mechanical equipment, a venerable British Nuffield tractor that had somehow found its way up from India into central Asia, part of a reinvigorated Silk Route trade that had come with the fall of the Soviet Union. Katya had become quite fond of it, despite the roar and the belches of black smoke. It was their warhorse, and as long as it fired up there was still hope. She jumped from rock to rock and came down in the small open space in front of the tractor, holding up her hand to Altamaty as she cast an eye over the chain and protective leather strap that extended from the tractor's bucket around a half-buried boulder. It had become their end-of-day ritual: Altamaty would maneuver the tractor to a promising boulder they had flagged earlier, near one of the rough tracks that ran up from the lake. She eyed today's candidate. In this case, the boulder that needed moving had fallen against a promising stone, and the space between had filled with hard earth which Altamaty had spent most of the afternoon digging out to get the chain around the rock.

Katya squatted down, inspecting the chain and the horsehide wrapped around it to protect the surface of the rock. The horsehide was getting frayed, but would be fine for today. Providing the chain held. She looked at the slack line of links leading to the tractor. Altamaty had salvaged the chain from an old patrol boat rusting in the shallows nearby, a legacy from the time when the Soviets had used the lake as a secret naval testing base. He had trained here himself as a marine conscript in the 1980s before being sent to the Soviet war in Afghanistan. He said he trusted old Soviet technology more than he did new Russian, even if it was rusty. Katya had to take his word for it. She stood, gave him a thumbs-up then retreated a safe distance over the boulders. She crouched behind one. Altamaty crouched too, behind a barrier of salvaged metal plates he had rigged in front of the steering wheel as protection if the chain should break. Katya put up her hand as a signal, then let it drop. She ducked her head and crossed her fingers. It was like scratching a lottery card each time, and usually about as successful. But this could be the one. They were close to the western defile, the eroded canyon that led up to the lake. If they were ever going to find an inscription from a traveler this would be the place, where the caravans would rest and recuperate, not up the slope where most of the Scythian petroglyphs had been found.

She shut her eyes tight. She heard Altamaty put the tractor in reverse gear, slowly lower the throttle lever until the engine was a roaring crescendo and then gently release the clutch. The entire surface of the ground seemed to throb. She opened her eyes and watched the tractor inch backward, a meter, then two. It came to a halt, and reared upward until the front wheels were off the ground, and then the noise abated and it lurched back down. Altamaty stood up and waved. Katya got to her feet, and saw that the boulder had been pulled upright, jamming against another rock to its rear. There was no way of pulling it out farther. But the rock they were trying to uncover looked accessible, covered only by a layer of loose dirt. Altamaty pulled on the hand brake, leaving the engine in idle, and jumped down with a trowel and brush in his hands. By the time Katya came over he was already in the hole cleaning the rock. It had clearly once been upright, and been pushed over by the boulder they had just moved, probably dislodged in a flash flood. She saw that the exposed surface was flat, at least a meter across in both directions. She held her camera at the ready. It looked perfect. But she steeled herself for disappointment. Her colleagues at the Institute had told her it was a wild-goose chase. Bactrians and Sogdians, the traders who passed through here, did not even carve stone inscriptions. But then she remembered Jack. He said you had a feeling, impossible to describe. She crossed her fingers tight.

Altamaty stood up, his back to her, blocking her view. She put her right hand on his faded old combat jacket. She realized she was bunching it up, holding it tight in her fist. For a moment they were still. Then she realized he was trembling, shaking. She had held him before, but never felt this. *He was laughing.* She relaxed completely, all the tension gone, let her hand drop, grinned insanely and began to shake with laughter herself, the first time since she could remember. Something had let go inside her, and she had not even seen the rock yet. Altamaty turned, and she saw his craggy, handsome face beaming at her. "I'm not a scholar of Latin," he said in Kyrgyz. "And I've never been west of Afghanistan, but when I was a boy I read all the books I could find on the Romans. I recognize that."

She followed his finger, then gasped and put her hand back on his shoulder, steadying herself. She knelt down, and looked hard. She remembered Jack again. *Those first few moments are crucial. You might never see it again. Forget the euphoria. Be a scientist.* With the sun low in the sky the contrast was perfect, and even the slightest undulation on the surface of the rock was visible. She quickly took a dozen photographs, using three different settings. She remained stock-still, fearful that the image would disappear.

It was an eagle. She pulled a clipboard out of her bag, and flipped through the pages until she found the right one. She was looking at a drawing made by her uncle in a cave in Uzbekistan, more than four hundred kilometers to the west of here. Beside the drawing was Jack's handwriting, notes made when they had pored over the drawing at the conference three months ago. She looked at the stone again, and back at the clipboard. There was no doubt about it. It was the same. *Carved by the same hand.* She stood up, staggering slightly. "I've got to go back to the yurt," she said, her voice shaking. "I need to get to the satellite phone."

"What is it?" Altamaty said. "What have we found?"

She looked at his weatherworn features, the beguiling blue eyes. She hugged him tight for a moment. She could smell his sheepskin jerkin, the tang of sweat, feel his stubble against her cheek. She felt extraordinarily good. She let go, and shouldered her bag. She also felt extraordinarily tired. She needed to make that call before she collapsed. But she wanted Altamaty to hear it first. "In all of your reading about the Romans," she said, "did you ever come across the story of Crassus' lost legionaries?"

12

Jack glanced back one last time through the entrance of the cave into the jungle clearing, and then flashed his torch over the wall of the tunnel. There was just enough room for him to stand upright behind Costas and Pradesh. He saw the dark green of algae, and maroon streaks that could have been some other form of growth. There was a strong smell of damp and decay, mixed in with odors that had crept in from the jungle outside. Pradesh aimed his flashlight along the wall ahead of them, then drew back, gasping. A garish shape had come into view, carved into the side of the boulder on their left, its head at their level. It was a fearsome demon, with popping eyes, a hooked beak and deadly fangs. Jack stepped up, panning his flashlight. "Incredible," he murmured. "It's got wings, like a griffin. I'd have said this was Persian, or carved by someone who'd spent a lot of time staring at images like this. Pradesh, I know ancient Indian sculpture is a passion of yours. Got any ideas?"

Pradesh touched the stone. "I persuaded my engineering tutors it was a good way of studying lithics technology, but really I was just as interested in the art." He stared at the demon. "It's a generic form. There's a lot in common between Persian and Indian art. But there's something distinctive about this, confident, not quite like anything I've seen before. You may be right. It could have been done by someone familiar with Persian monumental sculpture, maybe from the Parthian period."

Costas put his hand cautiously on the bulbous eye, then quickly removed it. "No wonder the Kóya never came in here," he murmured.

"Now look at the scene behind it," Pradesh said.

Jack peered at the wall beyond the demon's tail, angling his light. He saw more carving. It was shallow, but the image was clear. He drew in his breath sharply. It was some kind of narrative scene, with many human figures. He saw heads on poles, decapitated, with knives suspended beneath them. People were tied in front. Below them was a mottled strip of dull red, speckled with pyrites, evidently a mineral extrusion in the rock. It was as if the sculptor had positioned his image above the mineral to take advantage of it, to make it appear like a pool of blood. *Human blood.*

314

There was no doubt about it. "A sacrificial scene," he murmured. "A *meriah* sacrifice."

Pradesh nodded. "Yet not carved by a native. There was never any tradition of stone carving among the Kóya. And look. There are older carvings underneath."

Beneath the image, faintly, Jack could see another carving, much older, only discernible as he angled the flashlight to and fro. It was a cluster of concentric circles, about a meter across. In the center were four small parallel lines extending from a line like the head of a garden rake. It looked as if it should be symmetrical, with the same rake shape on the other side, but the superimposed carving of the sacrificial scene had obscured it. Pradesh looked closely. "The symbol of the labyrinth," he murmured. "They're found elsewhere in India and in central Asia, some in caves like this. The oldest ones are Neolithic, at least five thousand years old. Most of them have a stylized rectilinear shape in the middle, but I've never seen one as complex as this."

Costas reached out and touched the carving. He looked intently at Jack. "Correct me if I'm wrong."

"Incredible," Jack whispered. "The Atlantis symbol." He had been staring at it the day before, on the front cover of the monograph in his cabin on *Seaquest II*. He panned the light to and fro. It created a bizarre image, almost holographic, with the labyrinth appearing and disappearing beneath the shocking images of sacrifice. He wondered whether those who had carved the age-old symbol of a founder civilization were themselves interlopers, witness to primeval scenes of horror that some later artist would one day carve over their sacred symbol, half-obliterating it. The superimposition seemed to draw the ancient image closer, make it real. *A labyrinth, hot with human blood.*

"There's more. Lots more." Pradesh advanced cautiously down the passageway, his shoulders stooped, and then squatted down about five meters ahead of them. Jack and Costas joined him, and watched as he panned his light over the walls. "It's the same style as those sacrificial images, but we're not looking at a narrative here," he said. "There's a lingam, a phallus, the symbol of Shiva. And on the opposite wall you can see a coiled cobra, its head facing the entrance, its tongue flickering out. That could be a Hindu symbol too, but snake-gods are also relics of pre-Aryan cults. Remember back at Bebbie's monument, the fear the Kóya had of the *giringar,* the cobra spirit of the jungle? This carving would have put the fear of the gods in them. I think these two carvings were gateway guardians, to keep people out."

They advanced a few meters beyond the carvings, and Pradesh stopped again, moving

316

his light over the ceiling. It was painted deep blue, in places thick like lacquer, elsewhere patchy where the pigment had crumbled away. "The color of Shiva," Pradesh murmured. "In Hindu imagery, blue signifies eternity." He reached up and touched the rock, and then rubbed his fingers where some of the pigment had come away. "It's lapis lazuli. That's what they used to make blue pigment. They ground it up to make a paste. You'd never have seen anything as precious as lapis from Afghanistan traded up here in the jungle, so the artist must have brought it with him."

Jack reached up and put his palm on the ceiling, on a patch where the blue was still as thick as enamel. He remembered what his grandfather had told him about the little carved elephant in his chest of family artifacts. Pradesh had said it too. *Lapis lazuli, the color of immortality.*

They moved on. The passageway opened up into a chamber, about eight meters across. It was covered with carvings, an extraordinary jumble of human and animal forms, strange symbols and monstrous beings. Pradesh panned his flashlight around. "I recognize some of these. There's Vishnu, striding across a wall, vanquishing a demon. And Parvati, wife of Shiva, with her enraptured gaze, picked out in red. And Padmapani, bearer of the lotus, with her swaying torso. She's sup-

317

posed to radiate serenity, tranquility."

"And an elephant," Costas interrupted excitedly, pointing at a pillar carved as a trunk, with bulbous eyes and flapping ears at the top. "Odd though," he said. "With those ears, I'd swear that was an African elephant, not Indian. The type more familiar to someone in the ancient world of the Mediterranean, who'd maybe seen them in the amphitheater in Rome."

Pradesh nodded, then pointed at two other pillar carvings alongside. "Those are Buddhist stupas, with bulls on top. And there's another one, with a spoked wheel. And look at the wall behind us. Crowded figures, *bodhisattvas,* enlightened beings, turbaned, bejeweled, moustached. And check out the grotesque dwarflike creatures. They're male *yakśas* and female *yakśīs* figures, nature deities of the ancient religions, much older than Hinduism. The large one that looks like a Buddha is Kubera, a *yakśa* who was venerated as the god of wealth, the guardian spirit of treasure."

"It's all carved by the same hand," Jack said, looking around. "The same style, the same techniques."

"The figures are familiar to me, but the style isn't," Pradesh murmured. "I haven't seen anything like this in southern India."

"It's reminiscent of Gandharan art," Jack said. "The art of ancient Bactria, the kingdom

318

founded by Alexander the Great's successors in Afghanistan. A fusion of Indian and Greek styles."

"But here, it's not so much a fusion of styles," Pradesh added. "It's a fusion of Indian *images* with a foreign style. It's as if someone from a completely different artistic tradition is trying to copy what he's seen in India, maybe in Persia too, but using his own techniques and conventions."

Jack traced his fingers over the elephant trunk. "This is technically skilled work, but not distinguished. If I were to make a comparison with the Graeco-Roman world, I'd say it was done by a jobbing sculptor, the kind who did sarcophagi, household altars, inscriptions, routine architectural decoration. An artisan more than an artist."

"There's something not right in all this," Pradesh said, looking around.

"You mean the whole place is out of sync with the jungle?" Costas said. "I was thinking that. What you were saying earlier. The spirits, the gods of the jungle. The Kóya have no need to represent their gods. They see them already."

"That's one problem. But even if you buy into the idea that all this Hindu and Buddhist and animist worship did happen here, it's still not right."

"Go on," Jack said.

"When I was seconded to the Survey of

319

India two years ago, my first posting was to Badami, a cave complex about two hundred miles west of here. I'd studied ancient mining technology for my engineering dissertation, and we were assessing the safety of the caves. They're famous for the painting and sculpture, mainly sixth century AD. There are familiar mythological scenes, like this one, Vishnu striding across the universe. But at Badami they're part of a coherent whole, flowing into other scenes, a fluid, confident iconography. Here they're fragmented, like unmixed ingredients. The Badami sculptor knew his mythology and believed in it. Here they're like a collection of tourist snapshots. There's no soul to them, no depth. Hinduism is inclusive. Voraciously inclusive. It accepts all manner of different gods. But there's just too much here. It's too disjointed. I'm a practicing Hindu, and I can tell you, it doesn't feel right."

"It's as if someone wanted to keep people out of here, but was hedging his bets, using all the deities he thought the locals might fear," Costas said.

"Even including the odd Parthian one," Jack murmured.

"Maybe there was something to hide," Pradesh said.

Costas pointed at the gloom of the far wall, where dark cracks were visible between the shapes of the boulders. "Another chamber, maybe? That Kubera god, the god of treasure, could be the ultimate protector. If he's a god of the older religion, maybe the sculptor did understand that the people here would fear the ancient gods more than anything from Hinduism and Buddhism. Whoever did this must have had some contact with the local people. He saw them carry out human sacrifice. And he must have been fed, somehow."

Pradesh nodded. "Traditionally, the Kóya from Rampa village left food offerings outside here every day. They thought the god Rama was inside, cornered by the spirits of the jungle. As long as he was fed, he would stay there. Every night, the food offerings would disappear. The *muttadar* probably came at night and took away anything left over by the animals to keep up the pretense. And the rats used to grow to a huge size here. The legend was that if an offering was missed, Rama would break free and wreak his vengeance on the jungle people, taking on the guise of the *konda devata,* the tiger spirit, and cleaving them with his great broken sword."

"Broken sword?" Costas murmured. "That rings a bell, Jack."

"If we're going to seek history behind the mythology, the ritual makes sense," Pradesh continued. "In ancient times, Rama comes into the jungle, the prince who is later deified. But the jungle people resist the intrusion of Hinduism into their spiritual world.

321

The shrine becomes a focus of their cultural strength. They put Rama inside, the intruder. Their gods imprison him. So for the rebel leaders in 1879, this place was a rallying point, a focus of defiance against outsiders. They murder the police constables here, in the guise of sacrifice. But in the minds of the Kóya, Rama was then sealed inside by the earthquake, and the food offerings gradually ceased. And something had gone, the *vélpu* that disappeared in 1879. It was not Rama in the guise of the *konda devata* they now feared, but the *konda devata* itself, the tiger spirit of the jungle."

"So where's the image of Rama in all this?" Costas said, looking around. "I mean, isn't this supposed to be his shrine?"

Pradesh paused. "In Hindu belief, Rama was the descendent of an ancient solar dynasty. He could be represented by that image of Vishnu, or by a sun carving. Maybe we just need to look more closely."

Jack was staring at the chisel work on the neck of the Kubera god, seeing techniques that seemed remarkably familiar. He stepped back, sweeping his flashlight around the room, finding details, lingering on them, seeing what all his education made him want to deny, yet which years of incredible discoveries as an archaeologist made him know lay within the realm of possibility. His mind raced back to Egypt, to Hiebermeyer's discovery of the *Periplus,* to the first glimmerings of this trail they were on. An extraordinary discovery was beginning to take shape before his eyes, an imprint from the past that was becoming more real with every second.

"What's the date of all this?" Costas said.

"The *yaksas* and *yaksīs,* like the *naga,* the serpent, are idols to earth spirits, survivors of the early religion in India before Hinduism and Buddhism took over," Pradesh replied. "The earliest *yaksas* sculptures date from the third century BC, but these ones here could be first century BC, possibly first century AD. That was when the gods of early Hinduism, the ones you see here, started to make an appearance. After that, the Hindu gods rule supreme over the native cults, absorbing or extinguishing them. And there are no images of Buddha here, but there are Buddhist symbols, the bull on the pillar, the spoked wheel. It's a little like early Christianity, where symbols were used before Christ was represented anthropomorphically."

"So this could be, say, late first century BC," Costas said.

"That would fit with the sculptural style, if we were looking at Graeco-Roman influence," Jack said. "There are stylistic and technical details I'd put in the late Republican period, if this were Rome."

"We've got to eliminate the obvious," Pradesh said. "The Roman site at Arika-

323

medu's only four hundred miles south of here. No Roman from Arikamedu would ever have come into the jungle without a very good reason, but we have to consider the possibility."

Jack shook his head. "I don't see a sculptor at Arikamedu. Mud-brick buildings, wooden, purely utilitarian. Even at Berenikê on the Red Sea there was hardly anything made of stone. There was nothing for a sculptor to do."

"Maybe someone who'd been a sculptor, but changed careers, became a sailor or a trader," Costas said. "Maybe he came to India and then went native, found a bolthole in the jungle, rediscovered an old passion for carving. You always say it, Jack. Anything's possible."

Jack hesitated, thinking hard. "Sculpting, stonemasonry, was a hereditary profession, and you didn't move between trades that easily in the ancient world. And if we're talking Rome about the time of Augustus, it would have been madness to leave. Augustus rebuilt the city in stone. It was one of the biggest building programs in history." He paused, then voiced a suspicion that had dawned on him only moments before. "But you may have hit on something. There was one walk of Roman life that took men with all manner of skills, from every profession."

"The army," Pradesh said.

"Citizen-soldiers," Jack murmured. "But we need to think carefully about the date. At the time of Augustus, the army was becoming professional, recruiting eighteen-year-olds for twenty years' service. For the real citizen-soldier, we need to look back to the time of the civil wars, and before that to the Roman Republic, when fit men of any age would volunteer for a shorter period, usually no more than six years. I'm talking mid-first century BC or earlier. That's several decades before the main Roman period at Arikamedu. And there's another problem. There's no evidence whatsoever that the Romans ever sent legionaries to India."

"Maybe a mercenary?" Costas said. "Or a deserter? You told me about those maverick British and French officers in eighteenth century India, running native armies and setting themselves up as princes. Maybe the same thing happened in the Roman period?"

Jack panned the light over the walls. "It's possible. The *Periplus* mentions armed guards on ships, as defense against pirates." But Jack already knew what they were looking at, with utter certainty. His voice was tight with excitement. "Or something else. An escaped prisoner of war."

Costas edged around the far side of the chamber, inspecting the deep shadows around the boulders beside the sculpture of Kubera. He peered into one, his hand remaining on the belly of the god. "I was right. There's another tunnel here. It looks like another chamber beyond."

A muffled shout came down the entrance passageway in the opposite direction, a few urgent words in Hindi. Pradesh barked something back and then looked beyond Costas. He glanced at his watch, and shook his head in frustration. "I've got to go. Sergeant Amratavalli's returned from his recce. I need to confer with him. I'll leave you in here as long as I can, but we've got no more than an hour. The chopper pilot won't linger. He's an ex-army friend, but he's not going to want his machine to get shot up again. We'll need to leave before any more of the Maoists arrive. Good luck." Pradesh unholstered his revolver and disappeared back toward the entrance. Jack went ahead of Costas into the crack between the boulders, and Costas wedged himself in behind. The slick of damp on the rock acted as a lubricant, and he forced his ample frame through. Jack shone the flashlight back for him, illuminating the thick brown smear on what was left of his shirt. "Ruined," Costas muttered mournfully. "Completely ruined."

Jack swung the light around. The chamber was about the same size as the first, but the walls were different. Someone had gone to huge efforts to chip away and smooth the boulders to create flat surfaces, like sculptural canvases. Jack was aware of shapes behind him, but kept his light focused on the wall he had seen when he first entered the chamber. His mind was still attuned to the images they had seen before, Indian gods and demons, bold sculptures almost in the round. The wall ahead was the side of one massive boulder at least five meters long and three meters high. He stared in astonishment. The images were utterly unlike those of the previous chamber. Subtle relief carving covered almost the entire wall. He could see soldiers, weapons. It was a continuous scene, a narrative. And these images had nothing to do with Indian mythology. It was as if they had walked into a museum of Roman art. *Into a room created in the heart of Rome itself.* "My God," he whispered. "It looks just like the Battle of Issus. One of Alexander the Great's most famous battles, against the Persians."

Costas came alongside. "That's fourth century BC, right? You mentioned prisoners of war, Jack. I'm thinking Battle of Carrhae, first century BC. Is that where all this is leading us?"

Jack's mind was racing. "Alexander would have been much on the mind of the legionaries as they marched to Carrhae: Crassus probably saw himself as a born-again Alexander, and may have used Issus as a rallying cry. And when the Romans lost at Carrhae, Alexander's victory against the Persians

327

would have attained mystical status. Add to that the evidence of Alexander's eastern expedition seen by the escaped Roman prisoners, the altars described in that fragment of the *Periplus*. Alexander would have been a constant backdrop to what might have happened. An adventure that might have taken a citizen-soldier, a sculptor by trade, from Rome to Carrhae, then to imprisonment at Merv and then east into central Asia, on the route taken by Alexander and his Macedonians three centuries before. And then down here to the jungle of southern India."

"So how do you know this image is Alexander's battle?"

"The Battle of Issus is on the Alexander mosaic, from Pompeii," Jack said. "It was probably the way the battle was usually depicted. On the left is Alexander, with wavy hair, sweeping into battle on his horse, Bucephalus, wearing a breastplate depicting Medusa. He's placed lower than his opponent, Darius, who towers above his Persian soldiers, looking down on Alexander. There are lots of Persian troops, fewer Macedonians. It's a way of emphasizing the greatness of Alexander's victory, showing him riding against the seemingly invincible army of the god-king himself. And Darius is on the run, ordering his charioteer to whip his horses as he tries to escape, looking around at Alexander with fear in his eyes. His right arm is extended toward Alexander as if he's just thrown a spear, or maybe as a gesture of obeisance. He's acknowledging the victor."

"So how come a mosaic from Pompeii gets copied by a sculptor in the heart of darkness in central India?"

"Here's my theory," Jack murmured. "The guy who carved this was a soldier who'd been a sculptor in his former life. There's a lot of technique here that comes straight out of the school of Roman funerary sculpture of the first century BC. I'm talking about stock sculpture for clients of modest means, relief slabs to put in front of cremation urns, the occasional larger scene on a sarcophagus. But even a small-time sculptor would have been familiar with the great works of art. Rome was awash with art looted after the conquest of Greece in the second century BC. The Alexander mosaic was made about that time for a wealthy client in Pompeii. But even that was a copy of a famous painting, by the Greek artist Apelles or Philoxenos of Eretria. Pliny the Elder mentions it in his *Natural History*. The painting must have been on public display in Rome, and whoever sculpted this must have studied it during his apprenticeship."

Costas traced his hand over the sculpture. "But these soldiers don't look like Greeks to me. Or Persians."

Jack swept the torch over the wall. "You're

right. The soldiers to the left are Roman, not Greek. They've got chain mail, and early style helmets. They're carrying the *pilum,* the Roman spear, and the *gladius,* the thrusting sword. They're Roman legionaries of the first century BC, the time of Crassus."

"I can see Roman numerals." Costas peered closely at a standard carried above the soldiers. "The symbols XV, and the letters AP."

"Fifteenth Apollinaris," Jack exclaimed. "That's the legion mentioned on the cave inscription from Uzbekistan, the one Katya's uncle identified. The sculptor has replicated the Battle of Issus scene, but has substituted Romans for Greeks. This must be the Roman army marching into battle at Carrhae."

"And the tall guy in the center? Where Alexander should be? Is that Crassus, the Roman general?"

Jack shook his head. "No way. The legionaries who survived Carrhae, who survived imprisonment, who escaped east, would have been the toughest of the tough, probably including veterans of Caesar's campaigns in Gaul and Britain a few years before. But Crassus was an incompetent leader by comparison with the revered Caesar, and the soldiers would have been contemptuous of him. A veteran of Carrhae would never put Crassus in the position of Alexander. And I doubt whether it's a self-portrait, the sculptor himself. That wasn't the way of a Roman legionary. Your identity was with your section, your *contubernium.* But because of that bonding, close friends could be revered. That's what I think this is. The members of a *contubernium* called themselves brother, *frater.* That character's not dressed as a general. Maybe he's an *optio,* a section leader, or a centurion, but no more. He's shown as *primus inter pares,* a leader certainly, but definitely one of the men."

"But he's larger than life," Costas said.

Jack put the torch close to the carving. "No. Look again. Not larger than life, just tall. The anatomical proportions are the same as the others, he's just longer-limbed. And look at his face. Roman funerary sculptors churned out stock images, but when it came to the face they always carved actual portraits. Look at these soldiers. I can see faces from central Italy, men from Campania, Latium, Etruria, hard men, grizzled mountain men, farmers, fishermen. These are portraits, real individuals known to the sculptor. You can see it in the quirky features, the humanity. Then look at the taller man. His face is longer, leaner, with higher cheekbones. His hair's tied back under his helmet in a ponytail, and he's got a beard. You don't see that in any of the other legionaries. He's a Gaul, maybe from the Alps, maybe one of the former enemies recruited by Caesar. And look at his expression, the toughness, the fortitude, even the hint of humor in those eyes, the black humor of the soldier. There's a lot to admire in that face. He must have been a close friend of the sculptor, his *frater.*"

"It looks as if the sculptor knew something about perspective, anyway," Costas said. "I count a dozen legionaries down here around the tall man, but above them it looks like a whole legion in low relief, a separate body of men in midair."

"That's what clinched it for me," Jack said. "Even before I looked at their enemy to the right."

"Explain."

"That crowd of soldiers above. It isn't a distant scene, a crude way of showing perspective. It's a scene in another dimension. It's a ghost legion."

"A ghost legion?"

"That standard you spotted, the Fifteenth Legion? It's not being carried by the soldiers below, the real-life soldiers. It's being carried by the ghost legion. And look at the carving at the top of the standard. It's the *aquila,* the sacred eagle. Then look again at the real-life soldiers below, the dozen. They don't have a standard at all. Now that's bizarre. A Roman sculptor brought up with all the rules and conventions of iconography would never have done it. A legion in battle *always* has its eagle. For a sculptor who'd also been a soldier, not depicting it is almost unimaginable."

332

"These were the legionaries who lost their eagles at Carrhae," Costas murmured.

"Precisely. And that's why this isn't a depiction of Carrhae. It's another battle. *A later battle.* The iconography is perfect. The soldiers above, the ghost legion, are the men who fell at Carrhae, with their eagle. The men below are the survivors. Here's what I think. These are the escaped prisoners from Merv, fighting another battle of their own, far to the east, in a place where the legend of Alexander's conquests must have been on their minds, something that persuaded the sculptor to use the Battle of Issus as his template."

"But they're dressed in full legionary gear," Costas pointed out. "How on earth could they have retained all that from Carrhae, after years of imprisonment?"

"After escaping, they would have had to arm themselves on the way, pick up whatever they could find. But in their minds, they were still Roman legionaries. When they went into battle, they saw themselves this way. So that's how the sculptor depicted them."

"Okay. Now for the other warriors. The enemy."

Jack swung the flashlight to the right. It was an image that seemed impossibly at odds with Roman legionaries. Jack had a sudden flashback to standing with Rebecca in front of nearly identical images in the British Museum, the traveling exhibit he had taken her to see shortly after they had first met in New York. He trailed the beam over the entire image, coming back to linger on the central character, the one opposing the tall legionary. He stared hard. *There was no doubt about it.*

"I may be wrong about this," Costas murmured. "But are we looking at the terracotta warriors?"

Jack took a deep breath, his heart pounding with excitement. "Look at the armor. It's segmented, like fish scales. And look at the weapons. Long, straight blades, elaborate halberds, distinctive bows and arrows. In the ancient world, only one army wore armor like that. And this isn't just generic Chinese armor. The details here are very specific, exactingly observed. The sculptor had been a soldier himself and knew what he was looking at. What we've got here is a depiction of first-century-BC Roman soldiers confronting warriors dressed in the armor of the third-century-BC Qin dynasty, the First Emperor of China, a full two centuries before the time of Crassus' legionaries."

"How could Romans have seen the terracotta warriors?"

"Not terracotta warriors. Real warriors. Remember our Roman sculptor, the portrait tradition. If he can, he'll show real people as individuals. I saw the terracotta warriors with Rebecca. There are a number of facial types, but they only give the illusion of being individuals. They're like a CGI army for a film, with enough individuality to give the authenticity needed but not bearing close scrutiny. And the faces are of a fairly uniform central Chinese type, rounded, without much ethnic distinctiveness. Now get a load of these guys." Jack flashed the light along the row of figures who seemed to be jostling for position in the foreground, their legs wide apart, weapons at the ready, staring out at them. The faces were hard, scowling, with intense eyes and long moustaches, their hair braided high in topknots.

"They look like Katya's father did. A face that's burned into my memory," Costas murmured. "Like Genghis Khan."

"Exactly," Jack said. "These are steppe people, nomads, from the northern fringes of China. These are the First Emperor's own people. This is what the warriors who accompanied him to victory in China would have looked like. And these are real individuals. But they're not like the Romans opposite, where you can see affection, humanity. These are faces the sculptor has met in battle. You remember the faces of people who have tried to kill you."

"Check out the central figure," Costas murmured.

Jack shone the light again at the figure with its head twisted back toward the tall legionary. The figure was riding a horse, a sinewy charger with wide eyes that seemed to stare upward to the heavens. The sculptor had tried to show the horse twisting sideways, just as Darius' chariot was shown turning away from the Macedonians in the Issus mosaic. The perspective here was clumsy, but the sense of movement was arresting. The horse and the surrounding warriors were speckled in dull red, as if someone had flicked paint over the rock. Costas rubbed a finger against it, then sniffed the moist smudge that came off. "A ferrous base, like ochre."

Jack looked back at the wall. "The sculptor could have made up other pigments from mineral outcrops in the jungle, just as the Kóya do for body paint. And we know he had lapis lazuli for the ceiling. But it looks as if red was the only color he used here. It gives a powerful impression, like looking at a black and white projection through a red filter. This was a scene reduced to its essentials, seared into his consciousness. The individuality of the faces, the detail of the weapons, the armor. And the color of blood."

"A memory of battle."

"And of that warrior on the horse," Jack said. "Look at his headgear. In the Alexander mosaic, Darius wears a Persian hood, rising up around his chin and high above his head. It was probably made of felt, protection against the sun and cold on the steppe. That's what this headdress looks like too, until you inspect it closely." He handed the flashlight to Costas, who held it above his head with the beam angled down on the wall, enhancing the shadows. "I can see eyes," he murmured. "And fangs, big ones. It's the head of an animal. A lion."

Jack shook his head. "No. A tiger."

"A tiger."

"The south China tiger," Jack said. "Today there are only a few dozen left in the wild. At the time of the First Emperor, they were probably widespread."

Costas raised the light higher to the left, to the level of the ghost legion, near the ceiling of the cavern. There was another relief sculpture above the soldiers, a roundel about a meter across containing two sculpted faces. Costas stared at it. "What you were saying earlier, on the way to Arikamedu," he murmured. "About the arrival of Christianity in this region. That looks awfully like a mother and a child."

"I saw that when we first came in here," Jack said. "I wanted to work this whole scene through, but now I'm sure of it. It's too early for Christianity. I think this place was sculpted some time in the final decades BC, and that roundel's by the same hand, not some later addition. Those two portraits inside are real people too. You can see they were carved with special care. The woman's not exactly pretty, is she? A bit heavy round the jowls, a crooked nose. The little boy has protuberant ears, and his eyes are close together. But these details are carved with loving care. This was a mother and child he adored, real people in his memory."

"His wife and child," Costas murmured.

"The roundel's another Roman sculptural type, often funerary," Jack said. "Look how the sculptor's put it up there on the same plane as the ghost legion, as if the woman and child are in heaven. It's as if he's acknowledged the truth. Maybe his yearning for them brought him here, a trek across a continent to seek out his own kind. Maybe he met Romans at Arikamedu, and maybe they told him, a weather-beaten old tramp who arrived from the north, what he knew to be true, that the life he had left behind years before on the other side of the world was gone for good, that there was only one route left for him to join his loved ones."

"You really do believe this was one of Crassus' legionaries."

Jack nodded. "Decades beyond the time when he last saw his wife and child, when he marched off from Rome to Carrhae. Thirty, perhaps forty years have passed. Rome has been devastated by civil war. He'd heard about that at Arikamedu, before retreating to this place. He hopes that his son followed in his footsteps as a sculptor, or lived and died a legionary." Jack stared at the roundel. He would have known that the image was of loved ones long gone, who survived only in his memory. Standing here, chisel in hand, two thousand years ago, he knew he was never going back. It was easier for him to think of them in Elysium. And for the soldier who had left his family to go to war, there was a catharsis in this scene. Jack turned to Costas. "He and his comrades have fought for each other, for the honor of the legion. But they've also fought for their families. Putting the roundel there, above the battle scene, tells him that he did not abandon them. It reassures him, in his crushing moments of doubt." Jack wondered whether John Howard had seen this too, on that day in 1879 when he and Wauchope had stumbled into this place. *His own child, his little boy, left behind with his mother, an image that would only ever live on in his memory.* Had Howard felt it? Had he seen an image of a death foretold? Was that what he had feared most of all, a fear for his own child, so far away from him, when he turned from this place to leave, to escape from this darkness?

Costas panned the light down from the roundel and along the Chinese warrior's arm, showing where it extended toward the tall legionary. Between the two figures the stone was blackened and furrowed where water had dripped down the rock from an opening somewhere above, eroding the sculpture. He moved the flashlight to and fro. "His hand, where it looks as if he's raising a fist to the Romans. He's actually wearing some kind of glove. If I angle the light, you can see he's holding a sword."

Jack followed the beam. He stared at the hand, his mind racing. "It's a gauntlet," he said, his voice taut. "A gauntlet sword. A *pata*."

"You mean like the one you inherited?"

Jack took the flashlight from Costas, and angled the light in different directions. Suddenly he saw it, the distinctive ears, the mouth, the fangs bared. His voice was barely a whisper. "It's identical. The Roman must have taken it from the warrior, in this battle. He must have brought it here. And then Howard took it, that day in 1879." He reached out and touched the sculpted fist, just as he had touched the real *pata* in his cabin on *Seaquest II* the day before, tracing his fingers over the features so familiar to him since his grandfather had given it to him as a boy. History suddenly seemed to contract, so that he was there, standing with the ghostly form of the man who had sculpted this image, an old man scarcely recognizable as a Roman, chipping and rubbing, living out his final days in here, finishing the image of his loved ones before he went to join them in Elysium. Jack remembered the *Periplus* fragments, the first glimmerings of the incredible story that was playing out in the shadows on this wall. *It was all true.*

There was a clatter and a curse and Pradesh was beside them, revolver in hand. He stood rooted to the spot, staring, swaying slightly. "Good God," he whispered.

"Want a rundown?" Costas said.

"We don't have time. My sapper says there's a party of Maoists coming this way. He counted fifteen of them. They're only twenty, twenty-five minutes away. I've called in the chopper. We've got to get out of here. I've set some C-4 explosives at the entrance of the shrine. It'll blow it in, and keep this place safe until we can make it back here again."

"Five minutes," Jack said urgently, taking out his camera.

"No more." Pradesh stared at the sculpture again, a look of blank astonishment on his face, and then ducked back through the entrance tunnel. Jack passed Costas the flashlight. "Shut your eyes. I'm using flash." He began methodically photographing the wall, waiting a few seconds between each shot for the flash to recharge. Costas stumbled and slipped backward, swearing under his breath as he righted himself. "Keep the beam on the sculpture," Jack said urgently. "I need to see what I'm photographing."

"I think you might want to look at what

I've just bumped into."

Jack turned, and caught his breath. He had sensed some shapes behind them as they entered the chamber, and had assumed it was the boulders. But this was man-made. It was a large, rectilinear shape, about two and a half meters long and a meter and a half high, carved from the natural rock. Jack's eyes darted over it, measuring, estimating. He began to smile, shaking his head. It was the right size, the right dimensions. He could see that the upper surface was a stone lid. "It's a sarcophagus," he exclaimed. "You've found his sarcophagus. This place wasn't a shrine. It was a tomb."

Costas traced his fingers along the join below the lid. "So our sculptor carves out his own coffin, then sculpts the funerary scene on that wall. He takes one last look at the image of his loved ones, then gets inside and pulls the lid over himself."

"The last act of strength by the toughest of the tough, a legionary who had survived the Persian quarries at Merv."

"He blows out his candle, lies down and shuts his eyes, that final image seared in his mind."

"He's back in Rome, with his wife and child," Jack murmured. "Forgetting he was on the other side of the world, slowly dying in a hellhole in the jungle of southern India."

"And he'll still be in there."

Jack stared at the lid. There was something odd about it. He leaned over. The sandstone was encrusted with a layer of hard translucent material, like resin, evidently a calcite deposit that had formed over the centuries as condensation had dripped onto the tomb. In the center was a depression in the accretion layer, as if something had been removed. Jack shone the light closely. There was another thin accretion layer covering the depression and the thicker formation surrounding it, showing that whatever had been removed was taken decades ago, perhaps a century or more. He stood back and looked at the shape. Of course. *Twentieth August 1879.* "This is where the gauntlet was lying," he whispered. "You can see the shape of the fist, and the sword blade, broken off below the hilt."

Costas felt the dampness of the stone. "Amazing any of the blade survived from antiquity."

"If it was first-grade Chinese steel, chromium-plated, then it's possible."

"Chinese," Costas murmured. "You really think so?"

"My grandfather said that the *pata* did once have a blade, but that it was already broken when Howard found it. Howard removed and discarded the broken section in the Godavari River after they got out of the jungle. All he kept was the gauntlet."

"It seems strange that he took it," Costas

said. "This was a shrine of the Kóya, and maybe the gauntlet had become one of their sacred objects, one of those *vélpus.*"

"He and Wauchope were soldiers, remember? Soldiers first, engineers second, anthropologists a distant third. They'd been trained to fight with the sword. They'd have had their own weapons, but Howard reaches for another blade, even a broken one. If it came to a fight, they might have no time to reload their revolvers and two blades were better than one. It was little short of a miracle they'd made it this far without being cut down, and they'd have been pretty apprehensive. Howard had his own survival to think of, his own wife and child. Respecting the local culture would not have been high on their list at that point. They probably only had a short time in here, and the war drums would have been beating outside."

"Like they are now, Jack."

"Okay. Time's up."

"I spoke too soon. I should never do that."

"What is it?"

"There's an inscription. Where my hand was. I thought the rock felt pitted."

They could hear the sound of the helicopter now, the noise throbbing through the chamber. Jack swung his flashlight to where Costas was pointing at the side of the tomb. To his astonishment he saw five lines, in Latin. He squatted down and read out the words:

HIC IACET
LICINIUS OPTIO XV APOLLINARIS
SACRA IULIUM SACULARIA
IN SAPPHEIROS NIELO MINIUM
ALTA FABIA FRATER AD PONTUS AD AELIA
ACUNDUS

HERE LIES
LICINIUS, *OPTIO* OF THE 15TH
APOLLINARIS LEGION
GUARDIAN OF THE CELESTIAL JEWEL
IN THE DARK *SAPPHEIROS* MINES
THE OTHER IS WITH FABIUS, BROTHER,
ACROSS THE
LAKE TOWARD THE RISING SUN

"Sappheiros," Costas exclaimed. "I remember that from the *Periplus.* Doesn't that mean lapis lazuli?"

A voice bellowed down the passageway from outside. "Time to go!"

Costas swung the flashlight around the chamber one last time. There was another dark fissure at the back, where they had heard the sound of water trickling. He hesitated, then stumbled forward, holding the wall with one hand, and leaned through. For a few moments he was stock-still, the beam shining into the darkness. "Jack, it's my worst nightmare. I think I can smell it. Get me out of here."

345

There was another noise outside, the drumming of gunfire. Jack quickly joined Costas. He stared into the pool of light. At first it seemed like another sculpture, white, an extrusion of the rock. But this was different. He realized with horror what he was looking at. *A human body.* It was stretched out in the waterfall, the arms behind the back, the head tilted forward at a garish angle. The neck was reduced to bone and sinew. The face was grotesquely adiposed, unrecognizable. Costas swayed slightly, and Jack held him by the shoulder. He forced himself to look again. The head was held up by a noose, tied around a rock above the waterfall. It looked as if the man had died by slow hanging, left with just enough rope to stay alive as long as his feet could find some purchase on the rock. He could have survived like that for hours, even days. A scurry of black shapes left the legs, and Jack saw that the calves had been stripped almost to the bone. The man's shirt had been eaten away, revealing the skin of his left shoulder. Then Jack saw it. He felt a cold certainty. *It was a tiger tattoo.* It was distinct from the ones they had seen on the bodies outside, more elaborate. He remembered what Katya had told him about her uncle's tattoo. Then he realized. *She had known they might find him like this.*

"It's Hai Chen," he said hoarsely. "Katya's uncle." He swallowed hard. He had seen enough. There was another burst of automatic fire outside. He turned Costas around and pushed him back toward the chamber entrance. Jack glanced one last time at the sculpture on the wall. His mind was racing. Romans. *Raumanas.* Rama. *A shrine of Rama.* He saw the tall one, the legionary in the middle. *Was that Fabius?* He flashed his torch across the breastplate, the sword belt, the garlands. There was something he needed to see again. He had seen it before, but had dismissed it, some Roman Republican military decoration, lost to history. But now he knew what it was. A round shape, like a sun, with beams extending from it, carried inside a pouch on the legionary's belt. *A shape like a jewel.* There was another bellow outside, another burst of gunfire. He took out his Beretta and cocked it. "Let's get out of here."

13

The man with the rifle could see the two figures by the lakeside clearly now, motionless among the boulders near the shore, framed by the Tien Shan Mountains to the east, the edge of the celestial empire itself. He had been watching them all afternoon, waiting for the sun behind him to lower, to accentuate the forms, but before the shadows were too long. He had learned everything he could about their behavior, watched every intimate movement, just as his grandmother had taught him to do. The tall one, the man, was awkward, angular, given to sudden movements and gestures, especially when he was working the tractor. But he was also given to watching the woman when she was hunched over, scraping and brushing, photographing. When he did that, the tall man was still for many minutes, sometimes half an hour or more, as if he did not want the woman to know he was watching. The man with the rifle curled his lip. The Kyrgyz were steppe nomads like his own ancestors, but nomads who had given up the ways of the warrior and become little better than sheep. He despised them. He wished he could target the man first, but the woman was the priority. He shifted his gaze to her. She was raven-haired, finely built, the Lycra tight against her thighs as she squatted down, athletic but curvaceous. She aroused him, and that increased his fervor. *Her clan had strayed. The Brotherhood would exact its retribution.*

The light was perfect now. He looked up at the line of snowcapped mountains across the lake, and then let his eyes drop back to the two figures. Always start at the horizon, his grandmother had taught him, and then everything will fall into place. He remembered her face, the handsome Kazakh features that had adorned postage stamps and murals across the motherland, the very picture of the Zaitsev Soviet march of progress. Only her unit of production had been death. Her master had called her *Zaichatel,* "little hare," but the Germans called her *Todesengel,* the angel of death. Her tally at Stalingrad had been in the hundreds. *Gold Star of the Hero of the Soviet Union.* He remembered what she had told him on her deathbed, high in the mountains on the Chinese border, their homeland. She had told him that by the end, she had not killed for a cause. She had killed because it was what she did. She had seen that in his eyes too, as he looked down on her, devoid of emotion, only wanting to take up where she had left off.

He had her rifle now. He pushed himself back, lying on his front in the rocky hollow on the ridge. He opened up the long brown package beside him, the leather cover still supple after seventy years, impregnated with gun oil. He lifted out the rifle and cradled the forestock in his right hand, careful not to touch the scope. He brushed his left hand over the wood below the receiver, touching the dents and scars of war, wounds that had strengthened the weapon, not diminished it. The female Soviet snipers always gave their weapons names. *Fire dragon,* she had called it. He looked at the markings on the metal. Mosin-Nagant, 1917, made under contract in Williamsburg, Maryland. His grandmother had laughed at the irony of it, during the long years of the Cold War when she had trained generations of snipers to take on the Americans. But she had said the instruments of death held no allegiance. At her own death he had taken it from her, and he had come to know it as he knew himself. She had said that each kill was like an act of passion with a lover, and the more he fired it the more he would know its needs, and the more it would become part of his very soul.

He opened the bolt, touching the fresh

sheen of oil on the receiver. He took two cartridges from a leather pouch. He had hand-loaded them himself, using the same batch of primers, the same powder, measuring the loads to the microgram. She had taught him that too. He had polished the bullets until they gleamed. He pressed the cartridges into the magazine then pushed the bolt forward and down, chambering one round. He slowly raised the muzzle on the small sandbag wedged beside the boulder, careful not to press down on the end of the barrel, then edged himself forward on his elbows and knees, holding the butt against his shoulder. He had smeared chalk and dirt on his face, and there was nothing reflective on the rifle. He would be invisible against the setting sun. He saw the two figures again. 880 meters. *He sensed it.* That was his gift. He dialed in the scope, adjusting the turrets for windage and elevation. The air was thin, and there was little wind. The target was downslope, and gravity would pull the bullet down. He had already compensated for that, adding one eighth to the distance. He had seen a shimmer of air around the tractor engine, the optical distortion. He would aim a meter to the left of the woman's head, at the boulder with the carvings beside her. The bullet would take more than a second to arrive. She would not even hear the report. It would go through her neck, split her spinal cord. He inhaled deeply, then exhaled and stopped breathing. He slowed his heartbeat. *Synchronize with your very soul.* He curled the ball of his finger around the trigger, then lowered his eye to the scope. *Great is the virtue of the First Emperor. The entire universe is his realm.*

Then he stopped. He slid back down into the hollow and rolled over, face up to the heavens, pulling the rifle with him, holding it against his chest, opening the bolt. He had done it over and over again, bringing himself to the brink. His grandmother had said it was *shiatse,* self-discipline. He had already dealt with the woman's uncle, the one whose place he would soon take among the twelve. He had known the man would say nothing, a man trained in the way of the tiger warrior, so he had left him to die in squalor, to be devoured by rats inside the jungle shrine. He and his men had found the inscription inside, and there had been enough time before the Maoists stumbled on them to read the words and see where the quest for the sacred treasure would lead. But before that he had come here, to watch, to wait, to see whether the woman would lead them farther. He knew that her uncle had told her about his own quest, about the clues he had found. The Brotherhood had eyes and ears everywhere. And her fate was sealed. When one of the twelve strayed, his clan was forfeit. It had always been the way. But he had to remind himself. And he was here not just to kill, but to watch, to follow. It was his test, his duty set by the Brotherhood, his rite of passage before he could join the twelve. He drew back his sleeve, touching the image tattooed on his forearm, still raw and bleeding. He reached toward the horse which had been standing behind him in the hollow, its flanks rising and falling almost imperceptibly, eyes half-open, red-rimmed. He pressed the tattoo against its flank, and his whole forearm came up red, covered with the blood that was lying like sweat on the horse. He lay back again, exultant. Their blood had mingled. They had become one. The blood of the heavenly steed. *The blood of the tiger warrior.*

Jack awoke with a start as the plane lurched and shuddered, its engines increasing to a whine and then settling down again. He tightened his seat belt. Rebecca was sitting beside him, reading. Opposite them Costas and Pradesh were dozing fitfully. Jack glanced at the navigation map on the foldout screen in front of him, then looked out of the window to his right. He could see where the valley of the Indus had given way to the crumpled foothills of Baluchistan, the northwestern province of Pakistan. They were close to the border with Afghanistan, over the tribal lands which had changed little since the days of British rule. Beyond Afghanistan lay their destination, the former Soviet republic of Kyrgyzstan, wedged between the mountains that led to China on one side and Russia on the other, astride the lattice of caravan routes and rugged upland passes that made up the northern arm of the Silk Route. Jack stared into the haze, gripping the armrests. Katya was out there somewhere, in one of the most forbidding landscapes on earth. Up here the prospect of finding her seemed inconceivably remote, yet all being well they would be with her in a matter of hours.

Jack glanced over at the two men. Costas was wearing another Hawaiian shirt he had somehow kept in reserve on *Seaquest II,* replacing the one that had been shredded in the jungle. There was a bulge on his right shoulder where a dressing covered the bullet wound he had received from the Chinese gunman, fortunately only a graze. Pradesh was wearing Indian army khaki stripped of all identifying insignia, a sensible precaution in Pakistani airspace. The evening before, he and his two sappers had kept the Maoist terrorists at bay while the helicopter had landed in the jungle, allowing them to escape with only a few dings in the fuselage. Pradesh had known exactly what he was doing, and Jack was grateful to him. Once back on *Seaquest II* they had been able to wash and change, but there was no time to sleep. The IMU Embraer jet had flown out from England to meet them, and in the early hours of the morning the Lynx had taken them from the ship to a military airfield near Madras for the long flight north. Jack glanced at his watch. Almost four hours gone now. They should touch down at the U.S. base at Bishkek in Kyrgyzstan by mid-morning.

The horrifying image from the waterfall was still imprinted on Jack's mind. He had no doubt that the decomposed body was Hai Chen, Katya's uncle. The tattoo they had seen on his arm was more elaborate than those on the Chinese corpses outside, but showed the same image of a fearsome tiger, almost a dragon. It was clear that Hai Chen was not just an innocent victim, a naïve anthropologist in the wrong place at the wrong time. Someone had left him to die slowly, in a cruelly calculated way. He had been on a trail that seemed increasingly to parallel the quest Jack now found himself on, and the outcome looked decidedly unpleasant. There was more at stake here than mining speculation. Jack needed to talk to Katya, in person. She was going to have to tell him everything she knew.

Jack tried to forget the image and focus on the archaeology. His mind was still reeling from their discovery. *A Roman tomb in south India.* A tomb near the Roman site of Arikamedu had always been conceivable, perhaps

355

a merchant or a sea captain. But they had discovered the tomb of a Roman legionary. *A legionary who may have been a survivor of the Battle of Carrhae.* It was a remarkable link to the fragment of the ancient *Periplus* from Egypt, to the proof that some of those legionaries had escaped east into central Asia. If the legionary who had carved those battle scenes in the jungle had really been one of Crassus' men, he must have made his way south from the Silk Route, somewhere below their flight path now. And there was the extraordinary reference in the tomb inscription. Jack squinted through the window toward Afghanistan, still seeing nothing in the early morning haze. One word from the inscription kept going through his head. *Sappheiros.* Lapis lazuli. The legionary had found something, something so precious he had left a clue on his tomb inscription. Something that another legionary, Fabius, his brother-in-arms, the soldier in the carving, had also possessed, taken away with him. *Something in two parts.* Jack began drumming his fingers on the armrest. This had become more than a fantastic trail of escape and adventure from two thousand years ago. It had become a treasure hunt.

"Dad." Rebecca nudged him. "This book is incredible."

Rebecca had her reading light on, and he

could see the title page. *Lieutenant John Wood, Bengal Navy. A Personal Narrative of a Journey to the Source of the River Oxus.* Jack raised his seat upright. "It's one of my favorites. He wrote it in the 1830s, before the British had begun to interfere in Afghanistan," he said, sipping at a bottle of water. "Like other early British explorers who trekked out there you can see that he really empathized with the people. He was Scottish and says it's something to do with being born and bred in the mountains. It's also a great adventure story. On the trail of Alexander the Great. And that book was a treasured possession of your great-great-great-grandfather. He pored over it. When I put my hand on it, I feel close to him."

"So do I," Rebecca said. She closed the book on a slip of paper, and picked up a typescript Jack had also given her. "And this is incredible too. Your biography of Colonel Howard. I nearly cried when I read about his baby boy, taking ill and dying within a day in Bangalore, while his dad was hundreds of miles away in the jungle. It's heartwrenching. I can't imagine what the boy's mother felt like, waking up one morning with a baby boy in her arms, then watching him lowered into his grave that same evening." Rebecca was talking quietly, trying not to wake the other two, but her words were choked with emotion. "You don't hear much about the women, do you? These adventures, the wars, they're all about men. But the women had to deal with so much loss and anguish. You'd think that all the childhood deaths in those days would have made them used to it, but I bet it didn't. Maybe all that stiff upper lip stuff was a way of dealing with it."

Jack nodded. "It was a big adventure for the British out here, but life was fragile. Diseases like cholera, diphtheria, blackwater fever, could take you within a day, strike without warning. All those images we have of exaggerated Victorian gentility in India — tea parties, the gentle clink of croquet, cosseted families sitting on verandahs — all of that was a kind of veneer. This was a place where you woke up never knowing whether you'd be going to bed again that night, or be lowered into a grave. This was a place for risk-takers, for people who relished living on the edge."

"That's why you love it, isn't it, Dad? All of this history. You really wish you'd been one of these Royal Engineer officers, don't you? You'd get war, adventure, bossing people around, you know, even archaeology if you were a survey officer, plus all those leaves and furloughs they had when they could go off exploring the mountains and looking for lost treasure. Perfect."

Jack laughed. "Luckily, I can be all of those things in the present day, and I can transport myself into the past. To really strike out on the trail of discovery you have to empathize with those you're following, know their minds."

"Costas says your great gift is diversion. He says you're always going after one thing, then something else crops up. He says you need a woman to pin you down. Make you more reliable."

Jack nodded across at the crumpled, snoring figure opposite. "He can hardly talk."

"Does he have, you know, a friend?" Rebecca asked.

"Well, he's got me, and everyone at IMU."

"No, I mean a *girl*friend."

Jack snorted, pointing at Costas. "That? You must be kidding. They never last more than ten seconds. Can you blame them?"

Rebecca shook her head. "Men are so stupid about themselves. They don't even know what makes a man attractive to a woman."

"Yeah, well, he's a techno nerd. He couldn't care less."

Rebecca shook her head and sighed. The cabin lights flickered on and the pilot's voice came over the speaker. "Jack, you asked for a wake-up call over the Afghan border. We're less than two hours to destination." Costas and Pradesh stirred, and woke up. There was another jolt of turbulence, and Pradesh peered past Costas through the window. It was four a.m. local time and still dark, and lights were twinkling far below. "That turbulence was bang on time," he said. "It always seems to happen here. We've just passed Quetta in northern Pakistan, and we must be over the Bolan Pass now. We're flying over Afghanistan."

"Load and lock," Costas said, yawning and stretching extravagantly. He raised his seat and took an orange juice from the fridge beside them. "I've got a headache," he said. "I think it was the jungle. I got dehydrated." He gulped the juice, then took another can.

"It's that palm toddy you drank," Jack said. "I did warn you."

"I only had a few sips," Costas said. "But I'll stick to my rule from now on. Never drink on operations." He downed the second juice, and binned the can. "It'll make that first tequila on the beach all the more delightful. When we get to Hawaii. Tomorrow." He gave Jack a bleary, slightly accusatory glare.

"We're sort of heading there," Jack said. "In a roundabout way."

"North from India to Kyrgyzstan in central Asia," Costas said. "Yeah, right."

Kyrgyzstan. In less than two hours they would land at Bishkek airport, and a couple of hours after that he would be with Katya. A message from her had been awaiting him when they had returned from the jungle to *Seaquest II,* about an amazing new discovery she had made. He had called back immediately and told her about her uncle. Her response had been matter-of-fact, as he had expected it would be, but she had sounded distant. He had steered the conversation toward the archaeology. She had outlined her discovery to him and wanted his firsthand advice. That was a good enough reason to pull the schedule forward, but now there was added urgency. He had immediately put in another call to have the IMU Embraer fueled up and ready for them at the Madras airport when they arrived there less than two hours later.

"Okay, Jack," Costas said. "Bring us up to speed on your ancestor. Here's where I've got to so far. Howard and the other guy, the Irish-American officer, Wauchope, escape from the jungle. And my guess is, what happened to them after that has something to do with why we're flying up here now. And with the inscription in that tomb. We're not just coming up here to see Katya."

Jack took a deep breath and nodded. "Okay. The rest of the story. Howard and Wauchope made it with the sappers back to the steamer *Shamrock.* They had buried Bebbie in the jungle, not at the village where we saw the memorial inscription. But neither of them left any account of what had happened. We've got Lieutenant Hamilton's record of his skirmish in the jungle, and the folk memory of that day from the Kóya people, everything Pradesh told us. But nothing from Howard, who commanded the sapper detachment. His diary ends abruptly that morning on the *Shamrock.* It's at odds with his professionalism. That's what first set the alarm bells ringing for me."

"Maybe it was a cover-up for the death of that guy Bebbie," Costas said. "If he really was shot by the sappers."

"I think there was more to it than that," Jack replied carefully. "I think there was the shock of the sacrificial scene, what they saw from the *Shamrock.* Then I think they saw what we saw inside that shrine. They would both have been well-versed in Latin from school. Wauchope was known for reading Greek and Latin classics when he was on campaign. I think they saw that inscription. I think that was their binding pact. Not to tell anyone what they had read. They saw the earthquake seal in the shrine just after they'd escaped, so the secret was theirs."

"What happened to them after the rebellion?"

"Wauchope left the Madras Sappers to join the Survey of India, one of the most coveted appointments for an engineer officer. He spent most of the next twenty years on the northwest frontier, starting in Baluchistan and working east, carrying out surveys for the Boundary Commission on what became known as the Durant Line, delimiting the border of Afghanistan. His boundary markers are still there like latter-day altars of Alexander the Great. He was famed for his climbing ability and endurance, a born mountaineer. But the malaria he picked up in Rampa finally caught up with him and forced his early retirement, in 1900. After five years recovering his health in the mountains of Switzerland he returned to his beloved India, exploring the remote valleys of the borderland, adopting traditional garb and living with tribesmen. The last we hear of him was in Quetta in the early summer of 1909, when he was fifty-five years old."

"And Howard?"

"He was the last sapper officer out of Rampa, months later, the only one who could withstand the malaria, probably because of his Indian childhood. The death of his eighteen-month-old son Edward in Bangalore while he was in the jungle was a terrible blow. Howard had been slated for great things as a soldier but opted for the engineer route, joining the Indian Public Works Department and then returning to England, to the School of Military Engineering at Chatham. He taught survey to young officers and immersed himself in the academic life of the corps. He became an ardent supporter of the movement that eventually led to the universal language Esperanto. Perhaps the urge came from his experience in Rampa, where they hadn't been able to speak the Kóya language without an interpreter. Maybe it was some kind of atonement. He only returned to India once his children had grown up and gone to boarding school. I always assumed that his career decision had a lot to do with his son Edward, with his need to provide a better home for his children, in England. But now I think there was more to it than that. I think it goes back to that day in the jungle in 1879. And I don't mean what they might have seen in the shrine. I mean something else, something he saw or did, that traumatized him. Maybe it was human sacrifice. Something he was powerless to stop."

"Not exactly the glorious image of soldiering," Costas said.

Pradesh shifted and cleared his throat. "I can sympathize. The worst thing for a soldier is being sent on a mission where you don't have the political will or the resources to finish the job. I've experienced it, on a peacekeeping mission in Africa. Being powerless to stop genocide. If you do intervene, you may ease one person's suffering, but it can make the feeling of impotence worse. One of my sappers shot a woman who'd been terribly mutilated. He was haunted by her face. He said that all the faces that previously had been one mass of tormented humanity had suddenly become real individuals, and that was what made it intolerable for him. He had nightmares about them all coming to him, asking why he hadn't chosen to end their suffering too. He couldn't live with it, and shot himself."

Jack saw Rebecca's face, and he squeezed her hand. "It could have been like that for Howard," he said quietly. "So little knowledge of the emotional response to trauma has survived from the Victorian period. Yet men brought up on romance and courtly deeds ended up seeing and doing terrible things. They internalized these experiences all their lives, somehow using the reservoir of manly Victorian courage to live with it, bottling it up to the end."

"You said he went back to India," Costas said.

"That's where it gets really fascinating," Jack replied. "He returned to the Public Works Department, building bridges, canals, roads, and was principal of a college for native engineers. Then, in 1905, aged fifty, he finally returned to real soldiering. He became commanding royal engineer of the Quetta Division of the Indian army, up against the Afghan frontier in Baluchistan. It was one of the hot spots of the British Empire, about the most dangerous place in the world. Howard relished it, and for a while it was as if he were making up for lost time. But then, in 1907, a full colonel, he abruptly took half-pay and retired."

"Quetta," Costas murmured. "The same place Wauchope was?"

"Exactly," Jack exclaimed. "That's the linchpin of the story. After Rampa, the two men part ways. Perhaps in their pact in the jungle they mapped out their future, the time when they'd get together again. They coincide once, in 1889, when Wauchope takes a refresher course at the survey school at Chatham. They even co-author a paper, on the Roman coins of south India. They were meant to present it jointly at the Royal United Services Institute in London, but Wauchope was recalled to duty. Next, they appear together in Quetta almost twenty years later, in 1907, both retired. They dine as honored guests in the regimental messes, they meet the explorer Aurel Stein, they spend hours in the bazaar talking to travelers, equipping themselves. And then, one morning in April 1908, they gear themselves up, hobnailed boots and puttees, tweed jodhpurs, sheepskin coats, turbans, rucksacks, revolvers. Two old colonels off on a final great adventure. Quetta has seen this kind of thing before. Howard's Tibetan servant Huang-li waves them off. He's been with Howard over the years, since Howard was taken as a boy to a refuge in Tibet during the Indian Mutiny. Huang-li is never seen again either. The two colonels march off toward the Bolan Pass into

Afghanistan, and disappear into the great cleft in the mountains. That's the last anyone hears of them."

"That's so cool," Rebecca said. "Its just like *The Man Who Would Be King,* Kipling's story. Now I know why you put that on the top of the pile for me to read on *Seaquest II,* Dad. Two British soldiers disappearing into the mountains, in search of treasure."

"Treasure?" Costas said.

"I think Rebecca's one step ahead," Jack murmured.

"Chip off the old block," Pradesh said, grinning.

"So what's the pull for these guys, of Afghanistan?" Costas said.

"Adventure. War." Pradesh clicked open a small case on his lap. Inside was a row of eight medals — three elaborate stars on the left and three service medals on the right, two of them with multiple campaign clasps over the ribbons. "These are Wauchope's medals. Before disappearing he bequeathed all of his military possessions to the Regimental Mess of the Madras Sappers, with instructions that they should be auctioned among the officers and the proceeds distributed to famine relief charities. As a young officer before Rampa he had been in Madras during the terrible famine of 1877, and it affected him deeply. But by the time an inquest was held in 1924 into the disappearance and the two men were declared dead, there was little interest in the medals. They've been languishing in the museum storeroom at Bangalore ever since. I felt that they should be in the old headquarters of the Survey of India, where they'd be displayed alongside the memorabilia of the other pioneers. These men are remembered for committing their lives to mapping India and improving the welfare of the people. They are remembered by their Indian and Pakistani successors with pride and affection."

"Isn't the northwest frontier headquarters in what's now Pakistan?" Costas said.

"That's another reason why I'm coming with you to Kyrgyzstan," Pradesh replied cheerfully. "There's a Pakistani sapper contingent attached to the coalition base at Bishkek. I purchased the medals myself under the terms of Wauchope's will, and saw that the money went to charity. I'm going to pass them to the commanding officer of the Pakistani sappers and he'll see them safely to the museum."

"I thought you guys were at war," Costas said.

"Only our countries. Major Singh and I are close friends. We were both seconded at the same time to instruct in jungle survey at the School of Military Engineering at Chatham. That's how I knew something of Howard and Wauchope's later careers, from the records there. When Jack first told me about his interest in the Rampa Rebellion, I was stunned. I had no idea he was from the same Howard family."

Costas peered at the medals. "Those two on the right, with the clasps. Different campaigns?"

Pradesh nodded. "Those are the Indian General Service Medals, with clasps for Hazara, Waziristan, Tirah. As a survey officer, Wauchope was involved in almost all of the Afghan frontier expeditions of the 1880s and 1890s."

"But no clasp for Rampa," Jack said.

Pradesh shook his head. "The government considered the rebellion a civil disturbance. It was a matter of politics, keeping it hush-hush. Nobody wanted internal unrest to be advertised in the wake of the Indian Mutiny. They agreed to consider it as active service in the soldiers' records, but no medal was given."

"And this one?" Costas pointed at the third campaign medal.

"The Afghan War of 1878 to 1880. Wauchope was there, as assistant engineer in the Bazar Valley Field Force, before being deployed to Rampa." He lifted the medal up and turned it over.

Costas' eyes lit up. "An elephant!"

Jack grinned at Pradesh. "I have to apologize for my friend. He has an elephant fixa-

tion. We found some underwater off Egypt."

"Underwater?" Pradesh looked incredulous. "Did I hear you right? You found elephants underwater?"

"Later."

Rebecca leaned across and touched the medal. "It looks just like Hannibal in the Alps," she murmured. "My mother told me about that once when we met, and I did a drawing of it. So they used elephants in Afghanistan too. That's so cool." Jack smiled at her, and looked over. It was a beautiful medal, hanging from a red and green ribbon. On the obverse was Queen Victoria, Empress of India. On the reverse was a column on the march, with cavalry and infantry, dominated by an elephant carrying dismantled field guns on its back. Behind it was a towering mountain range, and in the exergue the word *Afghanistan* and the dates *1878–79–80*. It was the medal John Howard would have received had he joined the Khyber Field Force after the jungle, as he was slated to do. Had the Rampa Rebellion not strung on for months longer than expected. Had he not been the only officer to withstand the fever. Had his son Edward not become ill, and had another officer not offered to take his place in Afghanistan, to allow him to be closer to his family. It was a gesture of kindness that made no difference at all, as Edward had died so quickly while Howard was still in the jungle. To Jack the medal seemed to represent all the odd quirks of fate, and the anguish of loss. Plenty of sapper officers had died in Afghanistan. Had Howard gone there, it was possible that Jack would not have been here today.

Costas suddenly saw something, and pressed his nose against the window. "Holy cow. What was that?"

They followed his gaze. A line of red flashes punctuated the darkness far below. "Airstrike against a mountain ridge," Pradesh murmured. "American or British warplanes, maybe Pakistani, low-flying. We're over the Taliban heartland now. Bandit country."

"Do we have any countermeasures? The chaff dispensers?" Costas said, looking at Jack anxiously.

"We're flying high, over forty thousand feet. The Taliban have nothing that can get us. The Americans didn't supply the mujahedin in the 1980s with anything bigger than the Stinger, and those are mostly gone."

"Right," Costas said. "I forgot. We armed these guys."

"Before the Russians arrived, the Afghans mainly had old British weapons, hangovers from the Great Game," Pradesh said. "Lee-Enfield rifles, Martini-Henrys, even Snider-Enfields from the 1860s. They made their own imitations, the so-called Khyber Pass rifles. These weapons are still around today and not to be underestimated. The Afghans were brilliant marksmen with their own homegrown guns, the matchlock jezails. With British rifles they were superb. This is sniper country, huge vistas with lots of upland vantage points. The traditional Afghan marks-man despises the Taliban recruit who sprays the air with his Kalashnikov while shouting jihadist slogans. He despises him for his poor marksmanship as much as for his Wahabist fanaticism. Afghan society is one where violent death is omnipresent, but within an honorable tradition. No Afghan warrior wants to die. He's contemptuous of the suicide bomber. He loathes fundamentalism. The martyr mentality and the Kalashnikov, those are the two weak points in the Taliban armor."

"Sounds like this war should be won for us by the Afghans," Costas said.

"A few hundred Afghan mountain men armed with sniper rifles could cripple the Taliban. The Afghans just have to be persuaded that the Taliban are their worst enemy. And they need to know that the coalition will stay on afterward to rebuild the country."

"A lot of work for sappers," Costas said.

"We're all ready for it," Pradesh replied enthusiastically. "My fellow officers and I have pored over all the archives from the 1878 war, when the Madras Sappers built bridges in the Khyber Pass. We could do it again." They looked up as the copilot came down the aisle, gesturing at Pradesh. "My turn to fly," Pradesh said, getting up. "I need to get my fixed-wing log up to date. See you later."

"Dad." Rebecca was looking at the book on her lap again. "I've just noticed. There's something in pencil, in the margin. I can barely read it."

"What's the book?" Costas asked.

"Wood's *Source of the River Oxus*," Jack said. "From my cabin. Howard's own copy. I showed it to you earlier."

"Oh, yeah. Fascinating stuff on mining."

"While you were all snoring away, I got to

the part where he discovers the lapis lazuli mines," Rebecca said. "It's incredibly exciting. It's like an adventure novel. He says there were three grades of lapis." She read out a passage: "*These are the* Neeli, *or indigo color; the* Asmani, *or light blue; and the* Suvsi, *or green.* He says the Neeli is the most valuable. *The richest colors are found in the darkest rock, and the nearer the river the greater is said to be the purity of the stone.*"

"*Neeli,*" Costas said. "Sounds like *Nielo,* from the tomb inscription — *sappheiros nielo minium.*"

Jack nodded. "It's the same word, in Pashtun and in Latin. It must be the Indo-European root. If I'm right, the Roman sculptor in the jungle, the guy who did that inscription, had actually been to the mines in Afghanistan. His choice of that word for 'dark' may well have come from contact with locals who described the best lapis lazuli that way." He leaned over Rebecca. "The writing in the margin. Where am I looking?"

"Beside the paragraph I just read."

Jack peered closely. "You're right. I hadn't seen that. There are so many other notes by Howard in the margins of the book, and I hadn't looked at this page closely." He took the open book from her and peered at it under his seat light. "It's definitely Howard's handwriting, Howard's. It's absolutely distinctive, even though you can barely see the pencil." He peered again, and then slowly read it out. *"It is said, if you put together peridot and lapis lazuli, then you have the secret of eternal life. They must be the correct-shaped crystals. Ancient Chinese wisdom, told to me by my ayah."* He lowered the book. "Good God."

"Peridot and lapis lazuli," Costas exclaimed. "That combination again. Who was his ayah?"

"His nanny," Jack murmured. "She looked after him when he was a boy in Bihar, where his father had an indigo plantation near the border with Nepal. She was the great-aunt of Howard's servant Huang-li, the one who waved them off from Quetta in 1908. During the Indian Mutiny, when Howard was a little boy, she took him up into the Himalayas. Later she became his own children's ayah, and then the next generation's. Nobody ever knew how old she was, but she lived to be well over a hundred. In the 1930s, she retired and disappeared to live out her remaining life in the mountains of Tibet. She was never heard from again. She claimed that her ancestors came from far away in the east, from northern China. When my grandfather was a boy she told him stories of the First Emperor, the great emperor Qin who unified China in the third century BC. She told him she was descended from the guardian of the First

375

Emperor's tomb. A legend, perhaps, but it enthralled my grandfather. One of the other books he gave me was the *Records of the Grand Historian,* the account of the dynasty of Qin. It had been another one of John Howard's books, found in his study after he disappeared."

"Speaking of family legends, what about Howard's disappearance?" Costas said. "Talk about something that would have enthralled children. You must have wondered whether he and Wauchope found some fabled treasure and lived out their lives like kings in some hidden mountain fastness, just like Kipling's story."

"Well, there was one story. It was told by Howard's wife, my great-great-grandmother. Everyone except my grandfather dismissed what she said because she'd become unwell. Howard had done everything he could for her. But as soon as their children had grown up, she deteriorated. She'd never been able to deal with the death of her first son. She was looked after by her sisters, but then she went into an institution. Howard had money from his father's indigo fortune, and no expense was spared for her comfort. Only when he knew there was no hope did Howard return to India. But he saw her again in England several times before he disappeared, the last time in 1907 just after he retired. He took her away for a few days to a cottage on the Welsh border. It seemed to be a brief window of happiness. It was a beautiful early summer, and they walked in the hills. That was how she remembered it, in a moment of lucidity when my grandfather visited her in the hospital years later. After Howard met up with Wauchope in Quetta, he never saw his wife again. But she lived for many years longer, in a kind of shadowland, not dying until 1933."

"Did she remember anything else?" Rebecca said, her voice emotional.

"She told my grandfather that when she shut her eyes tight, she was standing, holding hands with her son Edward, looking into a place of sparkling beauty, like a magical cave. Only Edward was older than he ever was, a little boy, not a babe in arms. Then she saw Howard, a proud young man in uniform, a twinkle in his eye, little Edward's father, her beloved husband, and the little boy ran, arms outstretched, crying out the word *Dada* over and over again, a word he had barely been old enough to say in his short life. She said in that moment she was in the perfect place. She spent a lot of time in that hospital with her eyes shut tight."

Rebecca was in tears, and Jack held her hand. "She did say one other thing. Everyone dismissed it because the hospital was run by nuns, and they thought she was just repeating some religious mantra. She said her husband had gone in search of the Son of Heaven."

"A Christian nunnery?" Costas said. "They must have said that to a lot of widows."

"That's what everyone thought." Jack leaned forward, his eyes ablaze. "But for my grandfather, then a young naval officer, it struck a chord and stayed with him. Fifty years later, when he was an old man himself, he called me at school. He was incredibly excited, and I had to drop everything and visit him. That was when he gave me the *Records of the Grand Historian.* He'd been thumbing through it, and he saw those exact words. *Son of Heaven.* He suddenly remembered where he'd seen them before. As a naval cadet, he'd put in at Shanghai and traveled to Xian, to see the fabled tomb of the First Emperor. His photograph of it in 1924 was one of the earliest to reach the west. That was where he'd seen those words, *Son of Heaven.* It was the traditional title of the Chinese emperor."

Rebecca wiped her eyes. "I remember it. The terracotta warriors exhibit."

"But there's more to it than that," Jack continued. "My grandfather had dug out his old print of the vast tomb mound, as big as an Egyptian pyramid, still completely unexcavated, years before the terracotta warriors were discovered. The tomb of the First Emperor, of *Shihuangdi,* Son of Heaven. He had the *Records* with him, and read the passage describing what was inside. Fabulous treasures, a replica of the world in miniature, the chamber decorated to represent the heavens, with the greatest light of all falling on the tomb. Then he had a brainstorm. That was when he called me. Howard's wife wasn't saying Son of Heaven, but *Sun* of Heaven. The sun, the greatest light in the sky, the light that would ensure the emperor's immortality. The greatest jewel in the heavens. That's what Howard's wife had meant. He had told her he was going in search of a fabled lost jewel."

"I knew it." Costas grinned. "A treasure hunt."

"All that stuff," Rebecca murmured. "How you thought it out, Dad. Pretty cool."

Jack sat back. "All I've done is open up an old chest of drawers and let it spill out."

The red warning light flashed above them. Jack glanced at Rebecca's seat belt and then out of the window, into the gray light of dawn. The descent to Bishkek airport was bumpy, through fierce crosswinds. Through holes in the cloud he saw flashes of land below, a dull flat wasteland and the airfield perimeter. A line of giant C-7 Galaxy transport aircraft stood on the tarmac, where the U.S. transit base for Afghanistan shared the runway with the civilian airport. The engines of the Embraer suddenly revved up to a whine. They had been bumped down too low,

379

and were doing a circuit before landing. Jack sat back and shut his eyes, feeling tired enough to fall asleep in an instant. He suddenly had a vivid picture of his grandfather's face, from the day they had spent together poring over the Chinese records. His grandfather had told him about the age-old quest for eternal life, about the First Emperor's expeditions to find the sacred Isles of the Immortals. Jack had only been a boy, but he had told his grandfather how one day he would search for treasures like that. He remembered what his grandfather had told him as they parted, the last time he ever saw him. He said he had sailed over a million miles in his life at sea, and that it was the journeys he relished most, not the destinations. Now, years later, after half a lifetime spent hunting down the greatest treasures in the world, Jack thought he understood. And then he remembered his grandfather playfully jostling him, and pretending to be an old Chinese sage. *Beware the Sacred Isles. The quest for immortality is a fool's errand, and the First Emperor was the biggest fool of them all. Stray too close, and you face mortal danger.*

The plane jolted violently. Jack opened his eyes with a start. Costas was staring across at him, in some kind of droll amusement. Jack guessed what he was thinking.

"Looking forward to seeing Katya?" Costas asked.

"Looking forward to seeing what she's found," Jack replied.

"Dad." Rebecca gave him a scornful look.

"Okay, okay. Looking forward to seeing her," Jack said. "But she's stuck out there by the lake because I suggested it. I'm visiting her in a professional capacity. I have a vested interest in this project."

"When you meet her, Rebecca, just don't use the word *girlfriend,*" Costas muttered. "If you don't want to bring out the Genghis Khan in her."

"Give me a break," Rebecca said. "What's going on here? Sounds like you guys need a reality check. Katya and I are both women. We can talk."

"Fortunately," Jack said, smiling sweetly at her, "you're not going anywhere near Katya today. After finding those bodies in the jungle, I'm not taking any chances. Katya was close to her uncle and involved with his research. If he was on a hit list, then Katya might be too. And that puts anyone around her in potential danger."

"Have you told her about him?" Costas said.

Jack held up his cell phone. "Just before we took off. And she had some news to tell me too."

"So you're saying I can't come," Rebecca said defiantly.

"You're going to stay with Ben and Andy at

the base, and help them with the equipment. Then you're going to fly east with them in a U.S. Air Force Chinook to the far end of Lake Issyk-Kul. That's where submerged ruins have been found. I promised we'd check that out too, as well as seeing what Katya's got for us. You're going to help set things up there, and wait for us."

"So I miss all the action," Rebecca said.

"You're going to be with a team of U.S. Navy SEALs," Costas said. "Can't get much better than that."

"You speak Russian, don't you, Rebecca?" Jack said.

She nodded, then looked at Costas. "The people my mother sent me to live with in New York are Russian. Petra and Michael defected in the mid-1980s, while they were in America at a conference. They're both palaeolinguists. Petra had been allowed by the Soviets to study in Italy, where she became my mother's best friend. That was before you two met, Dad, so you wouldn't have known her. After she returned to Moscow she met Michael at the Institute of Palaeography."

"That's where Katya's based, isn't it?" Costas exclaimed.

Rebecca nodded. "I knew about Katya way before I first met you, Dad. The first time I ever saw you and Costas was when I was sitting down one evening at our summer cottage in the Hamptons with Petra and Michael, watching a documentary about Atlantis. Katya was being interviewed."

"Small world," Costas said.

Jack looked out of the window, suddenly overwhelmed. He still had so much to learn about his daughter. It seemed inconceivable that he had only known her for a few months. He took a deep breath, and sat back. They were on the final approach now, and the plane was rocking about in the turbulence. He looked at Rebecca. "It's a serious job. Your Russian will come in very handy. The place you'll be going to on the lake is a Russian submersible warfare testing facility, recently reopened on the site of the old Soviet base. It's been a major coup getting them to agree to an IMU team operating in their restricted area, and for the U.S. military this is a lot more than just an interesting holiday for Special Forces out of Afghanistan. It'll require tact, poise and charm. It'll be your first official IMU role."

"But Costas hasn't taught me to dive yet," Rebecca said.

"Because Costas hasn't been allowed to take you to Hawaii yet," Costas grumbled.

"You can drive the boat," Jack said.

Rebecca perked up. "Where is it?"

Jack pointed down to the aircraft's floor. "Packed up in the hold. Brand-new Zodiac 6.5 meter rigid inflatable boat, twin 80

Evinrudes, state-of-the-art GPS navigation, position-fixing and bottom-profiling equipment."

"Cool."

Jack grinned at Costas. The plane's wheels skidded on the tarmac, and the nose settled down. The engines went into reverse and Rebecca shouted over the noise. "So when will I see you?"

"Don't know." Jack's voice was shuddering with the plane. "Depends on what Katya's found. Could be with you later today. But could be a little diversion."

"A little what?"

"A little diversion."

Costas looked despondently at his Hawaiian shirt, then at Rebecca. "By now, you should know what that means."

14

Jack and Costas stood beside the lake and waved at the army truck as it trundled off east, revving through the gears and disappearing over the ridge. After leaving Pradesh and Rebecca at the air base they had endured an exhausting four-hour journey from Bishkek, crammed into the cabin with the Kyrgyz driver and his guard. The U.S. Army Chinook helicopter which was meant to have brought them here had developed mechanical trouble, and rather than wait in Bishkek and risk losing a day they had opted to hitch a lift on a supply truck heading to the naval test base at the far end of the lake. Jack's anticipation had risen over the last hour as the truck had lurched its way toward the lake, through an extraordinary landscape of ravines and ridges formed by the raging cataract that had once flowed from the lake, now shaped again by the wind. He had imagined the thoughts of travelers who had once braved the pass, knowing that each dark recess might conceal a robber band, ready to inflict the murderous fate that had befallen so many on the Silk Route. And then the truck had mounted the final rise and they had seen Lake Issyk-Kul stretched out before them, with the snow-capped peaks of the Tien Shan Mountains lining the far side. The driver had stopped abruptly and gestured across a rocky field toward a solitary yurt, a traditional Kyrgyz tent. They had thanked him and jumped out, and now they slung their rucksacks and began to pick their way across the rocky landscape. Jack began to see the features that had made this place so beguiling to Katya: swirling, curvilinear patterns on the boulders, carvings that looked as old as the rocks themselves. He stopped at one, putting the flat of his hand against it, feeling the hand of the sculptor more than two thousand years ago.

"A cemetery?" Costas said from behind. "They look like tombstones."

"Possibly," Jack said. "But there's lot of shamanistic stuff here too. It goes on for miles, where boulders have tumbled down the slopes and come to rest near the lake-shore. Katya thinks the earliest petroglyphs date from the Bronze Age, from the late second millennium BC, but nomads were carving here right through the period of the ancient Silk Route, to the later first millennium AD. As well as the nomads, traders made their way east or west among these boulders for thousands of years; stopping here after surviving that pass or before risking it. In addition to all the nomad art, there's a chance of finding something really amazing, inscriptions made by those people — Bactrian, Sogdian, Persian, Chinese, you name it. Those traders are what give this route its place in history, yet they hardly left an imprint at all. Any discovery could be a huge revelation."

Jack shaded his eyes and looked across the field of boulders, away from the lake and back toward the pass. The late afternoon sun was in his eyes, and it was impossible to see much, flashes of light off the weatherworn surfaces of the rock, shadows where there were gullies and ravines. It would be very easy to get lost in this place, and very easy never to be found again.

"There they are," Costas said. "I can see Katya. Come on." Costas looked faintly out of place in his baggy shorts, oversized Hawaiian shirt, hiking boots and wraparound aviator sunglasses, but he was surprisingly agile and leapt nimbly from rock to rock. He reached a tall man in a felt hat who stood up among the boulders and shook hands. Jack joined them and shook hands too. The man was about his own age, with blue eyes, his face etched by sun and wind in the way of steppeland people. Katya stood behind him, looking as if she also had taken on the hue of the landscape. She caught Jack's eye and flashed him a quick smile, but her expression gave little away. She turned to the man. "Meet Altamaty," she said. "He's curator of the Cholpon-Ata open-air petroglyph museum. As well as his native Kyrgyz, he speaks Russian and Pashtun, but he's only just started to learn English. He's got diving experience with the old Soviet navy. He wants to be involved in the underwater investigations at the eastern end of the lake. I spoke to you about him, Jack."

"Where's the museum?" Costas asked.

Katya gestured around. "You're standing in it. It's probably the largest museum in the world. And the most under-resourced. It's basically a one-man show."

Jack looked at Katya. She was wearing faded military-surplus trousers and a khaki T-shirt, her forearms caked with dirt. Her long black hair was tied back and her face was deeply tanned, accentuating her high cheekbones. She looked more tired and weatherworn than the last time he had seen her, at the conference three months ago, but the color suited her. Jack knew that her mother had come from this area, and her face seemed at one with the tall Kyrgyz man beside her.

"I've already briefed our people about Altamaty," Jack said. "As soon as the Chinook's airworthy, Ben and Andy are flying from Bishkek straight to the old Soviet naval base at the eastern end of the lake. The Americans have already got things up and running there, and I want divers in the water as soon as possible to show what we can do. Rebecca's going with them."

"Your daughter is with you?" Katya said.

Jack had told Katya about Rebecca for the first time at the conference. "I was going to bring her here, but not after what happened to your uncle in the jungle. This place might be over the danger threshold. And she'll have enough on her plate with the guys on the lake. This is her first IMU expedition, and I want it to be a good experience, especially so soon after losing her mother."

"I'm looking forward to meeting her," Katya said.

"The maintenance team thought the chopper would be grounded for another day. I'm hoping they'll get there soon enough for things to be up and running before we arrive. Last time we were diving was in Egypt a week ago. I've never dived in a central Asian lake. I'm looking forward to it."

"I might take a raincheck until I pass a Geiger counter over the water," Costas said, rubbing his stubble. "Forty-odd years of Soviet submersible and torpedo testing. I know exactly how they fueled their gear. It was my master's thesis at MIT."

"The biggest problem is the old Soviet early warning stations on the mountaintops, which were nuclear-powered so they could be left unmanned," Katya said. "Locals have raided them and come back with pockets full of uranium, and been dead within a week. The nightmare is that any of this stuff finds its way onto the black market. It's why the Americans are so keen to take over cleanup of the old naval base. It's not so much environmental concern, but the war on terrorism."

Jack thought he saw a flash of light in the distance. He glanced up at the boulder-strewn slope behind them. It could have been a reflection off glass or metal, or just a trick of the eye. He shaded his eyes against the sun, looking hard, then turned to Katya. "Anyone else out here?"

"The odd shepherd, sometimes a hunter who disappears up there and never seems to come back." She turned to Altamaty and spoke to him in Kyrgyz. He followed Jack's gaze up the ridge, then spoke quickly to Katya. "Altamaty has eagle eyes," she said. "He says he saw breath from a horse when it was cold early this morning, far up on the ridge. The hunters sometimes stay in one place for days, waiting for deer."

"You're sure it's a hunter?" Jack said.

Katya eyed him. "Who else do you think it could be?"

"Are you armed?" Costas asked.

"Altamaty has his old service Makarov pistol and an SKS rifle he liberated from navy stores here when the Soviet Empire collapsed. We go hunting together. It supplements the mutton that's the staple out here."

"I forgot," Costas murmured. "A palaeolinguist who knows about guns."

Katya gestured toward a cluster of boulders about fifty meters away, where the top of a tractor was just visible above the rocks. "Come on," she said. "The light's perfect now, just as it was yesterday when we found it. And Altamaty's got some stew simmering in a big pot outside the yurt. You're in for a traditional Kyrgyz feast this evening."

"I'm starving," Costas said. "And I know mutton's one of Jack's favorites." Jack gave him a withering look and swallowed hard. It was the one thing he had been dreading. He could stomach virtually anything, except boiled sheep. He had lived for several years as a child in New Zealand, and had once overindulged. Since then even the smell made him feel nauseous. He knew it was a matter of the utmost importance that he conquer the problem now. His manhood was at stake. He smiled at Altamaty, then followed Katya along a track between the boulders. The ground was hard, baked like brick, with only a few tufts of coarse vegetation growing around the edge of the boulders. It was as if a sea of mud and rock had slid down the mountainside and solidified in one mass, embedding the boulders. Jack saw more rocks with carved designs on them, some so eroded they were barely discernible. He stopped for a moment to peer at one, and Costas hurried past him to Katya. "I meant to say," Costas said quietly, "I'm sorry about your uncle."

Katya glanced at him and nodded, saying nothing. She walked ahead, and they followed her in silence through the rocks until they came to the tractor. Costas stopped dead in his tracks, like a boy who had just been given a dream present. "A four sixty-five," he murmured reverently. "A Nuffield four sixty-five. This was why I got into engineering. I had a summer job on a farm in Canada. This was the first-ever diesel four-cylinder I disassembled." Altamaty opened the engine cowling, and the two men peered inside. Costas glanced at Jack. "I think I can bond with this guy. I think we just found a common language."

"No way," Jack said. "We did not come here to disassemble a tractor." Costas sighed, patted Altamaty regretfully on the shoulder, then followed Jack to where Katya was kneeling in front of a boulder a few meters away. They could see where it had been dragged away by the tractor, revealing another boulder that had been partly buried. Between the two was a marked-off excavation area of about four by two meters. In the center was a carefully excavated pile of smaller rocks, about a meter across and two meters long. Jack squatted down and stared at the markings on the freshly exposed boulder. It was why Katya had called him here. "Well I'll be damned," he murmured.

"Another rock carving," Costas said. "It looks better preserved than the others."

"Not just another rock carving," Jack said. "It's fantastic." His mind was reeling. It was one thing hearing it on the phone from Katya, but another thing seeing it for real. He felt the power of the past as he touched it. *Letters in Latin.* "It's the same number as in the jungle shrine, the same symbol. XV Ap. The Fifteenth Apollinaris legion."

Costas knelt down beside Jack. "I can see it. And that Roman inscription from the cave in Uzbekistan. The one Katya's uncle recorded."

"It's definitely the same sculptor," Katya said. "I've photographed this and scanned it against the image from the cave. He has a distinctive way of doing his finials, ending each line by angling the chisel back and knocking out a triangular chunk of rock."

"A citizen-soldier," Jack murmured. "One who remembered his trade, and still practiced it with care. He was the one they called upon when they needed to make an inscription."

"In the cave in Uzbekistan, I think it was a

393

casual marking, 'Licinius was here,' " Katya said. "Maybe the cave was where they really felt they had escaped from Merv, where the desert of Uzbekistan became the foothills of central Asia. From there, the Silk Route follows the ravines and mountain passes that eventually lead to this place. But this inscription here by the lake was for a different reason. You can barely make out the first line above the legion inscription, but it's a different personal name, I think Appius. And look at those two letters at the bottom."

"D M," Jack said, tracing his fingers down. "*Dis Manibus.* That means given to Dis, the god of the underworld. A funerary inscription." He glanced at the pile of rocks between the boulders. "This is a grave."

Costas peered at the rock. "And that symbol above the inscription. It's an eagle, isn't it? Isn't that what we saw in the jungle shrine?"

"It's the same legion," Jack murmured. "Incredible."

"It's exactly what I dreamed we'd find," Katya said. "The burial place of someone who died here, or in the pass below. For some, this must have been a place for exultation, for recuperation before the next stage in the journey. For others, it would have been a place to die. There must have been many deaths among the traders, Persians, Bactrians, Sogdians, Chinese. But *Roman?* It's astonishing."

"Did you find anything in the grave?" Costas asked.

"It was a hasty burial, as you might expect," she replied. "The ground's rock-hard and there isn't enough wood here to fuel a cremation. The body was covered with stones, maybe cut turf. That inscription would only have taken an hour or so to cut, for a skilled mason."

"A skilled mason?" Costas said. "Are you really sure about that?"

"There's no doubt about it." Jack traced his fingers over the symbols. "He had somehow fashioned a chisel with the right width of head, and he knew precisely where to place each blow. He knew the characteristics of this kind of rock, that it could take a glancing blow without fragmenting the surface. It's what I said in the jungle shrine. A citizen-soldier."

"You think this is the same guy?" Costas said.

"Let's wait to see what else Katya has to show us."

Katya looked at him, took a deep breath and pointed to a wooden finds crate on the ground. "The soil's very alkaline, and any bones would have disappeared long ago. But when the tractor dislodged the boulder, it revealed this." She drew back the cloth covering the interior of the crate.

Costas whistled. "That's some weapon."

Inside was a magnificent socketed halberd-head, dull silver in color with patches of green where it had corroded. On one side was a vicious curved blade extending outward about ten inches, and on the other side a narrower straight blade, the shape of a cut-throat razor.

"I've seen one like that in the British Museum," Jack exclaimed. "Late Warring States, early Western Han period?"

Katya nodded. "The razor-shaped blade is similar in proportions to Han-period swords, which look like Japanese samurai swords."

"Isn't this bronze?" Costas said. "Wouldn't that be too early for us?"

Katya shook her head. "Not necessarily. Iron was introduced in China by the fifth century BC, but the early cast iron was brittle so bronze was still used. And this bronze has been coated with chromium, which would have made it harder, better to hold a sharp edge."

"And a weapon like this might have been prized, passed down the generations," Jack murmured, touching the blade. "It could have been made in the early Han period, not long after the time of the First Emperor. But it could have survived in use for two centuries or more, to the period when we think these Romans came here."

"But what's a prestigious Chinese weapon doing in this place?" Costas said. "A passing Imperial Chinese warrior dumps it on a Roman grave? I don't get it." He gazed at Katya, who stared back at him, her eyes gleaming. "Ah," Costas said. "That's uncannily like the look Jack gives me. It means you've found something else."

Katya picked up a small plastic finds tray from beside the crate. "The halberd was in the center of the grave, as if it had been placed on the torso of the body. These two objects were where the head might have been." There were two coins in the tray, one silver and one corroded green, a disk with a square hole in the center. Jack took the silver coin, holding it up in the fading sunlight. "It's a silver tetradrachm of Alexander the Great!"

"And it's uncirculated," Katya said. "It's like those Roman coins from south India you were telling me about, uncirculated bullion."

Jack passed the coin to Costas. They could see the portrait on the obverse, the familiar head of Alexander wearing the mane of a lion, the classical form giving sudden reality to the idea of travelers from the ancient Graeco-Roman world coming this far east, to the very borderlands with China. Costas rotated the coin, peering at the portrait again, and a puzzled look returned to his face. "If my history's right, Alexander the Great lived in the later fourth century BC. That's a hundred years before the First Emperor, and three hundred years before our Romans. There must have been old Greek coins that found their way out here, used as bullion, jewelry. But they would have been worn." He looked dubiously at the Latin inscription on the boulder, then back at the coin. "Does this mean we're not looking at a Roman here after all, but at a soldier of Alexander the Great?"

"You've read the *Periplus of the Erythraean Sea*?" Katya said.

"The merchant's guide? First century BC, Egyptian Greek. I'm becoming an expert."

"Well, it says ancient coins of the Greeks are still to be found in Barygaza, just as you suggest," Katya said. "Then there are those new lines of the *Periplus* from Hiebermeyer's excavation in Egypt, describing Crassus' legionaries. Jack filled me in about that on the phone. They specifically mention an altar of Alexander, passed as they went east. That would have been in Uzbekistan, close to the cave with that Fifteenth Legion inscription. The Roman soldiers would have heard legends of Alexander's lost treasure. Once they'd reached that windswept altar in the desert, the mountains of central Asia looming ahead, they'd probably shaken off any pursuers from Merv and could relax a little. So what do they do? They dig around, searching. If Alexander was going to bother building an altar, he would have included offerings, and what better than mint coins with perfect images of himself. The Romans could have found this coin there, and brought it with them."

Jack took the coin from Costas, turning it over. "And then they place it on an eye of the body as an offering to Charon, the boatman across the river Styx."

"And the other coin?" Costas said. "On the other eye? That coin looks Chinese to me. Talk me through that one, Katya."

She picked up the second coin, with the square hole in the center. "There are three Chinese symbols on it, one to the right of the square hole, two to the left. This is a coin of the Han dynasty, a *wushu,* which means five grains, equaling four grams, the same weight as a Greek drachma or Roman denarius. Millions of these were produced, and they're quite common finds in Chinese central Asia."

"Can you pin down the date?" Costas asked.

"The symbols to the left are those of the reigning emperor, as distinctive to the Chinese as the change of portrait was to a Roman. And just as in Rome, a new emperor would attempt to replace existing coins with his own new ones. Token coins such as these, with no bullion value like silver or gold, would have been worthless with the name of a former emperor, and may even have been dangerous to be seen with. So this coin is unlikely to have been in circulation beyond the reign of that emperor. And he was the Han emperor Cheng, who ruled from about 32 to 5 BC."

Jack exhaled slowly. "Perfect," he said softly. "That fits with my own best-guess date for the escape of Crassus' legionaries, 19 or 18 BC. That's about a decade into the reign of Augustus, about the time he negotiated peace with the Parthians and saw the return of the lost legions' eagles."

"So how do our escaped Romans get hold of a Chinese coin?" Costas asked.

Jack pursed his lips. "They would have been desperate men, trained killers with nothing to lose. Any morality would have been stripped away with the loss of the eagles at Carrhae, and they would have been brutalized by years of torture and hardship under the Parthians. They may have stolen Parthian gold when they escaped, but they still had to eat. Silk Route traders packed everything they needed for the journey. The Romans would have preyed on any caravan they came across, probably killing everyone, maybe taking the odd captive as a guide, gorging themselves on food and drink, looting anything of value they could carry. This coin may have been in the saddlebag of some ill-fated Sogdian trader. But it was of no bullion value, and was something they could afford to leave here to satisfy Charon and ease their comrade's journey into the afterlife."

"And the halberd?" Costas said. "That would have been a much bigger sacrifice."

"A warrior was always buried with his

weapon," Jack murmured. "With their eagles gone, the legionaries only had each other, and they probably cherished a dream that they would once again march alongside their dead comrades, heads held high in the fields of Elysium. Even if it meant reducing their own defenses, they would never have buried a comrade without a weapon for the afterlife. Even a weapon so much at odds with the normal equipment of a legionary."

"You think they looted that from a trader too?" Costas asked.

"The Romans would have armed themselves with whatever they could find," Jack replied. "Thrusting swords and spears would have been their favored weapons as legionaries, but anything would do."

Costas touched his finger on the curved blade. "This seems an unlikely sidearm for a trader."

"There were others on the Silk Route besides traders," Katya said quietly. "Mercenaries, employed as caravan guards. Marauding bands of robbers, preying on the caravans like highwaymen. It was like the Wild West out here. Up on the steppes, in the mountains, is the toughest place for an outsider to live, and only the most murderous gangs survived. No mercy was given. And there were others."

"Warriors from the east." Jack looked carefully at Katya. "Warriors who bore the tattoo

401

of a tiger."

Katya shot a glance at Jack, and looked down at the halberd again. "There were murder gangs out here, but there were also raiding parties from China, from the warrior empire itself. They were the most feared of all, superbly armed and equipped, on horseback, always accompanied by a drumbeat, rising in a crescendo as they swooped down on their prey. They would have seemed invincible. For the nomads who live out here, for my mother's people, the sound of a distant drumbeat still sends a shiver through the soul. Even I can sense it, when I let my imagination run free."

"So the Chinese raided their own traders?" Costas said incredulously.

"To understand why, you have to understand the nature of Chinese society. The empire was a totalitarian state, inward-looking, a universe unto itself. Control freaks always need a boundary, between the world they can dominate and the world outside, which is feared, rejected. There's no hazy middle ground. When you look at the Great Wall of China, remember that psychology. In extreme cases, the boundary acts like a prison wall, and the controller sends out tentacles to draw back anyone who steps beyond. At some periods, that's what happened with China."

"So how could Chinese traders operate on the Silk Route?" Costas asked.

"They didn't. Officially, at least. But the people of central Asia and western China are similar in physiognomy, and an intrepid Chinese trader could pass through unnoticed. There were probably plenty of them, disguised among parties of Sogdians. There were rich pickings to be had in the silk trade, and the temptations for a Chinese trader would have been great."

"So you're saying they were hunted down?"

Katya nodded. "But there was another side to that coin. The Chinese elite enjoyed their luxuries. Like all megalomaniacs, the emperors were prey to human temptation. Prized raw materials could only be got abroad, such as precious stone: lapis lazuli, peridot. The emperors turned a blind eye to the trade, as long as the traders were invisible. But if anyone was *known* to stray, they were ruthlessly sought. The *Records of the Grand Historian,* the Chinese imperial annals, are full of stories of aberrant younger sons or nephews seeking fortunes elsewhere, forming pacts with outsiders. In that sense the Chinese royal dynasties were like any other, but they were unique in their relentless quest to bring back and punish anyone who tried to leave." Katya gestured at the weapon in the box. "That halberd's an imperial Chinese weapon, a prized item like an officer's sword. You'd never have found a weapon like that in the hands of a mere caravan guard. That weapon was brought out here by a Chinese warrior."

"So how on earth does a Roman get hold of it?" Costas asked.

Katya eyed him. "Speculation built on speculation, right? We've got a party of Romans, desperate men, escaped prisoners, tough ex-legionaries going east. Their numbers are dwindling. They've been attacked again, maybe in that pass behind us. Their attackers are not just another robber band, but fearsome warriors, worthy opponents. The Romans have fought well, and have captured some weapons. But they are hard-pressed. One of their comrades has fallen, and they quickly lay him to rest. They set off again east."

"If their attackers were Chinese, why are they coming after the Romans?"

"Backtrack in time a day or two," Katya said. "Imagine a party of Sogdian traders, laden with silk. They've come across the lake, heading west. They leave their boats here, and transfer to the camels awaiting them. They make their way through the pass. Soon after that they're attacked, by a band of desperadoes far worse than any they've seen before, by the Romans. The traders are all massacred, except for one, kept alive to guide the Romans back through the pass. Only the trader they've got is not a Sogdian. He's Chinese. And he's being followed. He is one who had strayed."

"With something that he shouldn't have," Jack murmured. "With what we found out from the inscription in the shrine. A jewel."

Katya shot him a piercing glance, and Jack held her eyes for a moment. Costas pointed at the crate. "Anything else to show us?"

Katya lifted out another tray. "We did find something pretty fantastic. I was saving it until the end." She drew back the cloth. Beneath it was a blackened lump, like a shriveled rind of fruit that had been peeled open in strips and left to dry. "It's camel leather, local Bactrian camel," she said. "It's uncured, skin taken from a freshly dead animal. Altamaty says that when the nomads do this, they soak the leather in urine to keep it supple." She sniffed the lump. "You can still smell the uric acid. That's probably why this survived, under the rocks where the feet of the body would have been." She picked up a clipboard and showed them a design that looked as if it had been cut from folded paper, full of triangles and rhomboids. "I downloaded this from an excavation report of a legionary fortress on the German frontier," she said. "A Roman soldier who'd been trained to make something one way would always replicate it, especially such a tried and tested design."

Costas stared. "Okay, Katya. I give up."

"The indispensable camel," Jack said, smiling broadly. "To a Roman legionary in need of kit, the first thought when he sees a camel is not something to ride or carry gear, but leather for making boots."

"Boots," Costas exclaimed. "Of course. The bits sticking out are where it laces up."

"These are *caligae*," Jack said. "Every legionary wore them, wherever he was. The pattern was fixed about the time of Julius Caesar, when these guys were doing their basic training." He leaned down and sniffed. Katya was right. *He could smell them.* It was an extraordinary feeling, a heady rush from the past, and for a split second he could sense it all, the sweat, the adrenaline, the fear, the sickly-sweet odor of decay at this spot, the reek of men with the heightened animal intensity that comes with the proximity of death.

He looked away. He realized that Altamaty had disappeared. Another smell came wafting over them, from the direction of the yurt. Jack steeled himself. It might be time to break his taboo in the field and drink something fortifying. Very fortifying. He could toast the Kyrgyz people. Katya was looking at him, the hint of a smile on her lips. "Are you ready to do Altamaty a great honor and feast on some mutton, prepared in the traditional way as a great mark of esteem to our guests?" Jack swallowed hard, and nodded. She knew. She dropped her smile and looked at him seriously. "And then we'll go up that hill behind

406

us. There's something else I need to show you. You were right about that Sogdian, Jack. He had something he never should have had. Something of incalculable value. We might just be on the most extraordinary treasure hunt you could ever imagine."

15

Two hours later, Jack and Costas followed Katya up a rocky hillside at the western end of the lake, above the pass that dropped through a fractured landscape of ravines and gullies toward the central plain of Kyrgyzstan. It was early evening and the sun had nearly set, but it was due to be a full moon and the lake was bathed in an eerie glow. Katya found a ledge and sat down, and Jack and Costas sat on either side, looking back over the shimmering surface of the lake. A few hundred meters to the north there was a roar of diesel and a puff of smoke as Altamaty fired up the tractor and drove it back toward the yurt, his form lurching and bobbing over the uneven track that led from the site where they had excavated the Roman burial. Huge boulders lay embedded in the slope as far as they could see, like a vast inchoate army struggling to free itself from the earth.

Jack's mind returned to one small group who had passed this place over two thousand years before, men who bore fierce allegiance to their greatest symbol, the eagle of the legion, who had paused to carve it on the tombstone of a companion in this place where none but they would recognize it. He remembered something Pradesh had told him about Kashmir, where his unit had fought Pakistani troops for possession of a bleak mountain plateau. It was the age-old wisdom of the soldier, that when you fight you do it not for any higher cause but for your comrades, for your unit. Jack narrowed his eyes, and wondered whether those legionaries had looked up and sensed the proximity of the heavens, felt the tingle of the wind. For a moment he saw not just a ragged band of survivors but a fully formed legion on the march, shadow-warriors who had been with them since the battlefield at Carrhae, but were here closer than ever, in a place where the living might seem but one short step away from the fields of Elysium.

Costas passed a cup he had carried up from the yurt toward Jack, who shook his head firmly. "No thanks." He could smell the fermented milk. He had avoided disgrace at the feast by accepting the choicest morsels to chew on, tasteless rubbery lumps from the sheep's head that were reserved for the most honored guest. Then Rebecca had saved the day by calling on the satellite phone just as Altamaty was serving up the mutton stew, and Jack had taken his plate outside with the receiver, apparently eager not to lose a moment before tucking in. He had returned with a convincing pile of gristle on the side of the plate, and had even tossed it back into the cauldron to be softened up further, scrupulously following the custom Katya had explained to him. Costas had looked at him innocently from the other side of the low table, reaching for Jack's plate and the ladle, but Jack's eyes had bored into him. It had been a close-run thing, but it was only a temporary fix. As he had clearly passed the test, endless feasts were in the offing. He had an image of the eyes of the Kyrgyz people glued on him as swimming stews of mutton and grease were poured onto his plate. He glanced at his watch. The helicopter was due to whisk them away in less than an hour's time. He turned to Katya. "You had something more to tell us."

Katya looked at the cover of the book she had been carrying and cleared her throat. "Okay. The period in history when these legionaries were making their way through this place was the time of the greatest empire the west had ever known. When the legionaries left Italy for the east, Rome was still a republic, just before the civil wars. But by the time they escaped from the Parthians over three decades later, Rome was ruled by her first and greatest emperor, Augustus. Those legionaries were not emissaries of Rome. They may not even have known that Rome was ruled by an emperor. But unwittingly, they were a bridge between Rome and the greatest empire of the east, one that had begun in China two centuries before. That was the time of King Zheng of the Qin dynasty, the warlord who unified China and ruled from 221 to 210 BC. He was the one history knows as *Shihuangdi,* the First Emperor."

"The guy with the terracotta warriors," Costas said.

Katya nodded. "The warriors were buried with him, surrounding the greatest unexcavated tomb in history. For the legionaries the fantasized image of that tomb may even have been the light at the end of their tunnel, a legend of unplundered riches that may have persuaded them to go east when they had escaped the Parthians. I'll get to that in a moment. Jack, what do you know about the *Res Gestae?*"

"It means *things I have done,*" Jack said. "It was Augustus' record of achievements, inscribed on bronze plaques and set up all around the empire. Lists of conquests, buildings projects, benefactions, laws, that sort of thing. The record of a man who saw himself as *primus inter pares,* a citizen who had taken temporary charge to restore the republic. Above all it was a celebration of peace, the

411

pax Romana, the inspiration for the *pax Britannica* that led men like my great-great-grandfather to believe their purpose was a noble one, that a benign empire was truly possible."

"And now for *Shihuangdi,* the First Emperor," Katya said. "He also left a record of achievements, inscribed on bronze and stone and set up high in the mountains, in places he visited to carry out sacrifices to the cosmic powers. But it's frighteningly different. Instead of listing vanquished enemies, the First Emperor celebrates internal order. He's proud of establishing a totalitarian police state. The empire of Augustus, like the British Empire, was cosmopolitan, with a tolerance for cultural diversity that was a linchpin of the Imperial system. China was different. The empire of the First Emperor was an empire of the Chinese people, full stop. The outside world was barely acknowledged. Augustus was a man of the people, a Roman through and through. The First Emperor was an outsider, a warlord who swept down into the Chinese heartland just as Genghis Khan was to do centuries later. But whereas Genghis Khan expended his energy in endless conquests in the world beyond, the First Emperor stopped at the geographical limits of China while he was still bursting with warrior fury. He found his outlet in a mania for control. He didn't really rule an empire at all. He himself said it. He unified China. He *created* China. Before him, China was a chaotic land of warring states. He subsumed all that. He turned back the clock to zero."

"Plus ça change," Jack murmured.

Katya opened the book. "Virtually everything we know of him comes from the *Records of the Grand Historian* by Sima Qian, written about a century after the First Emperor's death. It records admonitions, edicts, laws, tirelessly issued by the Great One. He adjusts rules, sets standards for everything, 'the ten thousand things.' He regulates the seasons and the months, rectifies the days, makes uniform the sounds and measures. All under heaven are of one mind, one will. Listen to this. *'His great rule purifies the folkways, the whole empire acknowledges its sway; it blankets the world in splendid regulation. Posterity will obey his laws, his constant governance knowing not end. The bright virtue of the Great Emperor aligns and orders the whole universe.'* He even erased the concept of doubt."

Costas whistled. "Sounds like the mother of all control freaks."

Katya nodded. "Augustus' creed was feel-good, the creed of a golden age. The creed of the First Emperor was one of order, certainty. And with that came denial of anything that couldn't be controlled, denial of the outside world. Listen to this: *'In the twenty-sixth year of his rule he first united the world; there were none who did not come to him in submission.'* And again: *'Wherever human tracks may reach, there are none who are not his subjects.'* These are patent lies, as anyone who had been beyond the borders would know. But he tried to solve that by preventing anyone from leaving."

"So what about the gods?" Costas asked. "Or was this guy divine too?"

Katya put down the book and took out a ziplock bag with an object inside. It was the Chinese coin they had found in the burial, with the square hole in the center. "This coin represents two of the most powerful Chinese symbols of cosmological power, in which the earth is square and the heavens are circular. The coin shows the heavens as a delimited concept, as something finite." She slipped the bag back in her pocket. "To the steppe-dweller, surrounded by vast open spaces and sky, either you're overawed by it or you see it as the definition of your world. The ancient Chinese attempted to rationalize the heavens, to bring them within their grasp. Take a look at Altamaty's yurt. The dome shape is a representation of the heavens, like a plan-etarium. Sitting inside it, surrounded by the vastness of the steppe, you can feel that you've drawn the heavens toward you, that you control them. That's how to understand the First Emperor. His cities, his palaces,

414

were analogues of the heavens, and so was the underground world he created for his eternal existence."

"Tell us about that," Costas said.

"That was another difference from the Romans. Augustus may have been deified later, but he lived his life as a mortal. The First Emperor had no need for the afterlife. He'd created his own heaven on earth. When he went to the mountains and sacrificed to the cosmic powers, he was really sacrificing to himself. He couldn't bear to acknowledge his own mortality."

"You're talking about the concept of *wu di,* non-death," Jack said.

Katya nodded. "For many ancient Chinese, there was no spiritual world beyond the present. The dead formed a community on earth, an analogue of the world of the living. They could even intermingle, in places where the earth and the cosmos are close, where illusion and reality were interchangeable. Places like this, high in the mountains. And for an emperor, *wu di* was a control concept. Everyone retained their roles — soldiers, courtesans, the emperor himself. For him, it meant eternal power."

"Didn't the First Emperor try to prolong his actual life?" Costas asked.

Katya nodded wryly. "He sent expeditions to a place called Penglai, the Isles of the Immortals, the mythical dwelling place of the

Blessed. He ate from utensils of gold and jade, thought to dispel bodily decay. He employed spells and charms to battle the demons he thought caused aging. And according to Sima Qian, he took mercury, another supposed panacea. That was probably what killed him."

"And that gets us to his tomb," Jack said.

Katya flipped the book to a marked page. "The most famous passage of the *Records of the Grand Historian*." She read it out:

"In the ninth month the First Emperor was interred at Mount Li. When the emperor first came to the throne he began digging and shaping Mount Li. Later, when he unified the empire, he had over seven hundred thousand men from all over the empire transported to the spot. They dug down to the third layer of underground springs and poured in bronze to make the outer coffin. Replicas of palaces, scenic towers and the hundred officials, as well as rare utensils and wonderful objects, were brought to fill up the tomb. Craftsmen were ordered to set up crossbows and arrows, rigged so they would immediately shoot down anyone attempting to break in. Mercury was used to fashion imitations of the hundred rivers, the Yellow River and the Yangtse, and the seas, constructed in such a way that they seemed to flow. Above were representations of all

416

the heavenly bodies, below, the features of the earth."

"Incredible," Costas murmured. "And all that stuff's still there?"

Katya passed him a photograph. It showed a vast mound, surmounted by trees. "There's no reason to doubt Sima Qian's description, even though the tomb had been filled and sealed before he was born," she said. "The discovery of the terracotta warriors in pits outside suggests that his account of the burial chamber may not be exaggerated. Chinese scientists using remote-sensing equipment have even detected high concentrations of mercury under the mound."

"So you're saying he wasn't preparing for the afterlife, but for a kind of parallel existence."

"The First Emperor had already paved the way in real life, planning his palaces and temples in his capital Xian as imitations of the heavens, with the river Wei as the Milky Way. He aligned political and cosmological order, just as he'd proclaimed in his edicts. He was also mapping his palaces on the stars, imposing the dwellings of a supreme being on the cosmos."

"And for supreme being, read First Emperor," Costas said.

"Right. And now for the reason we're here."

Katya picked up the book and read the next passage:

"After the interment had been completed, someone pointed out that the artisans and craftsmen who had built the tomb knew what was buried there, and if they should leak word of the treasures, it would be a serious affair. Therefore, after the articles had been placed in the tomb, the inner gate was closed off and the outer gate lowered, so that all the artisans and craftsmen were shut in the tomb and were unable to get out. Trees and bushes were planted to give the appearance of a mountain."

She closed the book and spoke quietly. "What I've told you so far is all documented. What I'm about to tell you no other westerners have ever heard, and no one in China outside a small and secret fold that includes my own family."

"Here we go," Costas murmured, eyeing Katya.

"There's an ancient myth," she said. She paused, and Jack could see the burden on her, the decision to reveal something kept secret by generations of her forbears. She looked at him, and he nodded. She took a deep breath and carried on. "A myth about a pair of precious stones, set together in the First Emperor's tomb at the apex of the

418

heavens. A pair of stones that shone with dazzling light, a light the emperor believed would assure his immortal power. And a myth that the guardian of the tomb secretly took those stones before the burial chamber was sealed. That those who swore to protect the tomb, to assure the emperor's eternal reign, pursued the guardian and his descendents relentlessly, through the ages, but never found the stolen jewels."

"Good God," Jack murmured. "The inscription in the jungle shrine."

"Fast-forward two thousand years," Katya said. "To a foggy night in Victorian London, at the Royal United Service Institution. It was the usual Thursday night venue, sherry and sandwiches followed by a lecture." She took out a clear plastic sleeve containing a faded brown broadsheet, and passed it to Jack. He looked at it for a moment, stunned. "Well I'll be damned," he murmured. He read it out:

"An illustrated lecture at the Royal United Services Institute, 6.30 to 7.30 pm, Thursday, 26 November 1888. "Roman Antiquities of Southern India." Accompanied by lantern slides and artifacts on display. By Captain J. L. Howard, R.E., of the School of Military Engineering, formerly of the Queen's Own Madras Sappers and Miners."

Jack looked at Katya incredulously. "How on earth did you get this? I knew about Howard's lecture, but I've never seen an original broadsheet."

"It's covered in scribbled notes, in Chinese characters," Costas said, peering closely. "In pencil, so faded you can barely read it. As if someone were taking notes."

"It was a Chinese diplomat called Wu Che Sianghu, a Kazakh Mongolian," Katya said. "He'd been posted the year before to the Chinese embassy in London, and frequently attended public lectures. He had a special interest in India because he'd been sent by the Chinese government to investigate the opium trade, which was still flourishing despite Victorian moral opprobrium. He was particularly concerned about the spread of opium use among the hill tribes of the upper Godavari River, following the end of the Rampa Rebellion and the departure of the troops in early 1881. I know about this because Wu Che's papers came into my uncle's possession."

"Your uncle?" Costas said. "The uncle whose body we found in the jungle?"

Katya nodded. "But the broadsheet probably never would have been saved had it not been for one thing Howard said in that lecture, the one thing that explains how my uncle came to be in the jungle and to die there. It's in those pencil notes."

"Go on," Jack said.

She took the paper out of the plastic. "It's at the bottom. It says, *'Roman military-style carvings found in jungle.'* And then *'cave temple?'* The first note was taken from what Howard said, and the second was guesswork by Wu Che. Almost all ancient carvings then being found in southern India were from cave temples or shrines, so it was a reasonable surmise."

"Incredible," Jack murmured. "There are no surviving drafts of the lecture and it was never published. In Howard's papers I found an exchange of letters with the editor of the institute journal badgering Howard for a typescript. The paper had been co-authored with Robert Wauchope, who'd been posted back to the Survey of India. Howard claimed the two of them needed to collaborate to produce a polished version, but that evidently never happened. There was a new editor a few years later and the matter was dropped. It always struck me as odd for Howard not to publish. His collection of Roman coins from India was a passion of his. But what you've said might shed light on it. Something was holding him back."

"Something he said in the lecture he shouldn't have said?" Costas suggested.

"Here's what I know," Katya said. "At the bottom of this sheet Wu Che writes *'Spoke*

421

privately after the lecture to Captain Howard, no more information forthcoming.' But then I think he tried to contact Howard again."

Jack's mind was suddenly racing. "I knew this rang a bell. He *did* try again. It's in another letter in Howard's papers, in the chest in *Seaquest II.* It dates from a few years later, in 1891. Someone from the Chinese embassy in London wrote to Howard about the Rampa Rebellion. That's why I remember it. I'm certain it was the same Chinese name, Wu Che Sianghu. The letter was purportedly about opium. He knew that Howard had been one of the longest-serving British officers in Rampa. He wanted to know if Howard knew of any ritual contexts in which opium might be used by the jungle peoples, in ceremonies, in caves, temples."

"He was fishing for more details about that shrine," Costas suggested.

"Wu Che must have done some research after the lecture, worked out where Howard was during his time in India with the Madras Sappers, anywhere out of the ordinary. Details of officers' deployments were published in the annual *Army List.* He would have seen Howard's deployment to Rampa in 1879 and 1880. It was close to the area of Roman influence in southern India yet hardly explored by Europeans, with hundreds of square miles of jungle not even surveyed. It was just the kind of place where soldiers on patrol might have stumbled on an ancient shrine. The Royal Engineers officers and NCOs of the Madras Sappers were the only British army personnel with the Rampa Field Force, and it's possible that Howard was the only veteran in England at the time of his lecture. Wu Che might have played on that too. He might have expected Howard to be eager to respond to any query about the campaign. But Wu Che's letter has Howard's handwritten 'Not replied' across the top. It was obviously Howard's firm decision, but it was perhaps a mistake. Not replying at all might have rung alarm bells for Wu Che."

"I thought Howard had clammed up about the rebellion anyway," Costas said. "Something you think happened to him out there. Some trauma."

"But Wu Che wouldn't have known about that," Jack said. "He would have assumed the lack of reply was because Howard refused to be forthcoming about something he'd found."

"Howard may have regretted his slip in the lecture, mentioning the sculpture, and determined never to make the mistake again," Katya said. "When the letter arrived he would have remembered Wu Che from after the lecture, and that may have set off his own alarm bells too. He might have remembered the pact Jack thinks he and Wauchope made after leaving the shrine. That's maybe when he decided not to go ahead with publishing the paper."

Costas looked puzzled. "What is it that excites a Chinese diplomat in 1888 about reports of Roman sculpture in a jungle shrine in southern India? What's that got to do with opium?"

Katya paused. "That's why I told you about the First Emperor. There's a connection. A pretty astonishing one. And you are the first outsiders to hear this." She took a deep breath. "When the First Emperor was planning his afterlife, he entrusted the sanctity of his tomb to his most trusted bodyguards, to men of his clan who had ridden down with him into China from the Qin homeland in the northern steppes. They were Mongols, fierce nomad horsemen, from the stock who would one day spawn Genghis Khan and the most terrifying army the world has ever known. The emperor's bodyguard wore tiger skins over their armor, and wielded great swords. They called themselves tiger warriors."

Jack stared at Katya. "Go on."

"There were twelve of them, his closest bodyguard," Katya continued. "Six was the First Emperor's sacred number, and any multiples of it had special power. Even during his lifetime the warriors were secret, and they revealed themselves only to the emperor's enemies, to those they were sent to hunt down, those who would never live to tell what they saw. In time, one of them became the killer, the emperor's closest bodyguard, and he alone became known as the tiger warrior. On the emperor's deathbed, the twelve were entrusted with the outer ring of defenses of his tomb. The inner sanctum was entrusted to a hereditary family of guardians, who lived within the tomb precinct. The twelve were sworn to infiltrate Xian society for generations to come, as courtiers, officials, army officers, an invisible power always ready to pounce. They were promised immortality through endless reincarnation, the eternal earthly vanguard of the terracotta warrior army who were buried around the emperor's tomb. For more than two thousand years the tiger warriors have kept the tomb inviolate, from tomb robbers, from later emperors, from archaeologists. Inviolate, that is, with one exception."

"Something was taken," Jack murmured.

Katya nodded. "Of all the wondrous treasures of the tomb, only the guardian and the twelve knew what lay at the apex of the heavens, directly over the tomb itself. Sima Qian, author of the *Records of the Grand Historian,* knew nothing of it."

"A pair of precious stones," Jack murmured. "Stones that interacted to produce a light like a star in the heavens. A double jewel. The jewel of immortality."

Katya stared at him, then spoke quietly. "In

the last act of the burial ritual, the guardian alone was in the tomb, passing from the central chamber to the entrance before sealing the vault for all eternity. Something made the warriors suspect him of stealing the greatest treasure, and their suspicions hardened when the guardian lived to a great age, well over one hundred years. That was not uncommon for steppe Mongolians, but was enough to convince them that he had taken something that prolonged life, a treasure that should rightly have been left in the tomb to release them from their servitude and allow the emperor to rise again. They never saw the guardian die. He returned to the northern steppes, handing over the custodianship to his son, a tradition that continued. But then, five generations on, the son of the guardian himself disappeared. He did not return to the steppes but went west beyond the boundary of the empire, strayed to where he should not go. The twelve decided to act. The tiger warrior was unleashed."

"Let me guess," Jack murmured. "That was 18 BC, maybe a little earlier?"

Katya stared at him again, and continued. "The son of the guardian disguised himself as a Sogdian trader, and joined one Silk Route caravan, then another. The tiger warrior and his henchmen chased him across the Taklamakan Desert, toward the Tien Shan Mountains, up here to Lake Issyk-Kul, into the ravines and passes beyond. They had him in their grasp, but then something got in their way."

"A band of renegade Roman legionaries," Jack murmured.

"In their secret oral tradition, the twelve remembered them as *kauvanas,* an ancient Chinese word for westerners," Katya said. "But my uncle was convinced of who they were."

"I was wondering when your uncle was going to come into this," Costas said.

"This was the story he pieced together. It fits with your scenario, Jack. The Romans attack the caravan and seize the disguised Sogdian. They keep him alive, as a guide. The warriors realize the Romans have him, and attack, but are repulsed, by a foe stronger than any they have ever encountered before. One of their number is cut down in the ravines, and one of the Romans too. That's the grave we found by the lake. By now there are only a dozen of the Romans left. The tiger warrior and his henchmen pursue them to this place, then see the survivors embark on the lake and row east. They find the body of Liu Jinn, the guardian's son, but the treasure is gone. They follow the boat along the shore, until it disappears in a storm near the end of the lake. But they realize that the Romans in the boat were fewer in number than they should have been. *One is missing.* They return to the western end of the lake, to where they had found the murdered Liu Jinn. They track the missing Roman, follow the dripped blood from the weapon the man had used. They glimpse him, high in the passes of the mountains to the south. They pursue him relentlessly, for weeks, months, sometimes coming close, sometimes losing him. They follow him through the valleys of Afghanistan, through the Khyber Pass into India, down the Ganges to the Bay of Bengal. Then, in the jungles of the south, they lose him for good. They know he's in there somewhere, but it's as if the jungle has absorbed him. But the Chinese do not give up. They infiltrate the Roman trading colony at Arikamedu, posing as silk merchants. For generations they remain, watching, waiting. But then the Romans leave, and with the rise of the Arabs the sea trade with the west comes to an end. The Chinese return home, and with that the story of their quest moves into the realm of legend, part of the mythology of an obscure secret society who seem to disappear from living history."

"And now we know their names, the Romans," Jack said. "From the tomb inscription in the jungle. Fabius, leader of the group, who went off east over the lake. And his best friend Licinius, the one who escaped south. And we know that they had the treasure. Fabius had the one jewel, the peridot. Licinius

428

had the other, *sappheiros,* lapis lazuli. They must have parted ways unaware of what they had shared out between them, of the power of the jewels together. The Chinese must have thought Licinius had taken both parts of the jewel, and fled from his comrades knowing the power of what he had stolen, something that might make him an emperor in his own world."

"Katya's uncle may have read that inscription too, before he was murdered," Costas said. "And those who murdered him may have found out too."

"So what happened to the tiger warrior, and the twelve?" Jack asked.

Katya paused. "Their pledge to protect the tomb, to recover the lost treasure, remained strong, through all the vicissitudes of Chinese history, through all the emperors and dynasties who might have plundered the monuments of their forebears. The warriors nurtured the cult of the First Emperor, the mystique that still surrounds his name today. Wu Che, the Chinese diplomat who went to Howard's lecture, was one of them. He was a keen historian, and wrote down the story I've just told you, the oral tradition recounted at their secret meetings. And then it seemed that their quest might be rekindled. In the second half of the nineteenth century, European scholars were reading the newly translated *Periplus of the Erythraean Sea,* and were beginning to understand the truth of Roman mercantile involvement in south India. Wu Che kept his ear to the ground, seeking anything unusual, anything in the archaeological discoveries that might suggest a maverick Roman, a legionary. When Howard mentioned the jungle shrine with Roman carvings, the light began flashing."

"And that's really why you're here, by Lake Issyk-Kul," Jack said quietly. "It wasn't just to record petroglyphs and search for inscriptions from the Silk Route. You wanted to find that Roman. You're on this trail too. You and your uncle are part of all this."

Costas eyed Katya. "Well? Your uncle was one of the twelve, wasn't he?"

Katya paused. "My uncle and my father both knew the story, passed down to them. My father inherited the family papers, but he had little interest in the mythology of the brotherhood. To him the jewels were lost forever, if they even existed. He was into the antiquities black market and easier prizes. It was my uncle who encouraged my interest in ancient languages and archaeology. Two years ago while we were on the Black Sea after my father's death, my uncle came across those lecture notes of Wu Che, while he was hastily searching through my father's papers in Kazakhstan before Interpol arrived. My uncle had already made the connection between the tiger warrior legend and Crassus' lost legionaries. He took up where Wu Che left off. He went to the India Office archives in London to research the *Madras Military Proceedings* and pinpoint where Howard had been during the Rampa Rebellion."

"The same records I studied," Jack exclaimed.

Katya nodded. "You were both on the same trail. In a district gazetteer he came across mention of a shrine, to Rama. That was the clincher. And that's where you found him. His body."

"Have you told Katya your theory about that name, Jack?" Costas said.

Katya replied first. "My uncle might have been there already. *Rama* seemed a very similar word to *Roman.* He mentioned it to me, but we didn't want to voice it until we were on firmer ground. The similarity seemed too obvious."

"Nothing's too obvious in this game," Jack murmured, peering at Katya. "Is there anything else you haven't told us?"

"My uncle was being secretive, but for good reason. He knew that once he'd been targeted, so would all his immediate family. It has always been the way. If one of the twelve deviated, his entire clan would pay the price. That was the way the First Emperor had meted out his version of justice. And since there's nobody else left in my uncle's family, that means me."

"Okay, Katya," Costas said. "I take it you're on about those tattooed guys whose bodies we found near the shrine."

"Jack told me," Katya said quietly. "How many of them were there?"

"We counted six bodies. Apparently, seven had gone into the jungle, arriving by helicopter. They were all Chinese, wearing shirts with the logo of a mining corporation, INTA-CON. Bids have been put in to strip-mine the Rampa hills for bauxite, and the local Kóya people are used to seeing prospectors. All it does is drive them further into the hands of the Maoist terrorists who use the jungle as their hideaway. The Maoists occasionally attack the mining parties because it solidifies their support among the tribals, and as a result the police turn a blind eye when the mining groups go in armed to the teeth. What we saw at the shrine suggests that the Chinese got inside the cave, found and murdered your uncle, then were ambushed on the way out. Their bodies had been partly stripped and mutilated by the Maoists, and we could see the skin. They all had the same black tattoo on the upper left arm."

Katya scribbled on her notepad. "Like this?"

Costas nodded. "Exactly like that. Like a tiger head."

"Tiger warriors?" Jack said.

Katya shook her head. "Only one of the

twelve is called that. He goes out to do the dirty work, the newest of them, as a rite of initiation. The others call themselves the Brotherhood. And the Chinese you saw were mere foot soldiers, lesser clan members bound by birth to serve the Brotherhood."

"We encountered three Maoists, and one of them wasn't quite dead." Costas pointed at his bandaged shoulder. "I'm supposed to be on holiday, not nursing a gunshot wound. You need to come clean on this whole thing, Katya."

"Only six bodies," she said. "So one escaped?"

"Apparently, he made his way back through the jungle to the riverbank where the helicopter had landed. The Kóya we spoke to couldn't distinguish him from the other Chinese. But they did say the man was carrying a scoped bolt-action rifle in an old leather wrapping, an odd weapon for the jungle."

"Not odd at all," Katya murmured. "Not for him."

"You know this guy?"

Katya looked hard at Jack. "Do you think he saw what you saw? What was in the shrine? The carvings, the inscription?"

"It's possible," Jack replied quietly. "And your uncle could have told them. It's possible he was tortured."

"It's certain, you mean," Katya said.

"When Licinius carved that inscription on

his own tomb, he was probably living in a twilight world of his own. In his mind, the jewel may have become part of the imagery of his devotion to Fabius, the comrade he had virtually deified on that battle scene carving. Whether or not he was consciously leaving clues for some future treasure hunter, he chose to use that word *sappheiros,* for lapis lazuli. For anyone already on the trail, that would have had instant meaning."

"Is this guy somewhere here now?" Costas peered at the shadowy ridge to the west, where the sun had nearly set. "The seventh one, who survived the Maoists? Are we in someone's crosshairs?"

Katya pursed her lips. "INTACON has mining concessions in Kyrgyzstan, in the Tien Shan Mountains." She pointed at the snowy peaks in the distance. "Those men whose bodies you found were employees of the company, but all of them have clan connections with the Brotherhood. They have helicopters, and tough horses they use for prospecting expeditions, a famous breed originating in Mongolia. If he's here, he's watching us now. They need to see what I've found, and where we're going next. The killing comes later."

"Great," Costas said. "That's just great. So we're dealing with a mining company? Is that the modern-day face of these warriors?"

"INTACON's their most profitable operation." She turned to Jack. "How much time do we have?"

"A U.S. Marine Apache helicopter is due here in thirty minutes." He checked his watch. "The Embraer should be fueled up and waiting on the runway at Bishkek. The supplies we need are already stowed."

"Okay." Katya looked at Costas. "Those horses I just mentioned. They're the blood-sweating heavenly horses of Chinese mythology. According to legend, whoever rode them could never fail in battle. The horses were highly prized by the First Emperor, and helped to convince his subjects of his invincibility."

"Blood-sweating?" Costas said dubiously.

"They're called the *akhal-teke,* and they're incredibly rare, one of the purest breeds to survive from antiquity. They're renowned for their speed and stamina. It's thought the appearance of sweating blood is caused by a parasitic disease endemic to the breed, but nobody knows for sure."

"You ever seen one?" Costas asked.

Katya gave him a scornful look. "I'm the daughter of a Kazakh warlord, remember? My father made me learn to ride them when I was a girl. The *akhal-teke* lived in a few isolated valleys, in Kazakhstan, Turkmenistan, Afghanistan, bred in secrecy by families who maintained the purity of the breed. My father's horse-breeder said his lineage went back to the time of the First Emperor, who sent out emissaries to the valleys to swear the breeders to eternal vigilance, to ensure that the heavenly horses were waiting for his bodyguard when he once again entered the mortal world. In China today there's excitement about the breed, a symbol of national unity and strength from before the communist era."

"So did your riding master pass on any other wisdom?" Costas asked.

"He said that those with the blood of the tiger in their veins can sense the *akhal-teke,* and that the horses sense them too. He said that when the warriors prepared for battle they came up here, past the Tien Shan Mountains to Issyk-Kul, and summoned them with their war drums. The *akhal-teke* came galloping through the mountain passes and along the shores of the lake, foaming and sweating and spraying the air with a mist of blood."

"This gets better every second," Costas said. "Is this in your genes too?"

Katya looked pensively at the lake. "I feel things up here. Maybe it's the thin air. I never sleep well, and that's when dreamworld and reality intertwine. I've woken thinking my heartbeat was the ground shaking with the pounding of hooves and thudding drums. As if the warriors were coming for me too."

"Don't go all Genghis Khan on us, Katya."

She gave him a tired smile, then looked out over the lake again. "Lying half-awake at night, I've been seeing images of my father again, of him when I was a girl, when he was still an art history professor in Bishkek. I'd hardly thought of him since I left the Black Sea almost two years ago. My mind had shut him out."

Jack glanced at Katya, wondering at the complex emotions she had felt since her father's death: grief, release, anger with her father, with herself, with him. The best thing for him to do was to say nothing, to let the process take its course. Costas saw Jack's reticence, and looked at Katya as he spoke. "Your father, what he'd become, was sitting on a sunken Russian submarine full of ICBMs," he said. "He'd have sold a few to al-Qaeda, and that's just for starters. A lot of innocent people are alive today because of what we did." He got up, stretched, wiped the dust off the back of his shorts and turned toward a hollow in the hill behind them. "Time for me to disappear behind some rocks." He gave Jack a ghoulish look. "Must be all that sheep grease."

"Be careful." Katya waved him off, and turned back. Jack saw that Altamaty had stopped the tractor beside the yurt, and the smoke from his cooking fire had gone out. Two rucksacks were stacked outside the tent. "It seems a long time since we sat together by the shore of the Black Sea," he said quietly. Katya nodded, but said nothing. Jack was silent for a moment, then pointed at the yurt. "Are you still sure about coming along with us?"

She nodded. "Altamaty too. He respects your military experience, but he said Afghanistan's a different story. He was in the valley we're going to, as a marine conscript during the Soviet war in the 1980s. His helicopter was shot down and he was the only survivor. He fought off repeated attacks but ran out of ammunition. The mujahideen spared him because he was Kyrgyz. He lived with them in the mountains for more than a year."

Jack nodded. "Good. Someone else is coming with us, a guy called Pradesh. He's in charge of the underwater excavations at Arikamedu, and flew with us to Bishkek. He's a captain in the Indian Army Engineers, with combat experience in Kashmir. He's also an expert on ancient mining technology. He was with us in the jungle. I really want IMU activities to expand out here. If Altamaty's serious about taking on the underwater survey at the eastern end of the lake, then he and Pradesh might be just the people we need to get things moving here. Pradesh speaks Russian. I'd like to see how they get on."

There was a commotion from the rocks behind them. "Hey, guys," Costas shouted. "Come and check this out."

Jack stood up and turned around. "Do we really want to?"

"Just avoid the gully on your left. I'm a bit farther down."

Katya got up, and the two of them picked their way over the rocks toward Costas. Jack had his compact diving flashlight with him, and played it into the gloom. He saw Costas hunched over a cleft in the rock, and they slid down a small scree slope toward him. They were in a hollow in the side of the hill, with the lake just visible to the north, the ridges of the ravine behind them to the west and the snowcapped peaks of the mountains to the south.

"Well?" Jack said, squatting cautiously beside Costas.

"I was walking back from washing my hands in the stream, and I saw this," Costas said. He pointed at two jagged rocks embedded in the side of the ridge, a crack between them. "There's something metal stuck in there. It's probably modern, but I've got ancient swords on the brain after seeing that Chinese halberd."

Katya knelt down beside him, and Jack shone the flashlight. It was a length of metal, embedded in the crack, just like a snapped-off blade. Katya put her finger out and touched it. She grasped and pulled it, but it would not budge. "Look at that silvery stuff on my fingers. That's chromium," she said

439

excitedly. "The metal beneath is oxidized, but it was once high-grade steel, hand-forged. The Chinese plated their best blades with chromium to stop them rusting. This is an ancient Chinese sword blade. A fantastic find, Costas."

"Just give me a bowl of sheep grease, then send me out into the hills," Costas murmured. He peered closely. "It looks like someone jammed it into the rock, to break it off. Maybe they needed a shorter blade."

Jack was thinking hard. "Any idea what kind of sword?"

Katya felt along the blade. "I know exactly what kind," she replied quietly. "A long, straight cavalry sword, a type favored by the Mongols. A type that was only really practicable on horseback, so if you were on foot and desperate for a weapon you might want to break it to make a more useful thrusting sword."

Jack gasped. He remembered the tomb from the jungle. The warrior in the carving, the adversary of the Romans in the battle scene. *The warrior with the tiger headdress.* He turned to Katya. "You don't mean a gauntlet sword, do you? A *pata?*"

She nodded. "I grew up with images of these swords all around me. The gauntlet was always gleaming golden, in the shape of a tiger. That's what's missing here. That's why I was so stunned when you told me you had one. I knew your *pata* must be the sword of a tiger warrior, but I couldn't be sure of the connection. Well, here it is in front of us. I'm certain of it. The gauntlet from this blade is the one John Howard found inside that shrine in the jungle."

"Well I'll be damned," Jack said.

Katya touched the blade again, and breathed out slowly. "So the legend *is* true," she whispered.

"What is?" Costas said.

"Another part of the legend." She looked up and around. Jack sensed her apprehension. "We should move away from here." She picked up a flat stone and put it over the crack between the rocks, concealing the blade. She led them back up the hill to the ledge where they had been sitting, where she had left the book. "The legend of those who were dispatched to destroy the guardian of the tomb, the one who had transgressed," she said. "The one who followed his prey relentlessly over mountain and through jungle, whose successors maintained the watch over the centuries, seeking that which had been taken from the tomb of their emperor. The tiger warrior."

"And the sword?" Jack asked.

"The *pata* sword of the first tiger warrior was taken in battle by the *raumanas,* the Romans. The legend tells that when it is recovered, the tiger warrior will once again surge forward and defeat all, and find what he has been seeking."

"Before you ask, it's secure, locked in my cabin on *Seaquest II,*" Jack said.

"I can feel it again now," Katya murmured. "What you once said to me, Jack, about walking into the past, seeing it in your mind's eye. I felt it when I was searching among those boulders with Altamaty, looking at those rock carvings made by my ancestors. But touching that blade has done something else for me. It feels exhilarating."

"That's when I get frightened," Costas murmured.

Jack turned toward the lake. Starlight speckled across its surface, like phosphorescence left by a boat's wake, a ghostly trail from the past. He felt the tingle on his skin again. Once, an Innu hunter in the Arctic had told him that the tingle you feel in these places is the divine wind, a wind of stupendous speed that you hardly feel because the air is so thin. Another Innu had laughed, and said it was just the cold. Jack had often thought about that when he had been in high mountains. Maybe it was just dizziness, oxygen deprivation. And this time it was an uneasy feeling, something that raised the hairs on the back of his neck. He looked toward the mountains to the south, a forbidding wall of rock and snow. That was where Licinius must have gone. He sensed the Roman stumbling away from this ravine, glancing at his companions as they disappeared across the lake to the east, then turning to the mountain passes, running hard, every sinew in his body straining to a breaking point. Jack turned back toward the dark ridge behind them, and looked hard. A distant throbbing became a roar, and the landing lights of a helicopter swept over the ridge as it headed down to the shoreline.

Katya got up. She turned to Costas, and gave him a steely look. "Time to go. And to find out about the Brotherhood of the Tiger. The modern version."

Jack grinned at Costas. "You ever been to Afghanistan?"

16

"This is the pilot speaking. We're entering Afghan airspace now."

Jack shifted and stretched, then pressed the control to raise his seat to the upright position. He was in the forward cabin of the IMU Embraer jet, and he had spent the last three hours fitfully sleeping, two and a half of them on the tarmac at Bishkek airport in Kyrgyzstan while they waited for the optimum time for departure. The flight to Feyzabad in northeast Afghanistan was only an hour and a half, and the captain had wanted to arrive at dawn and return to Bishkek as soon as they had off-loaded. An airport in Afghanistan was no place to linger, even an airport under nominal ISAF control, and the Embraer would be fueled up to return from Bishkek to pick them up as soon as the call went in.

Jack had a sketch of the inscription in the jungle tomb clutched in his hand. He looked down and saw the Latin word. *Sappheiros.* In antiquity, that meant lapis lazuli, and that could only mean the lapis mined in the forbidding Koran Valley, high in the Hindu Kush Mountains of Afghanistan. One strand of the ancient treasure trail had pointed across the lake of Issyk-Kul in Kyrgyzstan toward the eastern shore, to the place where Jack had begun to think a boat might have gone down in a storm two thousand years ago. The other strand led deep into the heart of Afghanistan, their route now.

Jack looked at the words of the inscription again. *Hic iacet Licinius optio XV Apollinaris Sacra iulium sacularia, in sappheiros nielo minium. Alta Fabia frater ad Pontus ad aelia acundus.* Here lies Licinius, *optio* of the 15th Apollinaris legion. Guardian of the celestial jewel, in the dark *sappheiros* mines. The other is with Fabius, brother, across the lake toward the rising sun. So Licinius had not taken his jewel south with him into the jungle. The *vélpu,* the sacred bamboo tube of the Kóya, the safeguard taken by Howard and Wauchope from the *muttadar,* may have been sanctified by its association with the *raumana,* the one who had come to the jungle and died in the shrine. But the bamboo tube had contained only a phantom treasure. The real treasure had been hidden somewhere out here, in the wilds of Afghanistan, during Licinius' escape south from the lake. It was somewhere in the lapis lazuli mines, where the precious veins of blue had been worked

445

since the time of the Egyptian pharaohs.

Jack remembered what he had been thinking when he had dozed off. The valley with the mines was on a route south from Lake Issyk-Kul to India, toward the community of Roman traders half a world away that had been Licinius' destination. Licinius might have guessed that the warriors pursuing him were after what he had taken off the Sogdian. He might have seen the odds stacked against him and decided to stash the jewel. He might have known the value of what he had taken. Perhaps the Sogdian had spoken to him of it, told him of its power if it were to be reunited with the other jewel, the one taken by Fabius across the lake. Maybe the Sogdian had spoken in desperation, hoping his life would be spared. Or maybe he had warned Licinius, told him something that made him want to be rid of his treasure. Maybe he had been told that he would be pursued relentlessly, and that the mines were the only place the jewel could be safely concealed, where the power of the crystal would be absorbed into the rock of its source. Only there, perhaps, it would no longer attract those who would come after him, who would hunt him like the tiger, as if they had some sixth sense for it.

Jack slid out into the aisle, slipped on his boots and made his way aft into the main cabin, where several window blinds were open on the port side. The pilot had taken a counterclockwise route over Tajikistan to approach Feyzabad from the west, and Jack could see the faint glimmerings of dawn over the Pamir Mountains and the bleak wasteland of the Taklamakan Desert beyond. He leaned over the seats and stared at the awesome mountain landscape below. It was a place where the obstacles to human existence appeared insurmountable, yet for those who endured it the reward was to live halfway to heaven. He stood back and made his way down the aisle to the others. Altamaty and Pradesh were sitting beside each other, talking in Russian. Jack sat opposite and poured himself a coffee from the trolley. Costas had been with them when Jack had gone to lie down, describing in detail the layout of his beloved engineering wing at the IMU campus in Cornwall. Costas had gone away to sleep as well, and Jack saw that the other two men had been poring over diving equipment catalogs from the onboard library.

Jack was itching to be underwater again. He thought of Rebecca. She had spent half an hour with him on the tarmac at Bishkek, running through notes she had made on Wood's *Source of the River Oxus*. She had given Jack the book and hugged him before being whisked off toward the lake in the U.S. Marine Apache helicopter. Jack smiled at his last image of her, in a flight helmet surrounded by four burly U.S. Navy SEALs. She had been loving every second of it. If all went according to plan, they would be back together on the eastern shore of Lake Issyk-Kul in less than twenty-four hours, and by then the IMU equipment ordered by Costas would have been air-freighted in. The ruins submerged in the lake were tantalizing, and might be one of the greatest Silk Road finds ever. The lake had also been traversed by boats carrying traders, and there was always the possibility of a wreck. Jack thought of Fabius and the fate of the Romans who had rowed for their lives toward the east. He glanced at Katya, who was sitting by herself a few rows ahead, staring out of the window. They might also find petroglyphs underwater, if the boulders extended into the lake. There was a major collaborative project in the offing. He could see himself spending more time out here. He looked out of the window, and remembered where they were heading. *If they made it through the next twenty-four hours.*

Costas came stumbling down the aisle and slumped into the seat beside Jack. He looked out of the window, and Jack followed his gaze. They could clearly make out the ripple of hills and valleys and stretches of snowcapped peaks. Costas flipped open the monitor from his armrest and activated the map. "That's it," he said. "We've passed over the border into Afghanistan. Can't be much more than half an hour to go."

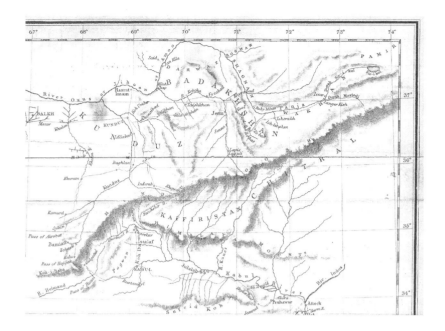

"You can just make out the Panjshir Valley," Jack said. "It's shrouded in mist with peaks on either side, stretching off to the east. It's the valley of the fabled river Oxus, the river that marked the eastern edge of Alexander the Great's expedition. Five hundred miles west from here it flows into the Aral Sea, a lake. On the way it passes Merv, where Crassus' legionaries were imprisoned. The escaped Romans may have come this way, but faced with the wall of mountains to the east they may have veered north on the spur of the Silk Road that led through Kyrgyzstan past Lake Issyk-Kul."

"And Howard and Wauchope?" Costas said. "Is this where they ended up, after they disappeared into Afghanistan in 1908?"

Jack pursed his lips. "They were experienced enough to make it this far. Both men knew the Afghan border region well from their army postings. Wauchope had actually been into Afghanistan before, during the second Afghan war."

"The medal Pradesh had, with the elephant?" Costas said.

Jack nodded. "That was in 1879, just before he joined Howard in the jungle. It was the time of the Great Game, the standoff between Britain and Russia. It was a decade of heroic defeats. Custer's Last Stand against the Sioux, 1876. The British defeat by the Zulus, at Isandlwana and Rorke's Drift, 1879. Then the battle of Maiwand in Afghanistan, in 1880. Almost a thousand British and Indian troops died on the plain outside Kandahar, fighting to the last. The Afghans desecrated the bodies just as the Sioux and the Zulu did. Thirty years before, during the first Afghan War, the British Army of the Indus had been massacred as they retreated toward the Khyber Pass, with only one British survivor making it out. These were painted as heroic failures, boosted in popular imagination to extol the virtues of the warrior. Many of the British officers had been steeped in chivalry. I have a complete set of Sir Walter Scott's *Waverley Novels,* signed by John Howard. He'd lived in that world as a boy, and subscribed to a new edition in the 1880s, as if he were trying to recapture the romance that was knocked out of him after he experienced the brutal reality. And the British should have known better with Afghanistan. They'd had men there from early on, explorers like John Wood. They knew the problems of the terrain, and they knew the people."

"What was the situation in 1908?"

"Uneasy peace. Afghanistan was still a no-go zone. The trek up here from Quetta would have taken Howard and Wauchope weeks, even months. For provisions they would have been reliant on the goodwill of the people they came across. Wauchope had much experience with the border tribesmen, but there would have been lengthy negotiations, social niceties to be observed, diversions as their guides took them around the territories of feuding warlords. Once they got to the Panjshir Valley, if they did, they would have been on their own. Winter was probably setting in, and it would have been an arduous trek into the mountains to get to where I think they were going."

Pradesh had been listening intently, and leaned forward. "What makes you so sure this was the place?"

"Because the Panjshir Valley is the route to the lapis lazuli mines," Jack said.

"Of course," Pradesh murmured. "*Sappheiros,* lapis lazuli. They'd seen that in the inscription in the jungle years before, and were looking for the place where you think Licinius hid the jewel."

Jack angled the map screen from Costas' armrest so they could all see it. He pointed at a series of ridges leading south from the main valley. "Here, deep in the Hindu Kush range. The mines are located in a narrow mountain valley. There are about twenty shafts, some of them open for thousands of years. The lapis lazuli decorating King Tut's coffin in Egypt came from here, traded west over a thousand years before the Romans came this way."

"Romans?" Costas said. "I thought it was just one, Licinius."

"He was alone when he came to hide the jewel, after he'd fled south from Issyk-Kul," Jack said. "But for him to know how to reach the mines, I think the band of escaped legionaries must have come in this direction during their trek from Merv into central Asia. The Panjshir Valley may have been where they were forced north, toward Kyrgyzstan. If you read Wood's *Source of the River Oxus,* you realize why. The mountains he describes at the eastern end of the valley sound like the end of the world, utterly impassable. But before turning away and going north, the Romans could have got far enough up the valley to hear of the fabled mines, maybe even to see them. If Licinius had been told by the Sogdian to take the jewel there, he would have known where to go."

Katya slipped into the seat in front of Pradesh. "And when he reached the jungle, he didn't need to leave a treasure map," she said. "All he had to inscribe on his tomb was the word for lapis lazuli. Everyone in India knows that lapis comes from Afghanistan. Everyone in Afghanistan knows it comes from the Panjshir Valley. And someone in the valley can always point you in the direction of the mines, where a miner might even show you the shaft that produces the darkest blue, the *nielo*. But it's like telling people about Shangri-la, because in truth hardly anyone would dream of going there, and anyone who did might stand little chance of survival. It was a prize that was only ever going to tempt the desperate, or fools. Or romantic old soldiers like Howard and Wauchope, with a yen for adventure."

"How sure are you that Howard and Wauchope were on this trail?" Costas asked.

Jack pointed at the book. "Lieutenant John Wood, Bengal Navy. *A Personal Narrative of a Journey to the Source of the River Oxus.* This was Howard's own copy, pored over by him, full of annotations. I found it in the lower drawer of that chest of family papers you saw in my cabin in *Seaquest II,* bundled up as if it were something he treasured but didn't want anyone else to see. The section on the Panjshir Valley and the lapis mines is so densely

453

covered with notes that it's virtually indecipherable."

"And there are notes in another hand too," Costas said, peering at the book.

"Robert Wauchope," Jack said. "I saw some of his manuscript papers in the India Office Library in London, and confirmed the handwriting."

"Odd that they didn't take the book with them, on their final journey," Costas said.

"They probably knew it by heart. And they would only have taken the bare minimum with them. Nobody wants to lug books around the Hindu Kush."

"But you say it contains clues for us."

"We've got Rebecca to thank for that. While we were at Issyk-Kul she had her head down, deciphering the notes. She thinks she's found clues to the mine entrance they were aiming to reach, among the many shafts in the mountainside."

"She's a great researcher," Costas said.

"She's got a fine eye for detail, and the patience for it. She's got a lot of her mother in her."

"Have you told her that?" Katya asked.

"When the time's right. It's still too raw."

"I'll talk to her. We have that in common. Losing a parent violently. When you want me to."

Jack nodded, and looked out of the window. They were dropping in altitude now, and the aircraft was below the level of the mountain peaks on either side of the valley. He could see occasional twinkling from houses and the odd splash of light from vehicle headlamps, on the same route that Wood must have taken almost two centuries before. He closed the book. "The beauty of Wood's account is that it predates the Great Game. To understand Afghanistan, you can go back to those travelers who came here before geopolitics came into play. Robert Wauchope in his notes at the end of this book says that, left to their own devices, the Afghans would shrug off all that history of outside interference in an instant."

The PA system crackled again. "This is the captain. Estimated touchdown thirty-five minutes. We're entering SAM missile range. We've armed the chaff dispensers. Just a precaution."

Costas grunted and checked his seat belt. "I got onto him about it when we landed at Bishkek. These ex-fighter jocks sometimes forget they're flying a bus."

Jack turned to Katya. "This is the last chance before we hit the road. If there's anything more to tell us, now's the time."

Katya drank some water, then nodded. "Okay. The Brotherhood of the Tiger. In the late nineteenth century, at the time of the diplomat Wu Che, the one who attended John Howard's lecture, the Brotherhood was one of many secret societies in China. But they were more secretive than most. Few other societies could claim an authentic lineage back to the First Emperor. And they never sought to expand their membership. The First Emperor had come from the Qin family, and as he rose to power he ennobled them, giving his brothers and cousins the land to rule as fiefdoms. Their pledge was to serve the emperor in life and in death. They took the names of their fiefdoms. There were twelve of them: the Xu, the Tan, the Ju, the Zhongli, the Yunyan, the Tuqiu, the Jiangliang, the Huang, the Jiang, the Xiuyu, the Baiming, and the Feilian. These were the original bodyguard. As each one died, the Brotherhood selected another from that clan to take his place. In time, the Brotherhood came to represent all the upper echelons of power in China. They were wealthy landowners, lords of their fiefdoms, but they were also generals, diplomats, ministers of state. All of them had been groomed from birth in the ways of the tiger warrior. Each clan provided a selection of boys ready for the next vacancy, trained in the martial arts, in the wielding of the great *pata* sword, in the art of becoming one with the *akhal-teke,* the blood-sweating heavenly horse. One of those would be chosen to enter the Brotherhood, to sit on the council of the twelve. The others would remain throughout their lives as his warriors, a murderous company of a hundred or more who could be called upon at a moment's notice to defend the creed of the First Emperor. And the one who was chosen, the newest of the Brotherhood, became the tiger warrior. It was his role to ride at the head of that company. To execute the orders of the Brotherhood. That was his initiation. The diplomat Wu Che was from the family of Jiang, and he was one of the twelve. My father's family, my uncle's, was the Huang. I am descended from many of those who were chosen for the mantle of tiger warrior."

"And today?" Costas said. "Are we basically looking at organized crime?"

Katya took a deep breath. "Their creed was to defend the emperor's tomb. Until the rise of communism, they retained their land and privileges, and had no need of more wealth. For generations they were behind the scenes in Xian, army officers, counselors to the emperor, bureaucrats, always close to the great tomb whose mound loomed beside the city, ensuring its sacred status. They fostered all of the superstitions about tampering with the First Emperor's legacy, superstitions that linger today even among Chinese archaeologists. They made sure that nobody ever dug into the tomb. And the Brotherhood were not thugs. The diplomat Wu Che was typical of the nineteenth century Brotherhood, a highly educated man, eager to represent China's

457

interests abroad. But that was when things began to change. For almost two thousand years the Brotherhood had been part of China's enclosed society, cut off from the outside world since returning empty-handed after losing the trail of Licinius in the Indian jungle. Wu Che reopened that quest, and once again the Brotherhood was on the warpath. The quest rekindled into a passion, an obsession. He also did something else. Unwittingly, he provided them with a temptation, one that some in the next generation of the Brotherhood could not resist."

"Let me guess," Jack murmured. "Opium."

Katya nodded. "Wu Che's travels in India had been an attempt to uncover the extent of opium use, to pinpoint the suppliers, to persuade the British government to clamp down on the trade. His papers show that his concerns were moral, and went far beyond Chinese official interests. He visited the Rampa jungle a couple of years after the rebellion and saw the extent of opium addiction among the hill tribesmen, easy prey to dealers after the troops had left. He would have found a sympathetic ear in John Howard. And there was something else. As a diplomat in London, Wu Che inspected the opium dens that were springing up in the port cities of Europe. When he returned to China for the last time in the 1890s, he took with him a prodigious amount of research, a detailed account of opium use and supply in the western world. It could have been the basis for quashing the opium trade. But it was open to huge abuse. It was a blueprint for control of the trade."

"We're talking about the time of the rise of communism?" Costas asked.

Katya nodded. "China was already fragmenting, and the republic was declared in 1912. The Nationalist Party had only a tenuous hold, and for years there was an uneasy alliance with the Communist Party. Much of the country was ruled by warlords. The abdication of the last emperor in 1912 marks the beginning of the modern Brotherhood of the Tiger. In the foundation mythology of the Brotherhood, the period of the Warring States had been followed by the rise of the First Emperor. They saw an analogue to this in what was happening around them in the 1920s and 1930s. It seemed as if a second coming of the emperor might be at hand. The foundation mythology began to twist, and new strands were fabricated. And something else happened. Their fiefdoms were lost, confiscated by the state. They needed another source of wealth."

"The opium trade," Jack said.

"Wu Che was murdered in 1912, a victim of the purge of the Chinese imperial court," Katya continued. "His son succeeded him in the Brotherhood. For the first time, one alone threatened to rule the twelve. He inherited all of his father's records, and built the largest, most secretive drug empire the world has ever known. British complicity in the opium trade had nearly ruined China in the nineteenth century, and he turned that on its head, using all the existing supply routes to feed more and more opium into the west, fueling the explosion in heroin use from the 1950s onward."

Costas jabbed his finger at the route map. "Afghanistan? The main supplier?"

Katya nodded. "For centuries the Brotherhood had been sending warriors up here to get purebred horses. Training with the heavenly steeds had always been part of their creed, an essential rite of passage for any who might become one of the twelve. By the 1920s, the horse trade had become a cover for the narcotics trade. Opium was channeled south into India, west into Europe. The Brotherhood relocated its hub of operations outside China, first to Hong Kong and Malaysia and then in the west itself, in London and America. They integrated themselves easily enough, ostensibly the scions of wealthy expatriate Hong Kong and Singapore families who were educating their sons in the elite schools of Europe and America, becoming part of the capitalist infrastructure of the west."

"They must be on the radar screens somewhere, if the drug involvement was as big as you say it was," Costas said.

Katya gave him a wry look. "They were clever. They were not gangsters like other Chinese secret societies. To the Brotherhood, the opium trade was less a criminal enterprise than a kind of payback for western complicity in opium exported to China in the nineteenth century. They had a romanticized notion of fealty to China, to a China that was already ancient history. But it did not serve their creed to become part of the criminal underworld, and they moved out of the drug trade after the Second World War. They reinvested in mineral prospecting and mining. That proved hugely profitable after the breakup of the Soviet Union. The new central Asian republics proved a ripe picking ground for outside entrepreneurs. Their company, INTACON, became massively profitable and overshadowed the other business concerns of the Brotherhood."

"What about 1949?" Jack said. "Mao Zedong, the communist takeover? Order returns to China."

"Communism had been part of the force that pulled down the old world in which the Brotherhood had existed for centuries, taking their land. But 1949 also represented the return of order over chaos, an analogue of the end of the Warring States and the rise of the Qin. The new certainty, the new control, was seductive to the Brotherhood. And the communist regime had its own power structure, its own hierarchy. The Brotherhood soon recovered their place in China, their watchful eye. They fueled the cult of Mao Ze-dong until it almost rivaled the cult of the First Emperor himself. But with Mao's death, they returned with renewed passion to the original creed."

"Cue the mythology," Jack murmured.

"According to *wu di,* the concept of non-death, they believe the First Emperor never left, but exists in a parallel world. They await a kind of folding of our reality into that world, the world of *wu di.* Only then will the emperor once again be able to impose his will on the universe. For the Brotherhood, this mystical hope became a fanatical dogma after 1912. Only with the merging of the two parallel worlds would order come again. They looked for signs in the ancient myth of the elemental powers. The First Emperor had risen under *shuide,* the power of water, overcoming the power of fire. The Brotherhood believe that the next age of the emperor will be heralded by the coming of *siandhe,* the power of light."

Jack stared at Katya. "That's it, isn't it? That's why the pair of jewels are so important. The power of light."

Katya nodded. "It was the diplomat Wu Che who reawakened the legend of the lost jewel from the tomb, the celestial jewel, whose two parts would combine to shine a dazzling light on the tomb of the emperor and breach the barrier of *wu di*. Only when the jewel is found can *siandhe* begin, the age of light."

"And when is this supposed to happen?" Costas asked.

"For the First Emperor, *shuide* was associated with the number six, as well as with winter, darkness, harshness, death. The Brotherhood is twelve, a multiple of six. They came to believe that the age of light would begin in the sixty-sixth generation after the tomb was sealed."

"Let me guess," Costas murmured. "That would be the current generation?"

Katya nodded. "That's why this has all heated up now. My uncle confided everything in me. He knew I was intimate enough with the history of the Brotherhood to share his fears, and he also knew the archaeological trail he was on would need someone with expertise to match his own. He'd groomed me for it. He had great faith in me. He knew time was against him, but I never thought it would end so soon." Katya looked down for a moment, then carried on. "My uncle took up where Wu Che left off. But when he realized that the celestial jewel might actually be found, he began to fear the consequences. A decade ago, the Brotherhood lost the representative of the Feilian clan, who suddenly died. He was succeeded by his son, Shang Yong. China was changing again. Communism was eroding, capitalism was in. Some profited hugely, many did not. In Russia, some look back on the time of the czars as a kind of mythical golden age. In China, they look back to the First Emperor. Shang Yong was part of this, though at the same time profiting hugely from the new opportunities. My uncle saw disturbing signs in Shang Yong. His family, the Feilian, controlled INTA-CON. With the increase in the wealth of the company, Shang became a megalomaniac. He turned the Brotherhood into his own council of war. It was he who took INTA-CON into exploitative mining, on aboriginal lands around the world. One of those areas was the Rampa jungle of eastern India. A huge fortune was to be had in strip-mining the jungle for bauxite. My uncle vehemently opposed the scheme. He was a committed anthropologist and a humanitarian, one of the Brotherhood who had not let the creed consume him. From the start he had opposed the ascendancy of Shang. My uncle had been naïve, and only realized the danger too late. By the time he told me the full story, he was a hunted man."

"And he paid the ultimate price," Jack murmured.

"So just like the diplomat Wu Che, he

unwittingly opened a can of worms," Costas said slowly. "Wu Che handed the Brotherhood the opium trade. Your uncle reopened the quest for the jewel, but also led them to a place where another treasure trove was to be found, in mining the jungle."

"That was something else that dawned on my uncle too late," Katya said. "And I fear he may even have entered into negotiations with the Maoist rebels. It would have been an act of desperation, but there may have been nobody else to turn to with the government about to draw up a contract with INTACON and the Kóya people powerless to resist. It would have been suicidal for him, but then he knew he was under a death sentence anyway. And I know he had rejected the Brotherhood. He saw the creed moving from the First Emperor to Shang Yong himself, as if Shang were seeing himself as emperor, as *Shihuangdi,* born again."

"So where is Shang Yong based?" Jack asked.

"In the Taklamakan Desert, on the other side of the Tien Shan Mountains," Katya replied. "A hundred thousand square kilometers of shifting sands and utter desolation, scarred by ferocious winds. For travelers going east on the Silk Road, the Taklamakan was the last great obstacle before dropping down into central China and reaching the end of the road at Xian, source of the silk and site of the First Emperor's tomb. Anyone who strayed into the desert risked being lost forever, and anyone who controlled the desert strongholds could prey at will on the caravans skirting its fringes. The desert remains one of the last great lawless tracts on earth. Even the communists couldn't control it. There are many ruined fortresses half-buried in sand, built beside oases long ago swallowed up. Shang Yong set himself up in one of these, hundreds of kilometers from the nearest road. He's built an airstrip and begun to convert the place into his own fantasy world. For the Brotherhood, the Taklamakan has always had huge symbolic significance, a bastion against the world outside, a place where they could seem to uphold the emperor's claim that there was nothing beyond. For Shang Yong, the desert is also a perfect headquarters for INTACON's mining enterprises in central Asia, in the Tien Shan and Karakoram Mountains. And my uncle knew more. INTACON prospectors have found evidence of huge oil reserves under the desert itself. The Taklamakan has become Shang's fiefdom. And it's no longer inward-looking. Shang threatens to control the whole of the western part of China, and to exert a frightening influence on the world outside."

"So that's what your uncle was really onto," Jack murmured.

"What do you mean about a fantasy

466

world?" Costas said.

Katya paused. "That's where the real significance of the jewel, the real danger, comes into play. For the last meeting of the Brotherhood that my uncle ever attended, he was flown to the desert headquarters. In the center of the ruins lay a domed structure, a former Nestorian church. He was ushered down a ramped passage and through great bronze doors. He sat in near darkness at a low table with the other eleven, Shang Yong at the head. What my uncle saw inside stunned and horrified him. It was instantly recognizable from the *Records of the Grand Historian*. Shang Yong had re-created the First Emperor's tomb inside the church. For the old Brotherhood, that would have been unimaginable heresy. Above them was the dome of the heavens, and on either side were rivers and mountains and palaces. Beyond that were images of the terracotta warriors. He said it was like sitting in a planetarium, with the latest CGI and holographic technology, even the sounds of water and wind, the baying of horses. Over the days he was there he realized that Shang Yong was spending more and more time alone in the chamber. My uncle had worried about Shang as a boy. He had been addicted to computer games, to the world of instant gratification and utter certainty, a world where morality and humanity are irrelevant. My uncle realized that

467

Shang Yong had moved from being a player in front of a screen to being inside the game itself, part of it."

"Computer whiz kids who barely know reality from fantasy," Costas murmured. "Who grow up and make fortunes and think they can take that extra step the boy in the basement can't, and walk into the screen, into a world they think they can control completely in a way they can never control reality."

Katya nodded. "Exactly. In Shang Yong's mind, it was an extension of the concept of *wu di,* the commingling of the worlds of the living and the dead that would come with the age of light, with the celestial jewel. But it was as if he had already found a portal to that other world. My uncle knew that the powers of the jewel might prove no more than a figment of myth, but for Shang Yong it could still have terrifying potency. If he believed that the jewel was the final key to his apotheosis, to some kind of melding with the First Emperor, then it might propel him into a terrifying megalomania. That's what frightened my uncle the most. That's when he determined to keep his research secret from others in the Brotherhood and try to discover the jewel himself."

"But Shang Yong already knew," Jack replied. "Your uncle would survive only as long as it took him to find the place where he thought the jewel was hidden."

"So who's the guy you think is shadowing us?" Costas said.

Katya stared at him. "You told me what the Kóya had seen in the jungle," she replied. "Seven men from INTACON went in, one came out, armed with a scoped rifle. He was the initiate. The murder of my uncle was his test. He has now become one of the Brotherhood. By tradition, when one of the Brotherhood strayed, he and his immediate family were eliminated. His replacement in the twelve came from another family in the same clan, chosen for their martial prowess by the other eleven in the Brotherhood."

"And this new one is the tiger warrior," Jack said quietly.

"A twisted version. A psychopath. And he has a particular speciality. His grandmother was a Kazakh Red Army sniper during the Second World War, one of those who chalked up hundreds of kills. He learned everything from her. He's a professional, and honed his art in Bosnia, Chechnya, Africa. His count may even exceed hers by now. He uses her old Mosin-Nagant rifle."

"A sniper's rifle is like an artist's favorite brush," Jack murmured. "An old Soviet bolt-action can kill as well as the latest Barrett."

"One question," Costas said. "Your family's been part of this since the time of the First Emperor. Sixty-six generations. How do we know you're not one of the bad guys?"

469

Katya cast him a baleful look. "Because they murdered my uncle. Because there are no others in my family. Because of a pledge my ancestors made more than two thousand years ago. And because the creed of Shang Yong has nothing to do with that history. It's an abomination. And because he will try to kill me — and all of us — as soon as we lead him to the jewel. It's as simple as that."

"So this valley we're heading to," Costas said, looking at Jack. "Sounds like sniper alley. Do we get any ISAF protection?"

"You could have a battalion of special forces up there combing the slopes, rangers, SAS, and they still wouldn't see a sniper that good," Jack replied.

Pradesh had been listening quietly, and glanced at Costas. "Jack and I have talked about this. If we want ISAF help to hunt one man and a rifle, that's a no go. Up here some of the local warlords are strong enough to confront the Taliban themselves. The ISAF commanders know that's the way forward. Let the warlords get on with it themselves, and don't make yourself their enemy too. The Taliban murdered and raped their way through here when they were in power, and Afghans have long memories. So we'll only get limited reactive assistance or medevac. Once we pass through the airbase at Feyzabad, we're on our own until we meet this former mujahideen chap Altamaty knows, the

470

local warlord. Then we have to run the gauntlet of a couple of villages where there might be Taliban infiltrators, and there's always the possibility of IEDs, suicide bombers. But if Altamaty really can get the warlord on our side, that's a big step forward."

"What's our cover story?" Costas asked. "Aren't they going to assume we're CIA or something?"

"Film crew," Jack said. "We're following the exploration of John Wood in 1836 in search of the source of the river Oxus. We've even got the battered old book for authenticity."

"Sounds like a dream project of yours, Jack," Katya said.

"One day." Jack flashed her a smile. "I'd love to. When the fighting's over."

Costas peered at the map. "What's the place with the mines called again?"

"The Koran Valley," Jack said.

The aircraft banked to port, and they heard the rumble of the undercarriage lowering. Altamaty had been staring out of the window, but turned as Jack spoke, hearing the word. He looked at Katya, and spoke softly:

"Agur janub doshukh na-kham buro
Zinaar Murrow ba janub tungee Koran."

Costas turned to her. "Meaning?"

She gave him a steely look. "It's Pashtun.

471

Something Altamaty learned when he was captured by the mujahideen up here. *If you wish not to go to destruction, avoid the narrow valley of Koran.*"

The plane bounced on the runway. "Perfect," Costas grumbled. "Another choice holiday hot spot."

17

Afghanistan, 22 September 1908

The two men bounced and tumbled down the pile of rock chippings that half filled the entrance to the mine, desperately scrabbling for handholds and kicking against the scree to find some kind of purchase. They came to a halt side-by-side, lying near the bottom of the pile. They could still see the mine entrance, the gray sky outside, a slit of light at the top of the mound about a pistol shot away. Beyond them the shaft continued into pitch darkness. At more than twelve thousand feet of altitude the air was thin, and they panted and coughed in the pall of dust they had raised as they slid down the slope. John Howard turned his head toward the figure beside him, then blinked hard and peered at the wall of the mineshaft. He could see pick marks, all over the rock. A shaft of light from the entrance lit up the ceiling. There was no doubting it. Streaks of blue, speckled with gold. He began to laugh, or cry, he hardly

473

knew which, then coughed painfully. "Robert," he whispered. "Have you seen? It's lazurite."

"I've just collected a specimen." Howard felt relief to hear Wauchope's voice, the Irish accent with its American twang still strong despite all his years in British service. In the desperate fight outside, Howard had wondered whether he would ever hear it again. He blinked hard, and tried to take stock. He was lying on his front, limbs splayed out, hands forward, his right hand still holding the old Colt revolver, a wisp of smoke coming from the chamber he had fired a few moments before. His left hand was clasped tight around the ancient tube of bamboo, ten inches long, blackened and shiny with age. They had taken it out to read the papyrus inside just before they were attacked, after they had stowed their bags on the valley floor, and he had clutched it close to him through the desperate climb to this place, seeking paths that the horse of their pursuer could not negotiate.

Wauchope rolled onto his back beside him. Howard watched him break open his Webley revolver, eject the spent cartridges and reload from a pouch on his belt, glancing up at the tunnel entrance as he did so. He put down the revolver and picked up something in his left hand. It was a fragment of blue rock. He fumbled with his other hand for a little leather pouch hanging from his neck, raising himself on one elbow, wincing as it bit into the rock. He took out a scratched old monocle from the bag, placed it over his left eye and then craned his neck forward, inspecting the fragment closely. "When Lieutenant Wood came to this place seventy years ago, he said there were three grades." Wauchope peered again. "This is the superior grade. That sparkle of gold is iron pyrites. It's the *nielo,* just as Licinius described it." He took off the monocle and slumped back. For a moment all Howard could hear was the sound of his own breathing, sharp, rasping. He watched his exhalation crystallize in the cold mountain air. Wauchope rolled his head over and looked at him. "You know what this means."

"It means," Howard said, "that by some act of divine providence those ghouls chased us into the right mineshaft. Wood said there was only one shaft that produced the superior grade. And look at those pick marks on the rock above us — and the soot from fires used to crack the rock. This shaft has been mined for thousands of years."

Howard closed his eyes. The rock chips he was lying on were jagged and unforgiving, but he seemed hardly to feel them at all. It was strange. He opened his eyes and peered at Wauchope. The two men were scarcely recognizable from three months before, when they had left Quetta one night and made their way toward the border, disappearing into the wilds of Afghanistan. And now here they were, thirty years after their escape from the jungle shrine, their faces sun-scorched and craggy like the mountain valleys, weather-beaten old men with matted gray beards. They both wore turbans, impregnated with dust, and heavy Afghan sheepskin overcoats tied around the middle, the matted wool turned inward as protection against the bitter cold that had begun to course through the mountains in their final treacherous approach to the mines. Beneath Wauchope's upturned collar, Howard could see the leather Sam Browne belt and khaki of his uniform, the colonel's pips and crown visible on one shoulder. They were both officially retired, but they knew they would be treated as spies by the Afghans if they went without uniform and would suffer a fate worse than death. It had been their profession for thirty-five years, as officers of the Corps of Royal Engineers, and it seemed the most natural thing to wear the uniforms they had worn all their adult lives, on their last and greatest adventure together.

Howard caught Wauchope's eye. They both grinned, and then began to shake, laughing uncontrollably. *They had made it.* Howard suddenly coughed, and spat blood over the rocks.

"Good God, man," Wauchope said, pushing himself upright and leaning over him. "You're wounded!"

"I took a sword thrust." Howard swallowed hard, tasting the tang of blood on his lips. "The horseman who came behind us on the trail. The one with the gauntlet sword. Just as we were scrambling up that rock on the way in here. In my back. Left side."

Howard felt Wauchope untie his sheepskin coat. He eased the bamboo tube out of Howard's left hand, placing it carefully on the rocks, and took his arm out of the sleeve. "Gently does it." He lifted the coat up, and felt the dampness down Howard's side. He let the coat back, tucking it carefully under him, and put his arm back in the sleeve, gently lying it on the rocks in its original position. He put his hand on Howard's right shoulder. Howard could feel the tenseness in the other man's fingers.

"It's bad, isn't it?" he said quietly.

"It missed the liver, that's for certain. It may have gone into the pleural cavity, beneath the lung. I've seen men bounce back from a wound like that, up and about in no time."

"It's gone into the lung, Robert. The blood's frothy. My breathing's getting shorter."

Howard saw Wauchope kneel up, stare hard at the entrance to the cave, take a deep breath then untie his waistband and shrug off his sheepskin. He adjusted his Sam Browne belt, slid his holster into the correct position and brushed off the front of his tunic. Howard shut his eyes. *So this was it.*

"We know it's in here somewhere. What we're after." Wauchope jerked his head toward the darkness behind them.

"They know too."

"They don't know which mine entrance we hid inside. When I emptied my revolver at them, they fell back. That bought us some time. And when they do find us, they won't know this is the one. They won't know that we happened to stumble into precisely the shaft we were looking for. The place where Licinius hid the jewel two thousand years ago."

"They'll search every one. They'll find us, then they'll find the jewel."

The jewel. Howard felt the blood well up in his throat. He felt as if he were slowly drowning. *He would show no fear.* He looked at the ancient bamboo cylinder that Wauchope had laid on the rock beside him. The *velpú*, the sacred relic they had taken from the jungle shrine nearly thirty years before, their guarantee of safe passage out of hell that dark night, so etched in Howard's consciousness it could have been yesterday. Howard had kept it, along with the tiger-headed gauntlet, the shape that had so terrifyingly reappeared on the arm of their pursuer only a few hours

478

ago. They had guessed that they were being followed, but their enemy had only struck on the valley floor below, once they had reached the fabled lapis lazuli mines of Sar-e-Sang. Howard had seen the mounted warrior who had led the phalanx of armed men up the valley toward them, masked like a tiger dragon, had glimpsed the flash of gold at his wrist as the warrior drew out his great gauntlet sword, the shape of the tiger head just like the one Howard had taken from the jungle tomb.

That gauntlet was not with him now, but they had brought the *velpú* for what it contained. Ten years after their jungle escape their paths had crossed again at the School of Military Engineering at Chatham, and one night they had locked themselves in the library and opened up the bamboo tube. What they had found was no idol, no god, but a roll of ancient papyrus, paper made from pressed reeds that Howard had recognized from his visits as a boy to the British Museum. *Egyptian papyrus, in the jungle of southern India.* That had been incredible enough. But it had writing on it, letters that Wauchope recognized as identical in style to the words he had glimpsed carved on the tomb in the jungle shrine. *Hic iacet Licinius, optio XV Apollinaris, sacra iulium sacularia.* Here lies Licinius, optio of the 15th Apollinaris, guardian of the celestial jewel. But the inscription on the papyrus was longer. And what it said was astonishing, words that had been etched in Howard's mind ever since. They had used their knowledge of Latin to decipher the message, hunched together over candlelight. They were words that had taken Howard back to his boyhood dreams, dreams of high adventure. They seemed to draw him from the darkness that had embraced his soul since that day in the jungle, given him something to strive for other than redemption for a deed he did not even know if he had committed, but which had lurked just beneath his consciousness every moment of his life since he had pulled that trigger on the river steamer. *The little Kóya boy, the weeping boy he could not allow to suffer, when his own son was crying out for him in his final hours.* Now, in this mineshaft, at the end of his journey, he looked up at Wauchope, and whispered the final words of the passage they had first read that night: *Cave tigris bellator. Beware the tiger warrior.*

Howard felt light-headed. He swallowed again, and felt the blood go down. He had seen the tattoo on the horseman's arm, the snarling dragon-tiger, as the rider had thundered toward them in the valley below. Somehow, those who had driven Licinius to his jungle hideout two thousand years before were still in existence, still stalking any who had chanced upon the trail, seeking what Licinius had found and hidden away. Howard had racked his brains as they scrambled up the mountainside, wondering how they could have been discovered. In Quetta, during their preparations, they had planned to let others know, who might ask, that they were intent on retracing Wood's expedition to find the source of the river Oxus, up the Panjshir Valley in northern Afghanistan. They had sought advice from the explorer Aurel Stein, but had not divulged their true intent. Stein thought they were suicidal going into the Hindu Kush without bearers or guides, but he had wished them godspeed. They were a pair of eccentric old colonels intent on a final adventure, in the best British tradition.

Then Howard had remembered. Years before, when he had returned to England after his service with the Madras Sappers. When he had tried to take his wife Helen away from their grief for little Edward, tried to give them a new life. He had been a newly promoted captain, teaching survey at the School of Military Engineering. He had given a lecture at the Royal United Service Institution in London on the Roman antiquities of southern India, a passion of his since boyhood when he had collected silver and gold Roman coins bought for him by his father and uncles in the bazaars of Madras and Bangalore. He had mentioned a rumor, nothing more, of a cave temple, one that contained carvings that appeared Roman. He had postulated scenes of battle. He had wanted to show that there could have been Roman soldiers as well as traders in southern India. It was an extraordinary possibility. It had been an extraordinary discovery.

He had let his enthusiasm get the better of him. He realized, now, that he had wanted something good to come of that experience in the jungle that so haunted him, and he had let his guard down. He had said nothing more than that, had intimated nothing about a location, about any truth behind the story. He and Wauchope had made a pact never to reveal what they had found inside the shrine, yet in the lecture there may have been something in his enthusiasm, a glint in his eye, the suppressed part of him that wanted to tell the world of their discovery, that revealed something to the careful observer.

Afterward, an official from the Imperial Chinese Embassy had come up to congratulate him, and to inquire about his sources. Howard had politely declined, repeating that it was merely a rumor. That was more than twenty years ago. Could it be that he had been followed, watched, for anything unusual, anything that might reveal what he knew? The bamboo *vélpu* had been concealed in a locked room in the School of Engineering at

Chatham, among a clutter of exotic artifacts brought back by officers over the decades. Howard had been the curator, and only he had the key. It was impossible that anyone else should have known about it. Then he thought about those who had served him over the years. Only one had been with him throughout, his faithful Huang-li, great-nephew of his beloved childhood *ayah* from Tibet. Huang-li had been with him from Bangalore to Chatham and then back again through his final postings in India. Huang-li had always had his oriental friends, coolies, sailors, men he met in the opium dens at night, but Howard had turned a blind eye, knowing it was better to tolerate the secret societies and rituals than to ban them. Huang-li had been there at the end, packing food into their rucksacks in Quetta, waving them off as they tramped up toward Afghanistan. He had been enthusiastic, perhaps strangely so for a man who might be seeing his master for the last time. He had packed their bags with more than they needed, Chinese medicines, herbal remedies, packages they had quickly discarded. He had been doing all he could to ensure that they stayed alive until they reached their destination. That had seemed only right for a faithful servant, and Howard had been touched. But now he thought again. Keeping them alive until they reached their destination, so they could lead others to it. *Could it be?*

Howard coughed. None of that was of any consequence now. He tried to move his head, and suddenly retched, bringing up a mouthful of frothy blood he tried to swallow. He felt excruciating pain. Huang-li had packed some laudanum, and he wished they had it now. Wauchope leaned over him, holding his head. Howard eyed him. "I'm not giving up the ghost just yet," he whispered hoarsely. "We still have to find that jewel."

Wauchope jerked his head back toward the darkness of the shaft. "It's in here somewhere. I'm sure of it."

"And then the other jewel. The jewel taken by the other Roman mentioned in the inscription, Fabius."

"One thing at a time, old boy."

Howard grimaced. "Immortality. That's what the celestial jewel is all about, isn't it? We could do with a dose of that now."

Wauchope looked at the entrance, scanning anxiously, then back down at Howard. "Maybe in the end, in the jungle, Licinius felt that too. I've wondered what manner of man he was. Whether we can see ourselves in him. Sometimes, that has seemed the only way of fathoming out this mysterious path we're on."

Howard gave a weak smile. He coughed and swallowed, breathed for a moment to calm himself, then carried on talking, his voice

484

little more than a murmur. "You remember that carving we saw on the shrine wall, the woman and the child? For Licinius to seek immortality would have been to seek an immortality where loss and grief are also there forever. What is the point if all those you have loved have gone before, and if you have expended your reservoir of love? I think he took his chance with mortality. Maybe Elysium was a better bet after all."

"So what are we doing here? You and I? In this place?"

"The same thing that drove Licinius and Fabius. Maybe they really were seeking Elysium, seeking death with glory, not immortality. Maybe the lure of immortality only came upon them by chance, along the way. Maybe Licinius only learned of it after Fabius had departed, when Licinius had struck off south. Maybe he had the man with him who had brought the two jewels from the east, maybe a trader they had robbed and enslaved, used as a guide. If the Romans had known about it earlier, it's hard to see why Licinius and Fabius would have parted company, and separated the jewels."

"Maybe the gods didn't want mankind to find the secret of immortality."

"Maybe the gods have our best interests at heart."

"You still haven't answered my question. What we're doing here." Wauchope was gazing intently at him, his eyes full of concern. Howard knew Wauchope was trying to keep him going, keep him conscious, squeeze every last drop from their friendship, relish all he could in these moments. Howard returned the gaze. "We're here for the same reason those Romans took their last great journey. Remember the inscription we saw all those years ago in the jungle shrine? *Fifteenth Apollinaris.* For the glory of the legion. They were marching alongside the dead of their legion, shadowing them, seeking the trick of fate that would propel them to the other side, death with glory. They were doing what they were trained to do. They were soldiers. Maybe that's why we're here. The glory of our legion. The Corps of Royal Engineers. For all who have gone before, for all who have fallen. *Ubique.*"

"*Ubique,*" Wauchope repeated softly. "Spoken like a true sapper."

Howard's vision had become a tunnel, the edges dark and blurred. All he could see was Wauchope's bearded, turbaned head, as if it were framed in an old sepia portrait. Howard seemed to be levitating, and to be pricked by a thousand pins and needles, a not unpleasant feeling. He felt he should try to move, but wondered if he were caught in a dream, one where movement would break the spell. If he stayed still, at any moment he might lift himself up, and walk down that tunnel toward the light. "Robert," he murmured. "I can't see so well anymore."

Wauchope clutched his hand and held it tight. There was a sudden commotion at the entrance. A sound of neighing, of pawing hooves. They both peered up the rocky slope. Warm exhalation, crystallized, blew inward, sucked from the mountain air outside and drawn toward them, like a lick of dragon's breath against the radiance of the rock. They heard more snorting, pawing, and then their eyes grew accustomed to the light, and they saw it. The silhouette of a horse framed against the red sun, a glow that seemed to make the sweat glisten like blood as it shook its mane, spraying flecks of crimson into the air. And riding it, the figure in the terrifying tiger mask, loins girt with plates of armor, the great sword with the gauntlet flashing against the sky, streaked red with freshly congealed blood. *My blood.* Howard's heart began to pound, pumping froth out of his mouth. A drumbeat started up, a slow, insistent beat that became louder, coming up the valley slope toward them.

"That horse won't come in here," Wauchope said. "But the others will be on us soon, those following on foot. We have a few minutes left."

Howard uncurled his left hand and clutched Wauchope's hand hard, then stared up toward him. "Did I do any good, Robert? I built canals and bridges and roads. I showed them how to map the land. Did I do any good?"

"You brought up a family. You were a loving father. There is no better good a man can do."

Howard's face collapsed. "My son Edward. My boy. I should never have left him in Bangalore. I should have been with him at the end."

"You were a sapper officer, and you were doing the Queen's duty."

"Duty? In the jungle? What were we doing there?"

Wauchope gripped Howard's hand. "Do you remember our friend Dr. Walker? He reported the terrible jungle fever that decimated our men back to Surgeon-Major Ross, and Ross came to the jungle to see for himself. If you hadn't told Walker your theory about mosquitoes and the fever, it might never have happened. Sir Ronald Ross, winner of the new Nobel Prize for medicine. Putting down that rebellion was a thankless task, but something came out of it for the common good."

"The common good." Howard coughed, and swallowed hard. "The Kóya were already immune to the fever. We killed scores of them. We burned their villages. The roads I traced with my sappers are still there, unfinished, grown over. The few we did finish only brought moneylenders, opium dealers, disease. We were there because our government tried to squeeze a few more rupees out of the Kóya, and we failed because our government couldn't be bothered with a place that was unprofitable. We do great deeds with high ideals, Robert, but this was not one of them, and it has shaped my life." Howard suddenly convulsed, wracked with coughing. Blood poured down his chin, and he clutched the wet patch on his side, the blood bubbling out of his lung. He looked Wauchope in the eyes, his face gray. His voice was a whisper. "I can't feel my legs anymore, Robert."

The drumbeat became louder. Wauchope put his hand on Howard's shoulder, and leaned close to him, wiping the blood from his mouth with his sleeve. "Steady on there, old boy."

Howard gripped Wauchope's hand. "Find the jewel, would you? Take it to the jungle, to Licinius. And return the sacred *vélpu* to the Kóya. We owe them." His voice was trailing off. He coughed again, then whispered, "Go back to the shrine, and put it in his tomb."

Wauchope squeezed his hand. "One thing at a time, old boy. And I'll need you to help me move the lid."

"Look underneath, at the base of the sarcophagus," Howard murmured. "There will be a hole, about the right size for that tube. Licinius was a stonemason, remember? Roman sarcophagi always had a hole in them,

489

to let the decay out. To let the soul fly free."

"I always said you should have been an archaeologist," Wauchope replied.

Howard forced a grin, his teeth glistening with blood. "We've had a great adventure, haven't we?"

"Indeed we have." Wauchope picked up the bamboo tube with his left hand, curling his fingers around it until they nearly touched, then reached down with his right hand and picked up his Webley. "And it's not over yet." He gestured at the pistol in Howard's hand, where it had remained after he fell. "Any chambers left?"

"Two."

"I can't believe you still use that old thing. Cap and ball. In this day and age. You really ought to get a cartridge revolver."

"That's what you said thirty years ago in the jungle. I've managed to avoid firing a shot in anger since then. It has served me well."

"Just as long as you keep your powder dry."

"A soldier always looks after his weapon, Robert."

"You are still a soldier. The best."

"But not always," Howard murmured, "a knight in shining armor."

"Did it feel good? Shooting again in anger, I mean? Just now?"

"I always enjoyed the smell of gunpowder."

"Well then. Let's see if we can make up for lost time, shall we?"

"Hann til Ragnaroks."

"What did you say?"

Howard raised his left hand. His fingers were curled as if he were still holding the bamboo tube, but he could not feel them. His voice was soft, almost a whisper. "Look at the signet ring. The family crest, with the anchor. It's made of Viking silver, brought to England by my Norse ancestors. *Hann til Ragnaroks* was their motto. It means 'until we meet in Ragnaroks' in Valhalla."

"How on earth do you know that?" Wauchope said.

Howard managed a weak smile. "Family history. Always been a passion. Don't expect it will pass on though. Nobody else interested. But at least I know what to say when I get there. To those who have gone before."

"Well, I'm deuced if I'm going to Valhalla without a fight," Wauchope said. "Come on."

"My hand, Robert," Howard whispered. "Have you seen? It's stopped shaking. It's had a tremor all those years, since the jungle. Since I pulled that trigger. Now I can't feel it at all."

Wauchope reached over and cocked Howard's Colt, wrapping his limp hand around the grip. "I'm going for a recce. Your job is to shoot anything that appears at that entranceway."

"Right-oh." Howard's voice was barely audible. "Soldier first, engineer second."

"*Quo fas et Gloria ducunt.* We are soldiers."

"Warriors," Howard whispered. "Knights."

"What was it you said? *Hann til Ragnaroks.*"

"*Hann til Ragnaroks.*" Howard whispered the words, then took a rasping breath, bringing up blood again, and clutched Wauchope's arm. He was shaking again, and his breathing was shallow. "Did I do it?" he whispered. "In the jungle? Did I do it? Did I shoot that little boy?" He looked up imploringly, but he could no longer see Wauchope. All he saw now was the imprint of the light at the end of the cave, and the aura of blue from the rock surrounding it. Wauchope held his hand and squeezed it, then reached into Howard's tunic to where he knew it was, and pulled out a faded photograph of a young woman holding a baby. He placed it in Howard's blood-soaked hand, and put his own hand around it. Howard was crying, tears streaming from sightless eyes, crying for the first time. "I can see him," he whispered. "Darling Edward." He watched them coming down the tunnel toward him, coming from the light, the woman and the boy. The boy ran ahead, stumbled into his arms, and he held him high, laughing, crying with joy. Wauchope leaned over and kissed him on the forehead, then pushed himself to his knees, staggering up on his feet, the Webley dangling from one hand and the bamboo tube from the other. The silhouette was gone, and all Howard could see was a blinding light, as the rising sun obliterated everything else in its beam. The blue on the walls lit up and channeled the light back out again, a beam of energy that seemed to lift him to his feet and carry him forward. Then he heard the drums again, closer now, reverberating through the cave, and he felt the wind from outside, sharp jabs of cold that seemed to pierce him like arrows, and he was gone.

18

Jack felt himself free-falling through the water, his limbs spread-eagled as he let the weight of his body take him down. At first he had kicked hard to descend to a depth where he was no longer buoyant, and then he had forced the remaining air in his lungs into his mouth and used it to equalize the pressure in his ears. He could taste the water now, fresh, sharp, a hint of salt. He could see the bottom of the lake below him, gray and flat, not rippled as it would have been in the sea. He saw the shape that had drawn him down, the outline of an ancient boat half-buried in the sediment. Inside it was a pulsing green glow, as if someone had dropped a strobe light into the sediment. He fell toward it, hit the bottom then reached his arm deep into the mud and grasped the object. He drew it out, and held it up. It was a brilliant jewel, green olivine, peridot from the island off Egypt. He felt a warmth from it, the glow suffusing his body. He was suddenly drowsy, weighted down by it, as if he had found what he had been searching for all his life and there was nowhere else to go, and all he wanted was to let the sediment envelop him and to sleep forever. But he jerked back to life, his heart pounding. He had to return to the surface. There was something more precious there. He pushed off, the jewel in his hand, and kicked hard, finning toward the sunlight that streamed down from the sparkling surface above. *I am calm. I am strong.* He repeated the mantra, but he did not need to. There was no craving for oxygen, no urge to breathe. But then, as he saw the outline of the dive boat above, the wavering figures leaning over the side, watching him, he again felt a heaviness, a tingling that moved up his limbs toward his core. The jewel, weighty on the lake bed, had become too heavy, an impossible burden. He saw Rebecca's face peering down, her long hair floating on the surface of the water. He tried to reach up to her, but the jewel was dragging him back down. He opened his mouth and breathed in, taking the lake into his lungs, falling back, feeling only a terrible emptiness, not knowing if he was crying, his hands outstretched toward a form which receded into the sparkle of the sunlight until it was no more.

"Jack. Wake up. Katya and Altamaty are returning." Jack felt a hand shaking him, and awoke with a start. He was sitting in the front passenger seat of the jeep, and Costas was beside him. He heard a crinkling sound, and saw that he was covered by a survival blanket. Costas must have found one in the jeep's medical kit. He felt a tingling in his hands, the circulation returning. He remembered how cold they had been when they had arrived at this place soon after dawn, the dew still heavy on the ground. He pulled his left hand out from under the blanket, and looked at his watch. It was almost noon. They had been here about three hours, and he must have been asleep for two of them. They had been poring over Lieutenant Wood's account of his final trek up to the lapis lazuli mines, somewhere in the valley ahead of them now. Jack remembered closing his eyes when Pradesh had gone to boil water for tea. He glanced at Costas. He was wearing a faded green army coat over a dark fleece, a Soviet tank driver's sheepskin hat pulled down tight over his head. They had not been prepared for the chill, and had supplemented their own gear with what they had found in the bin at the back of the jeep. Jack pushed the blanket down, and cleared his throat. "Sorry. I dozed off."

"I noticed. It sounded like the engine was still running."

"I don't snore."

"Of course not."

Pradesh appeared beside the jeep door.

"You needed sleep." He was also wearing a sheepskin hat, and an Indian Army green sweater. He squatted down over a small Primus stove, and passed a steaming cup up to Jack. "Fresh brew. Finest Darjeeling. I always carry some with me. It's one military tradition we inherited from you British and just can't shake off."

"Thanks." Jack took the metal cup and cradled it. He peered at the valley ahead. The mountains of the Hindu Kush rose beyond, huge folds of stark rock and scree, dusted white on the nearer ridges and carpeted with snow on the peaks beyond. Jack lifted the compact binoculars that were hanging around his neck and peered through them. He could make out Katya and Altamaty, coming down a path that skirted the side of the valley. There was another figure with them, in Afghan gear. Jack lowered the binoculars and glanced at Pradesh, who nodded. Everything seemed to be going according to plan. They had arrived at Feyzabad airport in northern Afghanistan just after dawn, and had walked out of the plane straight into the jeep. Jack had an old friend who ran an aid agency in Feyzabad, and he had arranged the vehicle, complete with the freshly painted letters *TV* on the roof and sides. They had wanted to keep a low profile, and avoid any kind of military reception from NATO. There was an ISAF reconstruction team in the region, but after a phone conversation with the Danish colonel they had decided against an escort. The colonel had warned them of the risk. Taliban attack was possible anywhere, even up here in the north of the country. But the local warlord was known to be an independent, a stalwart of the old Northern Alliance, and he was someone they needed to nurture, not provoke. The colonel had given them an assurance of a helicopter medevac if they needed it, but beyond that they were on their own.

Jack raised the binoculars again, scanning the opposite slope of the valley, looking for flashes of reflection, for hints of movement among the rocks, but knowing he would see nothing. Somewhere out there, somewhere ahead of them, was the sniper Katya was sure had watched them by the lake in Kyrgyzstan, and who would now be here. They would be safe until their destination was clear, until they had found what the Brotherhood wanted, but with every step closer they would become more vulnerable, until there was no reason left for the sniper not to strike. Jack felt powerless and exposed, but knew they now had no choice but to play the game out and hope they would find a way to even the odds. The others knew the score. Everything depended on whether Katya and Altamaty had succeeded in their objective in the two hours since they had left the jeep to reconnoiter up the valley.

Pradesh folded up the stove and stowed it in his rucksack. "Time to saddle up, boys."

Costas swung his legs out of the jeep. "I don't know where you get these expressions from, Pradesh."

"U.S. Army Engineer School, Fort Leonard Wood, Missouri. Six month secondment last year."

Costas stopped and peered at him. "Really? Did you come across Jim Praeder?"

"Submersibles technology, seconded from the Naval Academy? I did his course."

Costas looked at Jack, and jerked his thumb toward Pradesh. "We really need this guy. Big-time. Permanent IMU staff."

Jack flashed a smile at Pradesh, then got out of the jeep and stood up, stretching. He was wearing his own kit brought in the plane, his beaten-up leather hiking boots, a fleece with a green Gore-Tex outer shell, a cherished blue woolen cap he had been given as a boy by one of Captain Cousteau's team. He pushed his old khaki sidebag until it was comfortable, feeling the shape of the holster inside. It was reassuring, but they needed more than handguns. He squinted up the path, and saw the Afghan figure with Katya and Altamaty leave them, bounding up another path and disappearing out of sight. He took a deep breath and said a silent prayer. Altamaty had been up here before, twenty years earlier, and he had known where to go. He and Katya both spoke the main Dari language of Afghanistan, and they both knew the Pashtun code. It was better for them to make the first contact. Too many westerners had come here promising help and peace, but bringing only betrayal and death. Jack knew they already had one sniper to contend with, and if they antagonized the local warlord as well they stood no chance of making it out of the valley alive.

He reached back into the jeep and picked up Wood's *Source of the River Oxus.* He opened the old volume where he had bookmarked it, and saw the faded notes made by John Howard, his great-great-grandfather, and then the neat notes on an interleaved sheet by Rebecca, his own daughter. There seemed to be a flow between them, a continuity, and the book seemed to bridge the generations. He glanced at the text, at the sentence that had been in his head when he had nodded off. *After a long and toilsome march we reached the foot of the Ladjword Mountains.* Ladjword he knew was the old Persian name for the place where the lapis lazuli was mined. They were there now, where Wood had been, at the end of the road, at the farthest point they could reach by jeep. From here on in they would have to go by foot, just as Howard and Wauchope must have done if they really did make it this far. Jack closed the book and pushed it into his bag. He thought of Rebecca with the dive team on Lake Issyk-Kul. His dream of her a few moments ago was still visceral, sharp in his mind. He remembered what Katya had said about dreaming up here, on top of the world. Dreams were harder to distinguish from reality, as if you were always halfway in a dreamworld. She had said it was the thin air, the restless slumber. Jack shook himself, and concentrated on Katya and Altamaty as they came down to the jeep. It was time to focus on hard reality.

Katya was bundled in a thick down climber's coat but seemed in her element. "Okay. Here's the score. The good news is that we made contact with Altamaty's old friend."

"The mujahideen guy who captured him during the Soviet war?" Costas said.

Katya nodded. "His name's Rahid, Mohamed Rahid Khan. Word had already passed up here that we were on our way, a film crew. He knew your name, Jack. He knows who you are. He even knew there were Kyrgyz among us. Amazing how information travels here, in a place almost barren of people."

"Has he seen anyone else?" Pradesh said.

"I didn't ask. He's got other things on his mind. Earlier this morning the Taliban attacked a village in the next valley to the north. It was some act of vengeance dating back to the time when the Taliban were in power in Afghanistan, before 9/11. Vengeance against Rahid's cousin, a schoolteacher. You don't want to know the details. Rahid's sent all of his men with most of his weapons, and he's leaving himself in less than an hour."

"So no backup for us after all," Costas said.

"There might be. I told him what Jack wanted. I didn't tell him our real reason for being here, but he's no fool. Jack Howard doesn't come to a war zone to make a documentary film. But these people know when not to ask questions. With the Pashtun, you talk around intentions, guess at them, size each other up first. He said there are a few people living in the valley, and it's always possible there might be Taliban sympathizers. Where there's one attack, like this morning, there's a general simmering, and the sight of any foreigners might be provocation. He said we should keep to the high path, avoid the valley floor. When I told him what you requested, Jack, he asked whether there was anyone among us who could handle a Lee-Enfield rifle. I told him about you, the Canadian rangers. You told me once."

"Jack?" Pradesh said.

"When I was a teenager," Jack replied. "My father was a painter, and we spent a couple of summers in the Canadian Arctic. The Canadian rangers are militia, mainly Innu and Inuit. They're armed with the Lee-Enfield rifle. They use it to hunt. They taught me to shoot."

"They taught you to be a sniper, Jack," Costas said. "I've seen it."

"I'd never claim that in front of an Afghan warlord," Jack murmured. "The Pashtun can shoot before they walk. Anyway, Pradesh will be familiar with the Lee-Enfield too. It's still used in India. He's probably a better shot than me."

"You're our leader, Jack, and he knows it," Pradesh said. "A Pashtun chieftain is only going to respect a leader who can do the killing himself."

Katya looked at Jack. "He's in a cave complex about twenty minutes away, up the slope where you saw him disappear. We don't want to miss him. Let's move." She turned and led them back up the path. They rounded a corner, with the rocky valley spread out below them. Almost immediately they were among wreckage, large twisted fragments of metal, sections of fuselage, a rotor collapsed like a giant wilted flower. The fragments bore flaky paint that had once been a khaki camouflage, and in two places a dull red star could be seen. "Altamaty's Hind helicopter," Katya said quietly. "The one he was shot down in when he was eighteen, during the Soviet war. He was the only one who walked away. Two others were still alive, but were shot by Rahid."

"You mean the friendly guy we're about to

503

meet?" Costas said.

"That's what it's like up here," Pradesh said. "No quarter expected, none given."

Jack watched Altamaty make his way through the wreckage, saw his eyes unswerving, looking beyond the shattered fragments to the rocky path ahead. Somewhere far away there was a rumble, the sound of low-flying jets roaring through a distant valley. Then the noise was gone, and they had left the wreckage behind, and all they could see was the steep, narrow trail ahead of them, nothing but bare rock and scree. The war being waged now could have been any war of living memory, the wars fought by the British, the war with the Soviets, wars that trawled and smashed their way through the lowlands but left the mountains unscarred, barely changed since the day John Wood came searching for the mines in 1836. Up here, humans seemed tiny, inconsequential, and even the cultivation and settlements of the valleys looked ephemeral, as if they could be washed away in the blink of an eye. Pradesh had said the same thing about the jungle, about the Godavari River. The jungle and the mountains were both places that gave no quarter, places that humans could never master.

Jack scrambled up the slope ahead of the others. The path became less obvious as the slope steepened, but the route was clear from the shiny patches of rock, handholds, footholds, where many had made their way up here before. The rock was schist and dolomite, hard like the rock of north Wales where Jack had learned to climb. He relished it now, moving with speed over outcrops where he needed to use his hands, enjoying the cold, biting air in his lungs, feeling cleansed, revitalized. Mountains were places where he felt comfortable, at ease, as he did underwater. After about twenty minutes he came to a ledge that stuck out above him, close to the summit of the ridge. He paused to catch his breath, and looked up. A man was standing there, a few meters away. He was wearing a turban and an Afghan robe, and over it a thick sheepskin jacket. He stared at Jack with piercing green eyes. His face was dark and craggy, and his beard was streaked with gray. Jack guessed the man was about his own age, but his face had a timeless look about it, like the mountains that framed him. Jack scrambled up and reached out his hand. "Mohamed Rahid Khan. *Salaam.*"

"*Salaam.* Dr. Howard."

"You've heard of me."

"We get the History Channel too, you know," Rahid said, with a wry smile. "I was at boarding school in England, before the Soviet war brought me back here. My father was a minister in the old Afghan government. Since his murder, I have ruled here."

"I know you don't have much time." Jack

pulled the copy of Wood's *Source of the River Oxus* out of his bag, and handed it over.

"I have read this book." Rahid opened it with care, and perused it silently for a moment. "But I have never seen it annotated like this. I think you are not only following Lieutenant Wood, Dr. Howard. I think you are following in the footsteps of someone else."

"Two British officers, in 1908. Retired officers, on a quest. One of them was my great-great-grandfather. We think they came here, up this valley."

"Then our paths have crossed before. Your ancestors and mine."

"I know."

"There is an ancient proverb about this valley."

"This one?" Jack paused, then spoke:

"Agur janub doshukh na-kham buro
Zinaar Murrow ba janub tungee Koran
*If you wish not to go to destruction,
Avoid the narrow valley of Koran.*"

Rahid raised his eyes at Jack. "How do you know this?"

Jack jerked his head back. "A friend from Kyrgyzstan."

Rahid watched Altamaty coming up the slope. "He remembers well."

"You gave him the ring?"

506

"Did he tell you why we've come?"

Rahid narrowed his eyes. "My grandfather remembered the day, a century ago. Our tribesmen knew they had come, and saw those who pursued the two travelers up the valley to the mines. Afterward my grandfather went up there. He said he had seen something terrible, that the upper shafts were haunted, that no one should ever go. Only I was brave enough, as a boy."

"We think there's someone else now. Following us. Watching us. Already up there, waiting."

Rahid pursed his lips, then looked out across the valley. "This land is like my skin. I feel when vermin are crawling on it. Your enemy is my enemy. *Inshallah.* But today, my men are at war. We will have vengeance."

"Your enemy is my enemy."

Rahid peered at Jack, holding his gaze for a moment, then nodded. He reached into his coat and pulled out a photograph. "Do you have children?"

Jack nodded. "A daughter."

"This is my daughter." Jack looked at the picture of a smiling Afghan girl, unveiled, her black hair falling to her shoulders. "If I do not fight them, one day they will do to my daughter what they have just done to my cousin. They will whip her for going unveiled. They will mutilate her for reading books. And they will rape her because they are animals."

"These are not men. They have nothing to do with Allah."

Rahid curled his lip. "The Taliban? Al-Qaeda? The Wahabists have been here since the time of the British, trying to stir us up. They have nothing to do with Afghanistan. And now their recruits come from the west. They go to so-called training camps, young Muslims who think they have learned to shoot by playing video games, and spraying rounds at a hillside while chanting holy verse. Stupid boys, fat boys, with eyes too close together. They even make poor target practice. They die too easily."

Katya and Altamaty came onto the ledge, and Costas jumped up behind. He took off his mitt and shook Rahid's hand, his voice breathless. "Costas Kazantzakis."

"Ah." Rahid bowed slightly. "The submersibles expert with the Navy Cross."

"Jack has been telling you?"

"I read the newspapers."

Jack shot Costas a look. "Rahid and I have been discussing the Taliban. Our enemy."

"We're on the same side, I take it."

Rahid's eyes bore down on Costas. "When a Pashtun is being shot at, he kills the person who is shooting at him. When the British came, we killed them. When the Soviets came, we killed them. And now the Taliban have come, and we are killing them."

"And yet, twenty years ago, you spared Altamaty," Costas said.

"We occasionally took hostages. And he was Kyrgyz, not Russian. But perhaps I should have killed him."

"Well, now's your chance," Costas said.

Rahid curled his lip. "I can't. He brought me a sheep's head."

"What?"

"That bag, over there. When he came up here with the woman, Katya." Rahid pointed. Jack suddenly realized. That explained it. He had suffered the smell throughout the flight, then in the jeep. Thank God they had no time to boil it now. "When we captured him during the Soviet war, this is what I gave him to eat. And coming here again now, he remembered."

"That's why you spared him, back then," Costas said. "When you captured him, you sized him up. You knew he'd bring this, if he ever came here again."

Rahid looked at Jack, then gestured at Costas. "I like this man."

"It's the same in Greece," Costas said. "Where men are men."

"Men," Katya murmured, "are fools."

Rahid put away the photograph of his daughter. "Enough of this. I have to go soon. Come with me." He led them behind the ledge to a cave in the hillside, concealed behind a jumble of rock made to look like natural scree. They passed through a door into a corridor carved out of the rock. "This was a natural cave, then my ancestors chiseled it out as a refuge at the time of the first British war in the 1840s. The men who made it worked in the lapis lazuli mines, so they knew what they were doing. We lived here during the Soviet war. We've got our own generator, solar-powered. The Soviets tried to destroy the cave from the air, but they didn't have bunker-busting bombs. They tried ground assault, over and over again. That's what Altamaty was doing here. But the whole hillside is booby-trapped. Even now, you only made it alive up that path because I knew you were coming." He pushed open a sliding steel door at the end of the corridor, switched on a light and unplugged a dehumidifier that had been throbbing in the corner. "This room is our arsenal. My men have taken our modern weapons, but there's enough left here for what you need."

They filed in behind Rahid. The walls were lined with wooden gun racks, most of them empty but several dozen weapons still there. There was a whiff of gun oil in the air, and everything was spotless. Jack walked over to the nearest rack. At the top was a long, ornate gun, an antique muzzle-loader with an extravagantly curved stock and rings of decorative metalwork up the barrel. "A jezail," he said. "Matchlock, smoothbore, early nineteenth century."

Rahid looked at him appreciatively. "You know guns."

"A family tradition."

"My ancestors killed with these. They are all kept ready to shoot."

"So I see." Below the jezail were several percussion muskets, East India Company smoothbores similar to the one in Jack's cabin on *Seaquest II*. Below that were half a dozen Martini-Henry rifles, with the cipher of Queen Victoria on the receivers. In the middle was a Snider-Enfield breech-loader, with the date 1860 visible on the lock plate. Pradesh pointed at the buttstock. "Look at that," he said. "The stamped roundel of the Queen's Own Madras Sappers and Miners. My regiment, and John Howard's. He could have touched this, Jack."

"All of these rifles were taken from the British," Rahid said. "The Snider-Enfield was recovered from the battlefield at Maiwand, in October 1880. It was used by a British sergeant who fought to the last round, after all his Indian sappers had been killed. His name was O'Connell. That's what those Persian letters on the stock mean. They were carved by our tribesmen, who found his name on his medals. We respect our enemies when they are brave. We are honored to take and use their weapons."

Pradesh glanced at Jack. "Some of the sappers were redeployed up here from the

Rampa jungle, a few months after the incident with the river steamer. This chap could even have been one of Howard's NCOs."

Jack touched the rifle stock, seeing where there was a careful repair near the breech, a darker piece of Indian wood inserted into the English walnut. He thought for a moment of the sappers that day in 1879 on the Godavari River, a thousand miles from this place. He stood back. The rest of the rifles were Lee-Enfields: snub-nosed Mark 3 rifles, made by the Ishapore arms factory in India, as well as later Mark 4 rifles from the Canadian Long Branch factory, many of them refurbished in Indian mahogany.

"We still use these," Rahid said. "The .303 packs a bigger punch than modern standard-issue military rounds and the Lee-Enfield is highly accurate, with a remarkable rate of fire for a bolt-action. From the time of the jezail, we have been brought up to kill with a single round. One of my men with a Lee-Enfield can take out an entire party of Taliban, carrying automatic weapons they do not know how to use. They are not like the sapper sergeant. They are an enemy we despise. We desecrate their bodies and disdain their weapons."

Jack eyed the rifles, stopping at one with a scope. "Long Branch, Number 4 Mark 1, 1943," he murmured. "This was the rifle I learned to shoot." He lifted it off the rack, checked the buttstock length, then took the leather covers off the eyepieces. "Scope pattern 1918, Number 32 Mark 1," he murmured. "Three point five times magnification." He pushed the safety forward, disengaged the bolthead and drew the bolt out, then held the rifle up to the light and peered down the barrel. "Perfect bore."

"We look after our weapons," Rahid said.

Jack replaced the bolt, drew the handle up and back, pushed it forward and down to cock it, pulled the trigger, repeated the process but let the bolt snap back, then pushed it forward while pulling the trigger. He clicked out the magazine and pressed down the feed platform, feeling the tension of the spring. Rahid handed him a khaki bandolier with five pouches. Jack slung it over his left shoulder, feeling the weight of the ammunition. He opened one and took out a five round clip. "Three-oh-three British, Mark 7," he said. He drew back the bolt of the rifle, slotted the clip into the receiver and stripped the rounds into the magazine with his right thumb, then repeated the process with another clip. He closed the bolt over them, then flipped on the safety with his thumb. "I take it I won't need to sight this in."

"The scope is zeroed for three hundred yards. I did it myself."

"Not a very powerful scope," Costas murmured.

"We didn't have scopes when we destroyed the British Army of the Indus with our jezails in 1841," Rahid retorted sharply.

"Point taken."

Pradesh reached up and took down one of the Ishapore rifles from the rack above, giving it a quick inspection. "I'll borrow one of these, if you don't mind."

Jack passed two clips from the bandolier to Pradesh, who stripped them into his rifle. Rahid's radio receiver lit up, and he spoke into it quickly. He snapped it shut, then gave Jack a length of old gray turban cloth and a pair of thick sheepskin mitts. "Use the cloth to camouflage the rifle. Watch the sunlight off the scope. Keep those mitts on until you have to pull the trigger. We must part now." He led them back to the cave entrance, then turned and spoke to Jack, quietly. "I will tell you what you need to know. As boys we played in the lapis lazuli mines. I know them all, every last passage, every nook and cranny. Just below the upper ridge are three shafts, not visible from the valley floor. They are in a line above the main workings, away from the shafts where the lapis has been mined most recently. The upper workings are old shafts, very old, where there is no good lapis to be found anymore. We were told as boys that they were the shafts worked at the time of the ancient Egyptians, of Alexander the Great. That was where my grandfather told us never to go, or a guardian demon would devour us. But I told you, I went, once. What you seek lies in the central shaft, the one just visible from the path you will be taking above the valley floor."

"Nobody else ever goes there?"

"For generations we controlled the mines. During the Soviet war we sold lapis lazuli to buy guns. The mines were under my sway and that of my forefathers. Our word was law. We banned anyone from going to the old workings on pain of death. It was what my grandfather wanted. It is only since the rise of the Taliban that our control has slackened, as we have had to look elsewhere, to defend our villages like the one being attacked now across the valley. Even so I am certain they are undisturbed. It is only the lower shafts now that produce the high-grade lapis. And nobody who lives in these mountains climbs higher than they absolutely need to. Up there you will find only death."

While he was talking the others filed out behind. There was a whinnying from somewhere below, then a strange bellow and a stomping of hooves. Katya caught her breath. "You have the *akhal-teke!*"

Rahid stared at her. "You know," he said quietly. "Of course. You told me. Your Kazakh family."

"No other horse makes a sound like that," she said, her voice halting. "The war-cry of the *akhal-teke.*"

"They run wild in the valley. This is one of the last places where they are kept pure. That's one reason why we keep outsiders away."

"You breed them?" Costas said.

Rahid paused, then looked at him. "I am the direct male heir of Qais Abdul Rashid, progenitor of all the Pashtun tribes," he said. "He in turn was descended from the clan who lived in this valley from before the time of Alexander the Great. My ancestors bred the *akhal-teke* for the First Emperor of China, *Shihuangdi,* after his warriors came here looking for them."

Katya stared at him, stunned. "Your clan are imperial horse-breeders," she said. "We thought they had all passed into history."

"We are the last. Ours are the final remaining purebreds."

"Do you still heed the call?" Katya said quietly. "Do the warriors still come?"

"A Pashtun's word is his oath. My ancestor gave it sixty-six generations ago."

"When was the last time they came? Has Jack told you I think we are being followed?"

"The oath was one of secrecy."

"I sensed the *akhal-teke* near the lake at Issyk-Kul," Katya murmured. "I heard that noise, and smelled something. There was a presence nearby."

"Our oath was to *Shihuangdi,* and to those

516

who can prove to us that they are his eternal guardians."

"The Brotherhood of the Tiger," Costas said.

Katya pulled out a photograph from her front pocket. "You mean those who can show you this. The tattoo."

Rahid remained silent, staring at the valley. There was a sudden tension in the atmosphere. Jack shot Costas a warning look, and Katya saw it. She put away the photo and confronted Rahid. "You know the Brotherhood is corrupted. He who controls it now has been tempted, and rules as if he is the reincarnation of *Shihuangdi* himself. In doing so he has broken his oath to the emperor. The oath of your clan is no longer binding."

Rahid looked at her silently, and then spoke. "Two weeks ago, a group came to the valley from a mining company, claiming I owed them allegiance. Eight men, prospectors. They wanted me to take them to the lapis lazuli mines."

"A mining company," Jack murmured. "Chinese?"

"INTACON."

Jack drew in his breath. "What did you do?"

"I told you what we do." Rahid gestured at the rifle in Jack's hands. "My ancestor swore an oath to the emperor, to the true Brotherhood, not to these animals. I killed them all."

"And the other one?" Jack said quietly.

"The one who followed them, who is there now? Waiting for us?"

Rahid touched the rifle, and stared at Jack. "Your enemy is my enemy. God be with you. *Inshallah.*"

Jack looked him hard in the eyes, and understood. Through the entrance passageway they heard the staccato noise of distant gunfire, and then the bellow of the horse, a strange, unnerving sound. Katya still seemed distracted by it, disturbed. "Can I touch it?" she said. "I haven't touched one since I was a child."

Rahid shook his head. "Not now. When you return. When you bring that rifle back, with one round missing." He looked at Jack, then pointed at the path toward the mountains. "That's your route."

Jack held out his hand. "*Tashakkurr.* I owe you."

Rahid shook it. "It's our code. *Pashtunwali.* Hospitality to travelers."

"But not all of them," Costas said.

"No, not all of them. You've been lucky." Rahid slapped Costas on the back. "*Salaam.* Go now." He turned and disappeared over the ledge. A few moments later there was the sound of whinnying, then the clatter of hooves on shingle, receding down the slope. Then the noise was gone, and all Jack heard was a whispering of wind across the rock, a sharp, dry wind brought down from the peaks of the Hindu Kush. He slung the rifle over his left shoulder and squinted up the valley. He took the Beretta out of his bag and handed it to Costas. Pradesh slung his rifle and passed his revolver to Altamaty. They knew that Katya had her own sidearm. Costas snapped back the slider on the Beretta, cocking it, then eased the hammer to the safe position and tucked the pistol in the breast pocket of his coat. "I'm ready," he said.

"I'll take point," Jack said, walking forward.

"No." Pradesh niftily sidestepped Jack and took the lead, heading off up the path. Jack relented, and looked at his watch. "It'll take two hours to get there, according to Rahid. That puts us at mid-afternoon. And that's probably two hours Afghan time, for people who live in these mountains. The air's pretty thin and we're not acclimatized. We'd better get moving. We don't want to be stuck up there after dark."

Costas pulled on a pair of fleece gloves. "Roger that."

19

Just over two hours later Jack unslung the rifle and sat on a rock, waiting for the others to catch up. The penetrating chill of the early morning had gone, but he knew that a few minutes sitting here and the cold would return with a vengeance, made worse by lack of sleep and food. He pulled his binoculars out and scanned the narrowing cleft in the mountains ahead, looking for signs of movement, the telltale flash of sunlight against metal. Still nothing. He tucked the binoculars away, and made a mental note to avoid using them again unless absolutely necessary. If he did have to use the rifle, he needed to be attuned to what he could see with the naked eye, to be able to judge distances, to sense the difference at a thousand yards between rock and animate form. He glanced at the ridge far above, squinting in the harsh sunlight. The valley had become narrower and higher as they had trekked farther into the mountains. The cleft ahead was no more than two hundred meters wide, bare rock and scree on both sides, the ground between dry and cracked. They had followed Rahid's advice and kept to the upper path, a good hundred meters above the valley floor. Jack reached down and picked up a piece of rock. Despite the frigid air it was warm, baked by the sun. There was no blue in it, but it was jagged, fractured. The scree ahead could be mine tailings, debris from thousands of years of hacking and picking at the rock, by miners lighting fires to crack the stone and expose the veins of precious blue. Jack looked at the slopes again. It fitted exactly with the description in Lieutenant Wood's book. He realized that he must be looking at the fabled lapis lazuli mines of Sar-e-Sang. His heart began to pound. *This was it.*

The other four came up behind. Costas slumped down beside Jack, and Pradesh knelt back against a rock, his rifle on his knees. Altamaty pointed to a pall of dust above the valley floor, and Katya clambered up onto a rock to follow his gaze. Jack knew she had been looking out for the horses since they had left Rahid. They had seen none, but she had told Jack that Altamaty had seen signs that he'd been sensitized to by his nomad upbringing. Jack looked at the valley floor. He saw no horses, but he did see people, a man and a boy. They were standing in front of a tent that was stretched between boulders at the base of the opposite slope. They were bundled up in sheepskins, and wispy smoke was rising in front of them. They were six hundred meters away, maybe seven hundred. Jack made a mental note of their size at that distance, and let his eyes dart up the slope behind them, looking at the boulders and ridges, at points of concealment, gauging the gradient of the scree and the increased distance as the slope rose toward the ridge some five hundred meters above.

"Do we say hello?" Costas rubbed his mitts together against the cold, and shoved them in his fleece. "I like the look of that fire."

Jack shook his head. "Rahid said not to. When the miners come up here they use dynamite, and some of the people who've been attracted to work for them also work for the Taliban during the off-season when the miners have gone, making IEDs. That's probably what they're doing here now. It's too cold for mining and there are crops to harvest in the valleys. The Taliban like having their bombmakers up here because if something goes wrong, if there's an accident, nobody knows or cares. The bombs are mostly carried out to be used in Kabul and the south, but the Taliban in Feyzabad have recently put a bounty on killing westerners and these people up here might be tempted to use one on us. They have no land, no other income. And for desperate people, suicide bombing has become an easy route to paradise. We need to be careful."

"Won't they see our weapons?" Costas said.

"Everyone carries guns out here," Katya said. "They'll probably think we're prospectors. Others have come up here before."

"Including the one who's after us."

"He'll be invisible," Katya said. "He's a sniper. That man and the boy will have seen us by now, but not him."

"Let's take a look again at that passage in Wood's account," Costas said. "We need to get our bearings and keep moving." His teeth were chattering, and Pradesh passed over the thermos of tea he had made beside the jeep. Costas gratefully took it, unscrewing the top. While he poured himself a cup, Jack took out *Source of the River Oxus* and read out a marked page:

"Where the deposit of lapis lazuli occurs, the valley of the Kokcha is about 200 yards wide. On both sides the mountains are high and naked. The entrance to the mines is in the face of the mountain, on the right bank of the stream, and about 1500 feet above its level. The formation is of black and white limestone, unstratified, though plentifully veined with lines. The summit of the mountains is rugged, and their sides destitute of soil or vegetation. The path by which the

mines are approached is steep and dangerous."

Costas finished his tea and passed the thermos back to Pradesh, peering at the route
ahead. "Steep and dangerous," he muttered.
"You can say that again."

"You can see some of the mineshaft entrances along the slope ahead of us, on our
side of the valley," Katya said. Jack slung his
rifle and stood up. He felt the cold now,
touching his core. This place had stark
beauty, but also raw danger. *A place that gave
no quarter.* He climbed up beside Katya on
the rock, and followed her gaze. Above the
mine tailings he could see the entrances to
the shafts, at least half a dozen of them, black
holes in the rock. Somewhere higher up were
the ones they sought, three of them close to
the ridge. "If Howard and Wauchope came
here, they would have had no idea which
shaft contained what they were seeking."

"You mean the jewel," Costas said. "The
lapis lazuli one."

Jack nodded. "The only clue we know they
had was the inscription from the jungle
shrine, implying that Licinius had hidden his
treasure somewhere up here in the mines, on
his way south from the Silk Road toward
India. Howard and Wauchope could have
been here for days, searching all of the mine
shafts. We should appear to do what they did.

We don't want to give any clue that we know where we're going. If this is who Katya thinks it is and he's got his rifle with him, a beeline straight up to the shaft at the top identified by Rahid may be the last trek any of us takes."

"So what happens if he does rumble us?" Costas said. "He's not going to let us walk away from here."

Jack climbed off the rock. "Altamaty came up here once when he was a captive of Rahid, and remembers a couple of sangars made by the mujahideen, crude revetments of piled stone used as protection against air attack. Pradesh and I discussed this on the way up here. He's going to find one of them, and set himself up with his rifle. The sangars are about midway up the slope. Below that are the main shafts, the ones that are still mined. Katya and Altamaty, I suggest you explore those. Costas and I are going to climb above Pradesh, looking for those three upper shafts. Our sniper will be somewhere on the opposite side of the valley, with the best field of fire for the entire slope. If we split up, Altamaty and Katya below, Pradesh in the middle, and Costas and me above, then it divides his attention. He doesn't know yet which one is his target, and he can't concentrate on who may be targeting him. If he is here, he's seen us and knows that two of us have rifles."

Costas turned to Jack. "So what exactly are we looking for?"

"Rahid said it's up there. He seemed to know what I was after."

"Any detail? Like a treasure map?"

"He told me what I needed to know. All he said was that it's in the central cave. He went in there as a boy. Nobody else goes there. They think it's spooked."

"Oh, great." Costas paused. "If he found the jewel, wouldn't he have taken it? Or given us more detail, like told us where in the mine-shaft to look?"

"He told me what I needed to know," Jack repeated. "I trust him."

"You think there's something else up there."

Katya spoke quietly. "This isn't just about what we find. This is about Shang Yong. He thinks we're on the trail of the jewel taken by Licinius, that we're going to lead him to it. That's what the sniper wants to see. For years they thought the jewel was hidden in the jungle, ever since John Howard's lecture in London when the story of the tomb reached the Brotherhood. And now they're on the same trail as us, following the same clues. Even if they didn't torture the knowledge out of my uncle before he died, they may have seen the inscription themselves, that word *sappheiros,* lapis lazuli. And this is where it ends. The tiger warrior kills us, or we kill him. If we succeed, Shang Yong's power is broken. He only exerts power over the Brotherhood by force and intimidation. Without his henchman, the Brotherhood will rise against him, confront the corruption within. They will once again protect the eternity of the First Emperor, of *Shihuangdi*."

"And if we walk away now?" Costas said.

"Then there will be another confrontation, and the odds against us will be even greater. If we let Shang Yong believe he has won, then his world will seem inviolable. For him, the celestial jewel is a state of mind. This is what my uncle feared the most. In Shang Yong's re-creation of the First Emperor's tomb, in his fantasy projection of the heavens, he's halfway to believing that the jewel is already there, in its rightful place above him, giving him the immortality he craves. If we give up on the quest, then the delusion may become complete. We need him to believe that the jewel could still be found, to maintain the small doubt, the part of him still left that knows that what he has created is an illusion. We need to keep that door open. If he becomes locked inside his delusion, then the world becomes a much more frightening place. It will truly seem as if *Shihuangdi* has reawakened, and that is something we must do everything in our power to prevent. There is much more at stake here than an ancient lost jewel."

Jack's eyes were like steel. He glanced at Katya, then up the valley. He slung his rifle and looked at his watch. "We've only got three hours of daylight left. Let's move."

An hour later, Jack and Costas sat back against the rocky scree slope not far from the summit of the ridge, having followed a treacherous path up over ridges and sheer faces of fragile rock. They were high now, over twelve thousand feet, and Jack exhaled through his nose to equalize his ears. All the time they had been conscious that they were being watched, possibly through the sights of a rifle, but they had worked on the assumption that they would only become targets once they had shown some evidence of reaching the end of their search. They were less than a hundred meters below the three mine-shaft entrances that Rahid had told Jack to find. They dropped down into a gully formed by a bank of rocky mine tailings, concealing them from the opposite slope of the valley. Jack knelt down on the shingly rock and worked his way to the edge, the rifle beside him. He could see Pradesh in a depression in the shingle about a hundred and fifty meters below, his rifle positioned beside a rock. Somewhere far below were Katya and Alta-maty, exploring the line of shaft entrances closer to the valley floor.

"Shooting at ghosts hiding behind rocks on a hill," Jack murmured.

"What?"

"A line from a British soldier of the first

Afghan war," Jack said.

Costas settled down heavily on his front beside Jack, and rolled onto his elbows. He was panting, and his breath crystallized in clouds in the still air. "I should have brought my laser range finder."

"The Canadian rangers taught me to estimate distance on the tundra, where the white backdrop makes the target stand out. Their benchmark was the standard survey lot of a hundred acres. Each side's just under seven hundred meters. It's a distance people grow up with in Canada, as that's how the land was parceled out. The rangers reckoned that was about the maximum distance for a .303 shot with the unaided eye. Beyond that, you stand little chance of making out a stationary human form, especially with a rocky backdrop like this."

"Unless you've got eagle eyes, like our opponent."

Jack looked at the altimeter on his watch. "I downloaded a topographical map before we took off from Bishkek. The distance from the valley floor to the top of the ridge is about five hundred meters. Lieutenant Wood got that right in 1836, fifteen hundred feet. We're maybe a bit over a hundred meters below the ridge, and the slope we've come up must have averaged at least forty-five degrees."

"Isosceles triangle," Costas murmured. "That gives a distance to the valley floor of about six hundred meters. But our sniper could be anywhere up the opposite slope, and there's lateral distance too."

"You have to put yourself in his mind," Jack said. "Let's assume he arrived here with plenty of time to choose his position. He wants to have a view of all the mineshaft entrances, right? He doesn't know which one's going to be his target. The shafts up here, close to the ridge, are the farthest from the opposite slope. Rahid said they're just visible from the path running above the valley floor, the continuation of the one we came in on. That gives him a minimum distance to the most distant possible target, where we are now. He's going to want to position himself equidistant between the farthest possible targets on either side. That puts him in a cone of probability focusing on that large cleft you can see above the path opposite us."

"Remember what Katya said about how good this guy is. You're thinking of seven hundred yards, but maybe he can do nine hundred, eleven hundred, more."

Jack nodded. "He's also going to take counter-sniping into account. He's seen our rifles, but he's going to assume that none of us are trained. Remember what Rahid said about the Taliban recruits, their dismal marksmanship. That's what this guy's going to be used to, wherever he's worked in war zones around the world. Boy soldiers, terrorists spraying Kalashnikovs. Never much threat to him. In counter-sniper work, you always have to try to find a weakness in your opponent, and that's his. He thinks he's master of this valley, but he's not."

"You have to believe it, Jack."

"It's the psychology of the sniper. You need complete confidence in yourself. That's the sniper's ultimate strength, but also a weakness. Confidence breeds overconfidence."

Costas slid back down the mine tailings into the gully. "I just hope you don't get the shakes. My teeth are beginning to chatter, and I'm not sure if it's just the cold. I'm going to take a look in that shaft above us. But I'm going to drop down and see Pradesh first. He needs to know about that cone of probability."

"Good. The more movement our opponent sees, the longer we have."

"How much time?"

"Not much. He's going to want to strike before the light goes. And he'll have seen we're not equipped to spend a night up here. He'll be looking for any sign that we've found what we're seeking."

"You think he knows we're onto him?"

"He'll have seen Katya. He knows she'll have told us about him. He's seen us split up. He could guess why."

"If I'm sticking my head up, I want you to be covering me."

"Roger that."

Costas shuddered with the cold, beating his arms around him, then clambered over the tailings and made his way down the slope to where Pradesh was visible in the sangar below. Costas slid awkwardly on the scree, completely exposed. Jack was far more worried than he had let on. If the sniper was half as good as Katya said he was, his first target would be himself or Pradesh. He would want to get rid of the two rifles first, the only threat to him, then pick off the rest at leisure. Jack shut his eyes, and tried to put himself into the mind of the other man, somewhere on the opposite side of the valley, staring at them, his eye darting from Katya and Altamaty, to Pradesh, to him, seeing Costas moving down the slope. Jack opened his eyes and peered out, searching the opposite slope, still seeing nothing. The noise of Costas stumbling down the rock reverberated across the valley. Jack prayed that he had been right, that the rifle was trained on him first, not Pradesh. He took a deep breath and forced himself to stand up, holding the rifle, making himself a clear target for a few moments, then lay back down behind the rocks. His rifle had the scope, Pradesh's rifle did not. He took off his sheepskin mitts, remembering what Rahid had said. The cold would numb his fingers and make his shooting ineffective. By that simple act he was committing himself mentally to the task ahead. He had to believe that his opponent was also poised for action. He unwrapped the Lee-Enfield from the turban cloth. He tried to shut his mind from everything except his rifle and the target. He began breathing slowly, deeply, stopping every few breaths before inhaling again, trying to slow his pounding heart. He felt the forestock of the rifle, dried linseed oil on walnut, tested the grip. He held the rifle with his left hand and used his right hand to arrange the cloth where his elbows would be, cushioning them against the jagged chips of rock. He wrapped his right arm around the sling, but not too tight, remembering that the throb of arteries might be enough to throw his aim off completely at this distance.

Jack removed the lens covers and the elevation and windage turret caps from the scope, but kept a strip of turban cloth over the front lens to minimize the chance of glare. The slightest reflection, the slightest movement, could give the game away. As soon as his opponent knew that Jack was taking up position the waiting was over, and the others were suddenly targets. The slightest flinch could put all their lives in danger. He flipped off the safety on the rifle, then pulled the bolt handle back. He saw the gleam of the cartridge in the magazine, pushed the bolt forward, saw the cartridge jump up and nose into the chamber, and then felt the resistance as he pushed the bolt home and let the handle drop. He raised the rifle, careful not to let the muzzle show above the rocks. He edged up the slope, bringing the rifle level and then down, wedging the forestock into a rocky cleft, aiming at the path across the opposite slope of the valley. He looked along the side of the scope, trying to gauge the distance with his naked eye. He chose the rock he had spied with Costas. *Eight hundred yards.* It was downslope, but the air was thin, dry, and the decreased resistance would compensate for the extra gravity. He reached up and dialed in the elevation. There was no vegetation to gauge wind speed, but it was virtually nonexistent, only a tingle on his face from the north. He touched the dial on the windage turret, turning it one notch. He let his right hand fall to the trigger guard, then pulled the butt hard into his shoulder, bringing his cheek to bear against the raised wooden piece on the comb of the stock. Keeping both eyes open, he looked with his right eye down the scope, shifting back slightly to get the best eye relief. It was a simple crosshair reticule, and despite the three and a half times magnification the rock still seemed impossibly far away. He remembered what he had been taught. He projected his mind forward until he imagined the dark silhouette of a body in the rocks, then the bullet racing in, becoming smaller as the silhouette became larger. Without moving his head he looked around. The target could still be outside his point of aim visible through the scope. He curled his forefinger around the trigger, pulling it through its first stage, feeling the resistance. He took a deep breath, taking in the sharp, metallic smell of the rock, and exhaled halfway. He stopped breathing. He went still.

He stared through the scope. *Show yourself.*

Suddenly out of his left eye Jack saw movement on the valley floor. His heart began to pound. He willed it to slow down. Where the pall of dust had floated above the far end of the valley a shape had emerged. It was a horse, riderless, cantering along beside the dry riverbed that ran through the middle of the defile. The horse passed the tent they had seen among the boulders and came to a halt about a hundred yards beyond, tossing its head and pawing the ground. Jack kept stock-still. He saw another figure, walking from the edge of the slope below him toward the horse. Jack took his eye off the sights, and stared in disbelief. *It was Katya.* He remembered her fascination with the *akhal-teke,* the heavenly steeds. She walked toward the horse, hands outstretched, completely exposed. It was as if she were in a trance. Then Jack saw something else, a flash, a glint from the opposite slope. *That was it.* He instantly reacquired his target. The flash had been about twenty yards higher than his point of aim. He shifted the rifle up a fraction. The sniper had been thrown by the horse, by Katya, just as Jack had. He would have instantly known his mistake, and now would make up for it.

And Jack was the first target.

There was a vicious snap overhead, a smack on a rock behind and a ricochet that snarled off into the distance. The report and the echo seemed to come together, rebounding off the valley sides. Then it was gone, leaving Jack stunned. *Concentrate.* He had seen the muzzle flash in the rocks. He tightened his finger on the trigger again. He took a deep breath, and exhaled slowly.

Then there was something else. Katya was not the only figure on the valley floor. Another had emerged, running, stumbling from the direction of the tent. *It was the Afghan boy.* Katya had reached the horse and was stroking its neck. The boy was closing in on her, out of her view on the other side of the horse, a hundred yards, eighty. Jack had a sudden sick feeling. Something was terribly wrong. The boy had both arms out in front of him, and was wearing something bulky around his chest. He was shouting, screaming hoarsely, in a voice that had not yet fully broken, words that echoed up the valley, words of terrible defiance, of aggression. *Allah akbar. Allah akbar.*

Jack's mind reeled.

The cry of a suicide bomber.

Jack stared with sudden cold certainty. He had to make a decision. Now. *He might be the only chance Katya had.*

Another bullet cracked overhead, smiting the rock behind him and spraying him with rock splinters. This time Katya noticed the report, and looked up. She was holding the horse close now, stopping it from bolting. She must have heard the boy, but she had still not seen him. Jack's mouth was dry, his heart pounding. It was just another target. He angled the rifle down. The sniper knew where he was already. Jack had no choice. He brought the scope to bear. It was a moving target, almost impossible at this range. Suddenly the boy stumbled and fell, then struggled to his knees. It was a chance. Jack aimed at the torso. Katya leapt on the horse, and it reared upward. There was a sharp crack of a rifle shot from below. Jack remembered. *Pradesh.* Jack could see him out of his left eye, lying prone beside Costas in the sangar below, rifle aimed at the boy. Then Jack heard another snap, a ricochet that whined past him, and a report from the other side of the valley. He saw Pradesh thrown back in the sangar like a rag doll, his rifle clattering down the slope. Jack looked back at the valley floor. The boy was crumpled on the ground. Katya had begun to ride hard, and Jack saw Altamaty run out from the slope alongside, leaping up behind her. Suddenly there was a flash of dust and fire from where the boy had been, and a second later a dull boom. The dust cloud from the explosion seemed to chase the horse as it thundered down the valley. And then Jack saw the muzzle flash again from the opposite slope. The sniper had exposed his head, and was shooting at the horse. Jack's rifle was still on target. He was rock-steady. He squeezed the trigger. The rifle kicked hard, and there was a sucking sensation, as if the vortex of the bullet were taking all the sound with it, bringing all possible energy to bear on the target. *Eight hundred meters. One and a half seconds.* Jack's ears were ringing. He could hear nothing. And then there was another flash across the valley, and movement. Something went up in the air. Jack whipped out his binoculars. The movement had been a rifle, falling against the rocks. He looked hard into the shadows, and then he saw it. A human figure, sprawled back, motionless, a spatter of darkness on the rock behind the head. Jack closed his eyes, and forced the air out of his lungs. He began to shake uncontrollably. All he felt was cold, icy cold. He pulled on the mitts again, and crossed his arms tight against his chest, his hands stuffed under his armpits, lying on the scree, shaking.

"Man down!"

Costas was yelling from the sangar below.

Jack leapt over the rocks and stumbled down the slope, reaching them in seconds. Costas had opened Pradesh's bag and was ripping a large shell dressing out of its package. Pradesh was conscious, and looked at Jack, grinning weakly. Jack saw blood seeping out under his back, and knelt over him, panting. "How is it?"

"Not too bad." Pradesh's teeth were chattering, and he grimaced as Costas used a pair of scissors from the pack to cut away the fabric from his coat, revealing a neat hole the size of a quarter just below his right shoulder. Costas patted out coagulant powder from a plastic bottle and pressed on the dressing, then carefully eased Pradesh over and repeated the process on his back. "It's a clean exit wound," he exclaimed. "You were lucky. I think it was 7.62 millimeters, if he was using the Mosin-Nagant, ball rather than explosive. At this range, there's less cavitation and tissue damage. It doesn't look as if any major blood vessels were hit. What you've got is a nasty flesh wound. A few inches lower, and it'd have been a different story."

Pradesh looked at Jack. "The sniper?"

"A head shot."

Pradesh shut his eyes. "Congratulations." He opened them again and looked down at his wound, suddenly convulsed with pain. "And the boy," he said, grimacing. "That was my shot."

"The explosion came a few seconds after your bullet hit. He may have panicked and detonated the bomb himself when he saw Katya beginning to ride away."

"I was responsible," Pradesh said. "Either I shot him, or my round spooked him into killing himself."

"My rifle was trained on him too. It was just chance that you pulled the trigger first. He was going down either way. And you saved Katya's life."

"It meant you could take out the sniper."

"We did the job."

Pradesh gave Jack a fathomless look, then winced. "There's a radio in my pack. You can call in a chopper for a medevac. I think this counts as a Taliban incident. ISAF are going to want to send a recce team up here now. I expect they'll already be monitoring Rahid's attack on the Taliban at that village, so there will probably be a couple of helicopters on standby at Feyzabad."

Costas stared down the valley, his face whitened with dust. "What drives a child to do that," he murmured. Through the pall of dust they could see the man from the tent wandering about aimlessly, arms gesticulating, as if he were looking for something, where the boy had gone.

"It's not what drives the child," Jack said, shivering, holding his arms tight to his chest.

"It's what drives the father. That man down there strapped those bombs to his son and sent him to his death."

"He looks distraught."

"That's what the jihadists don't prepare you for."

"I just hope ISAF sends what's needed to take out all the Taliban in this area, those who led that poor man down the road to hell."

"I think Rahid can probably manage," Pradesh said weakly. "They've had enough outside interference here already. Where are Katya and Altamaty?"

"They rode off down the valley, the way we came in," Costas said. "We'll get the chopper to pick them up after you're safely out of here."

"Roger that," Pradesh said. "It'll take at least half an hour, which gives you time to see if there's anything to find up here."

"Anything more we can do for you?" Jack said.

"I could use a little morphine."

Costas took an ampoule out of the bag, tapped it, then slapped it on Pradesh's thigh. "That should do it." He pulled out an emergency blanket and tucked it around Pradesh, and Jack slipped off his coat and put it on top.

"Better. Much better." Pradesh closed his eyes, then waved his hand. "You can go now.

I think it's time you had a look in that mine shaft."

Twenty minutes later Jack and Costas stood in front of the central shaft entrance, looking into the dark hole above a large pile of mine tailing that partly blocked the way in. Costas had Jack's copy of Wood's *Source of the River Oxus* in his hands, and quickly read out the passage on the lapis lazuli mines:

"The shaft by which you descend to the gallery is about ten feet square, and is not so perpendicular as to prevent your walking down. The gallery is eighty paces long, with a gentle descent; but it terminates abruptly in a hole twenty feet in diameter and as many deep. The width and height of the gallery, though irregular, may be estimated at about twelve feet; but at some places where the roof has fallen in, its section is so contracted that the visitor is forced to advance upon his hands and knees. Accidents would appear to have been frequent and one place in the mine is named after some unhappy sufferers who were crushed by the falling roof. No precaution has been taken to support by means of pillars the top of the mine, which, formed of detached blocks wedged together, requires only a little more lateral expansion to drop into the cavity. Any further operations can only be carried out at the most imminent risk to the miners."

He shut the book carefully and handed it to Jack, who slipped it into his khaki bag. Costas began to trudge up the pile of rock chippings, slipping back down with each step. "Well, it doesn't sound less safe than anything else we've done today," he muttered. "You say no one else comes up here?"

"That's what Rahid told me. They think it's haunted."

Jack followed Costas. He felt heavy, suddenly tired. Each step seemed a monumental effort, as if he were walking in deep snow. His feet slipped back on the rock chippings, and halfway up the mound it seemed as if he was going nowhere. He felt as if he were constantly striving for an objective that was just beyond his grasp, like in a dream. Finally he stood at the top of the mound of tailings, the roof of the cavern entrance within arm's reach above him. Costas was ten meters or so ahead, inside the shaft below Jack, crouching down. Jack watched him take out a Mini Maglite and pan the light over the walls. The rock was dark, almost black. Jack remembered the description, the thick layer of carbon from the fires used over thousands of years by miners to crack open the veins of lazurite. He looked back at the entrance. He was not sure, but the light seemed to reflect a haze of blue off the walls, a blue like the azure of the sky. He turned back. Costas had advanced a few more steps down and was stooped over, close to the base of the mound where it sloped down into the cavern. He was motionless, staring hard at the chips of rock, shining the torch on one spot directly in front of him. He straightened, then looked back up. "Jack," he said quietly.

"I'm here."

There was silence for a moment. Costas cleared his throat. "That old Colt revolver of John Howard's. The other one of the pair, the one you said his father had used in the Indian Mutiny."

"Yes?" Jack's voice felt disembodied, as if he were hearing himself speak from a long distance away.

"Do you know where it was made?"

Jack's mind was a blank. He struggled to think. "It would have been Colt's London factory. The address would have been stamped on the barrel."

Costas got up, switched off the Maglite and made his way back to where Jack was standing. He looked him full in the face. "I know what Rahid found. I know why they never let anyone near this place."

Jack put his hand on Costas' shoulder. Costas offered him the Maglite, but Jack shook his head and reached deep into his bag, holding something tight. He left Costas, stumbling down, sliding on the rock chips, feeling where it was frozen underneath. He reached the spot where Costas had been, and dropped down on his knees. He let his eyes grow accustomed to the gloom. Then he saw what Costas had seen. It was half-buried in the tailings, but unmistakable. The revolver had been well-oiled so was not rusted, but had turned a deep plum color. He could see the address on the barrel. *Col. Colt, London.* The grip and the trigger guard were surrounded by rags, a coarse cloth, tightly wound. The fabric extended back under the rock chippings, then rose again in a mound, and then extended up again, a few feet away. The shape was symmetrical. Jack felt himself swaying. *Two arms, outstretched.* He looked at the other side. There was no pistol there, but a hollow where something had been, something that had once been grasped.

Jack peered again. The hollow could have been anything. It could have been the shape of a clenched hand, retracted in death. It could have held another weapon, a sword perhaps. But it could have been something else. The shape of a bamboo tube, the sacred *vélpu,* once held in that hand, now gone.

Jack swallowed hard. He was crying, and he did not know why. He took a deep breath, held it, and then exhaled slowly, blinking hard. He thought about what he knew of the man, of his love for his children, his family.

He hoped they had been there at the end. He hoped that whatever had tormented him, the anguish, the loss, had lifted from him here, in those final moments. He hoped he had found what he had been seeking all those years since the jungle, the greatest treasure imaginable.

Jack wiped his eyes, and looked up. There was a noise outside, pulsing into the cavern, the clatter of a helicopter coming up the valley. He heard a crunching of feet on the rock behind. Costas had left him alone with the body for a few minutes, but Jack had vaguely been aware of him skirting around and exploring the recess beyond. "I checked it out," Costas said, his breath crystallizing in the shaft of sunlight coming from the entrance. "The mine extends about twenty meters farther on, then drops into a well about five meters deep. If this was where Licinius hid that stone, my guess is that's where it would have been. There are ledges in the rock created by the ancient pick work, but I looked and there's nothing loose. It's as if someone has been in here and methodically worked through the entire place. If that jewel was here, it's gone now."

Jack cleared his throat, and pointed. His voice sounded hoarse. "Look at his hand, the empty one. It's exactly as if he were holding a Kóya bamboo *vélpu*. I think they brought that with them, the one they had taken from the jungle all those years before, and now that's gone too. And so is Robert Wauchope. There's no sign of another body here. Maybe when they came here the *vélpu* was empty, but when it was taken away it was heavy with a new weight. Maybe Wauchope took it from Howard's grasp, and escaped from here. Maybe they really did find the jewel."

Costas looked at Jack. "We've found what we came for, haven't we?"

Jack said nothing. He reached into his bag, grasping what he had been tightly holding as he entered the chamber. "I know we have to go. Just give me a moment."

"You want to be alone?"

"No. Stay." Jack took out his hand and opened it. He was holding the little lapis lazuli elephant, John Howard's childhood toy, worn smooth by years of little hands, played with by Jack himself when he was a boy. It had a sparkling ribbon tied around its neck, something Rebecca had put on it when she had taken it to her cabin on *Seaquest II.* Jack squeezed the elephant tight. *Lapis lazuli, born in this mountainside, now returned.* He put it down, and pushed it toward the twist of rags, the empty outstretched hand, carefully, gently. It touched, and he left it there, pulling his hand away.

The helicopter thundered past again. Jack got up, and straightened his bag. He took a deep breath, exhaling one last time into the depths of the cavern, watching his breath

547

crystallize and tumble into the darkness. He put his hand on Costas' shoulder. He remembered Pradesh. It was time to go.

20

Two days later Jack sat in the stern of the U.S. Navy patrol boat as it sped across the still waters of Issyk-Kul, its wake cutting a great V across the surface of the lake. The view was stupendous. Issyk-Kul was the deepest mountain lake on earth, three thousand square kilometers in area, five times the size of Lake Geneva. To Jack the wake seemed like a giant arrow pointing east, a final thrust of the central Asian massif toward the deserts of China. To the south, the mountains that cradled the lake loomed fantastically out of the haze, a strip of snowy peaks that seemed detached from the earth, floating in midair like a mirage. To the west lay the boulder-strewn shoreline where he and Costas had met Katya and Altamaty three days before. They had left her there again that morning, recording the Roman burial site, before a helicopter would fly her out to meet them. There was one place Jack insisted they visit, beyond the lake, beyond the Taklamakan

Desert near the end of the Silk Road. The visit would take a few days to set up, and meanwhile Jack was excited by the prospect of diving again for the first time since *Seaquest II* had left the Red Sea over a week earlier.

Jack thought again of Pradesh, of his gunshot wound in Afghanistan two days before. He would be in intensive care for weeks, but the prognosis was good. He was in the best possible hands at the U.S. medical facility at Bishkek, and would soon be sent to Landstuhl in Germany. After flying back with him from Afghanistan, Jack and the others had gone by helicopter to the lake to meet the patrol boat that had come out to join them from the old Soviet naval base on the eastern shore. Jack had wanted to travel the route the Romans under Fabius might have taken, east across the lake after Licinius had parted from them and fled south into the mountains. The patrol boat was now approaching the end of its journey, almost ten hours at maximum speed. It would have been an awesome endeavor two thousand years before for a few men in an open boat, already drained by the trek they had undergone since escaping from the Parthians at Merv. There was no way of knowing how far they had got, whether they had reached the eastern shore. Jack guessed they would have fought to the end, against the elements, against exhaustion, against the enemy who may have been awaiting their landfall. These were men who had been trained to confront every challenge head-on, who would fight to the last to uphold the honor of their legion, to earn the right to join the hallowed ranks of their brothers-in-arms who had gone before. And Fabius might not even have known he had the jewel, one of the pair, wrapped up in a bag of loot he had shared with Licinius. Jack peered into the steely waters, seeing only reflection, sky-colored, peppered with tiny clouds. Perhaps it really was here, lost in the wreck of their boat, just as he had seen it in his dream. *The celestial jewel.*

The engine revved down, and the warm water of the wake slopped up over the stern transom of the boat. The wind died away, and the air felt thin, cool. Looking back over the lake, Jack could see the shoreline disappearing off to the west, far enough to sense the curvature of the earth. He felt as if they had tipped the balance between east and west, and had reached a point where the Silk Road would channel travelers down the far slope of the mountainous plateau, into China. It was an illusion, with the death trap of the Taklamakan Desert beyond, but for travelers from the west the great mountain pass ahead might have been a sign of hope. Jack turned around, looking forward. Costas was still in the deckhouse where he had been since the morning, talking and peering at the navigation screens. Ahead of them, the shorelines of the lake were finally converging. Earlier, the lakeshore had seemed desiccated, eroded by the wind, but here the westerly wind that blew evaporation eastward had carpeted the ridges and valleys in olive-green. Nestled against the shoreline were buildings, drab concrete structures, the dilapidated remains of quays and jetties. As Jack watched, the surface of the lake shimmered and seemed to blur, and then was still again. He wondered if it was a seismic tremor. He looked at the shore again. Somewhere over there was Rebecca, with the IMU and U.S. Navy team. They had made a discovery already, the possible outlines of walls revealed by sub-bottom profiling. It was enough to give them a foothold on the archaeology of this place. Their job today was to check it out, before Katya joined them for the trip they had planned farther east over the mountain pass into China.

Costas swung back from the deckhouse and clambered over the diving gear stacked behind. He pulled two E-suits off the twenty-millimeter cannon behind the stern house and dropped one in front of Jack. "May as well suit-up now. We're heading straight to the site. Rebecca and a couple of the team are coming out to us in the Zodiac. We're going to be the first ones down."

"Rebecca won't be too happy about that."

"This is no place for her first-ever dive. No way. I don't trust lakes at the best of times, and this one should have a big red sticker on it."

Jack sloshed some water from the scuppers over his hands. "It's slightly saline. That helps to cleanse it. And the lake bed's two thousand feet deep in the center. Under a huge layer of silt. Anything toxic dumped out here's likely to be well buried."

Costas stopped pulling on his suit and looked incredulous. "You kidding? A Soviet submersibles testing site? We monitored these places when I was in the navy. You could almost warm your hands over the satellite images. And it didn't have to be weapons or reactors. In the early days, the Soviets would happily have used chunks of uranium to power toothbrushes."

"Altamaty told Katya that it was mainly torpedo testing out here, and whenever they lost one they went to huge efforts to find it. That's where the first report came from of these walls underwater, the ones Rebecca thinks our team may have found again. Altamaty liberated some of the files in 1991 when he was on reserve duty at the base, when the Soviet Union was in meltdown. He said any lost torpedoes they couldn't find were deemed unsalvageable and are probably best left where they are."

"Well, that's reassuring," Costas grumbled, poking his head through the rubber neck in the suit. "Any more words of wisdom before we go radioactive?"

"Katya says the Kyrgyz see the lake as a sacred place, full of treasures. Some of them think Genghis Khan is buried here. Their sagas talk of a golden coffin set on a silvery sea. And they think there's a sunken Nestorian monastery off the north shore. They think this place holds all the riches their ancestors saw pass along the Silk Road. But the waters are also sacred from before then. Some of the older Kyrgyz won't even swim in it."

"Sounds sensible to me." Costas grunted, straining his hands through the rubber wrist seals. "In this case, I'll go with the folk wisdom any day."

"Some of the stories may be true. If you study the shoreline, you can see where the level of the lake has fluctuated. It's a strange place. Hundreds of mountain streams empty into it, but hardly anything flows out. So the level of the lake goes up, or goes down when there are periods of high evaporation, like now. And on top of that, it's in a major earthquake zone."

Costas finished pulling on his suit and sat down, picking up a clipboard he had brought with him from the deckhouse. "I've got it here. The navy guys were briefed on it. At least three major quakes in recorded history, one about 250 BC, the Grigorevka, another 500 AD, the Toru-Aigir, and another 1475, the Balasogun, all probably eight to nine on the Richter scale, pretty hot stuff." He turned his back to Jack, arching his arms out to tense the shoulder zipper of the suit.

"Right." Jack yanked the zipper shut and slapped Costas' back. "The second of those, AD 500, might coincide with the sunken Christian monastery story. But the legend of Genghis Khan doesn't fit. Genghis died in the thirteenth century AD. His successors were notoriously secretive about his tomb, murdering everyone they encountered during the funerary procession. According to Mongol ritual, horses would have trampled over the site to conceal it. But I think the tomb was where history says it was, at a place called Burqan Qaldun in Mongolia, hundreds of miles to the east of here."

"What about decoys?" Costas said. "I mean, deliberately misleading stories. If they were so secretive, maybe they spread stories of the tomb being in different places. Hence the legend here."

Jack nodded. "It's possible. And not just for concealed tombs, but also for very visible tombs, extravagant ones. For those tombs, it's the exterior appearance that matters for posterity, for how later generations will see the dead. But the contents usually matter most for the deceased, their private insurance policy for the afterlife. So they can be concealed elsewhere, with the actual body. After all, even the Egyptian pyramids were robbed."

"And the First Emperor's tomb at Xian was robbed," Costas murmured. "By the caretaker, if the jewel story is true."

Jack stood up, peering at the shoreline. He looked for the Zodiac, for Rebecca, but there was still no sign. He sat down and began to pull the legs of his suit on. "So where exactly are we going in?"

Costas flipped over to another piece of paper on the clipboard. "I printed this off the navigational computer. About two o'clock from us now, half a kilometer out from shore. There's a creek with a few buildings at the edge."

Jack shielded his eyes. "I see it."

"It's where the profiler came up with that image of walls."

"It fits with the old Soviet report?"

"It fits exactly with the story from Altamaty, recounted to me by Katya. And I can't imagine Katya has anything to hide."

Jack raised his eyebrows, and was silent for a moment. "Well, to reassure you, Altamaty also spoke with Rebecca, in Russian. He said the first reports of underwater finds at this spot came from the Russian explorers who reached this place in the nineteenth century. You remember Sir Aurel Stein, the Silk Route explorer? Well, there were Russians who jumped on that bandwagon too, sent out by the Moscow Geographical Society. It was like an archaeological version of the Great Game, Russians against British. Nobody knows for sure what the Russians found. Such a lot disappeared after the Russian Revolution. But we know that two Russian explorers came down here, Nikolai Przhevalsky and Piotr Semyonov Tianshansky. They'd both heard stories of sunken ruins, cities under the lake. When they came here, the place seemed possessed by it. Tianshansky had been to Venice and found a fourteenth-century map showing an Armenian monastery by the lake. The legend of the tomb of Genghis seems to have been local. Undoubtedly the Russians were fed what they wanted to hear, but they were also shown genuine artifacts that had been found by fishermen."

"Then fast-forward through the Soviet period."

Jack nodded, pushing his head through the rubber seal on his suit. "The explorers left, but the legends grew. Nazi fantasists thought this was the Aryan homeland, drawing on local legends that this was a place of purity, a kind of heaven on earth. Then in the 1950s the Soviets established their torpedo testing base here, and divers went into the lake for the first time. As we know, they found something while searching for a lost torpedo, and

557

the Ministry of Interior Security became involved. That ended under Khrushchev in the early 60s as the Cold War heated up and attention was focused elsewhere. Then more years passed, more rumor, more legend. A professor in Bishkek started to talk about Atlantis. That's when Katya's father got interested."

"The family connection. I knew it."

"The professor was wrong, of course. And Katya's father never made it here. This place was next on his wish list when we drew a line under his plans two years ago."

"So what else does Altamaty know about what the Soviets found?"

"The records only give chart coordinates. There's a huge amount of silt down there, and no record of whether they found the torpedo. But rumors began circulating in Karakol, the local town, where the Soviet personnel lived. They told of ancient walls under the silt, like the converging walls of a great entrance passageway, with Chinese-style carvings. In Karakol there's a wooden mosque built about a hundred years ago by the Dungan Chinese, Muslims driven west by persecution in China. The mosque looks like a Chinese temple, with dragons on the cornice. The Dungans seem to have fueled the legend of Genghis' tomb. Katya thinks it's only a matter of time before the tourist department seizes on the idea and makes it into an embarrassing spectacle, with giant Soviet-style statues of Genghis Khan in the town square. She wants them to invest in the petroglyphs, the real archaeology out here, not some myth, and make that an international attraction."

Costas folded the sheet over on his clipboard and showed Jack a printout. "Well, whatever it was the divers saw, it seems to fit with the sub-bottom profiler data. To begin with, the profiler just showed linear striations coming down from shore, river runoff eroded into the bedrock. It was Rebecca who first saw how regular one of the channels looked. Almost an upside-down V shape, converging into shore."

"So it was Rebecca who actually spotted this? She didn't tell me that."

"She's modest. Like you."

Jack raised his eyebrows. "She's too busy being spoiled by a team of fifteen U.S. Navy SEALs, you mean."

"Every one of them a gentleman."

Jack looked serious. "I don't want navy divers out here right now. Just us."

"They're too busy anyway. There are ticking time bombs in the old Soviet port area, abandoned hulls with nuclear reactors. Where we're diving is officially a no-go zone. It's going to take them months to decontaminate out this far. This is our show. Remember, the only reason those Soviet divers came out here was to hunt for a lost torpedo, and they didn't find it."

Jack reached into the lake to splash some water on his helmet. "The water's warm. Just your cup of tea."

"If it gets any warmer as we go down, I'm out of here faster than you can say Geiger counter."

"That's what we've got these suits for. You designed them."

"We're still going to need a full scrubbing down after this."

"In Hawaii?"

Costas brightened. "That's the first time you've come out with the word. Actually said it, without being prompted."

Jack looked into the lake. In the bay the water was a brilliant blue, like lapis lazuli, like the aura that had emanated from the mine in Afghanistan where they had been two days before. But out here, away from the shore, it was different. The sun bore down directly overhead and bathed the water in an iridescent glow. Some quality of the water, or perhaps the sheer intensity of the sun, meant that the lake seemed to absorb the light and reflect it back a few meters below, as if a layer of liquid silver were floating just beneath the surface. He looked down, and could see no reflection of himself at all. The layer seemed real, like quicksilver spread up from some source below. Jack looked back at the shoreline opposite them. He saw a tall bird, a heron, standing stock-still at the entrance to the creek a few hundred meters away. It was serene, like a sculpture, then dipped its beak down into the water. Jack remembered his visit with Rebecca to the terracotta warriors exhibit in London a few months before, standing in front of an elegant bronze bird, which had once adorned a model shoreline inside the First Emperor's tomb. Jack looked across to the line of mountains to the south, breathtaking in their grandeur, and raised his hand to shade his eyes, dazzled by the reflection off the snowy peaks that seemed to float above as if they were in some other dimension.

Costas nudged him. "One thing's been bothering me, since Afghanistan," he said. "We know what happened to Howard, but not Wauchope. In the lapis lazuli mine there was no sign of the sacred *vélpu,* the bamboo tube you think they brought with them, taken years before in the jungle. Howard might have been grasping it when he fell, but then someone took it from him. If it was the bad guys, they may have found the jewel too, and the whole story would have been different. Shang Yong would have been sitting in his desert stronghold with the jewel of immortality stuck in his ceiling, planning world domination."

Jack nodded. Since leaving Afghanistan his

focus had been on Pradesh, as if his own survival instinct were being marshaled behind their friend. It was only with the assurance that Pradesh would pull through that he had begun to think of everything else, of the man he had shot, of the boy with the suicide bomb. For the man he felt indifference, for the boy a kind of numbness, as if he had seen the explosion on a news report. The shock of that death would sear into him, but not yet. The experience of confronting Howard's body, his great-great-grandfather, was still vivid, as if he were living it now, too early for reflection. But the fate of Wauchope had preoccupied him as they had sailed across the lake, as he had thought of the convergence of all their routes, the Roman legionaries, Howard and Wauchope, all the Silk Road explorers, of themselves, all focused on that mystical spot over the horizon where the sun rose on Chrysê, the fabled land of gold in the ancient *Periplus.*

He turned to Costas. "You remember Wood's *Source of the River Oxus,* the book we used to locate the lapis mines?"

"Sure. With all the annotations from Howard and Wauchope."

"One of their notes Rebecca pointed out was in the margin of the map at the beginning of the book. An arrow from the valley of the Oxus to the northeast, and the penciled name *Issyk-Kul,* underlined, beside the word

Przhevalsky."

"That Russian explorer?"

Jack nodded. "Przhevalsky actually died here, of typhus in 1888. Rebecca did some research. It turns out he was in London before that, and gave a lecture in the same series at the Royal United Service Institution where Howard gave his talk on the Romans in south India. That was just before Wauchope returned from leave to his job with the Survey of India, and both he and Howard attended Przhevalsky's lecture. It was about a rare breed of horses he had discovered in Mongolia, and he mentioned the blood-sweating horses. Then he talked of coming to this place, of the legendary treasures of the lake. He spoke of the Tien Shan range, of his explorations deep into the mountains. I think Wauchope would have been entranced by that, as a passionate mountaineer."

"So that's where you think Wauchope went?"

"Tien Shan means celestial mountains. From the Taklamakan Desert, they look closer to heaven than any of the peaks in China. The First Emperor was obsessed with those places, always trying to go as high as he could, to leave his proclamations. He must have looked to the Tien Shan when he sensed his own mortality." Jack swept his arm to the west. "If Wauchope survived the mine, he may have retraced Licinius' route and come toward Issyk-Kul, then made his way into the mountains. Maybe he was like the Romans, and felt he could never go back to his own world. Maybe he and Howard never had any intention of returning. Przhevalsky told of valleys that were not bleak and unforgiving like Afghanistan, but bountiful, lush, lost in time, like Shangri-la. Even if they didn't find the jewels, those stories could have tempted them with something of what the legend of the celestial jewel seemed to offer."

"Or they could have found the jewel in the mine. Wauchope could have gone back with it to the jungle. He could have put the jewel inside the bamboo tube and returned the sacred *vélpu* to the Kóya people. He could have found a way into the jungle shrine through the waterfall at the back, and hidden it there. Maybe inside Licinius' tomb. What they'd done in the jungle in 1879 must have been on Howard's mind in his final hours. That's the time when people think of atonement, redemption. Wauchope may have made a promise to him at the end, and then carried it out. That's the kind of thing friends do. They were soldiers, blood brothers. Like Licinius and Fabius."

Jack squinted at Costas. "Yes. Maybe."

"We're almost there." The boat slowed down, and began to trace a wide arc toward shore. "There's something more immediate we need to discuss."

"Go on."

Costas squinted at the water. "Have you noticed that when there's a breeze, it hardly ruffles the surface?"

Jack nodded. "It makes the water seem sluggish, heavy, like molten metal."

"It's because the westerly wind is funneled upward as it approaches land. But did you see the shimmer on the surface a few minutes ago?"

Jack nodded. "Seismic aftershock?"

"Worse. Seismic labor pains. There's been a big quake already, and there's almost certainly another one coming. Today, maybe tomorrow. Not the ideal diving conditions, but it could be good for us. We're looking at proximal and distal delta deposits, some glacial outwash, incised by basinward-converging channels. A lot of piled-up silt."

"You mean there could be a turbidite."

"A deformation, a sediment slip. It could reveal those walls, if they exist. They could be visible one moment, and then poof, another tremor and another sediment slip, and they're gone. We could be lucky. If there's anything there, now might be the time to see it."

"You remember the last time we were diving?"

Costas sighed. "Eight days ago. The Red Sea. Beautiful water, coral reefs. Paradise." He paused. "Elephants. Underwater elephants."

"That's what I was thinking about. Your elephants. Did you ever hear the old Hindu story of the blind men and the elephant?"

Costas looked back bemusedly. "Three blind men are led to an elephant, not having been told what it is. One feels the tail, and thinks it's a rope. One feels the trunk, and thinks it's a snake. One feels a tusk, and thinks it's a spear."

"Remember how I nearly didn't see that elephant on the seabed? I was too close to it. Remember that when we're down there today."

"What we'll see? A layer of brown, then darker brown. It becomes warmer, then hot. We start to glow. Then some Russian mobster fishes us out and sell us to terrorists as components of a dirty bomb."

Jack grinned. "The geologists say the lake is gradually emptying, you know."

"Emptying?"

"It's always been a mystery where all the glacial runoff goes, pouring down those slopes from the Tien Shan. The lake's like a huge ornamental pond, which the fountains never seem to fill up. It's as if somewhere in the depths there's a giant plug."

"That's another reason not to dive here. I'm not going to be sucked into some black hole."

"Speaking of black, did you know they say the Black Death came from here?"

"What?"

"The Black Death. The plague. Sometime in the fourteenth century, carried along the Silk Route on the backs of rats."

"You're kidding me. The Black Death. From this lake. The one I'm about to go swimming in."

"I wouldn't worry about it. Personally I think it's another myth, created to keep people away from this place. All the more reason to explore it, if you ask me."

"Hawaii," Costas muttered, raising his hands in prayer. "Why is it that every time there's a light at the end of the tunnel, you make me go through another nightmare?"

Jack slapped him cheerfully on the shoulder. "Because you're my dive buddy. And I need you to watch out for me."

The boat was on idle now. Jack sniffed the air. It was an unexpected smell, not the usual slightly rank odor of a lakeshore, but the scent of herbs, of lavender, of crushed dry leaves. The wind here came powerfully from the west, sweeping across the water like an army of ghosts, but the smell held the exotic fragrance of the east. On the shore Jack had glimpsed distant ramparts, the minaret of a fallen mosque, toppled by an earthquake, and he sensed a handhold from over the mountain pass, from the foothills of China beyond. The western end of the lake, where they had met Katya and Altamaty among the petroglyphs, was a place of desolation, a place people only passed through by necessity; but here to the east there was permanence, a place people had chosen to settle, Han traders of antiquity, Sogdian, Mongolian followers of Genghis Kahn and Dungan Muslims, expelled from the western fringes of China within living memory.

One of the crewmen made his way toward them from the deckhouse. "We've been in contact with shore. The seismic readout remains unaltered, but it's still condition orange. The navy divers have been clearing a collapsed jetty, which is why the Zodiac's been delayed. They hope to be heading out here in about fifteen minutes. We're over the GPS coordinates now. The advice is not to go in, but if you have to, do it now. Keep at least ten meters above the seafloor. And avoid any deep gullies. I repeat, the advice is not to go in."

"Advice understood, Brad," Costas said, struggling into the strap of his cylinder backpack. The crewman moved over to help him. "Jack and I have dived into a lava tube, you know," he said, gasping. "Into a live volcano. In Atlantis."

"Yeah? Cool."

"No. Hot." Costas peered up at the crew- man, who pointed skeptically into the water. They had spent most of the voyage together in the deckhouse talking about torpedoes and radiation leaks. "Don't say it, Brad," Costas said. "Just don't say anything at all."

"I was just going to say good luck, sir."

"Sir again," Costas grumbled. "Me, sir?"

"Lieutenant-commander, U.S. Navy, as I recall," Jack said.

"A nuts-and-bolts man. Just one of the guys. And I never pulled rank."

"That's because you're a born leader, and everyone always listens to you," Jack said, pushing his shoulder.

"Everyone except you."

"I don't need to listen. I just follow." Jack slapped Costas' back, then nodded at the crewman, who eased down the mask on Costas' helmet, snapping closed the locks, and then did the same for Jack. Both men ran through their life support systems, checking the computer screen readout inside their helmets, then double-checked each other. The crewman put up a splayed hand and pointed at his watch. Jack nodded at him. Five minutes to go. The engine revved slightly, and he felt the boat move as they repositioned. For a few moments before activating his intercom Jack was completely cut off. All he could hear was his own breathing, the pounding of his heart, a slight ringing in his ears, a legacy of gunfire. He thought again of Wauchope, and then of the Romans. Maybe one of the legionaries had survived too, made it ashore, escaped east over the

569

saddle of the mountains toward Chrysê, the land of gold. Maybe it was Fabius himself. Jack wondered whether they would ever know. He had only his instinct to go on, and that told him the story did not end in the waters here.

Jack looked down and saw the layer of reflection again, like quicksilver. He shook away the thought and switched on his intercom. Costas gave him the thumbs-down signal, and Jack repeated it. He felt the suck of the air from his regulator, and checked his gauge readout again. They slipped over the side together. Jack dropped down, under the surface, then floated back up again. He was in his element and was coursing with excitement. He suddenly knew they were in the right place. It was his instinct again. He glanced at Costas, who was bobbing in the water looking at him. Jack put his hand on his buoyancy valve, and pressed the intercom. They always said it. It was their ritual. Their good-luck talisman. He grinned at Costas. "Good to go?"

"Good to go."

Three minutes later they had descended more than twenty meters below the surface. There was no sign of the bottom, but Jack knew from his compass that they were facing the landward side of the lakebed as it sloped up to the shoreline half a kilometer to the east. To begin with the water had been remarkably clear, and Jack had rolled over and seen the dark shape of the boat's hull above, the figures of the two crewmen visible in wavering outline as they peered over the side. He rolled back again just as they hit a thermocline, indiscernible inside his E-suit but registered in a change in temperature on the readout inside his helmet.

"It's getting colder. This might not be radioactive soup after all," he said on the intercom.

"Just as long as all this seismic activity hasn't stirred up anything," Costas replied, his voice tinny with the increased pressure. "Like they said, whatever's down there is probably best left undisturbed."

"I'll remind you of that next time we see something that needs to be defused."

They continued down. Below the thermocline the visibility dramatically reduced, a result of particulate gray and brown matter in the water. Jack sensed a darkness underlying the gloom below them. He flicked on his headlamp but instantly regretted it, dazzled by the glare off the suspended particles in the water. He switched it off again, and blinked as his eyes readjusted to the gloom. He checked his depth readout. Thirty-five meters. Suddenly it was there, a gray, featureless plain about eight meters below them, gently undulating up the slope. "I take back what I said about radioactivity," he murmured. "Looks like something killed this place dead."

He neutralized his buoyancy two meters above the bottom, careful not to stir it up with his fins. "That's nowhere near as solid as it looks," Costas said. "With all this seismic activity, it's soup. Close your eyes, drop down and you wouldn't know you'd gone into it. After a while it'd become glutinous, and you'd be stuck. Only consolation is your body wouldn't be eaten by marine borers. Even they wouldn't live here."

Jack gazed at the sediment. "We're hardly going to see anything ancient sticking out of this stuff, are we?"

"We might. The earthquake's shaken it all up, and the silt that normally blankets the bedrock protuberances and other solid features may have slid down the slope. The brown haze in the water shows there's been movement, a turbitude. But the shake-up also leaves everything unstable. There could be another mass of sediment farther up the slope ready to drop down and bury whatever might have been revealed."

Jack looked around. "So the walls, the ravine, whatever it was Rebecca saw on the sonar readout, might actually be visible."

"They did the sub-bottom profiler run more than twenty-four hours ago. According to the bearings I programmed into my computer, we should follow this contour for about fifty meters, toward the south. That should put us over the gully, directly opposite that creek on the shoreline. The old Soviet seismological reports put this contour at about the level of the shoreline two and a half thousand years ago. Everything upslope was dry land. They think there was a single event that put it all underwater, a violent localized quake about 2,200 years ago."

They turned carefully and began to fin south, Costas in the lead. They were within a horizon of improved visibility, able to see five or six meters ahead, beneath the blanket of suspended sediment a few meters above them. Jack scanned the grayness below for anything solid, any protuberance. After about twenty meters Costas suddenly stopped finning. "I've got something," he said. Jack came up alongside. The lake floor was more mottled, irregular. Jack gingerly put out a hand. It was hard clay, smearing his glove. "Looks like a ridge, coming out from shore," he murmured. "It could be decayed mud-brick, but there's no visible stonework, no masonry."

"Check this out." Costas fanned his hand over something embedded in the clay. Jack switched on his headlamp, and gasped in astonishment. "It's a bronze handle," he exclaimed. Costas pulled it out. The handle was attached to a disk about the size of a dinner plate. Jack took it, wafting away the adhering clay. "It's a mirror," he said. "The surface has oxidized green, but it's intact."

"Weird thing to find in this place," Costas said.

Jack turned the object over. "Bronzes like this have been found along this shore before, hauled out by fishermen," he said. "Mirrors, elaborate horse harnesses, cauldrons. It was what first excited the attention of the Russian, Przhevalsky. The objects were all like this, intact, very high quality workmanship, not the kind of things people usually throw away. Rumors spread of a sunken palace, a drowned city."

"Or a tomb?" Costas said.

"That's my gut instinct," Jack said. "But these finds don't fit with the story of Genghis Khan. Mongol tombs were concealed, discreet. And I don't think a Mongol warlord would have had grave goods like these, mirrors, cauldrons. It doesn't add up. But I'll wager this must have been thrown up out of a burial site by the earthquake, something pretty prestigious. That would explain the past finds too. And these are not the result of tomb robbing in antiquity, when this slope was still dry land. Tomb robbers don't abandon valuable items like this."

Costas pointed to where fine lines of incision were visible on the handle, swirling shapes and bulbous eyes. "The decoration reminds me of that halberd Katya found in the Roman burial on the other side of the lake. It looks the same, Chinese."

"I agree," Jack replied. "The local population here includes those displaced Muslim Chinese from the fringes of the Taklamakan Desert, and there were earlier migrations, Uighurs. This mirror looks more than two thousand years old, but back then this end of the lake would have been a cultural melting pot, a staging post between west and east. Prestigious Chinese artifacts could have found their way here. But I don't think that accounts for these finds. Stuff like this wouldn't just be tossed into the lake. These people were traders."

Jack put down the bronze, and Costas placed a miniature electronic beacon beside it. Jack took the lead this time, finning along the forty-meter depth contour. The visibility was still only a few meters, but it was enough to see that the ridge of clay curved around to his left, and the lakebed dropped off to the right. "An erosion channel," Costas said from behind. "This must be the edge of the gully that leads down from the creek, cutting a ravine into the lakebed. It's consistent with the profiler readout. It should be dropping down ten meters deeper, and be twenty meters or so across. I think it's normally smothered in sediment, but the earthquake's shaken it away. This must be the converging feature Rebecca saw on the printout, that looked so promising. Maybe not man-made after all."

"I want to look a bit farther. Just to make sure."

"The mirror's a great find, Jack. We can surface with it like a pair of treasure hunters. Rebecca will be thrilled."

Jack was already finning ahead. "I've just got a feeling about this."

"Yeah, I've got a feeling too," Costas replied urgently. "And it's a bad one. Did you see that?" There was a shimmer in the water, then a shudder. "Jack, there's a wall of sediment about three meters above you. It's where the turbitude slipped down that revealed the channel. Any moment it's all going to come down. We need to get out of here. Now."

Jack looked up, saw the darkness of the sediment wall, then looked down again. He was motionless, spread-eagled above the lake floor. The shudder had lifted a veil of silt that had obscured his vision almost completely. The glow from the headlamp behind him diminished as Costas began to ascend. Jack knew Costas would remain a few meters to one side until he was certain Jack was following. He flicked on his own headlamp, so Costas could see him, and looked at his compass readout. He had come far enough. There was nothing more to be seen. "Roger that," he said. He reached for the buoyancy control on his E-suit. Costas was right. This was no place to die.

There was another shimmer in the water. Jack was suddenly wary, feeling that he himself was an active part of the forces around them, that his own movement could trigger the next quake. He looked down at the buoyancy valve on the front of his suit, checking that it was clear of sediment that might jam it open. It was a design glitch he had noticed before. He would have a word with Costas about it. He kept his right hand over the valve, then raised his head. His helmet bumped against something. He rolled over and looked up, seeing only the reflection off sediment. It would be unlike Costas to be so close overhead when he knew Jack was ascending. It must be something else. He rolled back, and felt forward with his left hand. It was a solid object, angled out of the lakebed toward him. It felt like a tree trunk. He suddenly remembered the lost torpedo. But this was wrong. The surface was like bark on an old maple, thickly segmented. He felt his way up with both hands, to where it angled above him. If it was an old tree trunk, it was hoary, twisted, with the remains of branches on either side. He felt the top. The trunk narrowed, then came out again before ending, like a bulbous growth.

Jack froze. He had seen something.

"You okay? You stopped." Costas' voice came harshly over the intercom.

Jack's voice faltered. "I've got something."

"Drop it. You need to get out of there. Now."

"Roger that." There was another shimmer, and the suspended sediment that had obscured his visibility suddenly flashed away, like a school of tiny fish. There was a moment of total clarity. Jack could see it clearly now.

It was a human head.

It was a statue, made of stone, larger than life, leaning out over the lake floor. He stared at the face. It was like a death mask, the eyes nearly shut, the mouth drawn back in a grimace. High cheekbones, flat nose, thin moustache hanging down, braided. The words of the Kyrgyz legend flashed across Jack's mind. *A golden coffin set on a silvery sea.* But that was about Genghis Khan. He had dismissed the story. *Had he been so wrong?* He looked again. What had felt like bark were scales of armor, segmented, overlapping. And he saw that the statue was cradling a sword, a great straight blade, finely shaped out of the stone. It had a long, rounded guard at the hilt, concealing the hand completely. Jack looked back up at the face, and then realized what he had seen. Not a hilt. *A gauntlet.* He hardly dared believe his eyes. He sank down, and looked closely. It was all there: the feline ears, the almond-shaped eyes, the grimacing mouth where the blade protruded. Jack stared in astonishment at the sculpted figure leaning over him.

A gauntlet sword.

A tiger warrior.

Jack looked up. He could just make out Costas a few meters above, releasing a marker buoy. There was a distant roaring in his ears, a noise that sounded like it came from the bowels of the earth, mixed with the sound of a boat engine. He saw the wall of silt behind the statue, and realized how close he had been. Now it was happening again. The silt was shimmering, blurred. He realized he was being pushed by some force in the water down the slope. He was suddenly over the edge of a black pit, the sides extending off into the swirling silt beyond. The shudder ended, and he sank down. He was fifty meters deep now. He could see where the pit had once been completely buried, where the earthquake had cracked open the hard clay surface and revealed a hollow space beneath, now almost choked with silt. He saw something white in his headlamp. It was a skull. *A human skull.* And then he saw more. There were skulls everywhere, human skulls, rows of them, eye sockets empty, jaws hanging down, dislocated, some lolling to left or right. Below the skulls were flashes of green and brown. He sank down farther, into a space in the pit, until he could see more. There was no doubt about it. The green-brown was metal, bronze. Segmented armor. Rows of skeletons, a whole regiment of them, buried upright in a pit, wearing segmented bronze armor. *Ancient Chinese armor.* He looked again, scarcely believing what he was seeing. Each skeleton had the remains of a rope around its neck, perfectly preserved in the freshwater of the lake. They were an army for the afterlife. *An army who had gone willingly to their deaths.*

Jack's mind was racing. The statue, the warrior, must be a guardian. He looked again at the skulls, rapidly disappearing beneath a cascade of silt. The words of an ancient chronicler flashed through his mind. *The hundred officials, as well as rare utensils and wonderful objects, were brought to fill up the tomb.* He looked up the slope at the statue, just visible in the gloom. Then he realized. The tiger warrior was not a guardian. *He was an executioner.* Jack looked back at the skulls. These were the true bodyguard, the loyal soldiers, the retainers, those who had built the tomb and brought the body, who had devoted themselves to the whims of their leader, who had sworn to protect the secret, sworn an oath that had failed to protect them. They were not a willing army for the afterlife. *They were the victims of mass murder.* They had been murdered not to satisfy the vanity of one who believed he would rule forever, but to satisfy the hunger for immortality of those who thought they were his most trusted lieges, the warriors whose guardianship of the secret would assure their power for all eternity. Suddenly Jack knew for certain. Rebecca had been right. There was something here, something in the darkness beyond, something so astonishing he could scarcely believe it. *The secret of the First Emperor's tomb.*

Suddenly it was happening again. Something was sucking him down. He began finning, kicking hard. For the first time on the dive he felt the icy grip of fear, as if there were some empty space in the macabre army reserved for him, for having dared to see what he had seen. He was going nowhere. He realized that the entire lakebed was moving, sliding down the slope. The statue and the pit had vanished. A massive surge threw him sideways, pushing him away from the gully. Then he was miraculously clear, floating above the storm of sediment, bathed in sunlight. He saw Costas only a few meters away. The intercom indicator inside his helmet was flashing red, and he realized that it must have failed. He flashed an okay signal to Costas with his hand, then saw Costas do the same. He looked down again, breathing hard, waiting for his pulse to slow before ascending.

He shut his eyes. He had seen something else. Something in the split second of that jolt. Something that had flashed into view while the sediment was sucked off the lakebed in a swirling vortex. He had seen walls, great stone walls, lining the sides of a passageway, converging at a dark entranceway in the side of the slope, sealed in with more stone. He opened his eyes. He was sure of it. He thought of what else he had seen down there, what he had touched. He looked up toward the surface, through water that was now sparklingly clear. They were less than twenty meters deep, and he was sure he saw the wavering line of snowy peaks to the south, cutting through the silvery reflection of sunlight on the surface. The words of the Chinese chronicler came into his head again. *Mercury was used to fashion imitations of the hundred rivers, the Yellow River and the Yangtse, and the seas, constructed in such a way that they seemed to flow. Above were representations of all the heavenly bodies, below, the features of the earth.* Then he realized. There, in the tomb at Xian, it had all been artifice. Here, below the celestial mountains, where the lake was liquid like mercury, it was all real. Here, where the realm of heaven was on the horizon to be seen, and the orb of the earth and the heavens could truly be the domain of one emperor.

One emperor. Jack was barely breathing

582

now. Not Genghis Khan. An emperor far greater than that. An emperor of all that is known under heaven.

Shihuangdi. *The First Emperor.*

Jack remembered the Sogdian, the man whose act more than two thousand years before had led them to this place, a man whose very existence was part surmise, part reality. Had they been right about him? Had he really stolen the celestial jewel from under the noses of the tiger warriors at Xian? Or had he been fulfilling a promise, one the first caretaker had made to the dying emperor, to take the jewel from Xian to this place, the real tomb? Had the emperor lost trust in the tiger warriors? Had he foreseen the future, seen how his legacy would be usurped by those who would profess to protect it? Had the brotherhood of the tiger been living a lie, propped up by murder, a fantasy of guardianship that had only ever been about their own greed and power?

Jack thought of the celestial jewel, the elusive treasure that had brought them on this extraordinary journey. Had the jewel been installed above the empty casket under Mount Li, a priceless heart of the emperor's dream they would be sworn to protect, yet which one day a descendant of the caretaker would spirit away and try to take to its rightful place? Jack remembered Katya's uncle, the story of the tiger warriors told by Katya herself, streams of knowledge that seemed to come from some reservoir deep in the past, exactingly remembered, passed down from generation to generation. Jack thought of Katya again. Had there been one among the Brotherhood, one entrusted by *Shihuangdi,* he who trusted so few, to keep the eyes of the others away from the truth? Had they lived a lie for sixty-six generations, protecting a tomb at Xian that one among them always knew was empty? Had Katya's uncle been after the jewel not just to keep it from Shang Yong, but to bring it secretly here? Jack thought of something Katya had said about her uncle. *He was grooming me.* Had she told them the whole story? *Who was the caretaker of the tomb now?*

His intercom crackled. "Jack. Can you hear me?"

"Loud and clear."

"I've been shouting myself hoarse. You need a ten minute decompression stop. The surge might have pressurized the water and put you beyond your no-stop time."

"Five minutes at twenty meters, five at ten."

"Roger that."

"The intercom interference must have been electromagnetic."

"I've been worried about that. The quake might have dislodged that lost torpedo, and reactivated something in the electronics."

"We'll want to cordon off the area," Jack

584

said. "This whole sector of coast becomes a no-go zone. That's our condition for working with NATO and the Russians. We'll fund the whole cleanup operation, put the Russians through any underwater training program they want. Once everything's ready, two years, maybe three years down the line, we'll initiate the search. Nobody goes in the water before then. Health and safety."

"Right, Jack. As if health and safety's ever been high on your list. So what exactly did you find down there? I take it we're looking at more than a bronze mirror."

"Is this a secure channel?"

"A closed system. Just you and me. The navy boat didn't have the right receiver and we couldn't get one freighted out in time."

Jack cleared his throat. "I found a statue and some bones."

"I said, what did you find, Jack?"

"That's what I saw for certain. That's what I touched."

"Right."

"Okay, I might have found a tomb."

"Genghis Khan?"

"Not sure. We need more to go on."

"You didn't find the jewel? The other one. The peridot."

"I didn't find the jewel. But it may be the right place. If Fabius and the others did reach the eastern shore of the lake and then went down in a storm, this is about where the wreck would have ended up. Everything they carried with them might still be here, somewhere in the silt below us now. Or Fabius may have escaped and taken it with him, into China toward Xian."

"Back toward the First Emperor's tomb."

"To the place that history calls the First Emperor's tomb."

There was a brief silence. "Are you saying what I think you're saying?"

"I only saw it for a second. Less than a second. But I'm sure of it."

Costas checked the old Rolex diving watch he wore over his suit and gave a thumbs-up. Jack repeated the gesture, and watched the depth gauge inside his helmet as they rose ten meters. Their buoyancy systems automatically adjusted to neutral and Costas turned to face Jack. "So, how are you going to explain to your daughter that she's been responsible for one of the greatest archaeological discoveries ever made, something that could change the perception of Asian history, but that we're going to say nothing about it and instead talk about a torpedo, or if pressed maybe mumble something about Genghis Khan?"

"I don't want to tell anyone. For the reason you just said. Asian history. There's too much at stake. A whole national myth. Right now, the Chinese might need that myth, the myth of the First Emperor's tomb at Xian, the myth of untold wealth buried with their greatest ruler. Revealing the truth might unleash a dangerous unfolding of control in China."

"You don't believe that. I've never known you to leave treasure unexcavated because you're worried about a national myth."

"Okay, I just want to wait until the seismic activity quiets down. That can take a couple of years out here. And that should give us time to develop equipment for getting through a mountain of lake sediment. Give you time, I should say."

"I was blueprinting a new sub-bottom excavator in my mind while you were ferreting around down there. I knew you'd got something, and that we'd be back. So what about Rebecca?"

"Two, maybe three years down the line. When we're ready to come back here. Then I'll tell her what I saw. I'd rather her first big discovery wasn't one that might upset the entire world order."

"Kids know everything. She'll be onto you as soon as she sees that look in your eyes. And show me one of our discoveries that didn't upset the course of history. If she sticks around, she's going to have to get used to that. She'll be up there on the boat by now," Costas added. "I bet you tell her, the moment we surface."

Jack looked up. They had only a few minutes now. He tasted a hint of salt from the lake. He remembered something Katya had told him, an old Kyrgyz legend about how the nomads kept the spirits of their ancestors at bay by weeping into the lake, along the shoreline beside the carved stones that marked their passing. If the mourners wept, the waters would rise around the ghosts, and they would drown. But now there were too few mourners, too few left to remember. Jack had seen the boulders left dry by the receding shoreline, the stain of a watermark meters above. Now the mountains themselves needed to mourn, to release meltwater in torrents, to keep the spirit below them at bay, the spirit of *Shihuangdi,* the First Emperor.

Jack thought about where they were again, the fabled Silk Road. A place swept by the divine wind, where little is left except myth and legend, stories that still adhere only because they are so light and insubstantial.

But not here. Not underwater. This was real.

There was another tremor, more violent this time, and a darkness swept over the lakebed below them, obscuring it completely. Jack checked his computer. It was time to go. Costas jerked his thumb upward. Jack looked up, and saw the shadow of the patrol boat, and moored beside it the Zodiac, its outboard directly overhead. A cluster of faces was visible over the stern of the patrol boat, around the ladder where Costas was already beginning to ascend, but a solitary face was peering down at him over the side of the Zodiac. The hulls were like dark clouds, but the faces reflected off the silvery surface of the water like stars, the brightest one directly above him. Jack rose up and broke surface, then flipped up the visor from his helmet and held on to the side of the Zodiac, looking up at the face with sunglasses and long dark hair gazing down at him. He kicked up and peered over the top of the pontoon, seeing that they were out of earshot of the others. He dropped down again and gestured for Rebecca to come closer. He snorted into the water and cleared his throat. He was as excited as he had ever been in his life.

"You remember our trip to the terracotta warriors exhibit in London?" he said. "Well, you are not going to believe what we've just found."

"Try me, Dad."

EPILOGUE

Gansu Province, China

Forty-eight hours later, Jack stood in front of a low wall, the remains of a rampart that had once been several meters thick inside a complex of ancient ruins. He knelt down and touched the surface, feeling it crumble in his fingers. It was loam, compacted clay with fragments of pink and gray granite. This place desperately needed rain, but the wall was so desiccated that rain would only hasten its destruction, washing it away rather than strengthening it. The loam looked like ancient concrete, like mortar, but was not. *This wall was not Roman.* He turned and waved to Costas, who was trudging up the path behind him, a slightly disconsolate figure in the dust. Farther back he could see Katya and Rebecca, picking their way together among the stones, and beyond them a dust cloud where the rotor of the Lynx helicopter was powering down. The helicopter had flown them here in stages from Lake Issyk-Kul in Kyrgyzstan, east over the mountain pass of the Tien Shan, skirting the northern fringes of the Taklamakan Desert, then down the narrowing funnel of the Gansu Corridor into the heart of the ancient Chinese empire. It had been a marvelous journey, following the Silk Road from the air, and they had camped on the site of a long-abandoned caravanserai. That morning they had swept in low over the Great Wall of China, over a section constructed during the Han dynasty two thousand years ago. They were within a few hours of Xian, the eastern anchor of the Silk Road and the site of the First Emperor's tomb. But for Jack the end of their quest was this place, the last hint of an extraordinary ancient journey they had been following from another world unimaginably far to the west.

A waft of breeze brought a hint of something exotic, heady even, some crop in the valley perhaps, but then the air was still, and all Jack could sense was the dusty smell of decay and dereliction, the familiar lifeblood of the archaeologist. He breathed it in, relishing it. He wished Maurice Hiebermeyer was with him now. He would have helped Jack to make sense of the walls, the jumble of ruins. Or perhaps it was too far gone to unravel, and there was nothing more to glean than what he could see in front of him.

Jack looked around. The place had a desolate beauty. They had passed ruinous houses, mud-brick walls bleached white by the sun, surrounded by patches of corn and barley that seemed doomed to lose the battle against the scorching sun. Rutted tracks led across stony fields, the scars of plowing and long-dry irrigation channels baked hard by the sun. In the distance the odd goat and sheep picked at the ground, finding something in the gravel and dust. The sky itself seemed scorched, colorless, and most of the time he could see nothing beyond the low plateau he stood upon, but then some upper wind would push apart the dust and the sky would streak with red. In those moments he saw the foothills of the Xaipan Mountains, great folds and spurs that rose up to a jagged skyline. To the north was another line of mountains, more distant, and between the two chains of mountains lay the Gansu Corridor, the eastern Silk Road. Here the pounding progress of the camel caravans had once stirred up a continuous storm of dust, a storm whose residue seemed to remain above the valley floor like the exhaust of history, a great exhalation from the past that was still unable to settle.

Jack realized that he had been to places like this before, on the edge of the Atlas Mountains in Morocco, in the north Syrian desert, in Andalusia in Spain. Places where ancient communities had once thrived on the periphery, but where exhaustion of the land and the spirit had overwhelmed all attempts to carve an existence out of the precious pockets of soil, so easily swept away by the whims of climate and erosion. He was told that it rained less and less here now, and the agriculture that had once sustained the village was being blown away in the wind. Soon, even the ancient walls would become part of the dust cloud that eddied and flowed along the Silk Road, caught between the endless chain of mountains that defined the corridor that had once linked the great empires of east and west.

Jack sat down on a stone revetment. Costas came up and sat beside him, wiping the dust from his face. He stared glumly at the wall. "This is when you know you're in the presence of a real archaeologist," he said. "One of the greatest wonders of history lies just over the horizon, the fabled tomb of the First Emperor, the terracotta army. But no, we come to sit in front of a crumbled wall in a wasteland in the choking dust and the burning heat. Hungry, thirsty, tired and needing a holiday very badly."

Jack passed him his water bottle. "But I can never make sense of it without you. Archaeology, I mean. You keep my feet on the ground."

"Right." Costas swigged from the bottle, then passed it back. "So what's the truth about this place, Jack? Is this what you brought us all the way to see?"

Jack passed Costas a piece of paper. "I printed this out from the helicopter's computer this morning. I knew you'd need an antidote to a ruined wall. Headline news, CNN. Your elephant ship off Egypt. Remember? I think that stands up to the terracotta warriors, don't you? And we found it."

Costas peered at the photo and his eyes lit up. "Look, they got my new submersible in the picture, the ROV-6. I asked the IMU film team to get that into the publicity shots. You can even see the new strobe array. Perfect."

"The elephants, Costas, the elephants."

"Yeah, that too." They stared for a moment at the extraordinary image they had first seen ten days before, the coral-encrusted shape of an elephant sitting on the bottom of the Red Sea. Costas read out the caption. *"Egyptologist Dr. Maurice Hiebermeyer announces sensational shipwreck find."* He slapped the paper. "I don't believe it. No mention of us anywhere. Just Hiebermeyer."

"We've got to allow the dirt archaeologist a moment of glory," Jack said. "After all, he was the one who got us out to Egypt in the first place."

"This happened when we found Atlantis," Costas grumbled. "I'd set up a special demonstration of the Advanced Deep Sea Anthropod. The press were all over Hiebermeyer and his wretched mummies."

"That's Egyptology for you."

"Anyway, it should be you doing the interviews."

"Maurice is better at it than me. He's got all that bubbly energy. And he's less threatening."

"Threatening?" Costas peered at him. "Let me guess. You don't want the world to know there's a real Indiana Jones around, do you? It might put the bad guys on their guard. You like to keep a low profile."

"Exactly."

"You didn't answer my question. The truth about this place."

Jack gestured at the crumbling wall. "It's what you see in front of you. A few years ago, Chinese archaeologists identified these walls as Han dynasty, contemporary with the Roman Empire. They thought this might be the site of Lijian, a settlement in the Gansu Corridor mentioned in Han records. Lijian might derive from a Han Chinese word for westerner, for those who lived beyond the Persians. Later this place might have been renamed Jielu, possibly meaning 'captives from the storming of a town.' It was common for the Han to settle their prisoners of war in places that were then named after their origin. The big leap of imagination was to connect this place with the theory that the Chinese employed Roman mercenaries, survivors of Crassus' legions who had escaped from Persian imprisonment."

"So that's it," Costas murmured. "That's why we're here."

"It's not clear-cut," Jack said. "The story of Fabius and the others in the boat might have ended on Lake Issyk-Kul. But it might not. There's another possibility. A really fascinating one."

"Go on."

"The Roman survivors of Carrhae were imprisoned in Merv in 53 BC. Licinius and Fabius and their comrades made their break about thirty years later. Over the years others must have tried to escape. Perhaps one group was successful, and word filtered back to Merv of the opportunities for mercenaries in the east, the great riches to be had. Perhaps that was what inspired Licinius and Fabius. And the hints about this place would seem to refer to an earlier group. The *History of the Former Han Dynasty* records soldiers fighting in 36 BC for a renegade Hun warlord, deploying in a formation reminiscent of the Roman *testudo* maneuver with interlocked shields above their heads. That's the one shred of evidence on which the whole theory hangs. A few who had been persuaded by the argument began to identify Lijian with the Roman settlement. And here we are."

"Any Roman artifacts?" Costas said, kicking the dust. They looked up as the two women joined them. Rebecca carried on, walking around the ruins in front of them, examining the walls. Costas shifted to make space for Katya on the wall.

Jack shook his head. "It's like Katya said at the Roman burial beside Lake Issyk-Kul. You wouldn't expect to find any. If Romans were here, they would have had nothing of their former life with them. It would have been stripped away from them on the battlefield, and then at Merv. But there's one fascinating feature of this place. Not artifacts or ruins, but people. There's a striking incidence of fair features, green eyes, flaxen hair, big noses. Some Chinese scholars who came here saw these features as western Asiatic, then someone remembered the Roman connection, and the idea caught on."

"What do they know about it?" Costas asked. "The local people, I mean?"

"It's impossible to tell. There might be some residual memory of their ancestry. But they're desperately poor, and buying into the Roman theory might be a ticket to tourist dollars."

Katya spoke. "Anywhere along the Silk Route you could have genetic input from the west — Persian, Sogdian, Bactrian, Indian and yes, Greek and Roman — but with input going as far back as the early Neolithic, even to Indo-Europeans who came this far. You just couldn't be certain."

Jack nodded. "DNA studies have been carried out and are pretty inconclusive. And the whole idea's based on a Chinese misapprehension about the Romans, that they were blue-eyed, blond-haired giants. Ironically, Roman legionaries from the heartland of Italy would have had more in common with the physiognomy of Han Chinese warriors — short, stocky, dark-haired, brown-eyed. What the Chinese were imagining is much closer to the Celtic or Nordic type. Of course, by the time of Julius Caesar and Crassus, there were plenty of men like that in the legions, Celts from northern Italy, Gauls, even Britons. The Huns weren't the only ones to employ mercenaries in their armies."

"What's your gut instinct?" Costas said.

Jack pursed his lips. In the distance he could see a farmer hacking at the ground, his implement bouncing off the rock-hard surface. Beyond him the mountains rose like crumpled paper, the folds and valleys in dark shadow. "My gut instinct," he replied. "This place would have been more fertile in antiquity, a more viable agricultural settlement, but always demanding, not a place of choice. My gut instinct is that prisoners of war could have been settled here."

Rebecca came over and stood in front of them. She had stripped off her fleece to reveal a gray T-shirt with the letters USMC stenciled across the front.

"You seem to have made some new friends," Jack said.

Costas inspected the shirt, nodding his approval. "Hoo-ah," he said.

"Hoo-ah," Rebecca replied, high-fiving him. Jack rolled his eyes. She flopped down on the low wall beside him and took off her cap, wiping her forehead. "It's deuced hot," she said.

Jack turned to her in astonishment. "What did you just say?"

"I said it's deuced hot." She looked at him sheepishly. "That's what John Howard would have said. I read it in a letter you have he wrote to his wife, from the jungle. When their little boy was ill. It was one of his favorite expressions. I've been thinking about him a lot. He so much wanted to be with them, but couldn't. I hope he found them in the end."

Jack put his arm around her and smiled. He remembered the lapis lazuli mine, the body. For a moment he saw them, Howard and Wauchope, standing together, not old men in ragged sheepskins but young officers, in white helmets and khaki tunics with telescopes and maps, staring off toward the horizon. He held Rebecca tight and then took his arm away. "You've just been on the cellphone to Bishkek, haven't you? How's Pradesh?"

"He's good." Rebecca suddenly looked downcast. "Altamaty and I went to see him at the U.S. medical complex at Bishkek just before we flew out here. The bullet missed

599

everything vital. But without the first aid he would have bled to death. He's grateful to you for saving his life."

"Costas did the triage. And I hardly saved him. I was the one who put him in danger."

"The army doctor said that if it had been an explosive bullet or a fifty-caliber Browning round, he'd have been dead on impact. He said that when the bullet hit Pradesh it was subsonic and must have been fired from an incredible distance, apparently from an old rifle. It was only one inch from the heart. He'd never seen anything like it."

"And he'll never see it again," Costas murmured.

"How's his archaeology reading getting on?" Jack said.

"He's lapping it up. He wants more. He said he was already seeing the Roman finds from Arikamedu in a new way, as evidence of trade, society, beliefs, Roman, Egyptian, Indian, his own history. He's itching to get back there."

"That's what I like to hear," Jack murmured.

"And Altamaty?" Jack glanced at Katya.

"He's staying with Pradesh until they fly him out. Pradesh is trying to teach him English. They get on like a house on fire. Altamaty even brought him a doggie bag of mutton stew. He says it'll cure anything."

Costas cleared his throat. "Well, Jack.

Maybe you'd like to join them. Maybe you'd like to eat some more sheep's lip."

Rebecca looked incredulous. *"What?"*

"It's true," Costas said. "In Kyrgyzstan, when we first met Altamaty. He ate sheep's lip. Your dad ate sheep's lip."

"Oh my God."

"I had to," Jack protested. "If I hadn't, it would have been deeply offensive. Altamaty would never have spoken to me again."

"I thought you hated mutton."

"It's the only food I can't eat."

"Couldn't you have chosen some other bit? Did it have to be, like, *lip?*"

"I had no choice." He eyed Katya despairingly. "It had to be lip."

"I have got," Rebecca said quietly, "the grossest dad. *Ever.*"

Jack grinned. "We need to show Pradesh and Altamaty the ropes. A crash course at the IMU campus, and some onboard experience with our research vessels. I need to talk to the commandant of the Madras Engineering Group to arrange a secondment. Pradesh'll need recuperation leave anyway and the campus in Cornwall is perfect. As for Altamaty, his training can be part of our funding for the underwater work at Issyk-Kul and the petroglyph research project. We can put temporary staff there while he's away."

"That would be wonderful," Katya murmured. "The funding."

"It's what I promised," Jack replied. "You may well find me back up there again soon."

"If Altamaty's away, Katya will definitely need company," Rebecca said. Costas coughed, and Rebecca continued. "When Costas finally teaches me to dive, in Hawaii, which he's promised to, I'm going to teach Altamaty all the English words for the equipment so he can order everything he needs from the IMU technical people without having to go through Costas. I told him Costas is a great guy, but usually he's obsessed with some new submersible or whatever, and if Altamaty wants stuff he should come to me." She leaned over and gave Costas a doe-eyed look.

"Good to see you're on top of things, Rebecca," Jack replied, raising his eyes at Costas.

"And the trouble with you, Dad, is that you hop from one adventure to the next. That's what Hiemy told me. You know, back in Egypt. He says that when he finds something, he sticks with it, teases out every possible scrap of information from the site. Obsessively."

"Tell me about it," Costas muttered.

"He says that he, Professor Hiebermeyer, is the true archaeologist. He said that when he found those fragments of pottery with the *Periplus* on them, he deliberately put them aside, didn't allow himself to get excited."

Jack narrowed his eyes. "He was on the phone to me in about ten seconds. You remember, Costas? He even came to visit us when we were digging up Istanbul harbor looking for the Jewish menorah. I was the one who was too busy. Sticking with my project."

"He said that if he hadn't spent months painstakingly excavating that Roman house by the Red Sea, this whole adventure would never have taken off. He said he always did the real work while you were off searching for the Holy Grail or something. He said it was like *Star Trek,* you'd gone over to the dark side. I said it was *Star Wars,* not *Star Trek.* I don't think he'd ever seen either of them. He said you'd become a treasure hunter, and he was only saying this because you still have potential, and it's for your own good."

"I think," Jack murmured, suppressing a smile, "I might need to have a word with old Hiemy."

"Don't worry," Rebecca replied. "Aysha's on the case. She says what he needs is a family. Kids, you know. She says she's working on it."

Costas nearly choked. "Working on it."

"Day and night," Rebecca said.

"Lucky old Hiemy," Jack said.

"And my next project is going to be south India," Rebecca said assertively.

"Your next project is school," Jack said.

"Ever since seeing all that stuff in the old chest, all our family history, I've become fascinated by it," Rebecca said, looking at Jack. "Pradesh has offered to take me to that jungle shrine, to see the carvings for myself. He thinks the next step is to get inside that tomb. See what's in there. He says that now the Indian government is sending in the sappers to build more roads, actually finishing several of the traces that were made by Howard and his men all those years ago."

"What about INTACON?" Costas asked. "And Shang Yong? Has terminating the sniper in Afghanistan finished him, Katya?"

She spoke quietly. "Without his henchman, the Brotherhood will disown him. But they will cling to their belief that they protect the legacy of *Shihuangdi,* and his tomb."

"And how long will that last?" Costas asked.

"The legacy of the First Emperor is safe, for now."

Jack looked hard at Katya, then turned again to Costas. "INTACON was owned by Shang Yong himself, and has been shut down. Pradesh reported back to his headquarters at Bangalore as soon as we got out of the jungle. He got a rap on the knuckles for going into bandit country without authority and taking those two sappers with him, but the colonel immediately dispatched an air assault company. The firefight with the Maoists was the excuse they needed to go in with an iron fist."

"Pradesh says the Indian government has withdrawn all mining contracts from the jungle districts," Rebecca said. "What we've set in motion could be the first big break for the jungle people, but Pradesh is worried that the withdrawal is only temporary and there's still a battle to be fought. We need to show them there's more revenue to be made from adventure tourism than allowing foreign companies to strip-mine the jungle. Pradesh says it depends on how deep the corruption is. Government officials can get bigger payoffs from mining multinationals than they can from start-up ecotourism companies."

"You should work for an NGO, Rebecca," Katya said, smiling.

"I was going to talk to Dad about that. You know, giving IMU another face. It isn't the first time your discoveries have opened a can of worms. And we can't just walk away and pass on the problems to someone else."

"When you do go to the jungle," Jack said, "I've got something for you to return."

"The tiger gauntlet?"

Jack nodded. "We can't return the sacred *vélpu,* as we don't have it," he said. "But the gauntlet had been in that shrine for two thousand years, and was venerated by the Kóya too, as the weapon brought to them by Rama, the god who had once lived among them. It may not be the jewel of immortality, but it might just give them an edge. You can do it for your great-great-great-grandfather."

"Maybe it'll mean closure for him, at last," she murmured.

"What do you mean?"

"Katya was talking to me about it just now, while we were walking up here," she said. "About my mother. About how we can never second-guess grief, how we should never let anyone tell us how it will pan out. Howard lived with grief for much of his life, and it was somehow wrapped up with what happened to him in the jungle. It's strange, it's as if I can feel it. Maybe you do inherit these things from your ancestors, unresolved things. He couldn't find closure in his lifetime, but maybe now we can do it."

Jack looked across at Katya. Their eyes met for a moment, and he looked away. She had said things to Rebecca that he himself did not know how to say. He knew there was still anger in Katya about her own father, still a yawning emptiness in Rebecca, but for a moment he felt as if there were a transcending bond that might protect them both. Rebecca had seen him looking at Katya. "After going to the shrine, Pradesh wants me to study the pottery they've been finding underwater off Arikamedu. Aysha might be able to come and help with the Egyptian and Roman stuff and get me going."

Costas cleared his throat. "If Hiemy can spare her."

"He might need a rest," Rebecca said, looking at him deadpan. Jack grinned. She swept her hair back. "Anyway, I think it's going to be my doctorate."

"Hang on," Jack said. "You haven't even finished high school yet."

"High school? After this? You must be joking. These last few days have been the biggest adventure of my life. Now I know what you mean about expeditions, about how close you get to people. I feel as if I've known all of you all my life."

Jack suddenly felt overwhelmed, and turned away, swallowing hard. He thought of what they had found in the lake, and his feeling of elation as he had looked up from underwater and seen Rebecca's face, gazing down on him. Costas put a hand on his shoulder, then stood up, stretching and scratching his bristles, squinting out over the ruins. He kicked a stone, then reached down and picked it up, turning it over and over in his hand, rubbing it clean. Jack realized that the ground was strewn with fragments — pottery, broken brick, all of it crumbling and decaying into the shroud of dust that seemed so close to removing this place from history. Costas turned to him, a quizzical look in his eyes. "I wonder if they did make it?"

"The Romans? Fabius and the others?"

"We're fifteen hundred kilometers east of Issyk-Kul. If any of them survived the wreck on the lake, that is. Let's say one survived, unknown to his pursuers, washed ashore somewhere, melded invisibly among the caravans of traders heading toward Xian, just as Liu Jian the trader may have melded among the Sogdians heading west."

"Maybe one did make it," Jack said, nodding slowly.

"This place isn't exactly a fabled eastern paradise, is it?"

Jack looked at the ruins again. In his mind's eye he saw those other places he had visited, in north Africa, in Germany, in the mountain valleys of Wales, placed at the periphery of the Roman Empire where the ground revealed a few clues to the discerning eye, the humps of buried walls, fragments of pottery, a clump of rusted chain mail, places where veterans had made their mark, had eked out their days. "It's what they were trained for," he murmured. "At a certain point, a soldier becomes an old soldier. He no longer yearns to die gloriously in battle. The legion of ghosts who have marched alongside him, his fallen comrades, march away to Elysium, where they will await him. He no longer needs to prove himself. He knows he will get there, and will join them. He has done enough."

"And old soldiers, veterans, gave the empire its true strength, settling the frontiers," Katya said.

Jack nodded. "It was the Roman way. A place with women, the chance to raise a family, building materials, a little plot of land. It was enough."

"Yet they would have been told the First Emperor's tomb was just over the horizon," Costas said. "Fabled riches, beyond their imagination."

"Maybe, for the old soldier, the adventurer, the fabled treasure is always just over the horizon, like Elysium," Katya murmured. "When you have spent all your life searching, it becomes the only way to live."

"And if it was Fabius, he may have had treasure already, remember?" Rebecca said. "The legionaries had what they could carry, the stuff they'd looted from the Parthians at Merv, from traders along the Silk Road. And maybe they did have the jewel, the peridot."

A little boy suddenly appeared in the ruins in front of them. "Look," Costas said. "There's some of that fair hair you were talking about." The small head bobbed up and down, coming toward them. He stopped, cocking his head, hearing but not understanding them. He darted into the dust again, then emerged above the loam wall, cautiously peering out. His hair was flaxen, more red than blond. They waved and smiled at him. Jack shaded his eyes, staring into the face. The boy's eyes were a striking green color, almost olive. And there was something strange about the features, something fleet-ingly familiar. The boy scrambled over the wall and dropped down in front of them, still standing a few meters back, cautiously. His clothes were rags, and he was barefoot. He seemed suddenly assured, with the confi-dence of a child. He grinned at them, and held out his hand.

"What do you give a child like that?" Katya murmured.

Costas was still fingering the stone he had picked up earlier. He stopped turning it in his hands, then held it up so the boy could see. A light flashed across Jack's eyes, and he realized that the stone was reflecting the hazy sunlight that was now breaking through. He glanced at it, and saw that it was a rich orange hue, translucent, like amber. He stared again. *Amber.* He could see an insect preserved inside, a mosquito. He saw that the stone had a hole in the center. It had evidently once had a cord through it, perhaps been worn as jewelry. It was old, worn. He saw marks on it. It looked like incised decoration, swirling. An animal, a swirling creature. Jack's heart began to pound. He reached out for it.

It was too late. Costas had not seen him, and tossed it to the boy. He caught it, and held it up, his face rapt with delight. The light shone through the stone. It was amber, there was no doubt about it. It could have come from thousands of miles away. *Amber from the Baltic.* Jack's mind was racing. The belongings of a Roman legionary? A legionary who hailed from the Celtic north, from Gaul or Germany, even Britain? He remembered Fabius, tall, ponytailed Fabius, from the tomb carving in the jungle. *Could it be?* An heirloom, somehow concealed over all those years of captivity? But then this was the Silk Road. All the riches of the world had once come this way. The boy smiled impishly, and held the stone tightly in his fist. He had seen Jack's hand. He was not giving it up. He stared at Jack with fathomless eyes. Then he was off, scampering away across the ruins. His flaxen hair suddenly seemed perfectly in place here, the color of the mountains, of the dust that rolled through the valley. The color of the Silk Road. But there was something else, something Jack knew with dead certainty. *Someone had been here.* He took a deep breath, then exhaled slowly. *Ave atque salve, frater.* He turned to the others. "I wonder whether we've just stared into the eyes of a Roman legionary."

Rebecca held his arm. "Do you think the jewel was here?"

Jack rubbed his chin. "We may just have found it. That boy. The legacy."

"She means the real jewel, Jack," Costas said.

"Maybe that's best left just beyond the horizon," Jack murmured.

"Yeah, right. Don't tell me you didn't want to find it. Don't tell me you didn't want to put those two jewels together, and see what would happen."

"I don't know." Jack narrowed his eyes. "I really don't know."

"It would have been fun to try though, wouldn't it?" Costas said. "Just once, I mean. To see what it was like. Immortality. Then we could have put the jewels in the IMU museum at Carthage, on opposite sides of the room. Close enough for a warm fuzzy feeling. People would come out of the museum feeling extra good. And make donations."

Jack looked at Rebecca, and jerked his head toward Costas. "That's what I mean. He brings things down to earth. With a crash."

Costas grinned. "I have got a lab though, and I can check out the properties of peridot and lapis lazuli. Pradesh talked about trying it. There may be something in it. Not immortality, you know, but something more than a trick of the light, a prismatic effect. Some channeling of energy. Some refractive quality."

Some refractive quality. Jack looked up toward the sun, shutting his eyes against it. The last few days had been a series of refractions, between past and present, between the world of a century ago and two millennia before that, between lives that seemed to run on parallel trajectories. For a moment he felt as if they were the same, Licinius the Roman legionary, John Howard his ancestor, himself, that they were fueled by the same yearning. Maybe the jewel did that, the idea of immortality, allowed those drawn by it to tap into a trackway far above the ephemeral. He took a deep breath, and put his arm around Rebecca. "I think mortality will do me for a while."

Costas looked down at his crumpled shirt, and picked at it despondently. He eyed Jack. "Immortality might give us time to get to Hawaii."

Jack got to his feet. "Point taken."

"Now I know what Costas means," Rebecca said.

"About what?"

"About diversions. He said your expeditions always end up being diversions. You never know where they're going to take you. He says that's what keeps him on his toes. This was one, wasn't it?"

Jack took a deep breath, and stared into the ruins. He reached into his bag, then remembered he no longer had the little lapis lazuli elephant. He remembered where they had been, and wondered how he had changed. He gave Rebecca a tired smile. "A bit more than a diversion, I fancy."

Costas looked at Jack expectantly. "So where do we go from here?"

"Got any ideas?"

"I thought we might go in search of the Isles of the Immortals. You know, that place Katya told us about. The First Emperor sent out expeditions to find them. Somewhere in the eastern ocean. In the center of the Pacific, to be exact. A small but delightful chain of volcanic islands."

"Aloha," Rebecca said.

"Aloha," Costas replied. He made a whirling motion with his fingers, and pointed at the helicopter. Jack scratched his chin, looking at Costas' sun-beaten face. "You know, you look as if you could do with a few days on a beach."

"Damn right I could."

"But Rebecca wants to go to the jungle. To the shrine."

Costas got up and stretched. "It can wait. Anyway, there's probably not much more to see. When we were there, I felt a hole in the base of the tomb. I remembered you showing me stone coffins in Rome, with the drainage hole to let the decomposition products flow out. If Licinius was in that tomb, there's probably not much left there now."

Jack stared at Costas. "A hole, you say."

Costas put up his hand, and curled his fingers around. "About this big."

Jack's mind was racing. "Big enough to shove a bamboo tube through?"

"I guess so. A small one."

Jack had remembered something. A possibility that Rebecca had mentioned. She looked at him now, reading his mind. "Robert Wauchope," she murmured. "The *vélpu?*"

Could it be? Could he have made it back there? Jack's heart was suddenly pounding. He felt the familiar thrill of excitement. He slung his old khaki bag on his shoulder.

"Oh no." Costas shook his head defiantly. "No way. I know that look."

"We've got to get back to *Seaquest II* anyway. She's in the Bay of Bengal. It would just be a diversion."

Costas looked despairingly at Rebecca. "See what I mean?"

Rebecca put her arm around Jack. "Don't worry, Dad. He'll follow you anywhere."

Jack looked questioningly at Costas. "Well?"

"You really think we might find it?"

"No promises."

Costas sighed. He glanced again at his Hawaiian shirt, then looked dolefully at Jack. They stared each other in the eye. Jack's face broke into a broad smile, and Costas looked down, shaking his head. "What can I say."

"Good to go?"

"Good to go."

AUTHOR'S NOTE

The seeds of this story were planted when I first stood as an archaeology student among the ancient ruins of Harran in southern Turkey, near the Syrian border. The heat was stifling, the sky was lowering, and a wind had whipped up the dust and obscured the light. It seemed a place on the very edge of existence, and it made a deep impression on me. This was the site of the Battle of Carrhae, where a Roman army under Crassus had been catastrophically defeated by the Parthians in 53 BC. It seemed inconceivable that a battle could have been fought in such heat. I had read the story of captured legionaries being marched east, never to be heard of again. Could the rumors be true, that some of them might have escaped and undertaken a fantastic trek as far as China? In the years that followed, my own travels took me deep into central Asia along the ancient Silk Route, and on the trail of Roman seafarers who had traded as far east as the Bay of Bengal. I became fascinated by the early history of archaeological exploration in India during the period of British rule, and with the lives of my own ancestors who had been soldiers and adventurers there in the nineteenth century. Always my mind returned to the question of Crassus' legionaries. Could there be a connection? Had these men truly risked everything to seek Chrysê, the land of gold known to the traders? What tales had they been told of the fabled riches of the east? What could have driven them on?

The fate of Crassus' lost legionaries from Carrhae is one of the most beguiling mysteries of ancient history. It exerted a strong pull on the Roman imagination; the poet Horace asked, "Did Crassus' troops live in scandalous marriage to barbarians . . . grow old bearing arms for alien fathers-in-law . . . ?" (*Odes*, iii, 5, trans. W. G. Shepherd). For the Emperor Augustus, who agreed to peace terms with the Parthians in 20 BC, the return of the captured legionary standards was one of the greatest triumphs of his reign, celebrated by a famous series of gold and silver coins bearing the legend *SIGNIS RECEPTIS*, "The standards returned."

The surviving ancient sources on Carrhae are all reliant on earlier histories, now lost. According to Plutarch, Crassus marched with "seven legions of men-at-arms, nearly four thousand horsemen and about as many light-armed troops" (*Crassus,* xx, 1), implying about forty thousand men. The identity of the legions is not known; however, Plutarch mentions that a thousand of the cavalry had "come from Caesar," presumably veterans of Julius Caesar's recent campaigns in Gaul and Britain. At that date, legionaries were still "citizen-soldiers" rather than career professionals, bound by terms of service not normally exceeding six years. The memories of the campaign in my prologue, including the ill omens on crossing the Euphrates, the death of Crassus and the humiliation of Caius Paccianus, are all from Plutarch (*Crassus* xix, xxxi–ii) and Dio Cassius (*Roman History* xl, 16–27); Plutarch has Crassus being killed by a Parthian, and Dio Cassius "either by one of his own men to prevent his capture alive, or by the enemy because he was badly wounded." Afterward, "the Parthians, as some say, poured molten gold into his mouth in mockery." Plutarch tells us that in the whole campaign "twenty thousand are said to have been killed, and ten thousand to have been taken alive."

The only indication of the fate of those prisoners is a single line in the *Natural History* of Pliny the Elder, who describes Margiana, a city east of the Caspian Sea, as "the place to which the Roman prisoners taken in the disaster of Crassus were brought" (vi, 47).

Margiana, present-day Merv in Turkmenistan, was a Parthian citadel and gateway to central Asia. The Roman prisoners could have been used to build the huge circuit of walls whose crumbling ramparts can still be seen at Merv today. The walls required rebuilding on numerous occasions, and it is intriguing to note that the Romans in Italy were first developing techniques of concrete construction at this time — the basis for the idea in the novel of how deliberate sabotage may have come about.

The suggestion that survivors of Carrhae may have escaped from Merv and made their way east comes from a controversial interpretation of Chinese written sources, first published in the 1950s. In 36 BC the Han Chinese mounted an expedition against the Hsiung-nu, the Huns, who were establishing a foothold in Sogdiana in central Asia. The ancient *History of the Former Han Dynasty* contains an account of the Han siege of the Hsiung-nu fortress, probably based on contemporary paintings, including a passage translated as more than a hundred foot-soldiers lined up in a "fish-scale" formation (chs. ix, xxiv–v). Some modern scholars have equated this with the *testudo,* the "tortoise," a Roman formation in which shield was locked with shield, as Plutarch put it in his account of Carrhae (*Crassus* xxiv, 3). The Han army also found a "double wooden palisade" outside the citadel, a description perhaps reminiscent of Roman fortification techniques. These two references have led some to imagine that the Hun army included Roman mercenaries.

Nothing definitive has yet been found in the archaeology of central Asia to support this idea. The most intriguing discovery is an inscription in southern Uzbekistan, some five hundred kilometers east of Merv, similar to the fictional inscription in chapter 3; it may refer to the Fifteenth Legion, possibly an Imperial legion of that number founded in AD 62, but conceivably a legion of the same number from the century before. A thousand kilometers northeast from there lies Cholpon-Ata, the extraordinary field of boulders with petroglyphs — rock carvings — beside Lake Issyk-Kul in Kyrgyzstan. The images mainly relate to the spiritual life of the local population, but Issyk-Kul was a staging post on the Silk Route and my own explorations there suggest the potential for discovering other inscriptions. In a mountain valley to the south, I rode a horse that may have descended from the fabled *akhal-teke,* the blood-sweating heavenly horses of Chinese mythology. The lake itself contains inundated ancient structures and artifacts, and rumors abound of sunken cities and tombs, even that of Genghis Khan himself; archaeological diving now underway in the lake could produce wonderful discoveries in the near future.

More than fifteen hundred kilometers southeast, past the forbidding Taklamakan Desert, lies the village of Zhelaizai in Gansu province of China. Some believe this to have been Lijian, a place where prisoners from the battle against the Huns in 36 BC may have been settled. The name Lijian — perhaps derived from "Alexander" — may have meant "westerner." The population today does indeed contain a striking number of green-eyed, fair-featured people, though DNA analyses to test for western origins have proved inconclusive. Silk Route travelers would have passed this place close to the end of their journey toward Xian, site of the tomb of the First Emperor, *Shihuangdi,* at Mount Li outside the city. The "Brotherhood of the Tiger" in this novel is fictional, but the idea is based on other Chinese secret societies, and the fiefdoms are those of the First Emperor's family (*Records of the Grand Historian,* Shi ji 5). "Tiger Cavalry" were employed as the Emperor Ts'ao Ts'ao's personal bodyguard in the third century AD, perhaps based on an earlier bodyguard; their weapons could have included prized bronze halberds such as the one in this novel, based on an actual halberd on display in the British Museum (OA 1949.5–18 1,2). The tomb itself was said to have been guarded by twenty households, supposedly the basis for twenty modern villages around Mount Li, so the idea of a hereditary custodian is rooted in the history of this extraordinary site, one of the remaining unexcavated wonders of the ancient world.

The *Periplus of the Erythraean Sea* survives as a tenth-century AD manuscript in a library in Heidelberg, copied from an original written in Greek about a thousand years earlier. It is one of the most remarkable documents from antiquity, detailing maritime trade from Roman Egypt down the African coast as far as Zanzibar, and across the Indian Ocean to the Bay of Bengal. In recent decades there has been an explosion of interest in the archaeology of the *Periplus,* especially with the excavation of the Red Sea port sites of Berenikê and Myos Hormos. The merchant's house in this novel is fictional, but the finds are representative of actual discoveries at these sites, including Italian wine amphoras reused as water containers, thousands of peppercorns from India, ballast stones from Arabia and India, Indian hardwood — reused ship's timbers, including teak — and south Indian pottery. One sherd had a Tamil *graffito* bearing a personal name also attested in south India. Many other potsherds with inscriptions — *ostraka* — are known, including part of the archive at Myos Hormos of a man named Maximus Priscus. In this novel, the *ostraka* with the text of the *Periplus,* and the previously unknown section — mentioning Crassus' legionaries — are fictional. Nevertheless, potsherds would have been a sensible writing material for a draft, before copying the final text onto papyrus.

The ancient site of Arikamedu, south of Pondicherry, was first extensively excavated by Sir Mortimer Wheeler and the Archaeological Survey of India in the 1940s, and has been the subject of renewed investigations since the early 1980s. Many still believe, as Wheeler did, that the sherds of Roman amphoras and fineware at the site indicate the presence of merchants from Egyptian ports such as Berenikê — or their local agents — who traded with merchants coming across the Bay of Bengal and down from central Asia, bringing exotic goods such as silk and lapis lazuli. Divers from the Archaeological Survey of India have begun to investigate the waters off Arikamedu and other sites mentioned in the *Periplus.* As more archaeologists see Roman involvement with India as a two-way cultural process — with as much Indian influence on the west as the other way around — we can look forward to the discovery of more sites that represent the trade in the *Periplus,* one of the most extraordinary episodes of maritime endeavor the world has ever seen.

Some thirty nautical miles southeast of

Cape Ras Banas in the Red Sea lies St. John's Island (Arabic Zeberged), the only source in antiquity of the gem peridot, undoubtedly the *topazai* mentioned by Strabo and Pliny as the product of an island close to Berenikê. One Red Sea port mentioned in the *Periplus* that has yet to be conclusively identified is Ptolemais Thêrên, "Ptolemy of the Hunts," nor has a seagoing elephant-carrier — an *elephantegos* — yet been found. Neverthless, several Roman wrecks containing wine amphoras are known in the Red Sea, very possibly ships destined for Arabia and India. The *Periplus* specifically mentions gold and silver coins as the main Roman export — for trade on the Malabar coast we are exhorted to take coin, "a great deal of it" — and this is consistent with the emperor Tiberius' lament about the bullion drain (Tacitus, *Annals,* iii, 54; also Pliny, *Natural History* vi, 101; xii, 84), as well as with the discovery of many thousands of gold and silver coins in south India. There can be no doubt that a Roman wreck will one day be discovered in the Red Sea or the Indian Ocean with a wealth of gold to rival the treasure wrecks of the Spanish Main.

The Rampa Rebellion of 1879–81 was the largest uprising of tribal people to occur in central India during the period of the British Raj, and was put down by a brigade-sized expedition of the Indian army. The immediate cause of the rebellion was a tax on toddy, the alcoholic drink made from palm sap, though the backdrop included discontent over forestry regulations and the corruption of the native police. It was a protracted campaign, beset by the terrible "jungle fever," and its history has never been properly written. The picture here is based on daily reports in the *Madras Military Proceedings* and *Madras Judicial Proceedings,* private correspondence, regimental records and biographical information on the British officers involved (in some contemporary accounts, "Rampa" appears as "Rumpa," a more phonetical spelling). There are no known personal reminiscences of the campaign, though a sense of the language and outlook of a Royal Engineers officer on a jungle campaign in the 1870s can be gleaned from Lieutenant R. G. Woodthorpe's *The Lushai Expedition 1871–1872,* describing a punitive expedition into Burma. The dramatic events early in the Rampa Rebellion were reported in the London *Times* and *The New York Times,* including the attack on the steamer *Shamrock* by over one thousand rebels and Lieutenant Hamilton's fight in the jungle, but interest waned as the rebellion dragged on and became mired in disease and monsoon. The wording of Hamilton's account is taken from his report of 20 August 1879 in the *Madras Military Proceedings,*

showing that his sappers expended 1050 rounds and killed at least ten rebels. Surgeon Walker's description of the jungle fever in chapter 5 is taken from a report by Surgeon-Major J. Bilderbeck, Thirty-sixth Madras Native Infantry, in May 1880, when all of the British officers and three-fifths of the sepoys in his regiment were struck down. The Kóya treated fever with the remedy described in chapter 9 (*Note on the Rampa Agency, East Godavari District,* Madras, 1931, p. 31). Rampa district today remains little changed from the 1880s, and the jungles of eastern India are a haven for Maoist terrorists as well as attracting mining prospectors backed by

627

foreign investment.

An account from 1876 describes the sacred *vélpus,* including the potent Lakkála (or Laka) Rámu. The *vélpus* were bamboo tubes, kept hidden away. The animistic spirits of the jungle, the *konda devátа,* included a tiger god. The Godavari volume of the *Imperial Gazetteer of India* notes that near Rampa village, "beside a waterfall about 25 feet high, is a shrine formed of three huge boulders, two of which make a kind of roof, and fitted with a doorway and one side-wall of cut stone. The water of the fall pours continually between the boulders. A rough lingam and other holy emblems have been carved out of the rock." In my fictional shrine, the Indian iconography is based on cave carvings at Badami and sculpture elsewhere in India, including the *yakśas* and *yakśīs* figures. The Rampa shrine is where several police captives were executed in 1879. A native eyewitness described one "sacrifice": "Chendrayya himself cut off his head with a sword. They sacrificed him to Gudapu Mavili." (*Madras Judicial Proceedings,* 5 September 1879). Other accounts describe *"meriahs"* being sacrificed or rescued, and headless bodies being found. The riverside sacrifice scene is a fictional representation of these events, and derives further detail from eyewitness accounts of human sacrifices recorded in Major-General John Campbell's *A Personal Narrative of Thirteen Years Service amongst the Wild Tribes of Khondistan for the Suppression of Human Sacrifice* (1864) — including Captain Frye's rescue of a *meriah,* quoted here in chapter 4 — and from Christoph and Elizabeth von Fürer-Haimendorf's *The Reddis of the Bison Hills: A Study of Acculturation* (1945), one of few detailed anthropological studies of the hill tribes of the upper Godavari.

Several of the characters in this novel are based on actual individuals in the Rampa Field Force, some with names altered. Joseph Fawcett Beddy was assistant commissioner for the Central Provinces, and accompanied Hamilton during his affray in the jungle. The official report on the rebellion to the Government of India states that Beddy "died from fever" after the affray (*Madras Judicial Proceedings,* 14 December 1881); but his tomb inscription at Wuddagudem recorded that he was "shot in the late Rampa Rebellion" (H. Le Fanu, *List of European Tombs in the Godaveri District with Inscriptions Thereon,* Cocanada 1895). Dr. George Lemon Walker, Surgeon to D and G Companies, Madras Sappers and Miners, during the Rampa Rebellion, was indeed born in Kingston, Canada, and received his medical training at Queen's University in Belfast. From 1884 his superior in medical charge of the Madras Sappers was Surgeon-Major Ronald Ross —

later Sir Ronald Ross, famous for identifying the *Anopheles* mosquito as the carrier of the malaria parasite, and whose patients would have included sapper veterans of Rampa suffering from the dreaded "jungle fever."

Of the Madras Sappers, the fictional Sergeant O'Connell is inspired by Sergeant John Brown, who embarked for India in 1860, served in the 1875–6 Perak campaign in Malaysia and was pensioned as a quartermaster sergeant in 1881. Sapper Narrainsamy served in Burma and the Chin Lushai expeditions in the late 1880s. Of the subalterns, Robert Ewen Hamilton died in 1885 from cholera, "his health shattered by continued attacks of malarial fever" during the Afghan war and the Rampa Rebellion. The fictional Lieutenant Wauchope is based on Robert Alexander Wahab (who later used the spelling Wauhope for his Irish name); he was indeed from an Irish family with American connections. His health was also eventually broken by malaria, causing his early retirement in 1905, though by then he was a colonel with a distinguished record in almost all of the northwest frontier military expeditions of the period.

The fictional Lieutenant Howard is based on Lieutenant Walter Andrew Gale, my great-great-grandfather, the longest-serving of all the Madras Sapper officers in the Rampa Field Force. He had been detailed for the second phase of the Afghan war in late 1879, but remained in Rampa as the deployment there dragged on through 1880. His son Edward died in Bangalore in April that year, aged one year and five months. After leaving the Madras Sappers in 1881 both he and Wahab became specialists in survey, developing skills honed in the Rampa jungle. Gale returned with his young family to England in 1885 and became an instructor in Survey at the School of Military Engineering, Chatham, where he edited the *Professional Papers of the Corps of Royal Engineers.* As Secretary of the R.E. Institute he was fully involved in the academic life of the Royal Engineers, and would have attended lectures on subjects ranging beyond purely military matters — including archaeology, which had developed in India as an offshoot of survey. The topic of Howard's fictional lecture at the Royal United Service Institution in London would have been in keeping with the remarkable range of interests pursued by engineer officers at this period. The Institution housed the only known collection of artifacts from the Rampa Rebellion — two matchlock muskets, two swords and a scabbard, two bamboo arrows, a bird arrow, a shield and four arrowheads — donated by a fellow Madras Sapper officer and Rampa veteran, Lieutenant A. C. Macdonnell, R.E. in 1882 (*Journal of the Royal United Service Institution,* xxv, p. xxxi); the museum was closed in 1962, when any of these artifacts still in the collection would have been dispersed.

Gale and Wahab were together again in 1889, when Wahab returned to Chatham for courses of training. The final disappearance of the two retired colonels into Afghanistan is fictional. However, both men were intensely familiar with the Afghan frontier region, and would have been poised for such an adventure. Wahab spent almost twenty years with the Survey of India demarking the boundary with Afghanistan, from Baluchistan to the Khyber Pass and beyond. He was famous as a mountaineer, and his boundary markers still survive on the frontier today. Gale returned to India and became Commanding Royal Engineer of the Quetta Division of the Indian army and Supervising Engineer in Baluchistan, responsible for the entire province including the volatile frontier region. One of his colleagues in the Baluchistan administration was Aurel Stein, the famous Silk Route explorer, then employed as archaeological surveyor by the government; his and Colonel Gale's reports appear together in the *Administration Report of the Baluchistan Agency* for 1904–1905. Stein was also a personal friend of Robert Wahab, who shared his passion for classical history and was responsible for the most likely identification of Aornos, the mountain spur that Alexander the Great famously captured; Wauhope (as he became) is acknowledged warmly in Stein's classic *On Alexander's Track to the Indus* (1929). Twenty years before that book was published, there were still parts of Afghanistan so remote that hardly any Europeans had ever visited them, including the fabled lapis lazuli mines described in Lieutenant John Wood's *A Personal Narrative of a Journey to the Source of the River Oxus* (1841), quoted here in chapters 13, 15 (including the Pashtun verse), 18 and 19. At different times in their careers, and possibly together, Gale and Wahab must have stood before the Bolan Pass on the route to Afghanistan, gazing at the awesome cleft in the mountains that had lured so many soldiers and adventurers to the land beyond, in search of glory and treasure but so often ending in death.

Royal Engineers officers were exhorted to be "soldiers first and engineers afterwards" in an instructional paper edited by Captain W. A. Gale in the *Professional Papers of the Corps of Royal Engineers* for 1889 (Colonel E. Wood, C.B., R.E., "The duties of Royal Engineers in the Field," vol xv, 69–96), and were fully trained to act as infantry. In India, officers not on campaign spent a great deal of time hunting, so were closely familiar with firearms and were often expert marksmen. In this novel, the 1851 Colt revolver with Upper Canada markings is a genuine piece that I have fired, as are the Snider-Enfield and Lee-Enfield rifles. Colt revolvers were used extensively by British officers during the 1857–8 Indian Mutiny, and cap-and-ball revolvers were still favored decades later by adventurers such as Sir Richard Burton in areas where cartridge ammunition was not readily available. The Madras Sappers were armed in 1879 with the Snider-Enfield rifle, though the British army had converted to the Martini-Henry several years earlier. Many old service rifles found their way to the northwest frontier and Afghanistan, where British rifles still used today include Lee-Enfields made at Long Branch in Canada. Scoped Lee-Enfields and Mosin-Nagants made highly effective sniper rifles during the Second World War. The Mosin-Nagant was used by the Soviet female snipers called *zaichata,* "little hares," after their mentor, Vasiliy Zaitsev; one of them, Lyudmila Pavlichenko, had more than 300 kills, and is the basis for the sniper in this novel.

The quotes from the *Periplus of the Erythraean Sea* are my translations of the original Greek, based on the text in Frisk, H., *Le Périple de la mer Érythrée (Göteborgs Högsko-*

las Årsskrift, 33, 1927); these are extracts from Frisk, chapter 63–6 for the front quote, and chapters 41 and 63 in chapter 3. The second front quote is from *Records of the Grand Historian* by Sima Qian (Columbia University Press, 1993, trans. Burton Watson), *Shi ji* 6; this is also the source of the verse on the virtue of the emperor in chapter 4 — a version of a stone inscription raised by *Shihuangdi* on Mount Langye — and the quote in chapter 15. In chapter 3, the quote from Cosmas on Sri Lanka is from J. W. Mc-Crindle, *The Christian Topography of Cosmas, an Egyptian Monk* (Hakluyt Society series 1, vol. 97, 1987), 365–8. In chapter 4, the extract from Lieutenant Howard's fictional diary on the problems of survey is from Captain W. A. Gale's preface to volume XIV (1888) of the *Professional Papers of the Corps of Royal Engineers,* a comment undoubtedly influenced by his Rampa experience; the quote following that is from the report of the Hon. David F. Carmichael, who was deputed to tour the Rampa tract after the rebellion and make recommendations (*Madras Judicial Proceedings,* 14 December 1881, 1027–53).

One of the artifacts brought back by Colonel Gale from India was the brass *pata* gauntlet sword described in this novel. A similar brass *pata* is on display in the British Museum (OA

1878. 12-30, 818). The history of these rare weapons may date as far back as the Mongol invasions of India, or even earlier. One of few images of a *pata* in use is a battle scene of the seventeenth century showing the Maratha prince Shivaji wielding a great *pata* (from a miniature reproduced in *Monuments Anciens et Modernes de l'Hindoustan,* L. Langlès, 1821); the composition of the scene is reminiscent of the Alexander mosaic from Pompeii, the inspiration for the cave carving in this novel. My grandfather had been told that the *pata* came from a "rebellion," but nothing more is known about it with certainty. Images of this artifact, as well as the camphor-wood officer's chest, the telescope, the old books, the ancient coins and the weapons in this novel, can be seen at www .davidgibbins.com.

ACKNOWLEDGMENTS

I am grateful to my agent, Luigi Bonomi of LBA, and my editors, Caitlin Alexander at Bantam Dell and Harriet Evans at Headline; to Gaia Banks, Alexandra Barlow, Alison Bonomi, Chen Huijin Cheryl, Raewyn Davies, Darragh Deering, Sam Edenborough, Mary Esdaile, Crystal Velasquez, Emily Furniss, George Gamble, Tessa Girvan, Janet Harron, Jenny Karat, Celine Kelly, Nicki Kennedy, Lea Beresford, Ann Ledden, Stacey Levitt, Kim McArthur, Tony McGrath, Taryn Manias, Peter Newsom, Amanda Preston, Jenny Robson, Barry Rudd, John Rush, Emma Rusher, Jane Seller, Molly Stirling, Adja Vucicevic, Katherine West and Leah Woodburn; to the entire teams at Headline and Bantam Dell, and to my many publishers in other languages. I owe a great deal to Ann Verrinder Gibbins, and to Angie and Molly, as well as to my brother Alan for help with my website www.davidgibbins.com.
For the field research associated with this

novel I am especially grateful to the late Alan Hall, of the British Institute of Archaeology at Ankara; to the chair of the NATO Life Sciences Committee, for inviting me to Kyrgyzstan; and to the curator of the Cholpon-Ata open-air petroglyph museum beside Lake Issyk-Kul. My fascination with the *Periplus of the Erythraean Sea* dates from my time as a graduate student at Cambridge University; I owe much to the stimulus of the late Dr. James Kirkman, O.B.E., F.S.A., former curator of the Fort Jesus Museum, Mombasa, and to my grandfather Captain Lawrance Wilfrid Gibbins, who spent a lifetime sailing the same routes to India as the ancient mariners of the *Periplus.* Both of these men helped me to see the extraordinary sea trade of two thousand years ago.

I am grateful to Dr. Guodong Liu for his advice on Chinese names. For help in acquiring and shooting a Snider-Enfield rifle, I am grateful to John Denner and David Hurbuthnot. For my research on the 1879–81 Rampa Rebellion, I am grateful to the staff of the former Oriental and India Office Collections at the British Library, the Royal Engineers Museum and Library at Chatham, the UK National Archives and the South Asia Division of the University of Michigan Library; to Lieutenant Colonel Prabhat Kumar of the Madras Sappers Museum and Archives, Bangalore; to Lieutenant Colonel Edward De

Santis, U.S. Army Corps of Engineers (retired); and, for befriending me as a boy, to the late Lieutenant Colonel John Ancrum Cameron, Royal Engineers, Madras Sapper from 1927–48, who provided a vivid link back to the time of my great-great-grandfather, Colonel Walter Andrew Gale, Royal Engineers, Madras Sapper and Rampa veteran, whose *pata* gauntlet sword provided an inspiration for this story.

Finally, I owe a special debt to the late Mrs. Rosemary Hobbs, whose bequest allowed me to acquire first editions of John Campbell's *A Personal Narrative of Thirteen Years Service amongst the Wild Tribes of Khondistan* and John Wood's *A Personal Narrative of a Journey to the Source of the River Oxus,* and for all of her support for my expeditions and adventures over the years.